REALM

FROZEN SEA

Grey Lady

THE VALE

Fellsmarch

Chalk
Cliffs

Marisa Pines Camp

Firehole R.

Fortress Rock

Way Camp

Hunter's
Camp

Queen
Court

Alyssa
Plateau

Wolf's
Head

Marisa Pines Pass

The Harlot

Spiritgate

Delphi

KINGDOM of ARDEN

Middlesea

North Rd.

Temple Church

White
Oaks Keep

Heartfang Mtns.

Bittersweet
Keep

Ardenscourt

East Rd.

Baston Bay

THE INDIO OCEAN

Ardenswater

Heartfang R.

Bright Stone
Keep

Bitter Springs R.

Watergate

Gryphon Pt.

The Claw

The Wastes

WE'ENHAVEN

Hidden Bay

Northern Islands

Demon's Wounds

SARTHIS

Deepwater Court

Salt Sea

Dragonback Mountains

Tarvos River

The Indio Ocean

Guardians · Tarvos

Scorched Lands

Midden Bay

Endru

Also by Cinda Williams Chima

THE SHATTERED REALMS SERIES
*Flamecaster*
*Shadowcaster*
*Stormcaster*

THE HEIR CHRONICLES
*The Warrior Heir*
*The Wizard Heir*
*The Dragon Heir*
*The Enchanter Heir*
*The Sorcerer Heir*

THE SEVEN REALMS SERIES
*The Demon King*
*The Exiled Queen*
*The Gray Wolf Throne*
*The Crimson Crown*

# DEATHCASTER

# CINDA WILLIAMS CHIMA

# DEATHCASTER

### A
## SHATTERED REALMS
### NOVEL

HARPER TEEN
An Imprint of HarperCollinsPublishers

ISBN 978-0-06-238103-3 (hardcover)
ISBN 978-0-06-290591-8 (international edition)

Typography by Erin Fitzsimmons
19 20 21 22 23   PC/LSCH   10 9 8 7 6 5 4 3 2 1

First Edition

*For Jen—thank you for adding a special kind of magic to all of our lives.*

# SHIP OF FOOLS

Adrian sul'Han shivered, drawing the collar of his clan-made stormcoat up to his chin. Spring might have come to the Realms he'd left behind, but sea ice and icebergs still cluttered the surface of Invaders Bay. He could hear Captain Hadley DeVilliers shouting orders from the quarterdeck to their mingled Carthian/Fellsian crew as the *Sea Wolf* threaded her way through the ice toward the open sea.

Sailing toward Lyss, if there was any justice in this shattered world. A debatable point.

It had been Hadley's idea to launch their mission from the Frozen Sea north of Wizard Head. For one thing, Empress Celestine now controlled the queendom's only deepwater port at Chalk Cliffs. For another, the success of this mission depended on absolute secrecy. It was unlikely they'd meet any other ships this far north at this time of year. After all, nobody in his right mind would *choose* to be here.

Nobody who wasn't desperate for a win in the wake of so many losses—Hana, Jenna, his father. Ash did not want to live on as the survivor of another failure. He would save his sister and save the Line or die in the attempt.

*Not a trade I'd make. Stay alive.*

Ash flinched. He looked around, but nobody was near enough to have been heard over the howl of the wind. He gripped the serpent amulet more tightly, his knuckles white, as if he could squeeze a response from the metal and stone.

"Da?"

Nothing.

Ash's breath hissed through his teeth. It had been this way since the night he and his father had partnered to bring his mother back from the dead. He'd hear a whisper in his ear, or feel a presence like the brush of a feather or the tendrils of a dream, or hear his father calling his name amid the shriek of the wind and the crash of the waves.

But it was all one way. No matter how hard Ash tried, he couldn't seem to enter the borderlands between life and death.

*Come see me in Aediion*, his father had said. *You and your mother and sister have enemies at court. Enemies on the council. Don't give your trust easily.*

"A little help here, healer?" The voice was edged with impatience.

Ash looked up. High above, the magemarked pirate Evan Strangward clung to the rigging like a spider, shining like a ship's lantern in the night. He'd been up there for hours, facing the brunt of the weather without complaint, manipulating wind and waves to open a path through the ice for the *Sea Wolf*. At the same time, he kept her sails filled, driving them forward as fast as they could safely go. Maybe faster.

"Sorry," Ash said, moving back into position in the bow of

the ship, receiving the blessing of freezing spray and stinging sleet. It was his job to clean up after the weather mage—to clear away the obstacles the pirate missed, blasting icebergs into bits, softening the slabs of ice that floated into their path so the ship's hull could penetrate them without damage.

Watching Strangward at work was like visual poetry, his amulet flaring under his fingers as he gathered power, then both arms sweeping forward, shaping, coaxing, cajoling, commanding, like a temple speaker, a conductor of wind, ice, and water. He was agile as a cat, maneuvering over the spars to get the right angle, swinging from mast to mast as if unaware that he was more than a hundred feet above the decks. He seemed impervious to bad weather. He'd left his stormcoat on the deck below, saying it only got in his way.

Maybe he hadn't the range of magic enjoyed by wizards in the Realms, courtesy of their ability to work charms, but there were clear advantages to being a specialist. Ash had seen limited weather wizardry from his parents' friend Fire Dancer. As a clan-born wizard, Dancer had combined the uplander's easy connection with the natural world with the raw magic of wizardry. But Dancer's weather magic was a whisper next to Strangward's roar.

*Evan's* roar. The pirate had asked them to call him Evan, but, given the history between them, that wasn't easy to do.

"If you'd have told me I'd be sailing under that bloodsucking pirate, I'd have laughed in your face."

Ash spun around. Two of Hadley's crew huddled next to the foremast shrouds, their eyes fixed on Evan, their faces clouded with resentment.

"My cousin's ship went down off Baston Bay, and it was the swiving Stormcaster that done it." The sailor shuddered and spat on the deck.

"Every time a ship is lost, they blame it on him," the other one said, jerking his head toward the pirate. "He can't have done for all of 'em. Anyway, we an't sailing under him. DeVilliers is captain, long as we're at sea."

"Mind the telltales," Strangward called down, causing the two of them to jump. "Trim the jib sheets—*now*."

"Tell *him* that," the first one said, hurrying to adjust the sheets. "Maybe Captain DeVilliers is the master on paper, but she'll go to the bottom with the rest of us if he decides to founder us."

Ash sighed. Though the pirate seemed painfully eager to win the rest of them over by proving his value to the mission, his efforts seemed to have the opposite effect. The Stormcaster was hated and feared all along the coast. Sailors were superstitious by nature. Plus, they were so often at the mercy of weather that the Stormcaster's command of it was intimidating and unsettling, even for those who'd been raised with wizardry.

"Impressive, isn't he? Almost scary."

Ash jumped and turned to find Finn standing next to him, his eyes fixed on the pirate.

"If you like a show-off," Ash said, stuffing his hands into his pockets.

That should have drawn a laugh from the Finn he remembered. Instead, his friend drew in a breath, then let it out slowly. "Do you think we can pull this off?"

Ash swiped water from his face with his sopping sleeve. "Pull what off?"

"Get in and out of Celesgarde? Rescue your sister?"

"I wouldn't be here if I didn't hope for that," Ash said. "Why? Are you having second thoughts?"

"Not really," Finn said. "I'm just trying to estimate the odds of success."

"Maybe it's better not to look at the odds at all," Ash said, rolling his eyes. "I was a little surprised that you agreed to come, since you had to postpone the wedding and all."

"Duty trumps desire," Finn said. "Julianna understands that we all must be willing to sacrifice for the greater good."

That sounded stuffy, even for bookish Finn. It was the kind of thing people say to you when *you're* the one who's going to be doing the sacrificing.

"I'm not sacrificing anyone if I can help it," Ash said. "I've already lost my father and my sister. My mother still hasn't recovered. Too many of my friends have died in this war, or been gravely wounded, you included. I think we've done our bit."

"It's never enough," Finn said, pain flickering across his face. He rubbed his forehead with the heel of his hand. Though he was bareheaded, his hair plastered down by the wet, he didn't seem to feel the cold.

"Are you all right?" Ash said, putting a hand on Finn's shoulder.

"It's just . . . I've been having these headaches, ever since I was wounded," Finn said. "They're getting worse instead of better. And sometimes—it's like I have these spells when I miss things. I just blank out." He shook his head. "I think I'm losing my mind."

Worry quivered through Ash. Once again, he was reminded

that while he'd pursued a career as an assassin in the south, Finn had waged a war on a different battlefield—one in which he saw his friends slaughtered, and probably blamed himself for surviving. Both of them were marked by what they'd seen and done—things they would prefer to forget.

"Listen," Ash said. "Sometimes that's how the mind works. When we're under stress, it protects us by giving us an out when we need one."

"Well," Finn said, with a bitter laugh, "stress is an appropriate response to stressful times."

I should have asked more questions, Ash thought. I should have made sure Finn had recovered enough to deal with this.

What kind of a healer are you?

Unable to help himself, Ash sent a tendril of soothing magic through his fingers into Finn's shoulder. He yanked back his hand, fingers stinging, as Finn twisted away.

His friend stood, his back to the rail, one hand on his amulet. "Do not presume to heal me, Adrian," Finn said between ragged breaths. "I am not broken."

"I'm sorry," Ash said, mortified. "I was only trying to—"

"I know what you were trying to do," Finn said. "Don't." He turned away and disappeared down the forward ladder.

Ash sucked his blistered fingers.

*The time will come when you will wish you were a better healer.*

It seemed that Taliesin's curse would be with him his entire life.

They'd been at it for hours, but now—finally—they were escaping into the open sea. Once out of the bay, the seas roughened and the winds intensified, but at least the minefield of ice thinned, suggesting that their watch was nearly over.

"Stand down, Your Highness," Hadley called from the quarterdeck. "You, too, Strangward. You've done a yeoman's job. Now go aft and get warm."

"I'll be down in a little while," Evan said, gripping the spar with his knees and leaning down toward her. He looked soaked through and half-frozen, the watch cap he always wore on deck was sodden, and yet, he seemed illuminated, as if energized by his connection to the elements. "I'd better make sure we're well out of the shallows and possible coastal traffic before I leave off."

Ash was close enough to Hadley's position at the rail to see the storm brewing in her expression. She opened her mouth, as if to respond. Then, spotting Ash, she shut it again, turned on her heel, and stalked back to the helm.

They were just a few days out, but friction was already growing between Strangward and his stormborn and Hadley and her veterans.

Evan was used to giving orders, not receiving them. Though they'd all agreed that Hadley would serve as ship's master during the seafaring portion of their journey, he seemed to view Hadley's commands as the beginning of a conversation and not the last word. When he ordered Hadley's crew around, they resented it.

For their part, the Carthian crew was unflaggingly loyal to the pirate, always looking to Evan to verify Hadley's orders before following them. Ash could tell that it was getting under her skin.

Ash knew he needed to do something, but he wasn't sure what. This is why Lyss is the officer and you're not, he thought.

# 2

# SECOND THOUGHTS

Ash swapped out his wet clothes and retreated to his berth in the crew bunk room, knowing he would have it to himself this time of day. Reaching into his sea bag, he pulled out a weather-beaten, leather-bound book. He could just make out the timeworn lettering stamped into the cover—*Kinley's Mastery*.

As a boy, Ash had been intrigued by his father's stories about meeting the mysterious Crow in Aediion—the dream world. Crow—who had turned out to be their ancestor Alger Waterlow, known as the Demon King. He'd mentored Ash's father in his battle for his birthright.

At first, Ash had assumed that the ability to cross boundaries had been unique to the two of them, a consequence of Waterlow's unfinished business and his thirst for revenge. But when his father gave him his first amulet, Ash had begun devouring the magical texts in his library. Halfway through *Kinley's Mastery*, Ash found a chapter with directions for travel to the dream world.

For someone with an interest in healing, this seemed like a critical skill. Ash had begged his father to allow him to try a crossing himself.

His father had refused, warning him that the borderlands were a dangerous place. "You never know who'll be waiting for you there," he'd said. "A wizard more skilled than you can change his appearance and change the setting you're in. You can get lost in Aediion and not find your way back to your body."

"I'll be careful," Ash had said, which got him nowhere. "You could come with me," he persisted.

But his father held firm. "There are enough dangers here in the real world. Wait until you get some academy training," he'd said. "They teach it in senior year for a reason. Even then, not many are able to do it. We'll work on it then."

Soon after that, his father was murdered, and Ash fled to Oden's Ford. There, he trained as a healer and launched his career as an assassin. He'd never had a chance to study travel to the dream world, since he never completed his senior year. His schooling had been interrupted by the arrival of the Darian assassins.

Now, it seemed, he had permission, even encouragement from his father.

*Come see me in Aediion*, his father had said. Easier said than done.

Ash flipped to the middle, to a page marked by a ribbon. Page 393. The title was *Portal to Aediion*. There followed several pages outlining the risks of travel to the dream world—a daunting collection of dire consequences for the unwary and untrained. Everything his father had mentioned and more.

*I cannot emphasize enough how important it is for the wizard to leave his corporeal self in a safe place while journeying to the dream world. . . . Not only will it be vulnerable to predators and enemies of all kinds, there is a risk that it will be committed to the funereal flame.*

There was more. If he was killed in Aediion, he would be dead in real life. If he ran out of flash—stored magic—he would have no way back.

Enemies could lie in wait in the dream world, disguised as friends. Worse, an enemy might hitch a ride back to the real world and possess his body.

Ash was beginning to understand why his father had warned him away from it.

Direct magic was the only effective weapon in the dream world. There followed several examples of ways to use flash against adversaries, most of which Ash was familiar with. The exception was a method of "inhaling" magic—of drawing power out of an opponent until he was an empty vessel.

*It is possible to strip magical energy from an adversary in Aediion and turn it to one's own use. This should be used as a last resort, as timing and mastery of the charm are critical.*

He reviewed the lines of spellwork—three for the portal, three for the return. He mouthed the words, practicing them until he knew them by heart.

As Ash understood it, he'd have to meet his father in a place they both knew well. But where? They'd never set a place and time to meet, so what were the chances that they would connect? It wasn't as if he could leave his body behind and go and sit there, day after day, waiting for his father to appear. Not now, when he was on his way to find Lyss.

He was about to close the book and return it to his sea bag, when he noticed something that he hadn't before. At the bottom of the page, writing had bled through from the other side.

He turned the page. On the other side, in neat hand lettering, was printed *Meet at Drovers' Inn*. He stared at it. Ran a finger over it. Drovers' Inn was where he and his father had breakfast at Ragmarket on the day he was murdered.

Had that been there all along? Ash hadn't looked at the book since the day his father died. It had languished on his shelf while Ash was exiled in the south. He'd brought it aboard with him so that he could study it during the crossing.

He examined the inscription, trying to determine if it was in his father's hand. His handwriting was rowdy, scrawling, nearly unreadable. But this was printed. So it could have been him, being careful to make it legible.

But it couldn't have been him. He'd died that same day.

Unless he'd written it there beforehand. Had he had a premonition that he was going to die? Had he wanted to lay the groundwork for a meeting after death?

Or was it some kind of a trick?

Ash would have to go. He knew he had to go—either to meet up with his father or confront his killers. But it would have to wait until this mission was done. He couldn't risk letting his sister down again.

Slowly, he closed the book and shoved it back into his sea bag.

Later that day, after dinner, Ash made his way aft, descending the midship ladder to the gun deck, then continuing on to the officers' quarters in the stern. Hadley had made this space available to Ash's hand-picked band for private discussions. The rest of the crew was housed on the berth deck below.

Ash could hear low voices when he reached the day cabin, but they stopped abruptly when he pushed the door open.

It was Talbot, Finn, and Hadley, blinking at him like guilty co-conspirators.

"Don't mind me," Ash said, taking the stool closest to the potbellied stove and extending his hands to warm them. "You were saying?"

They all looked at one another. Hadley cleared her throat. "This isn't working."

"What do you mean?" Ash said, though he had a guess.

"It—it's just that we think it's a mistake to trust Strangward and his crew," she said. "He's already betrayed you once. Every third word is a lie. He's been decimating our shipping for years. Who's to say that he isn't in league with the empress and this is an elaborate trap?"

"Didn't Julianna say that was unlikely, based on what she was hearing from her eyes and ears?" Ash said. "All reports suggest that Evan and Celestine are sworn enemies."

"Eyes and ears have their limits," Finn said, brushing his fingers over his betrothal ring. "Julianna would be the first to admit that."

Julianna wasn't there to admit that, or anything else. Although she'd been included in early planning, in the end she had elected to stay behind. With the queen in frail health, the realm needed a capable administrator to keep the engines of government going. Besides, as the queen's niece, she was in the line of succession to the throne if their mission failed. The last thing Ash wanted was to hand the empress another weapon.

"Isn't it late to be having second thoughts?" Ash said, knowing he was now the outsider in this group of longtime friends. "If you all had a concern, you should have raised it earlier, before we sailed."

"That was before we saw what he can do," Finn said. "I'm on third thoughts by now."

"It didn't seem to bother you earlier, when you were talking about how impressive he is," Ash said, blindsided by this about-face.

"He *is* impressive," Finn said. "That's what worries me. He can take this ship wherever he wants to go."

"It doesn't help that he's up there in the rigging, where everyone can see him work," Talbot said.

"In all fairness, he can't do that job from his cabin," Ash said. "He has to be able to see where we're going. Maybe he can leave off stormlord duty now that we're in the open ocean."

Hadley snorted. "I can *ask* him to leave off, I can *order* him to leave off, but he's not very good at following orders."

"Any minute, he could conjure up a storm, sink this ship, and drown us all," Finn said.

"At any moment, you, I, or Hadley could burn this ship to the waterline," Ash said. "I don't know about you, but I wouldn't do that because I'm not that good a swimmer."

His attempt to lighten the mood was met with grim faces.

"I trust *you*," Talbot said. "I don't trust *him*."

"Look," Ash said, "he's a pirate without a ship. The last thing he'd want to do is sink this one."

"So we sail to Tarvos, he throws us in prison, and *then* he takes our ship," Finn said.

"That is a risk," Ash said, wondering how the hell he'd gotten into the position of defending Strangward. "Before we left the Realms, didn't we all agree that we would go by way of Tarvos, so that we can take a small crew and a smaller ship to Celesgarde?"

Talbot scowled. "Those bloodsworn of his are—"

"Stormborn," Ash said.

Talbot rolled her eyes, dismissing the distinction. "Whatever they are, they make my skin crawl. They look at him like they're hungry and he's supper."

"My crew is in a panic," Hadley said. "They're afraid they'll end up the same way—as half-dead slaves to Strangward."

"They've lived with magic all their lives," Ash said. "*You're* a wizard. Why are they so skittish all of a sudden?"

"Sailors are skittish," Hadley said. "Even though they've been sailing with me for years, I still don't show off a lot of wizardry when we're at sea."

"Look," Ash said, his irritation rising, partly because he shared some of their reservations. "I have more reason to distrust Strangward than any of you, but this was a forced choice. We need him if we're to have any chance of finding Lyss."

"But . . . wouldn't it make sense to go straight to Celesgarde with the crew we have?" Talbot said. "If Strangward really wants to help us, he'll go along. The longer we delay, the more chance that—that something might happen to Lyss."

"I agree," Finn said. "Why risk detouring to his stronghold? We have a ship, and now we know that we have a crew large enough to sail it, and we know where we're going. You have the maps and charts, right, Hadley? Even if Strangward won't cooperate, can't you get us to the Northern Islands without a guide?"

"Wellll," Hadley said, shifting in her seat. "I've never sailed in those waters. Most of what I know is rumor and tales, and the maps and soundings I have are centuries old."

"Could it have changed that much?" Finn said. "Talbot, you're bound to Lyss. If we get close, you could find her, couldn't you?"

Talbot looked uncomfortable at having that draped around her shoulders. "I'll do my best, of course," she said. "But I don't know."

"What are you proposing?" Ash said, losing patience. "That we dump Strangward overboard?"

"No," Talbot said hastily. "Of course not. But this is *our* mission. He's agreed to help us, but shouldn't we be the ones to decide how to go about it?"

I'm paying the price for being away so long, Ash thought. They've been fighting together for years. Why should they trust my judgment? Last they knew, I was a thirteen-year-old healer who ran away.

"It's Hadley's call, as long as we're aboard ship," Ash said.

"And *yours* once we make landfall," Hadley said, as if throwing him a bone.

"All right, then, we're at sea," Ash said. "What's your decision, Captain?"

"It's risky either way," Hadley said. "If we sail straight to Celesgarde in *Sea Wolf*, there's a greater chance we'll be spotted and recognized, but I would feel a lot more comfortable sailing *Sea Wolf* into a storm line with my crew than Strangward's little ketch with his. If we make straight for Celesgarde, we avoid the risk of being double-crossed in Tarvos, and we get there faster, since there aren't many ships that can beat the *Wolf* for speed." She paused, as if waiting for Ash to pull rank on her. "So I say we bypass Tarvos and sail straight to Celesgarde."

"And I say that would be a mistake."

All eyes turned to the doorway. Evan Strangward stood there, leaning against the frame, one bare foot atop the other, the silver and blue streaks in his hair glittering in the lamplight.

How long has he been listening? Ash thought. Long enough, he guessed.

"I'm here because I want this mission to succeed," Evan said. "That's the only reason I'm here. I've been fighting Celestine since I was thirteen, so I know what I'm doing. You asked for my advice, and I gave it to you. You'd do well to follow it, if you want to get out of this alive."

"Is that a threat, pirate?" Hadley said, eyes narrowed.

"The empress is the threat," Evan said, "not me. But I make this promise—I will not be delivered into the empress's hands, which is what will happen if you try to sail this ship into Celesgarde. If that's your plan, just drop me off on the nearest point of land, and we'll go our separate ways."

"So you can send word to the empress that we're on our way?" Hadley shook her head. "I can't risk it. Whether you help us or not, you stay for the entire mission."

"If I were truly working for the empress, I would keep my mouth shut and let you sail straight to Celesgarde," Evan said, his voice trembling with anger. "That is exactly what she wants."

# 3

# THE DANCE BARBEAU

Captain Charles Barbeau hurried through the familiar corridors leading to the king's small council chamber, determined not to be late. As newly minted captain of King Jarat's guard, this would be his first big appearance before the king's council, the culmination of an investigation that had been going on for weeks. This would be his opportunity to exact revenge on the murderer of his friend Luc Granger in the streets of Ardenscourt.

King Jarat had practically anointed Granger a saint for giving his life in defense of the empire. Charles was good with that. Maybe Granger had sometimes acted like he was better than him, but he'd given him a hand up when he needed it. Plus, now Charles had Luc's old job, and so was now lord and master of the estates Granger had vacated. So he had nothing but good things to say about his late friend.

Everything was riding on this meeting—his new status as a thane, his promotion, maybe his very life. He'd spent half the night practicing what he had to say before drinking himself into a deep sleep. Now he had a hangover, which didn't help.

Charles examined himself in the looking glass at the top of

the stairs, straightening his uniform tunic. He'd paid a pretty price for custom-tailored blacks reflecting his new status. This is your day to shine, he thought, adjusting his sword belt.

A brace of blackbirds was stationed outside the council chamber, collecting weapons. The table behind them was already cluttered with blades and amulets.

Charles nodded approvingly at the guards and went to pass by, but one of them blocked his path.

"All weapons are to be left outside of our council chambers," the blackbird said. "His Majesty's orders."

"I *know* that," Charles snapped. "I cosigned the order. I don't think the king meant to include—"

"*Everyone,*" the blackbird said. "We'll return them to you as you leave."

Charles reluctantly gave up his sword and dagger, a fine matched set left behind by a previous occupant of one of his new estates. Though he'd made sure to arrive early, most of the council members were already there. King Jarat sat at the head of the table, his hands scrabbling through a stack of papers. The young hawk looked to be suffering from a bad case of nerves, too. Maybe, like Charles, he was worried about the confrontation to come. In any event, the king had forgone his usual finery. He was clad in dung-colored velvet, his face pale and haggard. As Charles watched, Jarat refilled his cup from a decanter of wine.

Charles recognized most of the others at the table: Father Fosnaught, principia of the Church of Malthus; Lord Botetort, one of the few old guard thanes who'd remained loyal.

And, of course, General Karn. He was scowling, drumming his fingers on the tabletop. People said that he and his son, the spymaster, despised each other. From what Charles had seen, that was true. Every conversation between them was a series of verbal thrusts and parries.

How would the general react to what Charles had to say?

Both of the Karns were mages. Both of them were dangerous.

There were only two empty seats. Charles prudently took the one farthest from the general.

Blessedly, his fellow thanes and drinking companions Beauchamp and LaRue were there, too. Beauchamp gave him a nod of encouragement. LaRue only smirked. Neither had a clue what was about to happen. Charles liked being in the know. Still, he wished it was all over but the toasts.

It didn't help that it was already hot and stuffy in the room. Charles loosened his collar and debated whether to get up and throw open the shutters. In the end, he let them be.

Everyone jumped as the door banged open, admitting Lieutenant Destin Karn. The spymaster was sleek in his usual King's Guard black. He paused in the doorway, scanning the room. His flinty eyes rested momentarily on Charles, then moved on.

Charles shivered, and his mouth went dry. The spymaster had to be younger than Charles. How did he get to be so intimidating?

Charles glanced at General Karn, then poured himself some very early ale. Hair of the dog, and all that.

"Here we are, finally," King Jarat snapped. "Give us some privacy, please, Lieutenant."

The lieutenant walked around the room, murmuring charms. When he'd finished, the blackbirds collected his amulet, too, then left, closing the door behind them.

King Jarat pointed to the one empty chair. "Sit, Lieutenant

Karn," he said. "I hope that you have brought us some intelligence regarding the recent attack on our city and the disappearance of our . . . guests."

The spymaster tented his fingers together and looked around the circle of councillors. He was as cold-blooded as any temple crow. "Any other requests before I begin?"

Charles gulped down some ale. "I hope you can offer an explanation for how such a disaster could have happened right in our capital and in the presence of representatives from all over the empire."

The spymaster raised an eyebrow, as if this well-prepared speech was just a little over the top, but said nothing.

"Perhaps we should offer a prayer for the safety of our beloved queen mother and Princess Madeleine," Fosnaught suggested.

Jarat waved that away. "Save that for the temple."

"Is this inquest really necessary, Your Majesty?" General Karn said, rubbing the back of his fleshy neck. "It's obvious who's behind the attack, and why. This likely means that the rebel forces will attack sooner rather than later. Instead of dithering, we should mobilize against them in order to choose the most advantageous battlefield."

"Your Majesty, I am all in favor of swagger and sword-brandishing where appropriate," Lieutenant Karn said, his voice dry as dust. He kept his eyes on the king, never glancing at the general. His own father. "My job is to make sure that we choose the most appropriate target."

"General Karn, surely we can spare a few minutes to hear what the lieutenant has learned," Jarat said. "Captain Barbeau, please join in when called upon."

Damned right, I will, Charles thought, first sitting back in his seat, then leaning forward, gripping the arms. Then sitting up straight.

"Thank you, Your Majesty," the spymaster said. "I'll cut to the bone. As you know, our original theory was that the attack on our capital was engineered by the traitorous thanes, seeking to—ah—to secure their families before launching a military operation against us. We were wrong." Young Karn paused, waiting until every eye was fixed on him. "All evidence suggests that the attack on our city was planned and executed by agents of the empress in the east."

A murmur of shock and disbelief rolled through the council. Fosnaught made the sign of Malthus and muttered, "Great saint, protect us."

"The empress in the east?" Botetort said. "As I recall, we sent her emissary packing."

General Karn's eyes narrowed, but his posture didn't change. "You mentioned evidence, Lieutenant?" he said, in a bored voice.

"We believe that Emissary Strangward's visit was for reconnaissance purposes," the lieutenant said. "The story about searching for a magemarked girl was a ruse to gain access to the castle close and assess the feasibility of an attack on our capital. Apparently, in view of the security here, they decided that the north was an easier target."

"But if they've invaded the north, why would they return here and kidnap our women and children?" Beauchamp said.

"Here I can only speculate," Lieutenant Karn said. "Either they saw an opportunity and took it, or they are looking to the future. Once they subdue the north, they'll come south. How better to soften us up than to encourage the thanes to march on the capital? How better to encourage the thanes than to remove the obstacle of the hostages?"

This produced a satisfactory sucking in of breath.

"The other possibility is that the empress is in collusion with the rebels." The spymaster shook his head. "If so, they'll find out how risky that is."

"We've still not heard anything that proves it was the empress and not the rebels," the general said. "Why complicate things?"

"Tell me, General, do the rebels have a navy?" Lieutenant Karn said, gazing up at the ceiling, as if the answer might be written there.

"What does that have to do with—?"

"If you'll let me finish, you'll find out," the spymaster said. "What we do know is that the hostages—and, presumably, Queen Marina and Princess Madeleine—were taken out of the ballroom via the servants' entrance, through the pantry, and into the street. After that, we lose track of them until they take ship from Southgate the next day."

"The next day!" Beauchamp shook his head. "How would nearly fifty women and children travel from Ardenscourt to Southgate in a day?"

"How indeed?" Lieutenant Karn said. "Here's the thing—my eyes and ears in Southgate have identified the ship as belonging to Empress Celestine."

Eyes widened all around.

"Why didn't you say so in the first place?" Botetort grumbled.

"Again, we lose track of the ship, until it lands on the northern coast somewhere between Chalk Cliffs and Spiritgate." The spymaster paused, then added, "North of the border."

Charles looked around the table, to see who was buying what

the lieutenant was selling. Everyone looked confused except the general, whose face had flushed an angry red. Sweat trickled down the center of Charles's back.

"That doesn't make sense," Father Fosnaught said. "Why would the empress deliver the hostages to the witch in the north? Have they formed an alliance?" He shuddered, as if to say the only thing worse than one witch is two.

"Because the empress controls that territory now," Lieutenant Karn said. "It may be that the empress made the same offer to the queen in the north that she made to our late king—an alliance and an army. An offer King Gerard was wise enough to decline. However it happened, the empress's armies attacked Chalk Cliffs, and now hold the city and the port. She has been off-loading soldiers, horses, and equipment in preparation for what appears to be a major invasion."

"A pirate queen from Carthis has taken Chalk Cliffs?" General Karn rolled his eyes. "That's hard to believe. Your eyes and ears are as trustworthy as a harlot's kiss."

"Actually, it's true," King Jarat said. "I have my own eyes and ears in the north, and they confirm what the lieutenant is saying. The empress now controls Chalk Cliffs, and shows every sign of mounting a major offensive." He paused. "However. I've not heard anything about the arrival of our women and children."

Both Karns—father and son—looked surprised. They'd finally found something to agree on.

Lieutenant Karn recovered first. Startlement slid off him like the skin from a snake. He nodded at the king, as if grateful for the support, and continued, "Celestine is more than a pirate. My agents in the east tell me that she now controls the entire

Desert Coast as well as the Northern Islands. There's nothing more to conquer on her home ground. I surmise that she's seeking new territories."

"That still doesn't explain why this pirate empress would send agents to kidnap the families of the rebels and members of our royal family," the general said.

"Isn't it obvious?" the spymaster said. "She's hoping we will blame the rebels. Right now, she'd prefer that we continue fighting each other. That keeps us out of her hair and weakens us so that we will be easy pickings when she turns her eyes south. And she will."

"So," Jarat said, "we'll turn their strategy on its ear. While the northerners are distracted by the attack on their port, we'll march north to Fellsmarch, take the capital, and confront the pirates on northern soil. They will wish they'd never set foot in Ardenscourt."

The general's face had grown darker and darker as the conversation proceeded. "Your Majesty, with all due respect, it's not that easy. We haven't penetrated anywhere close to the seat of the witch in over twenty-five years."

"Whose fault is that?" Jarat said, his voice cold and cutting. "Perhaps our luck is about to change. I have reason to believe that we may receive a warmer welcome in the north than previously. Once the Realms are united, our armies will drive the empress into the sea."

"Whoever sold you that story is shoveling scummer," the general said. "As I've said before, the loss of the hostages won't make a bit of difference when it comes to the rebellion. Lord Matelon was never going to negotiate anyway. He's never parleyed with a hostage-taker or redeemed a prisoner, and he won't begin now. The northerners are no threat to us. They won't set foot outside their mountain strongholds, expecially if they're being attacked from the east. Our greatest threat comes from the rebel thanes, who are used to fighting in the flatlands. Our best protection is the fact that I have a battle-tested army between here and Temple Church. If we march north, the rebels will be inside our walls in a fortnight. We need to handle them first."

"It's too bad that your battle-tested army didn't stand between us and whoever engineered the attack on the city," Charles said. "Lord Granger is dead, we've been embarrassed in front of our guests, the hostages are gone, and so far, nobody has answered for it."

The general gave Charles a look that all but turned his bowels to water, then shifted his attention to his usual target.

"Actually, internal security is the lieutenant's job," the general said, jutting his chin at his son.

"A job I take very seriously," the spymaster shot back.

"Your Majesty," General Karn said, "I'm still not convinced that the pirates—if it was the pirates—could have pulled off the kidnapping without help. Fifty people don't just disappear. Whoever did it knew his way around the city." Again, he fixed his gaze on Lieutenant Karn.

"No doubt the empress has operatives within the walls, as I do in the Fells," the younger Karn said. "What's important is that we act quickly to undo the damage that has been—"

"If I take my army haring off into the north, then we will be vulnerable to the rebel militias," the general said. "No doubt they will take that opportunity to attack the city in force. Or is that the idea?" Again, he looked at the lieutenant.

He's totally throwing his son to the wolves, Charles thought.

"What are you suggesting, General?" Botetort looked from father to son. "Are you saying that it was the thanes who engineered this, after all?"

The general nodded. "The thanes—in alliance with traitors on the inside."

This was the moment Charles had been waiting for. "Your Majesty," he said, "as you know, I have evidence pertaining to this. General Karn is right—there is a traitor in our midst."

The council members shifted in their seats, trying not to make eye contact with anyone else, each one of them wondering, *Which* midst? Present company? The castle close? The capital? Charles enjoyed watching them squirm.

"Who?" Lord Botetort blurted, catapulting to his feet, looking around wildly, reaching for his absent sword.

Charles glared at him, irritated at having his script interrupted. "When I was going through Luc's personal effects, I came across a strongbox containing a packet of correspondence from agents of the empress. Specifically, the pirate. Strangward."

Botetort's eyes widened. "Young Granger was a spy?"

"Certainly not," Charles snapped. "It was addressed to someone else. When I went through it, it became clear that this traitor has been working for the empress for years, and Luc had somehow discovered it. I believe that is what got him killed. So I brought my findings directly to His Majesty."

Jarat looked around the circle, seeming to enjoy the drama of the moment. "I told Captain Barbeau to gather more evidence so that we could measure the scope of the problem and determine what to do." He nodded at Charles, then turned and looked directly at Lieutenant Karn.

"Why don't you take it from here, Lieutenant?"

# A CHANGE IN THE
# WEATHER

The wetlanders didn't listen to Evan's warnings. Over his strenuous objections, the next day Captain DeVilliers charted a course due east, directly toward the Northern Islands. She refused to put into shore and allow him to disembark.

*You should have known this would happen,* Evan thought, trying to quell the despair and helplessness rising in him.

That sick, stupid feeling reminded him of the day he'd first met Celestine, back when he was crewing for Latham Strangward. He'd sat astride the tops'l yard, looking down at the crew he'd thought were his friends. Who'd kept secrets from him. Who'd lied to him. Who'd threatened to kill him.

He'd trusted them, and they betrayed him. He'd sworn that would never happen again.

Since then, the only people he'd ever trusted were Destin Karn and Destin's mother, Frances.

*You should have known not to trust these wetlanders. This is why you've always used stormborn in your crew—so you wouldn't risk betrayal at sea.*

And then, friendless orphan that he was, he'd put aside the good sense that had served him for so long. He'd been so eager to make an ally that he'd overlooked the danger. And now, once again, he was heading straight into Celestine's hands.

Still, when his stormborn crew, Brody and Jorani, came to him for direction, he told them to follow the Fellsian captain's orders to the letter. "There's only one captain on this ship," Evan said. "That's what we agreed on."

"Why should we keep our promises when they don't?" Jorani grumbled.

"Because I don't want you to pay the sailor's price for insubordination."

"We're willing to pay it," Brody said, and Jorani nodded.

"Because we need to win them over," Evan said.

They slouched away, with many backward looks.

What he didn't say was that there was more than one way to win them over. Or to win, at least. He'd tried the carrot. Now for the stick.

The day after that, the wind changed from the usual easterlies to blow strongly from the northwest. The entire crew worked like demons to stay ahead of the weather: deploying sails, trimming them, turning the ship into the wind, then turning again when the wind changed, struggling to make any headway at all. Every time they relaxed their vigilance, the ship was driven off course—always south.

The weather was known to be chancy in the northern Indio, but now waterspouts rose from the ocean all around them, smashing into them broadside. Sailors learned to cling to railings, masts, and other fixed objects as they navigated their way around the decks, since every so often a rogue wave would smash over the gunwales, threatening to wash crew members into the sea.

Evan stayed out of sight as much as possible, appearing only to work his watches and to take his meals in the galley. The rest of the time he spent reading in the day cabin or lurking on deck in out-of-the-way places, watching the skies and using his instruments and star charts to determine their position. He made sure to keep the wolf constellation to his right and the dragon of Carthis to his left.

After a day of this, DeVilliers hunted Evan down in the stern gallery, where he'd taken refuge from the weather. He was playing his third game of nicks and bones with Brody.

She minced no words. "Strangward! When you signed on for this, you agreed to follow my orders at sea."

Evan glanced about, pretending that he thought the wetland sea captain might be speaking to someone else. "I'm not sure what you mean," he said. "I haven't missed a watch, and I'm off duty now. Is something wrong?"

"Captain Strangward told us to do what you said," Brody volunteered. "He said you was the only captain on this ship."

The ship rocked violently as a wave struck it midships, and DeVilliers had to grab onto the rail to keep from being thrown off her feet. She pointed at Brody. "You. Go."

Brody packed up the game pieces, saluted them both, and hurried away.

"I'm talking about the bloody weather," DeVilliers said.

Evan parsed his words carefully. "All ship's masters are at the mercy of the weather gods."

"I honor the weather gods," DeVilliers said. "But wizard mischief is something else. I won't tolerate insubordination. Tell the truth, now—are you responsible for these rogue winds and relentless storms?"

Evan gave up the dance. "We agreed on a plan, Captain," he said. "Then you changed it. I told you that I would not allow you to deliver me into the empress's hands, and I won't."

The captain's eyes narrowed. "So you *are* interfering."

"Your word is law aboard ship, but out there . . ." He waved toward the rail. "I'll use every weapon at my command to survive."

"By capsizing us?"

"There's no need for that. Simply put me ashore and you can be on your way. I'll wish you fair winds and following seas."

"And what's to prevent you from sending word to the empress that we are on the way?"

Evan shrugged. "The fact that Celestine and I are enemies? The fact that I gave my word, and I mean to keep it?" *Unlike you.*

DeVilliers stuck out her hand. "Give me your amulet."

Evan curled his hand protectively around Destin's amulet. "It won't make any difference. You see, I don't use amulets in the same way that—"

"Give it here," she said, "and that's an order."

Reluctantly, he lifted the chain from around his neck and handed it over. Captain DeVilliers turned on her heel and stalked away.

The weather went from bad to worse. After three days, *Sea Wolf* had been driven nearly to Deepwater Court, instead of north, where DeVilliers wanted to go. The crew's efforts to force her north all but capsized them several times. Even experienced sailors spent much of the day heaving over the side.

Now DeVilliers relieved Evan of duty and ordered that he be confined belowdecks. The next day, the relentless winds died and the seas quieted until the surface was like glass. And then they sat. And sat. Becalmed. Not a breath of air stirred the sheets that hung limp on the mainmast. DeVilliers was a capable pilot, and the entire crew willing, but nothing is nothing, and they went nowhere.

The Fellsians came and went from the day cabin, glaring, until DeVilliers burst in, slapped Evan's book away, and said, "Do you think this is some kind of a joke?"

Evan blinked up at her, then leaned down and retrieved his book. "I thought you *wanted* calm weather," he said, trying to find his place again.

She ripped the book out of his hands and tossed it into the corner. "Tell me why I shouldn't bind you hand and foot and toss you overboard," she snapped.

"If you like the weather we're having, go ahead," Evan said. "You and your ship can sit here forever. Before long, you'll be down to drinking piss." Actually, he had no idea what would happen to the weather if he drowned, but DeVilliers didn't need to know that.

"But you'll be dead."

"Meaning I'll miss a lot of bad weather. And piss-drinking." Evan fanned himself.

"You're bluffing," DeVilliers said.

"I am not bluffing," Evan said. "I would rather be dead than be handed over to the empress."

And that was true.

The captain ordered him sent to the brig and stormed out.

Later that day, Evan was drowsing in his hammock, his book

lying forgotten on his chest. Wakened by some small sound, he opened his eyes to find the healer sitting opposite him, hands on his knees, looking at him as if he were an egg about to hatch.

Evan propped up on his elbows. "What is it now?" he said.

"Are you really willing to capsize this ship in order to get your own way?" the wolf prince said.

"I'm willing to capsize this ship in order to keep you from handing me over to the empress."

The healer scowled. "What the hell are you talking about?"

"Look," Evan said, "I'm not stupid. The empress has something you want, and you have something she wants. We sail directly to Celesgarde and you make the swap."

Comprehension dawned in the healer's eyes. "You think we intend to trade you for my sister."

"That is exactly what I think," Evan said, folding his arms across his chest, over the place his amulet should have been. "I knew I was taking a chance, signing on for this mission, but I did it because we ought to be on the same side. Betraying me may seem like the best way to get your sister back, but I know Celestine, and there's no way you can play this game with her and win."

"I won't double-cross you," Prince Adrian said.

"And I won't throw you in prison and steal your ship," Evan said.

"Look, I'm sorry you overheard that," the healer said. Embarrassment looked good on him.

"That's how I learn things," Evan said. "Why should I believe your assurances when you won't believe mine? Can you speak for all of your crewmates?"

"No," Prince Adrian said, "which is why I can't order them

to sail into a possible trap in Tarvos."

"It's a lovely city, really," Evan said. "Plenty of wind." When the healer kept on scowling, Evan sighed. "What's the point in being a prince if you cannot tell people what to do?"

"I'm not the heir—I'm the spare. Besides, we're a bit more democratic in the Fells than in the empire."

"Pity," Evan said. "Democracy won't get your sister back."

Prince Adrian studied him. "Tell me, pirate—what *is* the best way to get my sister back?"

"I've already told you. Small ship, small crew, weather magery, and me. I'm willing to go after her by myself, if you're worried I'm leading you into a trap. But, when I show up at Celestine's door, why would your 'Captain Gray' trust me?"

"Remind me why you would risk your life to go after my sister?"

"I need allies," Evan said. It was all he could do to keep his voice under control. "If I could defeat Celestine on my own, I would. I've been fighting her all my life. I assume you brought me along because of that experience. It does you no good if you won't listen to me. Forgive me, but if you insist on being stupid, I don't intend to fling myself into the flame alongside you." Evan paused, distracted by the sound of running feet.

The door to the brig banged open to reveal Captain Talbot. "Strangward. Captain DeVilliers wants you on deck on the double. There's a ship bearing down on us, and she's hoping you can identify it."

# THE SERPENT'S TOOTH

"Why don't you take it from here, Lieutenant?" the king had said. Now every member of the king's council was staring at Destin, waiting.

Destin took his time. He sighed and looked at the door as if he wished that he could escape through it. He fingered the heavy gold ring on his right hand for luck—the one engraved with his mother's Chambord bear signia. The one Evan had given back to him in a tavern in Baston Bay.

Finally, he turned back toward King Jarat. "I've said this before, but I'll say it again. I'm sorry, Your Majesty. I feel at least partially responsible for Lord Granger's death."

"Understood, Lieutenant," Jarat said. "But carry on."

Destin looked around the circle. "You see, Lord Granger was working for me."

This was met by stunned silence.

"Working . . . for *you?*" Beauchamp said finally, his face twisting as if he smelled something bad. "I thought it was the other way around."

"We both report directly to His Majesty," Destin said, struggling to be patient with this dog-eared question, "though there is, of course, some overlap. I focus on intelligence throughout the empire. Granger's focus was protecting the person of the king and his family and guests."

Botetort shuddered. "But why would a young man with such bright prospects want to involve himself in—?"

"Exactly," Destin said. "Spycraft is a nasty business, unsuitable for those of noble breeding. Yet Granger was always interested in expanding beyond his role as captain of the King's Guard and bailiff. He had a strong interest in the intelligence service. Perhaps he had a need for solving puzzles. Perhaps it reflected his dedication to using all possible strategies to protect our king. He kept bringing me bits of information that he thought I would find useful." Destin rubbed his temples. Shoveling scummer always gave him a headache.

"I swear by all the saints, I tried to persuade him to leave off, to serve our king in another way, but he was . . . determined. And, actually, quite good at espionage." He looked up at Jarat again. "I keep thinking that I should have come to you, Your Majesty, and asked you to intervene."

Jarat sighed. "He knew that I disapproved of his dabbling in spycraft, but I never forbade it," he said.

Destin took a breath, collecting his thoughts. "I finally agreed to allow him access to some of my sources, because I thought it would be safer for him to be working under my supervision. I told him that he needed to work closely with me, and bring me his findings straightaway so that we could determine how to proceed. That otherwise, he might be putting himself in grave danger."

Destin swallowed hard. "So, after Lord Granger was killed, Captain Barbeau came to me with the letters he'd found in Lord Granger's strongbox. I was devastated. I immediately offered to step aside and let someone else take over the investigation."

"I assured Lieutenant Karn that I had every confidence that he would pursue the evidence wherever it led," King Jarat said.

"You see—I'm speculating here—Lord Granger must have come across correspondence between a traitor here in the city and the empress's emissary. Due to the—to the identity of parties involved, he may have been afraid to come to me. He decided to investigate on his own. I now believe he had some warning of the attack the night of the party, and put himself in position to confront the culprits." He shook his head. "We all know what happened."

Thus far, Destin had avoided looking at the general, afraid that his father would somehow read his intentions in his face. Still, any discussion of secrets that he was not privy to always made the general uneasy. Especially with Destin in the coachman's seat. The general shifted in his chair and glared around the room, eyes narrowed, big sweat marks blossoming under his arms.

"Are you going to tell us what you found or not?" he growled. "Or do we have to watch you mince around it for the whole damned day?"

Destin looked at the king, who nodded. He rose, crossed to the door, and called in the half dozen blackbirds waiting outside. They swarmed in and stood in a rough semicircle around King Jarat.

Destin returned to his seat, reached under his coat and pulled out a chamois-wrapped bundle, resting it on his knees. "This is the knife I found with Lord Granger's body," he said. Slowly, methodically, he unrolled it from its wrapping, then held it up for all to see.

It was a sleek dagger, with a double-edged blade made for doing hard business. The handle, however, was distinctive. The quillions were a beautifully worked pair of stooping hawks, and the skull-crusher pommel cap was the head of a snarling bear. It was clan-made, in an era when northern metalcraft was almost impossible to come by.

Botetort leaned in so that he could take a closer look at it. "What are those devices on the hilt? It looks like a . . . a bear and—are those hawks?"

Destin heard his father's hard intake of breath. He looked up and met the general's gaze without flinching. "I believe this belongs to you," he said.

He turned toward the others. "This was a gift from my mother to the general on their wedding day." Not exactly true, but close enough. Destin traced the metalwork with his forefinger. "The bear is for my mother's family, the Chambords. The hawks represent the general's long service to the king."

The general had been smitten with it, representing as it did his rise from despised mage and soldier into the corridors of power. It was the one thing of beauty he'd protected, the only one he hadn't destroyed. He'd carried it constantly, displayed it often, and used it at the least provocation until he'd left it in a puddle of blood in the seaside cottage in Tarvos.

Evan had brought it to Destin at Baston Bay. Since then, Destin had carried it constantly, hoping to return it to his father at an appropriate time. In an appropriate way. Until the night of the party, when he'd given it to Harper Matelon for self-defense.

By now, the general's face was the color of fresh liver. "You lying, gutter-swiving, scummer-sucking—I haven't seen that thing for years. Where did you get it?"

"Like I said, I found it in the street next to Lord Granger's body, covered in his blood." *How many have died on the point of this blade, General?*

The general looked around at the other council members. "Does anyone here really think that I'm stupid enough to murder a thane with my own dagger—a weapon that could be traced back to me?"

"That's exactly what I thought," Destin said, "at least at first. As you all know, my father and I have had our differences, but I couldn't believe that he would murder one of the king's most important councillors. I launched an investigation, assuming I would find out that his blade had been stolen, or that there was some other explanation. But when Captain Barbeau came to me with the letters Lord Granger had found, I knew that I was wrong."

"What did young Granger find?" Botetort asked.

Destin nodded at Barbeau. "That's your story to tell, Captain."

Of course it was. After all, Barbeau had been the one to find the papers Destin had planted in Lord Granger's rooms. Therefore, the new captain of the King's Guard was invested in the truth of the contents and in position to back up Destin's story.

Barbeau puffed up like a black-feathered peacock. "It seems that General Karn has been collaborating with agents in the Fells for years," he said, "since before King Jarat came to the throne. It goes a long way toward explaining why we've never been able to gain an advantage over the queen in the north, despite our superior resources."

"You swiving cock-robin," the general muttered, too softly for any but Destin's trained ear to hear.

"It was all there—letters, messages, references to maps, diagrams of defenses, and the like. The northerners knew we had cannon on the heights overlooking Delphi, knew our numbers and weaponry, and knew our points of vulnerability. Captain Matelon may be a traitor, but the loss of Delphi was by design."

Barbeau glanced at Destin, who smiled faintly. After days of coaching, the new-made thane sounded almost . . . clever.

The general planted his thick hands on the arms of his chair and pushed to his feet, back rigid. The flock of blackbirds stirred and drew their weapons.

Barbeau looked from the general to the blackbirds, wet his lips with a gulp of ale, and continued. "Despite the general's efforts, the war dragged on with no end in sight. The thanes were getting restless, and he worried that he'd be replaced as commander of the empire's armies, especially after King Gerard's death. So he offered his services to the empress."

He unrolled a parchment sleeve, and pulled out a crumpled page. "This is dated the third of last month, a few weeks before the masquerade." He cleared his throat and read. "'Expect us at the river docks after midnight. Require five wagons and horse teams for transport of approximately fifty persons.'" He looked up. "It's unsigned."

"I'm surprised it isn't signed 'Your Friend, General Karn,'" Karn growled. "Like I'd be foolish enough to commit treason in writing. This is a farce, Your Majesty, and a forgery, and if you don't know it now, you will. I am not going to sit here in the meantime and listen to this stall-whimpering molly tell lies about me."

"General," King Jarat said, "is it possible that Lord Granger was targeted because he was under consideration to replace you as the commander of the imperial armies?"

The words landed with a thud in the suddenly silent room.

The general stood rigid, fists clenched, like an embattled bull deciding which way to charge. "I was . . . unaware of that, Your Majesty." He bowed stiffly to the king. "I'll be in the garrison house, preparing my defense."

"General Karn, I look forward to hearing the evidence you present in formal proceedings," King Jarat said. "But, in view of what we've seen and heard, I must insist that you be confined to the tower until we can sort this out."

The general halted, midturn, and stood, fists clenched, staring at the floor. "Surely that won't be necessary, Your Majesty."

"If you are innocent," Jarat said, "then we'll soon put this unpleasant business behind us."

"I have served your father for more than thirty years," the general said, "when nobody gave him a gnat's chance of winning the throne."

"All of that will be taken into consideration."

With that, the dam of malice broke, as Destin knew it would. "I won't be tossed into gaol by a candy-assed boy who can't even dress himself," the general snarled.

Jarat's eyes narrowed to slits, and in that moment he looked more like his father than he ever had before. "Guards! Take General Karn to the Pit."

The vein in the general's forehead pulsed, and Destin knew what was coming. He'd spent a lifetime learning to read those cues.

Still, when the explosion finally came, he was ambushed,

as always. If he'd thought Barbeau's performance would redirect his father's rage, he was mistaken. His father could move quickly for such a bulky man. Instead of bolting for the door, or charging the king, he lunged toward Destin, slamming into him with the force of a runaway slag wagon. They both toppled backward to the floor, the general on top.

The general gripped Destin's lapels, repeatedly slamming his head against the stone floor, igniting those familiar skyrockets behind his eyes. Kindling the familiar terror in his gut. There was a commotion all round them, the king shouting to his guards to take the general alive, the blackbirds swarming, trying to drag his father off him. Yet, somehow, the scene had been reduced to two players, each reprising the role he'd mastered long ago.

"I should have drowned you at birth," the general said, spraying spittle into Destin's face. "As soon as I laid eyes on you, I knew you were no son of mine. I may go to gaol, but you'll be dead, and I promise you, the bitch will pay."

"Didn't anyone tell you?" Destin gasped. "You're too late. Frances passed away three days ago."

With a roar like a bloodied bull, the general wrapped his thick fingers around Destin's throat and squeezed until black shadows swarmed before his eyes. Destin gripped his mother's dagger with both hands and plunged it into his father's black heart.

For several long moments, nothing happened. Hot blood welled up around the blade, soaking into Destin's coat. Then, gradually, the general's eyes glazed over, the spark of malice extinguished. His grip loosened, and Destin sucked in ragged gulps of air. Finally, the blackbirds were able to pull his father's dead body away.

# 6

# A SMALL MUTINY

By the time Ash raced up four levels from the brig to the quarterdeck, he was out of breath, his knees quivering. Strangward still beat him there, with Captain Talbot lagging a deck behind both of them. When Ash arrived, the pirate was standing on the quarterdeck with DeVilliers and Finn, sweeping the horizon with his spyglass. Just outside their circle of calm water, a three-masted ship was barreling toward them, her sails bellying out with a strong northeast wind.

Strangward lowered the glass and swore softly. Handing the glass back to DeVilliers, he pulled out a watch cap and yanked it down over his hair.

"Who is it?" Captain DeVilliers demanded.

"She's not flying colors, but I can tell by her lines and rigging that she's one of Celestine's," the pirate said. "I won't know which ship or who's at the helm until she gets a bit closer."

"I would prefer that she didn't. Get any closer, I mean," DeVilliers said, scowling.

Hands on hips, Strangward glared around at the mirrorlike sea, the flaccid sails. "It may be too late already. Here we are, sitting ducks on a duck pond in the middle of the ocean."

"Which is your fault," DeVilliers said. "Your gambit has given us away."

"No, Captain, what has given us away has been your insistence on ignoring my advice and sailing your fine flagship so close to the Northern Islands," Strangward said.

"I don't care whose fault it is," Ash hissed, his eyes fixed on the oncoming ship. "Could you give us some wind, Evan, so that we can maneuver, at least?"

Strangward stared up at the sky. "If Captain DeVilliers gives me my amulet back, I'll see what I can do."

"Captain?" Ash said, feeling like he was arbitrating a schoolyard squabble.

DeVilliers reached into her stormcoat, produced the pendant on a chain, and thrust it at Strangward. He slid the chain over his head, tucking the pendant under his coat. Then, with a snap of his wrist, he conjured a light wind that sent ripples across the water's surface and stirred the sheets hanging limp on the masts.

"We'll need more wind than that," DeVilliers growled.

"If I raise too much weather, I may as well run my standard up the mast," Strangward said. "We might get away, but the element of surprise will be lost. And that's the only way we win this. If Celestine finds out I'm here, in a matter of days, the entire Desert Coast will be swarming with ships, all hunting for us."

As Ash watched, the other ship crossed the invisible line, its sails deflating a bit but her momentum carrying her closer and closer. Strangward raised a cross breeze, and Ash could see the sailors aboard the enemy ship scrambling to adjust the sails, tacking a bit to starboard to find the wind again.

Ash squinted at the Carthian ship, shading his eyes, looking for the blue-white aura that marked the gifted. Members
of the crew glowed, but it was a dull indigo color. These must
be the—

"Bloodsworn," DeVilliers said, looking disappointed, as if
she'd harbored some hope that Strangward was mistaken. As
they watched, the empress's siren banner climbed the mast, followed by the black flag, demanding surrender.

"Do you think we can bluff our way out of this?" Ash said.

DeVilliers said, "Maybe," at the same time that Strangward
said, "No."

"They already know who we are—at least that we're aboard
a wetland ship," Strangward said.

"Even if they do, why would they challenge us?" DeVilliers
said. "They can tell we're heavily armed, and unlikely to be
carrying valuable goods. Pirates favor easier meat."

"But Celestine isn't thinking like a pirate these days,"
Strangward said. "She's thinking like an empress, with territory to protect. She'll want to know what we're doing so close
to their capital. How—and if—we get out of this will depend
on whether she's aboard. I don't feel her presence—yet. Let me
take another look."

DeVilliers slapped the spyglass into his hand. He looked
again.

"Well?" Ash whispered. "Do you see her?" He'd looked
forward to seeing the empress for himself, but not under these
circumstances.

Strangward shook his head. "It's Tully Samara, the empress's
admiral of the fleet. The ship is the *Hydra*. As far as I can tell,
they have no mages aboard, unless you count the bloodsworn.

The good news is that Samara can't erect magical barriers or work any fancy magic. On the other side of the ledger, the bloodsworn are unstoppable hand to hand. We cannot allow them to get close enough to board."

"We can't afford to get into a firefight, either," DeVilliers said. "We might lose crew, and we're at a minimum as it is. Look, we have four wizards on board, and from what you say, they have none. If we demonstrate what they're up against, don't you think they'll back off?"

"It's more likely to make them wonder why we're sailing off their coast with four wizards on board, at a time when all of our magical assets are needed for the fight at home," Ash said. "We'd have to sink them outright, or they'll carry that knowledge back to Celesgarde."

Strangward shot him a quizzical look, as if surprised by this display of logic.

"Then we'll run up the yellow flag," DeVilliers said, "and try and bluff our way out that way. At least it might explain why we're sitting offshore, going nowhere."

Strangward rubbed his chin. "Every freebooter from Sand Harbor to Deepwater Court knows that rig. Even if you scare off Samara, it won't bother the bloodsworn."

"What's the yellow flag?" Ash felt hopelessly unschooled in nautical matters.

"It signals disease on board," DeVilliers said. "A symbol of quarantine. It's an old trick to fend off pirates, but that, along with our firepower, might cause them to think twice."

Strangward shook his head. He leaned toward DeVilliers, speaking low and urgently. "Captain, now that we're in this, we need to hit them hard and fast with conventional weapons.

With the crew we have, we can't man the big guns, so we probably can't sink her. The best we can do is cripple her enough that we can sail away without revealing too much. My recommendation is to erect magical barriers, which Samara can't see, then open up with the eight-pounders with bar and chain, aiming for the masts and rigging. If they try to board, use the swivel cannon at the rails, loaded with grape and canister shot."

All traces of Strangward's usual self-deprecating charm were gone. In its place was the hard and ruthless Stormcaster of legend. And, once again, the pirate was telling the master of the Fellsian navy what to do. But in this case, at least, she bowed to the stormlord's expertise.

DeVilliers gazed at Strangward for a long moment, then nodded curtly. "That will require time to set up. We'll put up the yellow flag and stall for time. You give us a brisk northwest wind to hold the weather gage. Baines, you're on the gunnery deck. When the eight-pounders are primed and ready to go, run them out and fire when ready. Teza, you are sailmaster. Finn, you handle the barriers. Jorani, run up the yellow flag and then load the swivel cannon, but keep them out of sight for now. Prince Adrian, go forward and charm the Carthians. Keep them occupied and stop them if they try to board us."

"Captain," Captain Talbot said, her sword in her hand, practically vibrating with the need for action. "What can I do?"

"Help the prince," DeVilliers said. She reached into the slop chest and pulled out two long strips of yellow cloth—flags made from the remnants of sailor's shirts. "You'll be the last surviving crewmen." She turned away, toward the stairs.

Like a shell detonating, the crew dispersed to battle stations. Finn, Talbot, Ash, and Strangward sprinted forward.

Finn peeled off at midships, planting himself by the mainmast. Moments later, a glittering web of magic spun out from the waist of the ship, settling gently over the masts and rigging.

When they reached the forecastle, Ash could see bloodsworn lined up along *Hydra*'s rails, grappling hooks in hand. It didn't require close counting to tell that they were vastly outnumbered. Strangward peered around the foremast. "There's Samara," he murmured, pointing. "He's the only one who's not bloodsworn." The Stormcaster retreated to the aft side of the foremast, planting his back against it. Curling his fingers around his amulet, he raised his other hand, as if reaching for weather. The ship shuddered as the sails began to fill.

Ash gazed across the waves at the fleetmaster, who wore a lavishly brocaded coat, high boots, a broad gold belt, and a satisfied smile. He held a curved Carthian sword loosely in one hand.

"Greetings, wetlanders!" Samara called. "You have nothing to fear. Strike your colors and stand down, and you will find out just how merciful the empress can be."

Anger welled up in Ash. Would the empress display the same kind of mercy she'd shown at Chalk Cliffs? Had this fleetmaster seen his sister? Did he know where she was? Ash wanted to reach across the waves, grip him by the throat, and demand answers.

"Your Highness?" Talbot touched his sleeve, breaking into his dark daydream.

Ash collected himself, leaned toward Talbot, and murmured, "Let's buy some time." Ash stepped away from the mast, lunging forward to grip the rail as if worried that his legs wouldn't support his weight. Talbot came up beside him, following his cue. Ash couldn't help thinking that he and Talbot were poor choices to impersonate a pair of sailors. He hoped that Samara wouldn't ask them to recite the pirate code or demonstrate a sailor's knot.

"Halloo the ship!" Ash called.

Samara stared at Ash in his nondescript coat and mariner's cap, a makeshift scarf around his neck. His gaze slid to Talbot and then back to him. Clearly, this was not what the fleetmaster had expected.

"Who are you?" Samara said in Common. "I expected to be greeted by a wetlander naval commander. Instead, we have what looks like a pair of wetland scrubs. Or is it just that you couldn't find a uniform large enough to fit that one?" He nodded toward Talbot.

Ash saluted the empress's flag. Talbot squinted at him, then followed suit.

"Sir. We are privateers with a letter of marque from the king of Arden," Ash said. "We work the wetland coast off Bruinsport. We captured this Fellsian vessel, and wish to present it to Empress Celestine with our compliments."

"Is that so?" Samara scanned *Sea Wolf*'s decks for activity. "Where's the rest of your crew?"

Ash and Talbot exchanged glances, as if getting their story straight. "They're—uh—sleeping," Talbot said. "Below."

"The empress is always in need of good ships, sailors, and soldiers," Samara said. "But why would you want to give up your prize?"

"We're hoping the empress will take us on," Ash said eagerly. "The boy king in Arden—he is even more miserly than his father. We think we'd do better with you."

Samara eyed them skeptically. "Where's your captain? I want to speak with him."

"He—ah—he's resting," Ash said. "He can't be disturbed."

"I don't believe you," Samara said. He pointed to the yellow flag flying from *Sea Wolf*'s rigging. "What the hell is that?"

Ash stared up at the flag, as if surprised to find it there. "That? It's only . . ." He pretended to be overcome by a spell of dizziness, hanging on to the rail in order to remain upright.

"It's some kind of a northern banner, I reckon," Talbot said. "We just never took it down." She blotted at her face with her rag mask and shivered, as if from a sudden chill.

Finally recovering his balance, Ash called, "Would you like to come aboard, sir? Or should we pass a line and come to you?" Reflexively, Talbot gripped his arm, as if she thought he might follow through.

Samara looked up at the flag again. "What is it? Ship's fever? Bloody flux? The pox?"

"I don't know what you mean, sir," Ash said.

"I mean that you're trying to run a rig on us," Samara said. "Trying to gull us into letting you bring contagion onto our ship and back to our home port."

Ash tried to keep the astonishment off his face. Was this sketchy plan actually going to work?

"Please, sir," Talbot said. "We have to get off this ship. We don't want to end up like—like the rest."

Ash glared at her. "Shut up!" he hissed.

"It seems to me," Samara said, with a sharklike smile, "that the kindest thing to do would be to put the lot of you out of your misery. It will also teach you not to bring wetland diseases so close to our shore." He turned to his waiting bloodsworn.

"Put down your grappling hooks, men. We won't be boarding this one. Run out the guns and fire at my command."

The bloodsworn seemed to take this order quite literally. All along the rails, grapnels hit the deck with a clatter, and the crew swarmed to battle stations.

Well, Ash thought, they're not going to board us, but there's more than one way a plan can go wrong. What the hell was going on below? He knew they were shorthanded, but how long could it take to ready the smaller guns?

Then it seemed like everything happened at once. First, the creak of the hinges as *Sea Wolf*'s gun ports opened and the rattle of the side tackles as the eight-pounders slid into view. Strangward's stormborn sailor Jorani immediately began to roll one of the deck cannons to the rail. Talbot ran to help her, and together they got it secured and went back for another.

The deck shook as the eight-pounders roared beneath their feet, sending bar and chain shot pinwheeling into *Hydra*'s rigging, shearing off the foremast and shredding the sheets at midships. The second volley ripped into *Hydra*'s wheelhouse, which was emotionally satisfying but did little to arrest the enemy's battle preparations. The third volley took out the mainmast, sending it crashing sternward.

Jorani raked *Hydra*'s deck with grapeshot from one of the deck guns, sending the bloodsworn flying. When it was emptied, she raced to the next and put the match to it. She unloaded one more gun into the Carthian ship, and then they were done until they could reload.

Samara's shouted commands floated across the water as *Hydra*'s gun ports slid open.

"Prepare to come about!" DeVilliers shouted, and the ship

began a slow turn, presenting its stern to the *Hydra*. Ash and Talbot ran aft, meaning to keep the enemy ship in view. Just as they came abreast of the foremast, *Sea Wolf* lurched forward as her sails filled with air, and Ash fell flat on his back. Talbot was extending a hand to help him up when he was blinded by a flash of light and searing heat as the entire ship shuddered and pitched. The foremast and rigging crashed down on him, and he found himself entangled in lines and sailcloth, breathing in the scent of burning pitch and scorched wood.

Clearly, the *Hydra* had launched its first volley. But what had happened to the barriers?

Fighting free of the rigging, Ash looked aft. Finn stood alone in the waist of the ship, his stormcoat fluttering in the rising wind, one hand on his amulet, his eyes closed.

As Ash watched, Finn opened his eyes, wells of malice in a pale, grief-stricken face. The eyes of a stranger. Raising his free hand, he released a torrent of flame directly at Ash.

What the hell, Finn?

Ash flung himself to one side, but not quickly enough. He was conscious of searing heat, and a concussion all but cut him in half and left his ears ringing. Then he was in the water, wrapped up like a parcel in sailcloth and unable to tell which way was up.

Ash kicked strongly, hoping he wasn't weighed down too much to float to the surface. Before long, his mouth filled with salt water, and his lungs were bursting, and he still couldn't see a thing.

You're going to die, he thought. I'm sorry, Lyss. I'm sorry, Mother. I'm sorry, Jenna. He'd managed to fail all of the women in his life. The men, too.

Somebody wrapped a muscled arm around his chest from the
rear, towing him upward until his head broke the surface of the
water. Ash sucked in air gratefully, then began coughing, trying to expel seawater from his lungs. His rescuer took his hands
and planted them on something solid, made of ridged wood or
planks. "Hang on to this, healer," he said. "I'll be right back."

It was Strangward. Within the space of an hour, his erstwhile
friend had tried to kill him, and his erstwhile enemy had saved
his life. It was no wonder he couldn't tell which way was up.

Keeping one hand on his makeshift raft, Ash groped for
his belt dagger and carefully sliced away canvas and lines until
he uncovered his face and he could see. He found that he was
clinging to the overturned hull of the longboat that had been
mounted just above deck level on the *Sea Wolf.* He looked back
at the ship, and saw that there was a huge bite taken out of the
port side of the ship right where he and Talbot had been standing. The hull and decking were charred black, as if they'd been
flamed.

He squinted, blotting seawater from his eyes, and realized
that *Sea Wolf* was still under way, growing smaller and smaller
as she receded into the distance. When he looked around, he
saw that he was floating midway between *Sea Wolf* and the
*Hydra*, with nothing but ocean all around, no sign of land as far
as the eye could see. "Hey!" he shouted. "Sailors overboard!"
And then, "Help!" even though he realized that it was probably
futile as more and more ocean opened between them and *Sea
Wolf.*

"Will you shut *up?*" someone said, startling Ash so that he
almost lost his hold on the keel.

Strangward was back, this time towing an unconscious

Talbot, who was bleeding heavily from a head wound. "Sound carries over water, and we don't want Samara coming over to finish what he started."

"You'd rather drown?"

Strangward thought about this for a long moment, as if it were a hard question. Then he said, "We're not going to drown, healer, unless you panic." He brought Talbot up beside Ash, boosting her a little so that her chest and head rested on the side of the boat. "Here," he said. "Keep her head above water and try to stop the bleeding. There are enough predators around here without drawing any more."

Talbot was reviving, coughing and sputtering. It consumed all Ash's attention to keep her from foundering the boat before she came fully awake. She vomited out seawater, and then, eventually, began spewing words. "What the hell just happened? Where's the ship? What are we— Strangward! What are you doing here?" She eyed the pirate suspiciously. "Where's the rest of the crew?" She swung her head from side to side. By now, both ships were out of sight. Empty ocean stretched all the way to the horizon. "Why do I keep ending up in the ocean?" she moaned. "All my life until recently, I never even came close to drowning, and now twice in a couple of months—"

"Be quiet and hold still," Ash said, "and I'll try to close up the hole in your head." Fortunately, it was just a flesh wound, and he was able to deal with it quickly. His own head was thick with confusion. What had just happened? It had seemed like they were getting away. And then—

Strangward watched the horizon a little longer, waiting for rescue or enemy vessels to appear. Then he said, "All right, I'm going to flip this boat over. I don't want to lose either of you, so you need to grab onto the line, let go of the boat, and put as much distance between you and it as you can."

"You want us to let go of the boat?" Talbot said, her teeth chattering.

"I can't flip the boat with you clinging onto it like a barnacle," the pirate said. Ash and Talbot walked their way hand over hand down the length of the boat until they reached the tether line. Releasing their hold on the planking, they held tight to the line.

"Be ready for a high wave, all right?" Strangward said. Moving a short distance away from the boat, he held on to his amulet with one hand and made a kind of come-hither motion with the other. The longboat disappeared into a trough, then seemed at risk to be foundered by a high wave that slammed over the gunwales and flipped the boat right side up.

Ash had to admit, it was a slick move.

"You've done that before," Talbot said, almost accusingly. "Haven't you?"

"A time or two," Strangward said. "Now, hang tight a minute and let me get aboard first, so I can haul you both in safely."

"Why do you get in first?" Talbot said.

Strangward mopped wet hair out of his eyes. "Oh, I don't know—because I know how to do it without flipping the boat over again?"

"Is this some kind of trick?"

"Why would I play a trick on you now?" Strangward said. "I could have let you both drown." The humor faded from his eyes, replaced by the pain Ash had seen before. "That could still happen, you know."

"Talbot, please," Ash said. "He saved both of our lives. You have to give him credit for that."

Talbot looked from Ash to Strangward. She'd been unconscious, of course, during the pirate's heroics. "I'm just saying—"

"I don't want to argue while I'm treading water," Strangward snapped. "I'm getting aboard. Do whatever the hell you
want." The pirate swam up next to the longboat, put his back to
it, gripped the top edge with both hands, threw his head back,
drew his knees up, and flipped himself backward over the side.
Ash and Talbot stared at him, then stared at each other.

Planting his feet against the near side of the boat, and leaning
back over the gunwale on the other side, he gave them both a
hand up. He dragged an oilcloth sea bag out from under the aft
thwart, opened it, and pulled out two pails.

"Help me bail her out," he said, handing one of them to Talbot. After a moment's hesitation, Talbot joined in.

When the longboat was as dry as they could make it, Strangward unfastened the mast from its storage straps. "Here," he
said. "Help me raise the mast."

Understanding finally dawned. "You're planning to sail *this*
boat all the way to shore?" Ash eyed it skeptically.

"In the hands of a stormcaster, this is a *ship*," Strangward
said, the light of mischief back in his eyes. "Hang on a little
longer, and I'll show you what I mean."

All three of them put their backs into it, attached the shrouds,
and soon they had the gaff and staysails raised.

Talbot studied the rig, frowning. "Do you even know where
we are now?" she said. "Or where we're going?"

Strangward laughed. "I know exactly where we are, and
I know exactly where we're going," he said. "We're going to
Tarvos after all."

# DEADLY DANCING

After Lieutenant Quill Bosley took his unplanned leap off the volcano, Lyss slipped back into Celesgarde, hoping to avoid being connected with his disappearance. She worried that an investigation might expose the presence of Jenna and Flame-caster in the mountains overlooking Celesgarde.

Bosley was reported missing at morning muster. When he didn't show up by evening mess, Lyss reported his absence to the empress. Celestine sent search parties into the mountains, through the capital—even into nearby islands. They found nothing. She questioned Bosley's fellow wetland officers about his possible whereabouts. They had no answers for the empress. They had no questions, either. The consensus seemed to be, the less said, the better.

As days passed, Bosley was mentioned less and less often, and Lyss began to hope that she was in the clear. She had plenty of other worries to occupy her time.

She had to stay alive, and free of Celestine's blood bond, and somehow get back to the Realms. But she was marooned on this island surrounded by a stormwall. The only way out, it seemed, was to return to her homeland as commander of the empress's army.

And, then, somehow, escape.

Well, then.

Since the age of twelve, Lyss had spent three seasons of every year in military camps of one sort or another. While this was a different army, in a different place, with different strengths and weaknesses, many of the challenges were the same.

Most of Celestine's dryland soldiers shared physical features—narrow eyes, high cheekbones, bronze skin—suggesting that they had the same ancestry. Yet the peoples of the Desert Coast were as tribal as any she'd seen—loosely organized into clans and extended families. They were generous to a fault, but proud, thin-skinned, and alert to any real or imagined show of disrespect.

They seemed to have two arrows in their quiver—hit-and-run horsemanship and a wild, melee style of fighting. Neither would work well in the flatlands, which was where Lyss intended to fight.

It seemed she spent much of her time as referee, settling endless arguments about who should command a given unit. The desert warriors tended to choose their commanders by acclamation, and so their officers could change day to day. That might work in a band of twelve, but not in a salvo or a brigade.

"You can make the first choice," she said, since she didn't know the soldiers very well, anyway. "After that, I'll make any changes that are necessary. This is not a popularity contest."

"But what if the officer is no good?" one of the warriors said. "What if he favors fighters from his own city? What if they get first choice of the women and the spoils?"

"Then you'll need to bring that to me," Lyss said, thinking, Next, we need to talk about women and spoils.

"But why should you bother yourself with that?" the soldier persisted.

"Because that's my job," Lyss said. "Because I can't ask for a show of hands on a battlefield to figure out who I should be talking to today. Because all of the units need to work together." Eventually, she resorted to the time-tested response, "Because that's an order."

The empress approved. "You can't reason with them," she said, "and you don't have to. Just command them to obey. If they do not, kill them." Celestine's eyes narrowed as she read resistance in Lyss's face. "There is no place in my army for the slow, the stupid, or the scrupulous, General Gray. Even less so among my officers. I have waited four long years to regain my legacy. Help me do that, and you will be richly rewarded. Fail, and I will reshape you into an instrument I can use."

The meaning of that was clear enough.

Gradually, Lyss embedded her surviving Fellsian officers into the mix. She began by having them drill small groups of bloodsworn in standard military commands and maneuvers. Eventually, she assigned her experienced officers to command larger units of cavalry and infantry.

It was easier than she'd expected, because sometimes the newcomers were perceived as more impartial than the enemies and rivals they knew. Also, more and more of the new bloodsworn came from the wetlands, mostly from the Fells. It broke Lyss's heart to see men and women she'd commanded back home show up wearing Celestine's purple aura, their faces hungry with an insatiable need. Each time a new group arrived, she had to steel herself against the possibility that she would encounter someone like Sasha Talbot or Char Dunedain among the "recruits."

I wish there were a way to help them, Lyss thought. She began reading everything she could get her hands on about blood magic—which wasn't much. Celestine had looted an entire library of books from Deepwater Court, brought it here to her capital, and shelved it in her new palace. There it remained undisturbed until Lyss began pulling books down and poring through them. She found nothing about blood magic, or magemarks, or anything else useful.

Eventually, she mustered the courage to ask the empress about it.

"That's not your concern," Celestine said, instantly defensive. "I do what I have to do. I use the gifts I've been given."

"I'm not criticizing you," Lyss hurried to say. "In fact, we practice a kind of blood magic in the queendom."

That piqued Celestine's interest. "Really?" she said. "I'd not heard that."

"There's a blood ritual that binds the—that binds members of the Queen's Guard to her. I was curious whether this was something similar."

"Perhaps so," Celestine said, looking pleased. "After all, the Realms were settled by peoples from the Northern Islands centuries ago."

"Is there anything that will modify the bond? Or undo it?" Lyss knew this was striking perilously close to the bone.

The empress recognized the threat. "General Gray, if you are hoping to shatter the bond of loyalty between me and my bloodsworn, you are doomed to failure," she said, scowling.

"Your Eminence, I see evidence of their devotion every day," Lyss said. "I was merely hoping that something could be done to address their lack of independent decision-making skills. You've said that is a problem, and I agree. I'm looking for a solution."

"Best watch your step, General," Celestine said, eyes narrowed. "If you solve that problem, I'll no longer have a need for you."

"Understood, Your Eminence," Lyss murmured.

If Lyss hated this constant verbal sparring, she despised the weekly tournaments that the empress held between bloodsworn soldiers. Celestine would choose the players or, worse, demand that Lyss make the selection. Sometimes the empress would choose two women to fight, or a mixed pair, or three against three. In one case, she blinded two soldiers, and then set them against each other. She found their struggles amusing.

Lyss, Breon, Samara, courtesans, and any other officers or ships' captains in port were forced to watch from the terrace. Servants delivered food and drink as the carnage went on. Celestine loved to wager on the outcome, and award prizes to the winners. The losers, of course, were carried off the field in pieces. Even the "winners" were often maimed beyond repair.

Each spectator dealt with the tournaments in his own way. Breon kept his pipe close and passed the time in a fog of leaf. Tully Samara joined in the fun with a will, cheering on his favorites and calling out Lyss for her lack of enthusiasm.

Lyss was no stranger to bloodshed, of course. There'd been no need for tournaments back home because everybody had plenty of practice on the battlefield every summer. She suspected that this might be a message for Celestine's reluctant commander—a graphic illustration of the consequences of failure. See? This could be you!

Lyss sat through several of these grisly "tournaments," grim and silent, until the day the empress sent two twelve-year-olds onto the field. They bowed before the empress, a little awkwardly, and turned to face each other, weapons in hand.

If this was a test, Lyss failed it. She abruptly stood, threw down her napkin, and stalked from the terrace.

"General Gray!" the empress called after her. "I did not give you leave to go."

Lyss spun around to face her. "Forgive me, Your Eminence, but I have other things to do."

"So do we all," Celestine said, "but I asked you to be here."

"I do not find this entertaining," Lyss said.

"This is not being put on for *your* entertainment, General," Celestine snapped.

"Then what purpose does it serve for me to be here?"

Celestine seemed to be at a loss for a second. "It is not your place to question my decisions," she said.

"I am not questioning your decisions," Lyss said. "If you find it amusing, by all means, enjoy. I will better serve you by putting my time to a different use."

"What if it serves me to have you stay?" Celestine said, her voice brittle with rage.

Lyss set her feet, knowing that this might be the end of the Gray Wolf line.

"If you require me to stay, then I will put a stop to this." She gestured toward the two young soldiers. "That would hardly serve you, since you find it entertaining."

The empress slammed her cup down on the stone table with

such force that it chipped the tabletop. She gestured to her bloodsworn guards. "Seize her!" she cried.

Two of them moved in on either side of Lyss, gripping her arms. She did not resist. She was aware of the others on the terrace, watching, wide-eyed. Except for Samara, who was staring into his cup, a faint smile on his face.

Celestine stripped back her sleeve, sliced her forearm with her dagger, and allowed the blood to drip into the cup to mingle with her wine. Then she stalked across the terrace to stand in front of Lyss.

She thrust the cup under Lyss's nose. "And if this is the alternative?"

Lyss breathed in the perfume of wine mingled with the metallic scent of blood.

"That would not serve you, either, Your Eminence," she said, meeting Celestine's eyes. "You have no shortage of bloodsworn soldiers. What you need is a commander."

For a long moment, they stood facing each other.

She has to follow through, Lyss thought. I've confronted her in front of an audience, like a fool.

If she forces me to drink that, I just might spew it all over her.

Then, all at once, someone shoved between them, knocking the cup from the empress's hands so that the contents splashed onto the pavement. The cup bounced several times before it rolled off the terrace and onto the field.

It was Breon. He stood between Celestine and Lyss, both hands raised, shaking his head. It was the best he could do, since his voice had been taken from him.

"Get out of my way," the empress said.

Breon didn't budge.

"Do you dare defend her against me? Your own sister?"

Breon shook his head again.

"He's looking out for you, Your Eminence," Lyss said quickly. "He understands that you are disappointed and angry, but he knows that I can serve you better as an officer than as a soldier."

Breon nodded eagerly, taking hold of Celestine's hands.

Blessedly, that seemed to give Celestine the cover she needed to stand down. The empress looked down into Breon's face, then pulled him into her arms, stroking his hair.

"Very well," she said. "If it means that much to you, I will let this go."

Breon looked over Celestine's shoulder, meeting Lyss's eyes. And then, unmistakably, he winked.

Lyss mouthed, *Thank you*, so weak with relief that only the bloodsworn's grip kept her upright. The busker's intervention had saved her, but she knew it wouldn't work a second time.

# 8

# DRAGON DAYS

Jenna sat cross-legged, her back propped against a stone out-cropping, skinning a rabbit she'd caught in a snare. Though her friend Cas made fun of Jenna's attempts at hunting, she was proud of her snare and her rabbit. Anyway, these days, as the dragon grew larger, he could eat an entire sheep on his own. Two entire sheep, with no leftovers.

Besides, she preferred her meat cooked—just a little—and she didn't like getting wool or fur in her mouth. Hence the skinning.

It was still light out, but the shadows were lengthening. Soon the sun would dive behind the western mountains and night would come down like a stooping dragon.

While she worked, she sorted through her worries. Their mission had become more complicated since they'd met Alyssa Gray, Adam Wolf's littermate—his sister, she amended. Cas continued to express reservations about their new friend.

*She doesn't know dragons.*

"That's understandable," Jenna said. "You're the first one she's met."

*I talk to her. She doesn't listen.*

"She doesn't know you're talking to her. Work with her."

*She should work with me.*

"Once she hears your voice, she'll be able to find it again."

*She looks at me like I'm going to eat her. Smells like prey.* The dragon looked at Jenna sideways. *It makes me want to take a bite.*

"Don't bite her, Cas."

Lyssa was a wolf like her brother. Jenna had known that since the first time she'd laid eyes on her as she stood, sword in hand, ready to do battle.

*Wolf is hiding something.*

"I know," Jenna said.

Alyssa Gray was seething with secrets, but she was giving away more than she knew. When Jenna gripped the commander's hands, images slid through her mind—a much younger Adam and Alyssa, dressed in elaborately stitched clothing, holding hands, watching a funeral procession, both weeping. Captain Gray, singing and stomping and playing a basilka, the stringed instrument common in the Realms.

*We are children of the north.*

Alyssa Gray, kneeling in a snowy, cobbled street, cradling the body of a young guardsman. Wearing the spattercloth of the northern army, charging, howling, at the enemy. Gray, in a fancy gown, dancing—dancing with the lieutenant who'd attacked her on the ledge. Gray, surrounded by wolves, wearing a simple circlet on her head.

It shouldn't be surprising that Alyssa was Adam Wolf's sister. She was as full of secrets as her brother.

Jenna, of course, was keeping her own secrets. For instance, she'd not mentioned the magemark, or offered an explanation as to why she had an affiliation with dragons. The wolf couldn't reveal what she didn't know.

It made Jenna's head hurt, trying to figure it out. It didn't help that she was worried about Cas. They'd flown across the Indio, following Celestine's ship, meaning to end the empress's hunt one way or another. They'd followed her all the way to her capital in the Northern Islands, to find it protected by a fierce wall of wind and weather. They'd managed to get through it, but Cas's left wing had been damaged, and one of his legs badly sprained in an ugly crash landing in the mountains.

During the weeks following, the dragon had begun to recover from his injuries, his wing function improving, his flights in the uplands of the islands longer and higher and farther.

In the past week or two, however, Cas's steady progress seemed to have stalled. His limp returned, and he seemed to struggle to get off the ground. It was almost like he was pretending to be more disabled than he really was, because he'd fly off in the mornings and not return until late in the evening. Where was he spending his time? Could a dragon who spoke to her mind-to-mind have a secret life?

"You're not stealing horses from the empress's horse-line, are you?" Jenna had said. "Remember, we agreed—no more than one a week. We don't want them to come up here looking for us." The longer they stayed there, the greater the risk that they'd be discovered by someone other than the empress's commander of the armies.

*One a week.* The dragon gazed at her with wide-eyed innocence.

Well, she thought, I'll have to take his word for it. There's no way I can track a dragon in flight.

All she could do was hope that soon he would be ready to partner with her in their mission. As he put it: *find the nest, kill the hatchlings, steal the hoard.*

They would get their revenge on Empress Celestine, destroy her capital, and then return to the Seven Realms, where, Jenna hoped, she might find Adam Wolf Gray, or whatever his real name was. She hoped that she could persuade Cas to carry Alyssa Gray back to the wetlands. That wasn't going to happen unless Cas grew to trust the wetlander, or, at least, to tolerate her. There was nothing more stubborn than a dragon with a grudge.

When the rabbit was skinned, Jenna mounted it securely on two crossed sticks, butterflied so that it would cook quickly.

Jenna scented the wolf girl before she materialized out of the trees. As usual, she wore the garb of the empress's soldiers. As usual, she was a bit out of breath, which meant that she'd run straight up the mountain with a bulging pack on her back.

She was a strange girl.

"Lyss," Jenna said. "Sit. Have rabbit." She stopped, cheeks flaming, suddenly aware of her stripped-down speech. Before long, she'd be spitting flames along with her words. "I was just about to cook a rabbit. It shouldn't take long. I hope you'll have some."

Lyss sat on the ground across from Jenna. "Where's your— where's the—where's Cas?" she said, scanning the mountainside. The wolf girl still struggled to remember that Cas did not *belong* to Jenna, but was her equal—a friend and partner.

"He left this morning and I haven't seen him since," Jenna said vaguely. "I imagine he'll be back before too long." She set the rabbit on the grate (courtesy of one of Lyss's previous trips) over the fire and wiped blood from her hands with a rather stinky piece of leather. It was easy to forget the niceties of civilization when you spend all of your time with a dragon.

"Ah." Lyss put the pack between her knees and began to fuss with the buckles.

Jenna eyed the backpack greedily. Over the past two weeks, Lyss had been up and down the mountain nearly every other day, bringing supplies and foodstuffs that could not be foraged on the top of a mountain in this miserable place.

Lyss was rummaging through the backpack, pulling things out, and naming them before she set them aside. "Rags. Saddle soap. Leather needle and thread. Salt. Pepper. Field remedy kit, including willow bark, aloe, maidenweed, ginger, tay, and some others. Brick of sugar. Block of cheese. Ground cloth and stakes. Dried cherries. Two pounds walnuts. Ale. Wine. Iron skillet." She looked up. "I could not find dried grapes anywhere."

Jenna shook her head, amazed. "I don't know how you managed to find all that, and how you carried it up here in one trip. Thank you." The scent of roasting rabbit wafted to her, and she resisted the temptation to rip the meat from the bones before it was fully done. Lyss was not by any definition fragile, but after their initial meeting, Jenna had no desire to reinforce the notion that she had one foot in the dragon camp.

When the rabbit seemed suitably charred, Jenna pulled it from the fire with her bare hands. Lyss flinched, then tried to hide it.

Jenna ripped free a joint for herself, the juices dripping onto the ground, and extended the rest of the rabbit toward Lyss, who pulled off a hunk of meat and took a bite.

"What's going on in town?" Jenna said, chewing. "Has the empress asked what happened to the male who attacked you?"

"The . . . male?" Lyss said, brow furrowed. Then her confusion cleared. "Oh. Bosley. I reported him absent from morning report, and ordered a search of the city and the harbor area. We finally concluded that he either got drunk and fell into the harbor and drowned, or was carried off by a dragon."

"Do you think anyone will come hunting for him?"

"Not if I have anything to say about it," Lyss said, wiping her hands on some leaves. "I've tried to convince everyone that it's too dangerous up here."

"Did they believe you?"

Lyss shrugged, glancing toward the path she'd taken up from the harbor.

She's still worried, Jenna thought. So she changed the subject. "Will the empress sail with her army? Or stay here?"

Lyss shrugged. "I don't know. We've already sent shiploads of soldiers, horses, and gear. I have to think we'll go before long, ready or not. Celestine is getting restless." She paused, as if reluctant to nag. "If you're going to act, sooner would be better than later."

Well, Jenna thought, that was bad news. Had she chased the empress all the way across the ocean only to chase her back again? Still, a ship on the expanse of the ocean makes a very good target. She'd learned from experience that ships readily burn.

"I'd like to go now, if I could, but Cas still isn't back to normal. He needs to be in good shape, because as soon as we deal with Celestine, I want to fly back to the Fells." She licked her fingers and set the bones aside. Just then, she heard a frantic, ragged flapping of wings. A shadow fell across their makeshift cooking site.

Cas landed hard and skidded a little before he came to a stop. He folded his wings and wrapped his tail around his feet to keep it from knocking over the tent.

Ignoring Lyss, Cas extended his wing to the ground, an invitation to Jenna to climb up. *Jenna come now.*

"Cas, can't it wait a little while? Lyss and I were just eating. . . ."

*No! Can't wait. Come now. Wolves.* The dragon dropped his head so that he was eye to eye with Jenna. Pleading. Jenna reached out and touched his face, and the dragon's worry, pain, and grief came down on her like a brick wall.

That didn't make sense. Wolves wouldn't be a problem for a nearly grown dragon. "Cas. Tell me what's going on."

Cas shot a look at Lyss, as if wishing she would disappear. *Hatchlings hurt. Hungry. Please come.*

Jenna was bewildered. The only "hatchlings" they'd discussed were related to their planned attack on Celestine's stronghold.

"What hatchlings? How did they get hurt? Where are they?"

*Please. Come now.* Cas nudged her with his head, practically toppling her.

"What's wrong?" Lyss said, standing, dropping the remains of the rabbit carcass into the fire.

"Cas is telling me some hatchlings are hurt, but I don't know what he's talking about or where they are," Jenna said.

"Hatchlings?" Lyss said. "Baby dragons?"

Jenna stared at Lyss. Baby dragons? That possibility had never occurred to her. What would baby dragons be . . . She turned back to Cas. "Baby dragons?"

*Please come. Wolves.* Cas pressed his head against her hand, and images of a cave littered with blood and scales sent her reeling.

Jenna's heart sank. She might be a miner, an explosives expert, and a soul mate to dragons, but what she knew about healing could fit on the head of a pin. And if she touched a dying dragon, or one mortally injured, she wasn't sure she could stand it, let alone treat it. She thought of Adam Wolf, recalling his strong, gentle hands, his quiet confidence, the magic in his touch. It was yet another reason to wish he was here.

Lyss's voice broke into her thoughts. "Well? What is it? What happened?" The captain was standing, fists clenched, balanced on the balls of her feet, as if prepared to leap into action.

"Cas says a pack of wolves found a nest of baby dragons," Jenna told Lyss. "They're injured, and—and he hopes I can help them. But I—" She didn't want to admit to her fear of failure with Cas looking on, but Lyss seemed to read it in her face.

"I just brought up a kit of medical supplies," Lyss said. "I've treated a lot of wounds in the field. Maybe I could help, though I don't really know anything about—"

"Lyss can help us," Jenna said to Cas. "Can she come with us?"

Cas eyed Lyss. *Wolf.*

"I know, but her littermate was one of the best healers I ever knew. He saved my life."

Worry about the hatchlings seemed to have crowded every other worry away, because the dragon said, *Yes. Bring wolf girl. And rope. Hurry.*

# MEETING OF MATELONS

Spring had always been Hal Matelon's favorite season—a time when each day dawned more fragrant than the last, the rich soil itself proclaiming the life below its surface, ready to burst into view. The rivers surged out of their banks, fed by the melting snow in the Heartfangs. The new leaves formed like a green mist around the treetops of the Tamron Forest. It was then, between the rainy winters and torrid summers, that the dourest southerner might believe in magic.

Since Hal had joined the army as a stripling of eleven, springtime also brought reunions with fellow soldiers and officers he hadn't seen since Solstice, the scent of leather and horses and woodfires. There was always hope at the start of a new campaign that this time they would achieve a decisive victory against the most tenacious and savvy fighters he'd ever come up against. He'd always preferred the discipline of military life to the mincing dance of the social season.

Until this spring, when his king called him a traitor, his father thought he'd been bewitched, and his heart called him north to the aid of people he'd always considered to be his enemies. Now he'd been at least partly responsible for sending his mother and sister into northern hands. If Lila Barrowhill was telling the truth. There was no way to know.

His gut told him that they were safer in the hands of Queen Raisa than under the control of his own king. Which said a lot about how his life had been going.

Now the fertile plains between Ardenscourt and Temple Church had become a no-man's-land of burnt-out farmhouses and abandoned fields. The few working farms that remained were guarded by grim-faced men and women with cudgels and rusty blades from long-ago battles. The green tips of the new crops were showing, but there was no livestock in the fields. Either it had already been confiscated by foraging soldiers or it was locked away from view in barns and sheds so as not to draw a hungry eye.

Hal and Robert wore nondescript clothing, but Robert's horse was standard military issue, and Hal's was the one he'd stolen from the empress's army before he came south. He suspected that neither of them could pass for farmers.

Robert reined in beside him, his gelding dancing and tossing his head in his eagerness to go forward. That was something—he and Robert were out of Newgate Prison and on their way home. He just didn't know what kind of reception they'd get to the message they had to deliver.

When they reached the checkpoint that marked the boundary of rebel-controlled territory, it was staffed with militiamen that Hal didn't know. It took a lot of talking and a safe passage letter from their father to get them through.

The encampment at Temple Church was a busy place—

wagons loaded and lined up, ready to hitch to teams, cannon mounted on their wheeled carts, prepared for transport, squires and orderlies rushing around in service of the thanes and higher-level officers. Raoul Bouchard, the blacksmith for White Oaks, sweated at the outdoor forge, reshoeing dun-colored military horses. Clearly, the massed armies of the rebellious thanes were finally getting ready to march somewhere.

But where? Hal thought.

Hal and Robert handed their horses off to the young boy who seemed to be managing the paddocks. When they asked after Thane Matelon, he pointed them to one of the barns. Inside, Hal could see that the building had been pressed into use as a warehouse, with gear and ordnance and staples piled nearly to the ceiling. He found his father deep in conversation with Jan Rives, the quartermaster.

Matelon looked up as Hal and Robert entered, and his frown faded. "Thank the Maker," he said, and embraced each of them in turn, which was about as demonstrative as Hal had ever seen him. He followed with, "Now we can finally get moving. I hate feeding an army sitting on its ass."

Matelon dismissed Rives and motioned them to a bench between the shelves of supplies, while he leaned against a stall door. Hal couldn't help thinking his father had grown visibly older, more haggard than before, in the scant few weeks since Hal had seen him.

"Did you run into any trouble on your way here?" he asked.

They shook their heads. "I think the king has his hands full with what's been going on in the capital," Robert said, swelled up with news, like a bubble about to burst.

"I've heard some of it, I think," Lord Matelon said. "I heard that there was another northern attack on the capital while you were there."

"There was another attack," Hal said, narrowing his eyes at his brother—a warning. Their father was not someone who liked dealing with complicated messes, and this was the most complicated mess they'd ever been involved with. They'd come up with a marginally plausible, straightforward story—a mingle of truth and lies. Now it was up to him to deliver it convincingly.

Blessedly, Robert pressed his lips together and looked up at the rafters. Hal's little brother had learned some hard lessons about playing his cards close.

"Apparently," Hal said, "Mother and Harper and the other hostages were at a party the king was throwing for guests from the downrealms when somebody blew up the Cathedral Temple."

"What were they doing there?" Matelon looked from Hal to Robert. "Why would the king invite his prisoners to a party?"

Hal shrugged. "He keeps calling them guests. I assume he wanted to show them off to demonstrate to the downrealms representatives that life at court was back to normal."

"They found out differently in a hurry," Robert said. "Like Hal said, somebody blew up the Cathedral Temple and several other buildings. When the smoke cleared, Princess Madeleine, Queen Marina, and all of the hostages were gone."

"Gone? Gone where?" Matelon looked from Hal to Robert.

"Nobody knows," Hal said. "Not only that, Luc Granger, one of the king's favorites, was killed during the attack."

"Granger? The upstart gaoler Jarat gifted Whitehall to?"

Hal nodded.

"I was so looking forward to giving him a warm welcome

when he came to claim it," Matelon said, with his tiger's smile. "I suppose that won't be necessary."

"No," Hal said, wondering what his father would say if he knew it had been Harper who did the deed.

"Where were you two during all of this?" Their father hadn't survived this long in the deadly world of Ardenine politics by overlooking important details.

"I had just tracked down Robert in the city. When we learned that Jarat was keeping the hostages in the Pit, we gave up the idea of a rescue. So we made preparations to return here."

"The Pit." A muscle in his father's jaw twitched, and two spots of color appeared on his cheeks—never a good sign. When Hal and Robert were children, that expression would have sent them fleeing into hiding.

"Aye, sir."

"So he was keeping them in the Pit except for when he trotted them out for parties?" Matelon took a long breath, then slowly let it out. "I suppose they're blaming us for the attack."

"I wish it *had* been us," Robert said, with some heat. Then he clamped his mouth shut and looked at Hal.

Good touch, little brother, Hal thought. He chose his words carefully. "King Jarat's spymaster, Lieutenant Karn, claims he has evidence that Empress Celestine is behind it."

"Really?" Matelon said, skeptically. "The empress again. How do you know what Karn's claiming? I suppose you and the spymaster discussed it?"

Actually, we did, Hal thought, and this was the best we could come up with after Lila landed this situation in our laps. "Most of this is barracks gossip," he said, "but from people who have been reliable in the past."

"Why would the empress want to kidnap our families?" Matelon said. "Isn't she busy enough in the north?"

"Maybe that's the difference between an empress and a king," Robert said. "An empress can meddle in more than one country at a time."

"Surely Jarat could have intercepted the kidnappers between Ardenscourt and the eastern coast," their father said. "They couldn't move quickly with such a large group of women and children."

Hal shook his head. "They went south, instead of east, and took ship from Southgate." He paused, then added, "The ship was of Carthian registry."

"Huh." Matelon rubbed his jaw. "How has the king reacted to all of this?"

"Obviously, he's looking for a scapegoat—someone to blame for an attack that bold, and that successful, in front of his guests from the captive realms. He is determined to seek revenge, to discourage any thoughts of rebellion on their part. Rumor has it that he's planning to take his army north to free them."

"You seem remarkably well informed of what the king is thinking and doing." His father paused, as if expecting Hal to explain. When that didn't happen, he said, "Why would he expect to succeed where his father has failed for nearly thirty years?"

Robert jumped in. "Because Jarat wasn't personally involved in those earlier missions," he said. "He seems to think he can do better."

Matelon laughed sourly. "A common affliction among the young," he said, giving Hal a measured look. "If you ask me, that's a fool's errand. Jarat will end up fighting both the northern witch and the empress. If we're lucky, he'll get himself killed before he gets himself an heir."

Now was the time for Hal to lay his cards on the table and see if he held a winning hand. "We should march north, too," Hal said, "and join the fight before it's too late."

His father scowled at him, as if a good story had just come to a bad ending. "Now you've lost me. Why would we do that? We are named traitors, marked for death. Do you think Jarat would pardon us if we waded in on his side?"

"I'm not suggesting that we join Jarat. I'm saying that we should join the Fells against Jarat and the empress."

If he'd lost his father before, now Hal had left him way behind. Matelon looked at Robert, as if he might weigh in, then back at Hal.

"That's not our fight," Matelon said flatly.

"It will be," Hal said, looking his father in the eyes.

"It's not our fight right now," Matelon said. "Right now, if Jarat's foolish enough to go north with our army ready to march, then *right now*, we need to take advantage of it."

"Harper and Mother are in Celestine's hands," Hal said, "or soon will be."

"This empress really has you spooked, Son," Matelon said gruffly.

"Maybe you should listen to me for once," Hal said, his impatience boiling over.

The Matelon men looked at each other, like three unyielding rock pillars.

Hal took a deep breath. "All right," he said. "Here's another option. From what I've seen, you have men ready to march. It will take King Jarat a little longer to get under way. Give me a brigade, and I'll march north and rescue our families before the king's armies arrive. Then we can meet Jarat's forces in the borderlands, while you come up from the south. They won't be expecting that, and it will mean they don't have the advantage of the fortifications in the capital. That way, we'll avoid a siege. Once we handle Jarat and his army, the city will fall easily."

Matelon snorted. "I am not an empress, Son, I am a simple thane, with considerable fighting experience behind me. I've found it best not to fight on too many fronts at once. Let Jarat go north if he wants to. While he's chasing through the mountains, we'll march on Ardenscourt."

"There's no reason to change those plans, Father," Hal said. "As soon as I'm finished in the north, I'll come south and join you."

Matelon shook his head. "You've seen who my allies are. They're all sharpening their knives, waiting for the opportunity to stab me in the back. I need someone I can trust at the head of our forces, and you're the only one with the talent, skill, and ability to claim the command."

It was the same old story. No negotiation. No compromise.

"You're making a mistake, Father," Hal said, his voice even, his gaze direct. "You're going to win one battle and lose the war."

His father stared at him, eyes narrowing, as if seeing something he hadn't seen before. Then he ran his hand over his face, wiping it away.

"If we don't win this civil war, we'll be tried and executed," he said. "Is that what you want? You'd let down your family, risk your legacy, and allow this house that has stood since the

Breaking to fall so that you can rush to the aid of the queen in the north?"

They'd had this argument too many times before, and it always came down to this—honor, duty, and loyalty to the Matelon banner. Worse, the thane militias had no loyalty to Hal—he'd been away for seven years, fighting with the army of Arden. The men he knew would be preparing to march with General Bellamy and King Jarat.

Without the support of his father, he'd be marching north by himself.

"Very well, Father," Hal said, teeth gritted. "I'll take the city for you. But, after that, I'm taking a brigade and I'm marching north."

# 10

# SMUGGLER'S COVE

Lila Barrowhill Byrne peered down at the wreckage of the harbor at Wolf's Head. The long pier was gone, as were most of the smaller docks. The water's surface prickled with broken masts and the burnt-out shells of the small ships that had been her playground as a child.

All along Smuggler's Coast, it was the same story. Harbor-front businesses burned, ships broken and sunk, the people dead or gone. Everything left to rot. It wasn't as if Celestine's soldiers had taken over the hamlets and towns and left a garrison there. The empress's blue-water ships had no use for these small, shallow harbors. They just came ashore, destroyed everything, carried the people off as prisoners, and moved on.

Her smuggler relatives were resilient, flexible survivors. But they couldn't survive this.

"Maybe your people fled before the drylanders arrived," Shadow said, behind her. "They would be smart enough to know that this was a battle they couldn't win."

Like the people at Fortress Rocks? Lila wanted to spit back. But she didn't. Shadow had lost his betrothed in that Ardenine sneak attack, and that wound was too raw to poke at. She wouldn't engage in a battle of the brokenhearted.

Shadow was not the enemy.

But he was wrong about her family. They wouldn't flee. At first, they wouldn't see the need. They were used to being overlooked, tolerated, left alone for a price. The war had been going on for thirty years, but neither side devoted time and treasure to rooting out smugglers. Their money spent just fine on both sides of the border. A deal was a deal.

For centuries, her mother's family had been driven from place to place by humorless people who did not understand the exquisite art of bargaining and resented being outfoxed. Who were suspicious of the islanders' clannish ways. They'd been driven out of the Southern Islands two generations ago, when Arden took control. They'd landed here, at a place on the northern coast that came to be known as Smuggler's Cove. It was cold in the north, and the terrain was rugged, the sea less forgiving, but the fishing was good in the shoals off Wizard Head. Lila knew all this from the stories her aunts and uncles told.

Uncle Chas and Aunt Leah had been her surrogate parents— so different from sober, duty-bound Amon Byrne, with his eyes always fixed on the Gray Wolf queen. Had Lila been cut from the same cloth as her brother, Simon, she could have stepped in to replace him. She could have joined the family business. But she was not, and she had not.

At first, Lila had moved back and forth between her aunt Lydia Byrne in Chalk Cliffs and her mother's family at Smuggler's Cove. Soon she was living with the smugglers full-time.

Her uncle Chas played the fiddle and basilka, and he and

Aunt Leah sang the songs that told stories. They had taught her how to dance, barefooted in fish houses with the tables shoved against the walls.

Uncle Chas had also taught her how to dance on both sides of the law. He was the master of finding his way to yes, lubricated by a sly, self-deprecating humor that made people underestimate him. Her cousin Mack had taught her to navigate the coastal waters in the dark. "If you pay attention," he said, "you can see the shoreline in your mind, you can feel the bottom coming up beneath your boat, you can skim across the surface like a water strider."

"Where will we go, when we have to leave here?" a six-year-old Lila had asked, upon hearing the old stories.

"Next time, we will not run," Uncle Chas had said, with no trace of humor. "Next time, we fight."

Lila knew, in her heart of hearts, that if she went down to the compound by the docks, where she learned all of those important lessons, she would find the bodies of those she loved. Unless they'd been carried off alive across the Indio.

I should have been here, she thought. Not roaming the south, nannying the runaway prince, sabotaging Ardenine military capability, spying on King Gerard. She'd thrown in with a father who had all but abandoned her, leaving the family that had raised her unprotected.

"It wouldn't have made a difference," Shadow said, as if reading her thoughts.

"It would have made a difference to me," she snapped.

"You're right," Shadow said. "You'd be dead, too, or crewing for the empress."

"You don't know that," Lila said, swiping at her eyes with

her sleeve. "I'm so damned good. I just stole thirty women and children from under the nose of the king of Arden while my real family was being slaughtered." She paused, and when he said nothing, broke her promise to herself. "Tell me you've never wished you'd been at Fortress Rocks when the Ardenine army attacked."

"Lila. Please. We have to go before we're spotted."

"You go ahead," she said. "I'm going to find my family and bury them." And then I'm going after the empress. I'll show her smuggler justice or die trying.

This conversation was rich with irony. Lila was the one who was constantly trying to talk Shadow back from the abyss, to persuade him to go easy on his self-destructive habits. To talk him out of throwing his life away with some rash scheme. Now the tide was flowing in a different direction.

"We can't defeat the empress on our own," Shadow said, returning like a dog to his favorite bone. "We have to work the plan."

"The plan is broken," Lila said, staring down at the ruins of her childhood. "There is no plan."

"Then we have to make a new one."

Shadow, she thought, I don't even know you anymore. But her gut said that if she insisted on going down to the water, he would insist on going down with her, and then he'd pay the price for her need for revenge. It could keep. A little while.

"Fine. Let's go," Lila said, standing and dusting off the seat of her breeches. They returned to their horses and mounted up, turning their heads back west.

They'd made this plan together—the plan to spirit away the thane families. Shadow had arranged for the wagons, lodging along the way—everything. Lila had planned on leaving their Ardenine refugees with her family on the coast while she returned south to work with Destin Karn to convince the southern king of the value of cooperation. Shadow was supposed to travel to Fellsmarch to pitch the notion of rapprochement with the south in order to fight the greater threat from the east.

Ordinarily, Shadow was the last person she'd have picked as an ambassador for peace, but beggars can't be choosers. She'd hoped that, coming from him, that argument would be more convincing. Now she had more incentive than ever to succeed, but Shadow was right. She needed a different plan for the hostages. Something that would allow her to be on her way as soon as possible.

One thing she knew—she didn't want to lose custody of her southern guests. They were the seawall that she hoped would prevent her life from washing away under her feet. If she took them to Fellsmarch, Queen Raisa and Captain Byrne would take control of them. They would be the ones making the decisions.

Not only that, she'd worked out this complicated story with Matelon and Karn—to blame the kidnapping on the empress in an effort to bring the southerners into an alliance against Carthis. (If they believed that story, she had some flashcraft to sell them.) If the thanes' families arrived in the capital, it would be only a matter of time before both the empress and King Jarat heard about it. Especially since Jarat seemed to have his own spies and sources in the north.

Who? Not even Destin Karn seemed to know.

Which meant that she needed to come up with an alternative hidey-hole before they reached Fortress Rocks, where they'd left the hostages while they traveled on to Wolf's Head. It was a place that had once seemed impregnable, but not any longer.

"Where can we put them where we can keep it a secret?" she mused aloud.

"What about Hunter's Camp?" Shadow said.

"Hunter's Camp?" Lila rolled her eyes. "That's in the middle of nowhere." Lila felt most at home in cities and towns, where she could melt into a crowd of scoundrels and people were in too much of a hurry to pay much attention to a girl working a scheme.

"Isn't that what you want? The flatlanders have never penetrated anywhere close to there. The hostages aren't likely to run off with hundreds of miles of mountains to get through. Anywhere else, you'll have to lock them up in a keep. I know you don't want that."

"How do you know what I want?"

Shadow just rolled his eyes and thrust his hands into his coat pockets. Shadow, who fit in everywhere and nowhere. "Marisa Pines Camp is another possibility. Willo Cennestre— my grandmother—is there. She would see to the health of the lýtlings—everything thrives under her care."

Truth be told, Lila wasn't eager to have the clans assume control of the Southerners, either. Shadow's father and grandmother were close to the queen. No doubt she would know of their presence in the time it took a bird to fly from Marisa Pines to Fellsmarch. She would probably send a salvo of Highlanders down to escort them to the palace.

"One thing for sure—they cannot go to the capital. Then everyone will know."

Lila did her best not to stare at Shadow. How did he read her so easily? How did he know what she was worried about? She looked up, met his eyes.

"Have you ever heard the expression, 'it takes a thief'?" he said. "It's obvious that there are traitors in the capital. If you want your story to hold, the presence of the southerners must be kept hidden."

Lila raked a hand through her curls. "Let's see how our guests are getting along with the uplanders at Fortress Rocks," she said. "Then we'll decide."

# FORTRESS ROCKS REUNION

Parts of the town of Fortress Rocks had been rebuilt since it was all but destroyed in the Ardenine attack a year ago. There was a halfhearted, tentative look to the new buildings, as if confidence in the future of the town had waned. The temple was the single largest structure. It had been the first to be rebuilt, right after the completion of a stone perimeter wall, meant to make sure the town would have more warning in the event of another attack.

This is like some kind of a disasters tour, Lila thought, shooting a look at Shadow. Back at Wolf's Head, Lila had lost her past—the life and family she intended to return to. At Fortress Rocks, Shadow had lost his dream of a future. When they passed through the gate, he took a quick look around. They'd both learned not to assume that what you left behind would be there when you returned.

Still, in the time since the massacre, Shadow had been back to Fortress Rocks a number of times. Does it ever get any easier? Lila wondered. Will I grow a thicker skin through constant exposure to pain?

Most of the hostages had chosen to be housed in the temple, where they could stay together. It was crowded, but it was a palace compared to their quarters in King Gerard's pits. The food was better, too, though it was a stretch for the town to feed fifty extra mouths.

Shadow and Lila left their mounts at the town livery with orders for extra fodder, grain, and water.

When they entered the temple, the evening meal was under way, served at a long table that ran down the center of the sanctuary. Lila's mouth watered at the scents that wafted from the sideboard. Some of the lýtlings were already lined up for seconds. Three people stood behind the serving table, a man and two women, all in clan garb, ladling up stew.

Lila squinted at one of the servers, a woman whose curly hair was pulled back with a leather tie. "Is that Queen Marina?" As soon as she said it, she knew it was true. King Jarat's mother was serving up food to her son's former hostages.

Shadow stopped in his tracks. "Blood and bones," he muttered. "The one next to her—that's my grandmother."

"Shadow Dancer!" the second woman called. "It does my heart good to see you." So the handsome older woman with the graying hair and the coat embroidered with Clan symbols was Shadow's grandmother Willo Watersong. As matriarch of Marisa Pines Camp and a renowned healer, she was called Willo Cennestre in the uplands, signifying wisdom. Even Lila had heard of her, though they'd never met—until now.

"Come share our hearth and all that we have," the man said. It was Fire Dancer, Shadow's father. Lila knew Dancer slightly—he and Shadow had worked together to supply flashcraft for some of her dodgy deals with Arden.

But Willo was close to the queen. Lila's heart sank. So much for keeping the presence of the hostages quiet.

Shadow walked forward, with Lila trailing awkwardly behind. This was the world Shadow had chosen—scoured clean by the winds from the Spirit Mountains. High above the tawdriness of waterfronts and cities. A world she could never fit into.

"Father. I'm surprised to see you here," Shadow said, embracing Dancer and speaking Common for Lila's benefit. "When did you leave the coast?"

"The coast is not a good place to be right now," Dancer said. "But I am going back soon, to join the fighting." He smiled at Lila. "Lila, it's good to see that you are back in the north again. Especially now."

"Right," Lila said, distracted. She was watching Shadow greet his grandmother out of the corner of her eye. They embraced, and then the matriarch put her hands on either side of his face and looked him in the eyes, murmuring something to him.

They remained like that for a moment or two, and then the matriarch dropped her hands and Shadow looked away. Willo shifted her attention to Lila.

"Will you introduce me to your friend, Shadow?" Willo said, smiling.

"Grandmother, this is Lila B-Barrowhill," Shadow said, stumbling a bit over the last name. "She grew up on the coast. She is a trader of sorts."

When Lila took the matriarch's hand, all of her usual bravado faded away. It was if Willo was gazing directly into her soul.

"Ah," Willo said. "It is a pleasure to meet you at long last."

At long last? What did that mean? Had people been telling stories about her? Had Shadow been telling stories? If so, what kind of stories?

"Yes, ma'am," Lila said, surfacing manners from somewhere. "The pleasure is mine."

"I've enjoyed visiting with your guests from the south," Willo said. "It has been too long since I've seen Queen Marina." She looked back at the southern queen, and the two women smiled at each other. "We've agreed that the last time must have been Briar Rose's name day party. So many people were there who are no longer with us."

"I was telling Willo Cennestre that I'm worried about some of the lýtlings," Queen Marina said. "This the first fresh, nourishing food they've had for some time."

"I know," Lila said, feeling guilty, even though she hadn't been responsible. "They've been held captive in the south for several months under poor conditions. Options on the road are limited."

"Options *here* are limited," Willo said, "but we will do our best. Her Majesty has authorized the Demonai to bring food-stuffs up from Way Camp, since the long winter is over now."

"Her . . . Majesty?" Lila said. She cleared her throat. "Queen Raisa knows that they are here?"

Willo hesitated. "Yes. She would have come herself to meet with you, but she is still quite ill."

"From the poisoning?" Shadow said. "I thought by now she would be recovering."

"She's not left her chambers since it happened," Dancer said.

Lila looked from Shadow to Willo. "The queen was poisoned?"

Shadow nodded. "Right before I came south to help with your operation in Ardenscourt."

"You never said anything," Lila said, scowling at Shadow.

"We've been busy," Shadow said. "Besides, things are happening so fast, it's hard to keep up in the telling."

How could I not know that? Lila thought. Miss a month, miss a lot.

The Gray Wolf queen had always been a part of Lila's life, whether she liked it or not. She had assumed that Queen Raisa would always be there, like Hanalea Peak, stones in her boots, or mosquitoes in the summer. It was oddly unsettling—the thought that she might not be immortal.

"Who poisoned her?" Lila said.

"I don't think they know," Dancer said.

"Is the prince with her?" Lila didn't ask about Captain Byrne. She knew he would be.

Dancer shook his head. "I'm sorry I don't have more details. We were in Marisa Pines Camp when we received a bird from Fellsmarch. The note was understandably brief."

"Well," Lila said, eager to change the subject at a time when every possible topic seemed like a minefield. "You—you're probably wondering what this is all about." She gestured rather vaguely at the families, some of whom were washing up, preparing for bed.

"Queen Marina has told us some of it," Willo said, "although it seems that their arrival in the north was a surprise to them." She raised an eyebrow.

"It's complicated," Lila said, which seemed like the kindest word to apply to it. "Shadow is going to travel on to Fellsmarch and meet with the queen's council to explain."

"That's why we're here," Dancer said. "Your father sent me to speak with you before you go to the capital."

Lila stiffened, gooseflesh rising on the back of her neck. She planted a puzzled look on her face. "My . . . father? I don't know what you—"

"Captain Byrne," Willo said. "He needs your help. He asks that you come to the capital with Shadow."

Lila looked from the matriarch to her grandson. She'd sneaked out of Fellsmarch after escorting the runaway prince back home in order to avoid being identified as Captain Byrne's daughter and drawn into an awkward reunion and a tangled skein of questions.

"Captain Byrne said this. Directly. To you?"

Willo nodded.

A person would think the captain of the Queen's Guard would know how to keep a secret, especially one that she had so carefully nurtured. Lila took a quick look around, making sure nobody was close enough to hear. "I don't know what he'd want with me," she said, her voice low and hurried. "I've done some work for the queendom up to now, but as soon as I meet with the queen's council, I need to go back east and—"

"He says to tell you that it's important," Willo said. "He says, please come and hear him out."

Now Dancer spoke up. "Captain Byrne also said not to bring the southerners to Fellsmarch under any circumstances, and not to speak to anyone at court about them without speaking with him first."

Lila and Shadow looked at each other. She'd expected the queen to insist that the hostages be brought to the palace for debriefing and safekeeping. She felt a little deflated, like she'd been training for a fight that wasn't going to happen.

Why was the queen trying to keep the presence of the

hostages secret? And from whom?

"They would be welcome at Marisa Pines," Willo said. "Or any of the upland camps."

"Not Marisa Pines," Shadow said quickly. "It's too close to the border. Maybe if we . . ." He looked up, startled, as the door banged open and four young women in clan garb burst in.

"There he is!" one of them cried. "I told you he was here."

Instantly, two of the girls launched themselves at Shadow, while the last two held back, restrained by the dignity of age. Shadow grinned and embraced the two of them. Then said to one of the younglings, "Flicker! How did you skin your knees?"

"I was walking up the waterfall with Harper," the girl said. She pointed at one of the older girls, and Lila realized that it was Harper Matelon, clad head to toe in clan gear.

We were only gone two days, Lila thought, and Harper has shed the flatlands like a too-warm coat.

Shadow looked over Flicker's head to the other older girl. "Sparrow—how is business?"

"Too many orders to keep up with," Sparrow said. "So many that we asked Harper to help us."

Harper laughed. "They let me sweep up the leather scraps," she said. Pointing at the food table, she said, "Let's get something to eat before it's gone."

And all four girls rushed off.

All at once, it connected. The other three girls are the sisters of Shadow's dead fiancée, Lila thought. She felt more out of place than ever.

"Let's go to Sparrow's hearth," Shadow said. "We can talk there without interruption."

# HATCHLINGS

Lyss stood, a kit full of supplies slung over one shoulder, a coil of rope over the other, watching Jenna Bandelow run up the side of a dragon the size of—well, she couldn't think of anything that compared. Her father always said that courage wasn't lack of fear—it was doing what needed doing in the face of it. By that measure, this had to be one of the bravest things she'd ever done.

"Captain Gray?" High above her, Jenna was leaning down, extending a hand to help her up.

She thought of the girl she'd once been—the one who loved to paint and play the basilka. If she survived this, she'd have images to paint and songs to sing for the rest of her life.

Fortunately, the spines that prickled the dragon's back offered Lyss some footing. She literally walked up Cas's side until she could put her foot in the stirrup.

"You sit in the saddle," Jenna said. "It will give you a more secure seat. Besides, Cas gives off a lot of heat. I'm more resistant to it."

Lyss swung her leg over and settled into the saddle in front of Jenna.

"Stow the gear in the panniers," Jenna said, "along with anything else that isn't strapped down." Lyss slid the rope and medical kit into one of the heavy leather bags.

Lyss was tall, but the dragon's back was so broad that it felt like her legs were sticking straight out.

"Bend your knees and hold your lower legs nearly horizontal for a better grip," Jenna said. "Lean forward along his neck. That will make you feel less awkward."

Lyss wasn't sure *awkward* was the word for it. Jenna was right—she could feel the dragon's heat through a thick blanket and the leather saddle. Her eyes stung a little from his slightly smoky breath.

Cas swung his head back so that he could look at the two of them. The message was obvious. *Ready?*

Lyss looked forward along the dragon's neck and saw no bridle, nothing to direct or control him. She looked back at Jenna. "Um, are there reins, or—?" She had time to hear Cas's soft snort of derision before he leapt forward with a rattle of claws on rock. It was only Jenna's body behind her that kept her from pitching head over tail off the back as Cas literally ran off the ledge.

Jenna reached forward, steadying Lyss with her arms. She took several hitching breaths, and Lyss realized that she was trying to suppress laughter.

"Cas doesn't need reins," Jenna said, "and he's a little miffed that you brought it up. We communicate mind-to-mind. Anyway, in this case, he's the one who knows where we're going."

"Oh. Ah, tell him I'm sorry."

"I don't have to. He hears and understands you. You just have to learn to hear him."

Remembering Jenna's directions, Lyss pressed her body forward against the dragon's neck, sliding her arms loosely across his chest, careful to avoid the wicked spines that stippled his hide.

In her winter gear and gloves, Lyss found that the dragon wasn't scorching hot, just a roasting warmth that was pleasant, given the cold night.

"It *can* be uncomfortable in summer," Jenna said, nearly into her ear. "That's one reason we like to fly high in the sky, where it's cooler."

Lyss stiffened, and the hairs rose on the back of her neck. "Hang on," she said. "Did you just read my mind?"

"Well, not exactly," Jenna said quickly, as if she was used to this reaction. "When I touch someone, images come to me. It's not always clear what it means, but in this case I got an image of a woodstove, so it was pretty obvious."

The thought was terrifying. How could she hope to keep any secrets from this girl that she was just beginning to trust? Lyss tried her best to empty her mind.

"That doesn't work very well," Jenna said. "What happens is that you think of all the images you don't want to think of. It's better to conjure up a really strong image and try to stay with it."

Well, then. Lyss immediately envisioned Hal Matelon, as he'd been that day in his cell, fending off Lyss and her bitter drinking game. Wearing only his breeches, his hair mussed from sleep, green eyes shadowed with wariness. She saw herself reach up, cradle his stubbled chin in her hands, and kiss the last drops of blue ruin from his lips.

"Getting a little steamy in here," Jenna said, fanning herself.

"You asked for it," Lyss said. "Deal with it."

They'd been flying through a layer of icy cloud, so that it was hard to tell up from down. Ice glazed the dragon's hide, melted, and then sizzled away into vapor. Finally, Cas slowed, dropping his head as if to search the ground, though Lyss could see nothing but a sea of white. When he folded his wings and plummeted toward earth, Lyss's stomach was left behind in the sky.

"Jenna!" she croaked. "Is this—?" Safe? Intentional? Suicidal?

"Don't worry," Jenna said. "This is how a dragon stoops on prey."

Lyss swatted at her ears, which felt like they were stopped up.

"That happens when we lose altitude quickly," Jenna said. "Keep swallowing and it will go away. Don't look down."

Of course, Lyss had to look down, in time to see the ground hurtling toward them. Just as she squeezed her eyes shut, they landed hard, a little awkwardly. Lyss's breath exploded from her lungs and she bit her tongue.

"Not his best," Jenna murmured to her. "He's getting better every day, but the extra weight probably didn't—"

Again, Cas thrust his big head toward them, smoke and flame bleeding from his nostrils, one baleful eye fixed on them. What was the word Jenna used? *Miffed?* Lyss found it amazing that a dragon with such an effective suit of armor was so thin-skinned.

"I'll get down first," Jenna said, already sliding down Cas's wing, then leaping lightly to the ground. Lyss tossed down the panniers, then climbed down herself. She tried to mimic what Jenna had done, but managed to remove a layer of skin on her forearms sliding down the dragon's scaly side.

"Not *my* best," she muttered. They looked to be perched high on a ledge on the side of a mountain. When she looked off the edge, all she could see were layers of cloud below.

Jenna pointed. "Cas says the hatchlings are this way." Lyss shouldered the saddlebags and followed.

They seemed to be walking toward a sheer cliff, but as they got closer, Lyss could see that it was pocked with fissures and cracks, studded with the scrubby alpine shrubs that were the only vegetation that could grow at this altitude, this far north. They circled around in back of a massive rockfall. Jenna pulled aside a twisted juniper to reveal an outcropping. Behind it was the mouth of a cave. It looked just barely large enough for Cas to squeeze through. Beside the cave, a waterfall spilled into a pool. In the mud around the entrance were mingled tracks—wolf and reptilian prints that must have been made by dragons.

Lyss scanned the skies and the peaks of the surrounding mountains, wondering if dragon parents were going to come flaming down on them. "Do dragons stay with their young?" she asked.

"I believe they do, until they can fly and hunt on their own," Jenna said. She turned toward Cas, body canted forward, speaking without audible words. Then Jenna motioned for Lyss to follow and ducked through the opening.

Just inside the entrance, the walls and ceiling seemed to disappear as they stepped into an even larger cave. Lyss reeled back, all but overpowered by the stench of rotting flesh, burnt flesh, and what might be dragon scummer. It smelled like the worst-kept field hospital ever.

The reason for the stench was immediately apparent. At the rear of the chamber lay a dead dragon, with eight dead wolves in a circle around it. Obviously, the dragon had gone down fighting the wolves. The wolves' bodies were charred, their bodies broken, lips pulled back in frozen snarls.

A lesson for all wolves, Lyss thought, kneeling next to one of them, fingering the blood-matted fur. Don't go up against a dragon.

From behind them came an earsplitting cry of grief and fury. They turned to see Cas just inside the entrance to the cave. Jenna ran to him, placing her hands on either side of the dragon's head and resting her forehead between his eyes. Her shoulders shook with weeping.

Lyss could feel *something* pushing at the edges of her thoughts. Not words, but—images? Images of the dead dragon, alive again, lifting her head in greeting.

Stepping over the dead wolves, Lyss examined the dragon's corpse. Though the carcass was relatively untouched, one of the dragon's wings was missing, and the wound where it had been torn away had obviously festered.

"It looks like it was this older wound that killed it, and not the wolves," Lyss said.

Jenna spoke, her voice muffled. "Cas says her wing was torn off in the flight through the Boil, and she crashed into the mountainside. She found this cave, and laid a clutch of eggs, which hatched. But she's been unable to hunt to feed them. Cas has been hunting for them."

"Where are they now?" Lyss said. "The hatchlings, I mean?" She paused, listening. "Is that them?" Now that she was next to the dead mother, she could hear faint cries coming from somewhere close by. She scanned the ceiling, the walls, the floor, but saw no obvious source.

There was a brief pause, while Jenna asked, and Cas answered.

"They're in a smaller cave behind their mother's body. She wanted to prevent the wolves from getting to them. But now that means that they are trapped."

"So we'll need to move her," Lyss said.

"That's why Cas asked us to bring a rope," Jenna said.

It took all three of them, working together. Lyss fashioned a rudimentary harness that they fastened around the dead dragon's body. They threaded the other end of the rope out through the entrance to the cave and around Cas's front quarters. With Cas pulling from outside, and Lyss and Jenna guiding the carcass, they managed to pull the body a few yards away from the wall, creating an opening large enough for Lyss and Jenna to squeeze through.

Inside the smaller cave, the cries were shrill, earsplitting, even. They seemed to be coming from one corner, from a kind of fortress made of piled rocks. The area around it was blackened with soot, and a reddish light flickered and danced on the ceiling as if coals were smoldering down inside.

Lyss heard a scrabbling sound inside the cairn, and something clambered up from inside, balancing precariously on the top. It was a baby dragon, armored in scales in all the colors of gemstones. It was painfully thin, its wings as frail and delicate as spiderwebs. One of its legs appeared to be broken. It flapped its wings, hissed at them, and toppled onto the cave floor.

Lyss's heart melted. She strode toward the nest, unshouldering her pack of supplies as she went. The injured hatchling screamed and sent a gout of flame roaring toward her. Jenna stepped in front of Lyss in time to catch the brunt of it. Still, Lyss could smell her own hair burning, and the skin on her face felt seared. She shifted her backpack full of medical supplies. It wouldn't do much good if she couldn't get close enough to examine their patient.

"I should have warned you," Jenna said. Her skin glittered as scales surfaced.

Lyss tried not to stare. She resisted the temptation to reach out and touch them.

"That hiss is a warning to stay back," Jenna said. "Even when they're that little, they can be dangerous. Their flaming capabilities seem to develop at a very early age."

So. In addition to being small and adorable, it was a pissed-off, dangerous baby dragon determined to defend its nest.

"What do we do?"

"I'll try to talk to it."

It looked more like a standoff than a conversation, with Jenna trying to make eye contact, the dragon hissing and screaming, flapping its wings. "It would help if I could touch him," Jenna said, edging closer.

Just then, another head popped up, over the side. And another, accompanied by more hissing. Jenna took a quick step back.

"How many are there?" Lyss said.

Jenna shook her head. "I don't know. Four, maybe?"

"They look like they're starving."

Jenna nodded. "At this age, they seem to require constant feeding. Cas says he hasn't been able to get food to them since their mother died."

"What would they eat at this stage?"

"Dragons eat meat from the time they hatch," Jenna said. "I don't think we're going to get anywhere until they get something to eat. Right now, they're hungry enough to eat the two of us."

*That* was a thought to ponder. "Should I go see if Cas can bring some fresh meat?"

"He's on it," Jenna said. "In fact, I think I hear him. He's already back with a kill."

I've got to quit underestimating this dragon, Lyss thought. "I'll go out and meet him."

Lyss squeezed past the dead female, passed through the outer cave, and burst out into the fresh air. Cas had a sheep's carcass pinned to the stone ledge and was ripping at the flesh and spitting out wool. For a moment, Lyss thought he was eating it himself, but then realized that he was tearing it into portable chunks. As if in answer to that thought, the dragon nudged a large shoulder joint toward her.

Lyss slid her arms under the raw meat, cradling it to her body, wondering how she would explain the state of her uniform if she ever made it back to the palace.

As soon as Lyss entered the rear cave with the mutton, five heads popped up from the nest, all screaming the dragon equivalent of "Meeee!" The injured hatchling must have returned to the nest.

Lyss dropped to her knees and used her belt knife to cut the meat into five pieces.

"Maybe you'd better feed them," she said to Jenna. Truth be told, she was worried that the baby dragons wouldn't be able to distinguish friend from food.

"No," Jenna said, "you feed them. Nothing wins a dragon over like food. I'll go get more." When Lyss still hesitated, she added, "Don't worry. It's not like they'll flame you. Dragons prefer their meat raw."

That was marginally reassuring. Lyss approached the stone

nest, and the hatchlings thrust their heads toward her, their open mouths displaying an already-impressive array of teeth. She went down the line, giving each little dragon its portion. By the time she'd finished, Jenna was back with another helping. They ran a kind of relay until the entire sheep was consumed. By now, the hatchlings were nudging at Lyss's bloody fingers, begging for more.

Jenna put her hands on either side of the injured baby dragon's head. A silent message passed between them. She turned to Lyss. "I told him that if he'll hold still while you fix his leg and wing, there'll be more to eat after that."

Laboriously, the little dragon climbed back to the top of the nest, teetering on the edge. Jenna and Lyss made a kind of cradle with their arms and helped him down to the cave floor.

With that, the other hatchlings set up an earsplitting clamor. Either they were worried about their brother, or they were convinced that their nestmate was getting some sort of special treats.

"They're saying another one of them has a torn wing," Jenna reported.

"One at a time," Lyss said. "Let's carry him out to where the light is better and it's not quite so noisy."

When they reached the outer cave, Cas was halfway in, blocking the light from outside. He pulled back from the entrance, and Lyss and Jenna passed through and set their patient down on the ledge outside. When the hatchling saw Cas, it cried out a greeting and tried to scramble closer. Cas lay down, forming a kind of scaly boundary with Lyss, Jenna, and the little dragon at the center.

Lyss unbuckled her backpack and pulled out bandages and

splints. "Can you ask Cas if this one has a name?" she said. When tending soldiers in the field, she'd found it helped if she kept talking.

After an exchange, Jenna said, "He likes to be called 'Slayer.' That's the closest I can come."

"*Slayer?*" Lyss eyed the hatchling dubiously.

Jenna laughed at Lyss's expression. "Don't worry, he'll grow into it faster than you think."

"Do dragons get to choose their own names?"

Jenna shrugged. "It makes sense, doesn't it? If you have to answer to something all your life, you might as well choose, right?"

Lyss had to admit, that did make sense. "Where I come from, you receive a new name at sixteen, after you've figured out who you are."

"Even better," Jenna said.

"Now. Here goes. Could you translate for me?"

Jenna laid her hand on Slayer's back. "Just speak to him like you would a peer. Cas understands human speech, though not as clearly as direct communication mind-to-mind."

"All right, Slayer," Lyss said, feeling a little foolish. "I'm going to fix your leg if I can." She tried to picture the process in her mind. "But you'll have to hold very still. Once we're done, there will be more meat."

Slayer's head came up at the word *meat*.

Gently, she straightened and aligned the bone in the dragon's leg, then bound it to a splint. She ran her hands over the dragon's scales from nose to toes, looking for other damage. In places, the scales were softer, thinner, as if recently regrown, but otherwise they seemed intact.

"Scales regrow quickly," Jenna said. "Bones take longer."

The only open wound seemed to be a large gash across Slayer's face, where the scales were thinner and not as densely packed. One end was dangerously close to his eye. She gently cleaned it out. Several times, Slayer tried to twist away, and once he set Lyss's sleeve on fire, but Jenna was apparently soothing him mind-to-mind. Lyss packed the gash with a salve that prevented infection.

Leaving Slayer in Cas's care, they returned to the inner cave for the second casualty. This one had a badly mangled wing. Lyss did her best, but it was difficult to construct an apparatus that would keep him from disturbing the splints while allowing him freedom of movement.

She wondered if he would ever fly again. What would that do for his odds of survival?

By the time Lyss was finished, darkness was falling, and she knew she'd better head down the mountain before someone came looking for her.

"Do you think there's any chance of persuading them to stay quiet for a few days?" Lyss said.

Jenna rocked her hand. "Maybe, if we wait on them hand and foot, and make sure they're never hungry," she said.

"It won't be 'we,'" Lyss said. "It has to be you. I've got to get back, or the empress will send a search party."

"Don't go back," Jenna said bluntly. "Stay here. Let the empress come. We'll give her a welcome."

"I wish I could," Lyss said. "But I have to play the long game, and that involves going back to the Fells and fighting for my homeland."

Still, it was hard to turn her back on new friends on the mountain and descend into the snake pit below.

# TARVOS

Ash couldn't help feeling like a helpless crate of cargo with Strangward at the helm of the longboat and in command of the weather. The pirate pulled a bag of hardtack, sausage, and dried fruit from under the thwarts and a large skin of water from the chest wedged into the bow. He handled the sails and tiller in a calm, methodical way, as if this was all part of an overarching plan.

It wouldn't be hard to believe that Strangward had somehow engineered this disaster so that he could sail them straight into a trap he'd set for them.

But it wasn't Strangward who'd attacked them. It was Finn.

Or was it? As the details of the attack on *Sea Wolf* grew fuzzier in his mind, Ash began to question what he'd actually seen. Could Finn have been aiming for the *Hydra* but the motion of the ship caused his shot to go astray?

Or had the trauma of the bombardment surfaced the pain Finn had buried since he was wounded? Everyone said that Finn had been changed by his experiences in the war. Right before they'd met *Hydra*, he'd confessed that he was struggling.

Maybe he'd lashed out blindly, mistaking friends for enemies.

You shouldn't have asked him to come, Ash thought. You, of all people, know what the trauma of war does to people, even the so-called survivors.

What about Talbot? What did she see? From the looks Talbot was sending Strangward, she was planning a mutiny. Ash wanted to ask her about it in private, but with the three of them packed into such a small space, there was little to no opportunity.

Anyway, a mutiny against a stormcaster seemed like a bone-headed move, especially since that stormcaster was the only one aboard with sailing experience.

Experience Evan seemed eager to share. He spent considerable time teaching Ash and Talbot the ins and outs of sailing, even when it seemed like it would have been easier just to do it himself. With Talbot on the tiller and Ash handling the sails, the pirate would conjure up shifts in wind and wave, challenging them to adjust to constantly changing weather.

"Big ship, small ship—the principles are the same," he said, scrambling fore and aft, showing them how to take the best advantage of a variety of conditions.

Gradually, he began to give over to his novice crew. He'd lie on his back, cloud shadows sliding over his face, fingering that odd-looking amulet he wore, as if his mind was a thousand miles away.

Ash found himself mimicking Strangward's behavior at night, when he couldn't sleep. He'd cradle his father's serpent amulet, tempted to reach for a connection. He heard the echo of his father's voice, heartbreakingly familiar, when his mother was dying.

*Come see me in Aediion.*

Present circumstances seemed to violate Kinley's stipulation that the corporeal self be left in a safe place.

Is it ever going to be the right time? Ash thought.

I'll wait until we make landfall, he thought. If we ever do. And then decide whether to risk a visit to the Drovers' Inn.

The rest of the time, he stared up at the sky and wondered if Jenna might be looking up at the same sky. Was she in the Fells, as Strangward claimed, or a captive in the empress's dungeon, or dead?

Finally, one night, while Strangward slept, curled up in the stern, his fair hair glittering in the moonlight, Talbot crept up next to Ash and hissed into his ear, "You know the bastard planned this all along."

"No," Ash said.

"You *know* he did," Talbot said, shooting a dark look at the pirate. "There just *happened* to be supplies in this boat, and dry clothes, and—"

"I made sure that all of the longboats were stocked with provisions before we left, just in case," Ash said.

"And we just *happened* to run into a Carthian ship when we—"

"Strangward told us that would happen if we sailed north," Ash said. "We didn't listen."

"That could've been a trick to *get* us to sail north," Talbot said, the way people do when they are grasping at straws.

"If that was his plan, it could've gone wrong in so many ways," Ash said.

"Then the ship blew up—which I don't understand, because Finn had put up barriers, and Strangward claimed that the empress wasn't even there."

Ash looked aft, to where the pirate lay, apparently sound asleep. "The barriers were down."

"What do you mean, they were down?"

"I don't know what happened, but they were," Ash said.

That stopped the conversation in its tracks for a moment. Then Talbot returned to her original tack. "And then Strangward just *happened* to save us, and—"

"Strangward *did* save us. Otherwise, we'd have drowned," Ash said.

Talbot lowered her voice further. "How do you know it wasn't Strangward who blew up the ship? Maybe he and the empress are working together, and he means to turn us over to her as soon as we get to shore." Talbot's knuckles whitened as she gripped the sides of the boat. "For all we know, *Sea Wolf* is at the bottom of the sea, and we're the only ones left with a chance to save Lyss, and—"

"It wasn't Strangward who attacked us," Ash said. "It was Finn."

Talbot looked as if she'd been clubbed. "No," she said. "I don't believe you."

"Look," Ash said. "I could have misinterpreted what I saw, but I don't think so. After the first explosion, I looked back to see what had happened to Finn, why the barriers were down. I saw him take direct aim at me and let loose."

"No," she said. "No. I know Finn. He's been fighting for the Fells since he was thirteen." She paused, and when Ash didn't respond, said, "Maybe he was aiming at the other ship and missed. I mean, both ships were moving."

"Maybe," Ash said. "Whatever happened, and whatever Strangward's involvement, he has us in a box. We can't sail into

Tarvos or Celesgarde without him. We're just going to have to wait and see what happens when we get to shore. We must be getting close."

By dawn, Ash began to see bits of vegetation in the water. Shorebirds began to appear, resting in the rigging, carrying images of rocky cliffs and desert landscapes. It was heartening to be able to connect with them again. He'd been walking the narrow path of revenge and survival for so long that he'd nearly forgotten how to open his mind to the creatures around him.

The next morning, a dun-colored streak appeared on the horizon. At first it looked like someone had drawn a brown chalk across the impossible blue-green of the ocean. As they drew closer, Ash could see the sheer sandstone cliffs that rose hundreds of feet above a sea that frothed and churned and seethed along the base. Eventually, he could make out the whitewashed shapes of buildings at the tops of the cliffs and two huge pillars of stone on either side of a narrow channel. Strangward seemed to be aiming for that.

"Sweet Hanalea in chains," Talbot muttered. "Are those dragons?"

Ash squinted, shading his eyes. Talbot was right. The stone pillars were mammoth stone dragons that faced each other across the channel, guarding the entrance to the harbor.

Strangward must have heard, because he glanced back at them. "Those are the guardians, protectors of the port," he said.

"Did—did *you* build those?" Talbot said.

"No," Strangward said, with a wry smile. "I cannot take credit for them. They were erected by stormcasters long ago. You'll get to see them in action. You'll be among the select few who live to tell about it."

Ash took another look and saw what he hadn't before—that the air shimmered and danced between the Guardians and the sea boiled, so that he couldn't see past the channel into the harbor beyond.

Strangward drew an ornate mirror from his pocket and turned it so it caught the rays of the sun, directing it into the eyes of the stone dragon to the left of the ship, then the one on the right, then left again. And, all at once, the air cleared before them and the surface of the sea settled, now only pleated with the wind. Their little boat hung almost motionless for a moment, then plunged into the cut. They passed through the straits, and Strangward quickly dropped sail.

"I developed the mirror system," Strangward said, "so that my harbormasters could control the port in my absence."

Inside the harbor, the water was clear and deep, indigo against the rocky shore. Two large ships rocked gently at anchor, Strangward's dragon standard flying from the masts. They looked to be sisters to the ship Strangward had sailed into Ardenscourt half a year ago. The ship that had carried a dragon to Ardenscourt. The dragon that Jenna had insisted that Ash free before he and Lila blew the ship to splinters.

It seemed he'd lived a lifetime since then.

Several other tall ships prickled the bay—one bearing the name *Scorpion* and another, *Viper*. Three small schooners were lined up along the wharf, alongside a small ketch, her sails furled and stowed.

Using sails and rudder, Strangward threaded their longboat through the traffic in the harbor and brought it up beside the smallest of the docks. He leapt lightly onto the quay and looped the line over the nearest cleat. He turned back and extended his hand toward Talbot, meaning to help her out of the boat.

Talbot hesitated, then grudgingly took the pirate's hand and clambered up onto the pier. After, she scrubbed her hand on her breeches, as if to wipe the magic off, then turned and gave Ash her hand. When they finally stood side by side, they both looked shoreward.

Spread out before them was the city of Tarvos.

Ash half-expected to find the empress's banner flying from the palace roof, the bloodsworn swarming over the shore like the deadly scorpions in the deserts of Bruinswallow.

But no. What struck him first was the color—white stone and stucco buildings, red tile roofs, blue sea, flowers spilling from every niche. Most waterfronts were a jumble of old and new, good ideas and bad, sailors' chapels and clicket-houses. Here were the usual warehouses, taverns, inns, and other marine businesses. Yet they seemed somehow organized, as if, in the recent past, the waterfront had been knocked down and rebuilt to a standard.

"Celestine burned the port a few years ago," Strangward said, like he'd read Ash's mind. "Most of this is new within the past five years."

The ground sloped sharply up from the quays, ending in another massive wall of sandstone a mile or so away. Beyond the few narrow streets along the water, the city climbed the steep terraces of the hillside, seemingly chiseled out of the rock. More whitewashed and pastel buildings capped with red tile roofs, more flowers, cascading down from terraces and spraying from hanging baskets and packed into every level patch of ground. It was spectacular, completely unexpected in a desert town like this.

"It's beautiful," Talbot whispered.

Strangward blinked at her, as if surprised to hear this coming from her, then nodded and smiled, visibly pleased. "Thank you," he said. "You could say that's my mission in life—stubbornly growing flowers in the desert."

"Do all of these ships belong to you?" Ash swept his hand, taking in the harbor.

The pirate shook his head. "I share the port with a handful of other ships' captains brave enough to defy Celestine. I take a piece of whatever comes in—that's the price of harborage and protection." He pointed toward the two largest ships. "Those are mine—*Sun Spirit* and *Free Spirit*. Plus our ship, the little ketch—*Destiny*." For some reason, he stumbled over that name.

Their arrival had not gone unnoticed. A small crowd had gathered at the landward end of the dock, simmering with excitement. Some of them shone with the same reddish glow as the rest of Strangward's crew. They were stormborn, then, and seemingly riveted by the arrival of their stormlord.

Talbot leaned toward Ash. "The way they look at him reminds me of the way the busker looks at a wad of leaf," she said.

A handful of men and women stood off to one side, arms folded, their stances challenging, their expressions grim.

The pirate's lips tightened as he looked over the welcoming committee. "The ones without auras are the independent shiplords," he said, nodding toward the surly group. "I've been away for a while, and I'll need to catch up with what's been going on in my absence. In the meantime," he said, "trust none of them. No doubt the empress has eyes and ears here, as she does everywhere." Lifting his sea bag from the longboat, he slung it over his shoulder and led the way toward shore.

A formidable-looking woman in leather and linen stood, muscled arms folded, at the front of the delegation. She'd shaved her head save one long, braided lock that dangled over one shoulder. Like the shiplords, she wasn't bloodsworn.

"Maslin," Strangward said, smiling with what seemed like real affection. "It's been too long."

She ran a critical eye over the longboat. "Lord Strangward," she said, "if you traded *Sun Spirit* for *that*, you must have been deep in your cups."

Ash and Talbot looked at each other. *Lord* Strangward?

"These wetland traders are merciless," Strangward said, shooting a look at his companions. "I was lucky to escape with the clothes on my back."

"Where are Teza and the others? Did you trade them away, too?" Ash could read the worry behind the words.

"No," Strangward said. "We got separated. It's a long story. But I have two new crew members with me." He gestured toward Ash and Talbot. "Freeman and Talbot, meet Akira Maslin, my harbormaster."

She eyed them, making it clear that they didn't measure up to Teza and the others. "They are not stormborn," she said finally.

"No," Strangward said.

"But your orders are that everyone who crews under your banner who isn't—"

"Let me worry about that." There was an edge to his voice now, a not-so-subtle message to back off.

"I will worry anyway," Maslin said. Then changed the subject. "The shiplords are eager to meet, my lord, at your earliest convenience."

"I see that Jagger and Jasmina are here. Who else?"

"Sangway, Blazon, Heff, and the Mongrel. We also have messages from two coastal smugglers and a fisherman seeking access and protection."

"Do they know the price of protection?" Strangward's voice was cool, transactional.

She nodded. "They are willing to pay it. I have drawn up the contracts for you to look over."

"I'll talk to the smugglers. Tell the fisherman that he's better off finding protection elsewhere. He should avoid entangling himself with me or Celestine."

Maslin nodded. "Yes, my lord. Also, the factors want to bid on your shares in the warehouses, and the stable master asks that you deal with the dreki. Their attacks on the paddocks get bolder every week."

It reminded Ash of when he was little, and his parents would return home after months on the battlefield. Ash and Lyss wanted them all to themselves, but every other official and lordling in the capital had a claim on them, too.

Strangward rolled his eyes and shifted the sea bag on his shoulders. "They need to understand that you have full authority in my absence. My comings and goings are my own business."

"Should I tell them that or will you?" Maslin said, clipping off each word.

Unexpectedly, Strangward laughed. "Sorry, Maslin. You're always the messenger. I'll meet with the shiplords tonight, the factors tomorrow afternoon, and the bloodsworn tomorrow evening," he said.

"Tomorrow evening," Maslin said, making a note.

"I'll see the smugglers the day after that at a place to be

determined." He leaned in closer to the harbormaster. "One more thing. I'll need provisions for a crew of five for a month-long voyage ready in two days' time."

"So soon?" She couldn't hide her disappointment. "But you've only just arrived."

"Yes. And I'm sailing again day after tomorrow."

"For which ship, my lord?"

"*Destiny.*"

"*Destiny?*" Maslin slowly turned her head and eyed the little ship with grave misgivings. "Do you know if she's even seaworthy?"

"She's seaworthy," Strangward said. "I built her."

Ash and Talbot looked at each other, exchanging silent messages of concern.

"Who'll crew for you?"

Strangward nodded at Ash and Talbot. "The wetlanders are well on their way to being sailors."

"No, my lord," Maslin protested. "You should not be taking such a long voyage in such a small vessel, with . . . such an inexperienced crew."

Maslin has a point, Ash thought, but Strangward was unmoved.

"She suits my purpose this time. As do they."

When Maslin opened her mouth, he raised his hand to stop further protests. "Don't worry," he said. "We'll have time to talk before I leave again. Right now, I'm going to escort my guests to Cliff House and get them settled. Tell the shiplords to meet me on the seaward terrace an hour before sunset. I'll dine with my guests immediately after."

Now that we're on dry land, Ash thought, maybe we'll get some answers.

# NO REST FOR PIRATES

It was a long hike uphill to Cliff House, but Evan liked to use the climb to gain his land legs and focus his mind. The heat hit like a club after the cool weather in the wetlands and the moderation of their week at sea. The sun seemed to reverberate off sand and rock. Even in the gardens that covered the long slope to the ocean, there was not a shadow to be found anywhere.

Evan could learn to live in any climate, not necessarily liking it, but this moving back and forth between was killing. Soon he was sweating freely, the moisture evaporating in the dry air almost as soon as it appeared. Still, he resisted the temptation to tease up a little onshore breeze. He couldn't afford to squander power just to make himself more comfortable. He never knew when he'd need every bit just to stay alive.

As usual, the handsome healer said nothing and revealed nothing, but Talbot scowled and sweated the entire way. Evan couldn't help liking the brusque corporal, and wished he could win her over. So far, that wasn't happening.

Having cleared the gardens, they toiled up the steep stone staircase to the house itself. It resembled a part of the landscape, built of buff-colored sandstone, with the same red tile roof as the harborside buildings, holding off the relentless sun. He nodded to the guards at the top of the staircase and headed around to the right, avoiding the main entrance. He spoke the charm that allowed him to access the hidden entrance to his apartments. That way they could enter without being seen.

Inside, out of the sun, it was remarkably cooler, leaving Evan dizzy with relief. He took a moment to allow his eyes to adjust to the change in light. Then he led his guests through the back hallways and into a small reception area. It was attended by Helesa, a slender woman in a long, divided skirt, a shirt emblazoned with a dragon, and simple sandals, and Kel, a man in linen trousers and shirt whose muscular build had softened somewhat with age. Among Evan's paid associates, Helesa and Kel were the closest to bodyguards. They'd been assassins in the service of the empress. Now they served him.

"Good morning, Helesa, Kelsang," he said, as if it had not been several cycles of the moon and a thousand miles since they had last met.

"Lord Strangward!" Kelsang said, flinging himself facedown on the tiles. "Forgive me. They said you had arrived, but I did not expect you to come straight here, else I would have greeted you properly."

Helesa was marginally less demonstrative. She bowed deeply, fluidly, spreading her arms wide.

Evan shifted from foot to foot. As always, this kind of display made him uneasy, especially with the wetlanders looking on. He'd lived most of his life aboard ships, where there was a minimum of ceremony and protocol. And he'd seen nothing like this in the queendom of the Fells.

Besides, this was the kind of fealty Celestine demanded. She was his personal benchmark for what not to do. He'd tried unsuccessfully to change the habits of the bloodsworn-turned-stormborn, but had pretty much given up. He still had hopes for Helesa and Kel, who were free of the blood binding.

At least he'd persuaded them not to call him "emperor of the wind and wave" or other such title.

Between them, Helesa and Kel could kill a person twenty-five different ways. They had no business kneeling to an eighteen-year-old orphan with a price on his head.

"Please. Kel. Get up," he said, grimacing. He turned to his reluctant allies. "I have things to do. Kel will see to your immediate needs. You'll have time to rest and bathe before dinner. After dinner, we'll—"

"No," Prince Adrian said, folding his arms and planting his feet like he was growing roots.

"No?" Evan stared at him, nonplussed. "Are you against the resting or the bathing part? Or is it the waiting for dinner that—?"

"We've been two weeks on the water," the healer said. "A week sailing north, and another week sailing south. Meanwhile, the empress is landing her armies in my homeland and my sister is being held captive."

"I'm not the one who insisted on sailing north, into the arms of the empress," Evan said. "If we'd stuck to the original plan, we'd be halfway to Celesgarde by now, with a skilled crew." Kel and Helesa shifted their weight, their eyes fixed on Evan for direction. He gave them a firm head shake and waved them away. They retreated to the far end of the room and stood, bodies canted forward, waiting for the wetlanders to make a move.

"So now we want some answers," Talbot said.

"We've been packed together in a small boat for a week," he said. "If you had questions, why didn't you ask them before?"

"I didn't think we'd need answers because I wasn't sure we'd make it to dry land," Talbot said.

"Thank you for your confidence," Evan said, with a sigh. When they said nothing, he gestured toward a sitting area by the cold hearth. "Would you like to sit down?"

The prince shook his head. "This shouldn't take long."

Can't anything be easy? Evan thought. He'd never realized that allies were such a pain in the ass.

"Ask your questions standing up, then. I promise that I'll be honest, though I won't guarantee you'll like my answers."

"I heard what the harbormaster said, down at the docks, about only sailing with a bloodsworn crew," Talbot said, thrusting her chin out. "I'll tell you right now, I am not signing on as one of your blood slaves."

Evan folded his arms. "Noted," he said. "Would it help if I told you that I had no intention of enslaving you?" Seeing the suspicious expression on Talbot's face, he added, "I suppose not. Frankly, I have more blood captives than I can manage already. You saw what happened down at the harbor. Everybody wants a piece of me." Literally. Different pieces.

"Do you think this is some kind of a *joke*?" Talbot growled.

"No, it's not a joke," Evan said. "In fact, if I were a betting man, I'd say we're unlikely to survive the next two months. I neither want nor need slavish devotion from you. If we can't be friends, I would appreciate a little gratitude, at least. I'm not the one who betrayed you, after all."

Talbot and Prince Adrian exchanged furtive glances. They

know, Evan thought, seeing their expressions. Or at least they suspect something.

"What do you mean?" the healer said.

"It was your friend, the fanatical mage. Finn."

"Finn?" Prince Adrian said.

"I was focusing on managing the winds, on driving the two ships apart without being too obvious. You two were in the stern, charming Samara. Captain DeVilliers had gone down to the gundeck, to move things along. When I looked up to judge our position relative to *Hydra*, I realized that the shields were down."

The healer was looking at Talbot as if to say, *I told you so.*

"Are you sure? You can see them?" Talbot said.

"I'm a mage, and I've seen them before. I'm sure. I looked for Finn, to see if he'd been hit, or he'd run out of flash, or had gone to the head or what. He was just standing there, staring at *Hydra*, as if waiting for the slaughter to begin. It didn't, though, because just then we opened fire. I slammed *Hydra* with a wall of water and then put everything I had into our sails. When Finn saw that we were getting out of range, he took matters into his own hands and blasted half of the stern away."

"You're saying he tried to blow up the boat he was sailing on?" Talbot said.

"I think he was aiming at the two of you."

"Finn was aiming at *us*," Adrian said, slowly, deliberately, looking at Talbot as if this was the evidence needed to convict.

"But why would he do that?" Talbot said.

"You would know better than me," Evan said. "Sometimes friends grow apart. Perhaps the empress offered to build him a hospital. When I saw that the two of you were in the water, I dove in after you. The rest you know."

The wetlanders just stared at him, and the confusion on their faces told him that they were going back over past events, looking for evidence, some way to predict this. Evan almost felt sorry for them.

"Why didn't you say anything?" Talbot muttered.

Why didn't *you* say anything to *me*? Evan thought, exasperated. "I thought you knew," he snapped. "I thought it might be rude to, you know, rub it in that the person you'd thrown into the brig saved your asses after the friend you trusted tried to kill you."

"Oh," Talbot said, in a small voice.

"Expect betrayal," Evan said, "and you're less likely to be disappointed. Plus, you might live longer. Now. Please go get settled in. Plan on having dinner with me after I meet with the sharks that are already circling."

"Sharks?" Talbot said.

"My allies," Evan said. "The ones who are no doubt conspiring to betray me."

# 15

# BRAWL AT THE DROVERS' INN

Strangward's bodyguard Kel led Ash and Talbot to adjoining rooms overlooking the bay. They were furnished simply, but offered beautiful views of the sun gilding the Guardians as it descended toward the Indio.

"I will return in two hours and take you to the baths," Kel said, bowing out of the room.

Could we go now? Ash thought, fingering his filthy, salt-encrusted clothes.

On the other hand, this was the first hour he'd had to himself since they'd set sail from Wizard Head.

I could really use some advice, Ash thought.

That need was beginning to outweigh his concerns about traveling to Aediion. Finn's betrayal had shaken him. He'd left his mother back in Fellsmarch, guarded by people he trusted implicitly. But if Finn had turned, who else?

*You and your mother and sister have enemies at court,* his father had said on the night his mother was poisoned. *Don't give your trust easily.*

Were there four-year-old secrets that Ash needed to know—secrets that only his father could tell him?

Kinley's book was long gone. He'd left it in his sea bag, aboard *Sea Wolf*. He couldn't study or obsess over the words printed in the chapter about the portal to the dream world. But he had them memorized.

*Tell me where to meet you.*

*Drovers' Inn.*

He had two hours. He had to try.

He acted quickly, so he wouldn't have time to second-guess himself. Taking hold of the serpent amulet, he spoke the charm to open the portal, half-convinced that nothing would happen. Instead, he was swept into a swirling black vortex. Gradually, he rebuilt the scene at Drovers' Inn from memory—the walls smudged with the soot from generations of fires, the battered wood surface of the table pocked with half-moons, where people slammed down their tankards, requesting a refill. Bowls of porridge decorated with precious bits of ham and a hunk of brown bread to sop up the leavings.

And there, at a corner table, was his father. He'd leaned his sword against the wall, draped his cloak over the back of his chair. As usual, he sat facing the door, a legacy from his days as lord of these same streets.

For a moment, Ash stood frozen, afraid to speak for fear it would shatter the scene before him.

"Da!" The cry seemed to clamor in Ash's head, but it came out as a whisper.

But his father heard, of course. "Ash," he said, pushing to his feet. "Thank the Maker. I was close to giving up."

The image flickered, changed. Here was the shaggy-haired

streetlord, not much older than Ash was now, wearing silver cuffs on his wrists and an attitude. Gradually, he aged, until he was much as Ash remembered him. His clothes changed, too, from nondescript Ragmarket clothing, to student's robes, to the clan garb he often wore to travel in rough country, to his High Wizard robes, to his funeral coat.

His father stared at him, eagerly drinking him in, and Ash realized that he must be shifting and changing, too. From court dress to Ardenine healer's browns, to the student robes at Oden's Ford, to the stormcoat he'd worn on board *Sea Wolf*. Putting on and taking off all the roles he'd played since last they'd met.

"You've grown so tall," his father said, finally. "You've traveled"—his voice caught—"a long way since I last saw you. I have missed so much."

Ash thought his heart would explode. He took one step forward, then another. "Da—I'm so sorry," he said.

His father held up both hands, palms out. "We all have sins enough on our shoulders," he said, his voice rough with emotion. "So don't take the fall for somebody else's crimes. You have nothing to apologize for."

"Can—can I touch you?" Ash wasn't sure what the rules were.

His father nodded, opening his arms. "Just—a word of warning. Creating yourself in this place involves a stampede of choices. The more senses involved, the more complicated it is. It's exhausting."

They embraced, sensation coming at Ash in fits and starts—the rough feel of the embroidered coat against his skin, the scent of dust and faraway places, the brilliant blue eyes, now on a level with his own. The scar from a long-ago knife fight.

When they stepped apart, Ash all but toppled over. He felt like he often did at the end of a strenuous healing—wrung out.

His father smiled, as if he understood. "It takes some getting used to." He gestured to the other seat at the table. "Please. Sit down. Let's make the most of the time we have."

Ash sat, feeling his way, keeping his eyes fastened on his father.

His father shifted self-consciously under the scrutiny. "Don't worry. I won't disappear if you blink. Close your eyes if it makes it easier."

Ash kept his eyes open. He did not want to miss a minute.

"How is your mother?" his father said.

"She seemed to be recovering when I left," Ash said.

"When you *left*?" His father's head came up, his fingers pressing against the table until the knuckles whitened. "Who's with her now?"

"Magret Gray, Captain Byrne, and Ty Gryphon. I had to leave. Lyss . . ." Ash swallowed, then went on to bring his father up to date on what had happened to Lyss, and the betrayal by Finn sul'Mander.

"Sul'Mander? Bayar's nephew?" His father's jaw tightened. "I might've known."

"The thing is, Finn was my friend. He's been fighting for the queendom every summer while I've been in the south. He was badly wounded in the borderlands—"

"People are complicated," his father said with a bleak smile.

"—and he couldn't have been responsible for Hana's death—he would have been twelve years old. There's got to be somebody else."

"I agree," his father said. "Finn may be involved, but

something and someone connects all of this, and we won't be able to protect the Gray Wolf line unless we figure out what it is. It began with Hana and Simon, then Cat, then you and me. I'd hoped it had stopped with me, but obviously, it hasn't."

"No," Ash said. "It hasn't."

For a long moment, they sat in silence, his father toying with the ring on his finger, the match to the ring his mother never took off.

It was odd. Whenever they were deep in conversation, it was as if the rest of the room disappeared, their world reduced to the table they shared. If he looked around, the common room would reappear, as if emerging from the mist.

Out of mind, out of sight, Ash thought.

If Ash had hoped his father would shovel answers into his lap, he was disappointed. Instead, he seemed to be coming around to blaming himself.

"I should have been there," his father said. "I should have been there to look out for all of you. Instead, I—"

"If I don't get to apologize for running off, you don't get to apologize for getting killed," Ash said bluntly.

His father stared at him. And then, unexpectedly, began to laugh. He spit in his hand and offered it. They shook, sealing the deal.

Then Ash asked the question that had dogged him for four long years. "The day you died, you said you were on your way to meet someone . . . ?"

His father nodded. "After Hana was killed, I suspected that someone at court had betrayed us. I was supposed to meet a splitter—a source—that morning in Southbridge name of Darian. Said he had a—"

"Hang on," Ash said. *"Darian?"*

"Aye," his father said, with a puzzled frown. "Have you heard of him?"

"There's a sect in the Church of Malthus that hunts wizards," Ash said, his heart beating faster. "They call themselves the Darian Brothers. They're the ones who tried to murder me at Oden's Ford, and they've made at least two more attempts since then. They said their leader, Lord Darian, was working to cleanse the Realms of wizards. They came after me because I'm the get of an unholy union between a powerful mage, Han sul'Alger, and the witch queen in the north."

"Well," his father said, rubbing his chin, "they've got you there."

"There's more. When they caught the busker who led Lyss into an ambush, he had Lyss's locket, the one you gave her. He said he was given the job—and the locket—by someone named Darian." Ash took a breath, then pushed on. "I think the brothers are being used by someone who's coming after us, specifically."

"It has to be someone at court," his father said, "someone who could get hold of the locket, who would know why it was important. Did the busker provide a description?"

Ash nodded. "Keep in mind—I never spoke to the busker. All this is secondhand. He described Darian as tall, gaunt, and gifted." He paused. "The day you were murdered, remember, someone grabbed me in the street. I was smaller then, but I remember him as somebody who fit that description."

His father thought a moment. "Does the name Darian mean anything to you?"

"I looked it up in the Temple library at Ardenscourt.

Apparently, the original Darian was a founder and saint of the Malthusian church."

"Was he a wizard?"

"Yes." Something in his father's face impelled him to add, "Since that was a thousand years ago, I think we can assume this isn't the same person. Just somebody inspired by him."

"You're probably right," his father said slowly, "though you never know. After all, our thousand-year-old ancestor Alger Waterlow came back in the form of a character named Crow."

"In Aediion," Ash said. "Not in real life."

"He could have shown up in real life," his father said, "if he'd caught a ride back with a living person."

"What do you mean—caught a ride back?" Ash said. "I never heard of that."

"Early on, Crow demonstrated that he could come back with me to real life and control my actions and use my magic. I always worried that he would possess me in order to take revenge on his enemies. The descendants of his enemies, anyway."

That's when Ash remembered—he'd read about that in Kinley.

He shivered, the hairs standing up on the back of his neck as if a cold draft had come in through the tavern door. And, indeed, the lanterns flickered and popped.

"So the attacks involve someone tall, gaunt, and gifted, using the name Darian," his father summarized. "Someone at court, or at least knowledgeable about it. Someone with access to the royal family."

"Could it be—do you think it's Micah Bayar? He and Finn were always close. And you and he were . . . not."

His father considered this, absently fingering his scarred

wrists where the cuffs had been. Then shook his head. "I would like to pin this on Micah, and I might have done until we got to the point of poisoning Raisa. That, he would never do. I think Raisa was the only topic we ever agreed on. For all of his faults, he has always loved her. I think he would die before he would see her come to harm. And the notion of him throwing in with a bunch of fanatics is too ludicrous to stomach."

"All right. Not Micah," Ash said, crossing the High Wizard off his mental list. "So. It would have to be someone skilled with poisons, or with access to that expertise. Not all of the killings were poisonings, but I believe the same poison was used on Mother as what was used to kill you. It's called two-step lily—rare and relatively unknown. Amateurs and jilted lovers tend to use gedden, which is readily recognized, or moonflower, sometimes mixed with flowering oak, to mask the—" He cut off abruptly at the mixed sorrow and guilt on his father's face. "What?"

His father sighed. "Like I said—you've traveled a long way since we last met, to places I hoped you'd never have to go. Back in my Ragmarket days, I gave no quarter. I destroyed my rivals in the hopes that one day my children wouldn't have to live that life. And now here we are."

He knows, Ash thought. He knows I'm a killer. Tall, gaunt, and gifted, with a talent for poisons—that could describe me.

"There's still time, Da," Ash said softly. "It's not too late."

"Maybe," his father said. "I wish we'd have talked sooner."

Since the day his mother was poisoned, a question had been plaguing Ash. "I— Why didn't you reach out before? I didn't know this was possible. I thought what you did with our grandfather was a one-off thing. I would have tried to connect before now, if I'd known."

"I have no memory of the time right after the attack," his father said, drawing circles on the tabletop with his forefinger. "It was as if I didn't exist. I suspect that I just wasn't bitter enough to keep fighting."

"What do you mean?"

His father smiled faintly. "I mean that I was beginning to think I deserved what I got. I was tired. I'd been fighting for the queendom and the line for more than twenty-five years, yet the war showed no sign of ending. I'd lost Hana, and Simon Byrne, and Cat Tyburn, and was beginning to think someone else would do a better job."

Ash made as if to protest, but his father shook his head. "It was Alger—Crow—who wouldn't let me rest. Remember, he'd been betrayed by his best friend. He never had a life with Hanalea.

"So. It irked him that after all the trouble he'd taken to restore the Line, I let myself be taken down by assassins on the street like a nick-ninny mark." He paused. "He wouldn't use that word, of course," he said drily. "He's too fancy for that. Even after Alger intervened, I couldn't make a connection. As you said, nobody knew I was here, so nobody came looking. Alger waited a thousand years for me to wander into Aediion. It wasn't until Raisa—until Raisa was dying that I had a way of communicating with you, through her."

But if his father hadn't planned for this, then—?

"But you told me where to meet you," Ash said. "You told me to meet you here."

"What do you mean?" His father looked lost.

"The note. In Kinley. *Drovers' Inn*, it said."

"I never wrote a note in Kinley," his father said.

"Then who did?" Ash said. Who else even knew they'd had breakfast at the inn that morning?

The answer blazed across his consciousness before he'd properly finished the question.

The killers.

So. This was not a message from his dead father, desperate for a meeting. It was, most likely, a trap set by his murderers for his son.

It might also be a chance to get some answers.

The Alisters, father and son, looked at each other, understanding kindling between them. Then both scanned the room, then looked toward the door. Nothing seemed awry.

His father reached across the table, closing his hand over Ash's. "Go back," he said. "Now. I'll wait here and have a chat with them. We'll meet up later, and I'll let you know what I find out."

"I'm staying," Ash said.

"Use your head," his father said. "I'm already dead. You're alive. The whole point is to keep it that way."

"Look," Ash said. "It's taken me four years to arrange one meeting with you. Who knows when it will happen again? If I don't find out who's behind this, I might not make it to that next meeting. I'll stay, but I promise I'll go when the time is right."

"How much power do you have on board?" his father asked, gesturing toward his amulet. "I can create illusions and the like, but I have no actual magical energy. If you're still here when you run out of flash, you'll have no way of getting back."

"I'm good," Ash said, fingering his amulet.

"Remember, swords and that lot don't work here." He

gestured toward his sword, leaning against the wall. "That's all illusion. The only weapon you or anyone else has is magic. Drop an illusory anvil on your enemy, and it won't make a bit of difference. Killing charms, immobilization charms, and the like, are the thing."

"Got it," Ash said, with more confidence than he actually felt. He reviewed what he'd read in Kinley about weapons to use in the dream world.

His father hesitated. "Now. If you insist on staying, it will help if those who come don't know I'm here. Would it be all right if I join forces with you?"

"What do you mean?"

"I'll inhabit your person alongside you. Alger did that with me, once or twice. You'll hear my voice in your head, and I'll act through you if I think I can help."

"Go ahead," Ash said warily.

His father disappeared from his seat at the corner table. When he slipped into Ash's consciousness, it was more like being embraced than anything else. Ash felt a warm presence, like he had an ally and counselor in his head. It was more mental and emotional than physical—the knowledge that someone had his back.

*Now that we're joined, we can communicate without an enemy overhearing.*

*Okay.* Ash kept scanning the taproom, pushing the margins out, wanting to put distance between him and whomever might be coming.

*If you keep your amulet in your hand or your pocket, you won't signal to them when you reach for it.*

Ash lifted the chain over his head, looped it around his wrist, and gripped his amulet in his right hand.

*This is a mind game. Put on your street face. You may find that you— We have company.*

Ash could see the shadows all around the room deepening, becoming more solid, moving and sliding past each other.

*Most of them are not real. The trick is to find the wizard hosts among the rest and target them. They will try to fool you into using up all of your flash lobbing at phantoms. Then you're done. Remember, they can't hurt you except through direct magic.*

The shades swarmed toward them, shredding, reassembling, stretching into new shapes, with Ash desperately resisting the temptation to let fly.

Which one of these is not like the others? Ash thought.

That one, perhaps. It was moving with more purpose than the others. He aimed carefully, fired, and the shadow dissipated into nothingness.

*Just a shade. You'll see a glow when your real target accesses magic. That will pinpoint him and let you know when he's about to make his move.*

It took everything Ash had to stand fast with shades flying into his face, swirling around his body, sliding under his clothes. It was like being swallowed by a mob, knowing that someone in the crowd was packing.

A faint glow kindled in the midst of the shades. Ash threw himself flat as a killing charm rocketed through the spot where he'd been moments before. He fired back at where he guessed the shot had come from, but he must have missed, because it had no apparent effect.

Now, inky blackness descended over everything.

"So, mage, I have taken your eyes," a soft voice said. "We'll see how well you do when I hunt you in the dark."

Dread sluiced over Ash. Those were the very words used by the dark priest who'd nearly blinded him in the cellars of Ardenscourt.

"You like to hide in the dark," Han Alister said, speaking aloud through Ash, seeming to echo inside his head. "Let's see how you look in daylight." Brilliant light flooded in, lighting every corner of the Drovers' Inn, driving the shades and shadows away. Leaving one standing alone.

It wasn't Bayar, or Finn, or anyone Ash expected. It was Lyss, clad in the spattercloth of the Highlander army. She looked around, as if bewildered, her hand on the hilt of her sword.

Ash might not have recognized her, except that his mother had shown him a recent portrait of his sister in her captain's uniform, her honey-colored braid draped over her shoulder.

"What is this place?" she demanded. She lifted her chin, focusing on Ash. "Who the hell are you?"

"Lyss," Ash said. "It's me. Ash."

She stared at him, brow furrowed, shaking her head. Her clothing wavered, shifted, settled again.

"It's Ash," he said again, extending his arms.

He was conscious of his father, clamoring in his head. *Ash. Remember what I said. That could be anyone.* And then, more urgently, *Ash. That's not Lyss. It's a rig. Don't fall for it.*

*I've got this, Da.*

"Ash?" Lyss took a step forward, and then another. "But how? Is this a dream?"

"Lyss," Ash said. "I don't understand—how did you get here?"

A smile broke across her face, wiping away the confusion. "It *is* you!"

She charged toward him, the image fragmenting momentarily, then coalescing into a bolt of elemental flame.

Ash raised the hand with the amulet and clasped it with his other hand, extending it out in front of him. As flame torrented toward him, he spoke the ancient charm from Kinley. The flash was intercepted by his amulet, drawing it in, heating in his hands as flash accumulated.

*Slick*, his father said.

Lyss screamed, her voice changing midscream, as her form and features changed as well. For a moment, Ash was facing off with Finn sul'Mander, his features twisted in agony, and then another face—unfamiliar.

It resembled a demon's face—thin-lipped, hollow-cheeked in a cowl and prelate's robes.

"You have temporarily broken the thread that connects me to the living," the demon said, "and that is all."

Ash sent flame spiraling toward him, but it appeared to pass straight through the spectre.

"You cannot kill me, mage," it said. "I am already dead."

*Is that true? There's no way to kill him?* Ash silently asked his father.

*That's true. He and I belong here, you don't. But without a connection to the world of the living, he has no access to magic.*

"Surrender, mage," the demon said. "I have been fighting this war for five hundred years. You cannot match my knowledge and determination."

"You must be Darian the dead and depleted," Ash said. "Knowledge and determination are no match for magic."

"Ah, but there's where you're wrong," Darian said. "Knowledge and determination are what enable me to acquire magic."

Ash heard the warning in the priest's voice, but still, when Darian attacked it was almost impossible to resist. He felt an intense and painful pressure, as if someone were pounding on the borders of his brain, demanding to be let in. Tendrils of someone else's memory were sliding through tiny cracks in his mental wall, scenes and biases from someone else's experience. Ash stiffened his resistance, pushed back.

And then, with a force like an explosion against the inside of Ash's skull, Darian was driven back, every trace of his presence excised.

"Leave off, Darian," Han said. "You claim to be a priest, but you serve the Breaker. This is Ragmarket, and this is my blood. If you come onto my turf again, you'll answer to the Demon King."

And then, to Ash, *Time to go. Come back when it's safe. Southbridge Temple next time.*

*Southbridge Temple.* Ash gripped his amulet and spoke the portal charm.

# 16

# NEWS FROM THE CAPITAL

As Hal assessed the battalions of soldiers contributed by the rebel thanes, he couldn't help feeling like he was reliving the debacle at Queen Court. Once again, he was being asked to lead poorly trained troops against a better-prepared and more experienced enemy.

Hal was beginning to appreciate King Gerard's genius in collecting taxes instead of troops from his liege lords. That way, he could hire and equip a full-time professional army—one that didn't come and go with the seasons or whims of the thanes.

The nobility grumbled about taxes but could not afford to send their bannermen and tenants away during the summer growing season, year after year.

That allowed Gerard to fight his semipermanent war in the north. It also prevented the thanes from fielding experienced armies of their own.

Each of the rebel thanes planned to lead his own troops into battle. Which was either brave or foolhardy on their part, but it also meant that launching a battle plan was like herding cats.

Each lord was endeavoring to preserve his own army while jockeying for a dominant or advantageous position in the end.

How about we focus on defeating the Ardenine army? Hal thought. If we're successful, you can fight over the spoils. If not, our heads will be decorating the palisades in Ardenscourt.

"General Matelon?" His aide-de-camp poked his head into the room. "Corporal Matelon has returned, sir, and has asked to see you."

"Show him in," Hal said, pushing his diagrams and sketches aside, hoping his brother brought good news.

Robert entered, followed by Jan Rives, his father's longtime quartermaster. Hal had sent the two of them to Ardenscourt on what he preferred to call a reconnaissance mission. He'd hoped Rives would be the check on Robert's penchant for impulse. Hal could tell by their appearance that they'd come straight from the paddocks. He could tell by his brother's face that he brought news, and at least some of it was good.

"Welcome back," Hal said, relieved that they'd made it back safely. He hated sending his fourteen-year-old brother into harm's way. But Robert was smart and unquestionably loyal—two traits that were hard to come by in this command. And, in this instance, Robert was the emissary he needed.

There are no children in a civil war.

"Are you hungry? Thirsty?" An unnecessary question, because soldiers were always both. "There's cider on the sideboard, cheese and bread and fruit. If you want something more, I can—"

"This will do," Robert said, already pouring.

It was all Hal could do to wait until they had settled down to eat before he said, "Well? How did it go?"

"Karn's disgraced, dead, and hanging from the city walls,"
Robert said.

Hal stared at Robert, his heart sinking. Since the night
they'd escaped from Ardenscourt, Hal had been trying to
devise a way to save Destin Karn if and when they took the
city. He might be a ruthless, conniving bastard, but he'd saved
their lives and spirited the hostages away from the king. Plus,
if he could be persuaded to talk, Hal was sure he'd have plenty
to say.

Had the king found out about the spymaster's involvement
in the attack on the capital? If so, what else did the king know?

Then he noticed that Robert was smirking at him.

"*What?*" he said.

"I'm talking about *General* Karn," Robert said, biting off a
hunk of bread. "Not Lieutenant Karn."

"*General* Karn is dead?" Hal stared at him with mingled
delight and disbelief. If there was a grave he would dance on,
that was it.

Robert's mouth was full, so Rives continued the story. "The
scum-sucking bastard's dead, thank the Maker. There's all kinds
of rumors flying about what happened. Some say it started
when Karn disagreed with the kinglet about whether to send
the army to meet us or go after the witch in the north."

"Let me guess—General Karn wanted to come after us."

"Right," Rives said. "Maybe he thought he'd have better
luck against us than he's had subduing the queendom."

To be honest, it was the decision any field commander would
make. You protect your rear. You deal with the bear charging
at you before you go hunting wolves in the mountains. In over
twenty-five years of war, except for the debacle in Delphi, the

northerners had never come south. Still, it seemed improbable that General Karn would go toe-to-toe with Jarat on a matter of strategy.

"There's more," Robert said. "Apparently, General Karn was spying for the empress all along. He was in league with that pirate who came here just after Solstice."

Hal practically choked on his cider. "General Karn . . . was spying for the empress? *That's* what they're saying?" Somehow, in Hal's heart of hearts, he knew that wasn't true. It would be easier to believe that about the younger Karn, the spymaster and keeper of secrets.

Rives picked up the story. "I guess they found all kinds of evidence that the general had been feeding information to the empress. In fact, General Karn and the empress were behind the attack on the capital." Rives leaned closer. "*In fact*, General Karn killed Luc Granger, the captain of the King's Guard, himself, and left him lying in the street."

Hal looked up and met Robert's eyes. Robert winked. Hal decided to pour himself more cider.

"When he was confronted," Rives went on, "the general attacked the king and was killed by his own son—Lieutenant Karn. People are saying the spymaster's a hero."

Hal shook his head in wonder. How the hell did Destin Karn pull that off? He hoped they'd both live long enough that he could find out.

Rives stood. "By your leave, General, I'd better go see how much ordnance was stolen while we were gone."

"Dismissed, Sergeant. And thank you."

With that, Rives saluted, then departed, leaving the Matelon brothers on their own.

"What about . . . the other thing?" Hal said. "Were you able to speak with any of the officers on my list?"

Robert nodded. "Three said no, but four are in." He handed Hal a coded list, with the four marked off.

"Four?" Hal stared at his brother. "I thought maybe two would sign on, at most."

Hal had given Robert a list of seven officers who'd fought under him in the past—good, experienced men that he trusted. He hadn't much to offer, put up against the risk of court-martial and execution, but these were men who wouldn't turn his brother in. Especially since most had known Robert since he was little. Some had even fought beside him during his brief career.

"There seem to be lots of men eager to fight with you, big brother. Part of it is your godlike reputation . . ." Robert paused, while Hal rolled his eyes. "But there's a lot of resentment, too. Here, they've been busting their asses in the north every summer, getting blamed for every setback. Then rumors were flying that Jarat was going to put his man Granger in to replace General Karn. Not going to happen now, of course, but it left a sour taste in everyone's mouth."

"What about enlisted men? Did they think it was feasible to bring some of them along?" That was definitely the tricky part. It wasn't like his officers could put out a general call for traitors willing to fight against their king.

"We might get more than we thought. Jarat's still inconsistent about paying his soldiers, especially in the winter months," Robert said. "Stupid, really, if a war is staring you in the face. If your army is there for the money, then you'd better make sure they get it. You can't treat them like a farmer's militia."

"So who's in command of the army?" Hal said. "Have they chosen anyone?"

"King Jarat has promoted Colonel Bellamy."

"Bellamy!" Bellamy had been on Hal's wish list.

Robert nodded. "He said no to us."

"Saints," Hal said. "I wish Jarat had picked somebody else." He didn't relish the idea of going up against his friend, who was by far the most talented officer, the most skilled tactician still fighting for the king. He'd much rather have met Granger in the field.

Robert looked to his right and left, then leaned toward Hal. "No worries. Jarat's not coming here. He's still planning to march on the northern capital."

"He hasn't changed his mind?"

"Jarat seems determined to take his talents north. He says it's high time to add the queendom to the empire." Robert laughed. "Apparently, he doesn't see you as much of a threat, big brother."

Hal shook his head. "Maybe it's a ruse. He'll take the North Road, pretending to be marching on the Fells, but he'll turn off when he reaches Temple Church."

Robert shrugged. "You may be right, but that's not what I'm hearing."

What is it about the north that turns our kings into fools? Hal thought. Either Jarat's still hot to prove he can succeed where his father failed, or he's made some kind of deal with the empress to split the Fells between them.

Hal scanned his list, considering assets and liabilities. "I wish we had some mages on our side," he said. "Even a few would make a big difference."

"The officers who are coming over are going to try and recruit some mages," Robert said. "They have no love for the empire, either."

"Maybe not, but if they're in the army, they're collared and under the king's control." Hal wasn't forgetting his experience in Queen Court, where mages that were supposedly on his side turned on him.

"Speaking of mages," Robert said, "that reminds me. I received a peculiar message while I was in Ardenscourt." He leaned toward Hal. "I'd gone outside of the inn we were staying at, to use the privy. This drunk stumbled up to me, and I thought she was going to ask me for money or something, but she gripped my arm and said, sober as could be, 'Corporal Matelon. You and your brother should know that nearly all the flashcraft in the Ardenine armory is special issue.'"

"Special issue?" Hal said. "What does that mean?"

"I asked her, and she handed me a pouch and said, 'This is a gift from the clans in the north. You can thank Lila Barrowhill.'"

"Barrowhill?" Hal rubbed his chin, remembering what she'd said. *Everybody's girl.*

"She said they'd send more information later. She turned to leave, and I grabbed her arm, and . . . she decked me."

"This drunk girl decked you?" Hal couldn't help grinning, even though Captain Alyssa Gray had done pretty much the same thing to him.

"Like I said, she wasn't drunk," Robert said defensively. "Anyway, I was lying there in a puddle of piss and she leaned down and said, 'You'll need at least one loyal mage in order to use this.' Then she left."

"What was in the pouch?"

"Have a look," Robert said, fishing inside his coat and handing it over.

The pouch was heavy and clinked with the sound of metal on metal. Hal dumped the contents into his hand. It was a pendant, gold and silver, obviously clan-made. It resembled a key, with a long shank connecting the bow end and the toothed blade. When he looked more closely, he could see a clever joint where the grip met the shank. As he turned the grip, notches on the edge lined up with tick marks on the shank. He pulled on the two ends, but they didn't come apart. What was it? An amulet with power settings? A locket with a combination to open it? An explosive device with a detonator?

Or was it an actual key to something?

Knowing Lila, it was probably some kind of trick that would move ahead her secret agenda. And yet—what if it really was a tool that could help them?

"Any ideas?" Robert said.

Hal ran his fingers over the pendant and returned it to its leather pouch. "Like Barrowhill's messenger said—maybe what we need is a loyal mage."

Hal locked the pouch away in his strongbox and unfurled his maps again. He didn't need more mysteries—he needed a battle plan. While he was dithering around in the south, the empress was marching in the north, where his sister and mother were, and Alyssa Gray was still a captive in the east, if she wasn't already dead. He couldn't shake the notion that he was running out of time. That by the time this was over, everything and everyone he cared about would be lost.

# 17

# SHIPLORDS

After settling Prince Adrian and Talbot in their rooms, Evan and his bodyguard Helesa made their way toward the seaward gallery, where he was to meet with his shiplords.

Evan wasn't looking forward to it. When he'd received the message from Destin, he'd bought the baby dragon at the market and sailed the next day. It wasn't unusual for him to slip away unannounced—it was the one way he could make sure the empress couldn't intercept him. But he'd never stayed away this long before.

Evan had once hoped that Tarvos could be more than a pirate's stronghold—that it could be a center of commerce and scholarship for the entire coast. He believed that a free port should be a marketplace of ideas as well as goods. He wanted peers, not subjects.

He'd made a start. His library was the best in Carthis, built with books in a multitude of languages, carried in from all corners of the known world.

But pressure from the empress had prevented his sanctuary from becoming the commercial center he'd hoped for. Trading ships gave the Desert Coast a wide berth. Only the cagiest, bravest, most ruthless ship's masters were willing to risk drawing Celestine's enmity by signing on with the stormlord. Which meant that, whatever shine you put on it, it was still a nest of pirates, struggling for power over a shrinking dominion.

For Evan, power was just a means to an end, the price of survival. Before he met Jenna Bandelow, he'd always assumed that if he tired of the game, he could leave the fight and find a hole deep enough to hide in. But if Celestine could find Jenna in the mines of Delphi, she would find Evan eventually. Worse, she might discover that the way to Evan led straight through Destin Karn.

Sometimes it seemed that his entire life had consisted of the steady dismantling of dreams, the narrowing of horizons, a battlefield that would one day shrink to this narrow strip along the sea. It was risky, allowing other ship's masters the use of his harbor. But he couldn't quite let go of his dream of a free port, and the businesses in Tarvos needed a steady stream of commerce to survive.

The gallery was cool and high-ceilinged, with stuccoed walls and tiled floors, built for the climate. Its large, arched windows caught the breezes that came off the water, and a fountain splashed in one corner. It was a peaceful setting, but Evan knew he would find no peace here.

Eight pairs of eyes turned toward him when he walked onto the terrace, each face hungry in its own way. Five men, three women. All older than him, and none of them gifted. All of them bound by their need for this sanctuary that Evan had created where the sea met the shore.

Here, they could ply their trade independently, knowing

they had a safe harbor to return to, where Celestine couldn't reach them.

At best, the alternative would be bending the knee to the empress, who extracted exorbitant port fees; at worst, there was the possibility of blood enslavement, although, these days, fewer and fewer of Celestine's ship's masters were bloodsworn. She'd learned that they couldn't outsmart Evan's free shiplords, let alone Evan himself.

While the ships' masters were free, the ships' crews were all blood-bound, to Celestine or Evan, respectively. They were unfailingly loyal, hardworking, and reliable—as long as they were told what to do. And as long as they were convinced that the orders served their bloodlords. Any whiff of betrayal, and they were likely to tear their officers to bits.

Evan walked a tightrope every day. Fear of Celestine kept the shiplords in line. Fear of Evan's magic kept the empress at a distance. And the threat of the empress had been the driving force in Evan's life for nearly as long as he could remember. It was a delicate balance that could fail at any time.

Deep down, Evan knew that he would eventually lose this battle of strength and wits, because he would never match the empress for ruthlessness. He could justify binding the already bloodsworn. He couldn't bring himself to bind free men and women, nor did he want the burden of their unquenchable need.

The shiplords knew his expectations by now. The burners were going, the water was heating, the cups were prepared— waiting for the Stormcaster to provide the final ingredient, if he cared to. Evan always insisted that they participate in the ritual of tay whenever they came together. That gave him the option of forging a stronger bond, if need be, by adding his blood to the brew. Any who refused lost access to the harbor at Tarvos.

So far, he'd served up only unadulterated tay.

Jagger spoke up first, as always. "Strangward," he said, rising to his feet, spreading his arms in a deep bow. "You have been missed." He moved toward him like the predator he was, silent as death save the soft music of his jewelry—necklaces, bangles, multiple earrings, gold beads threaded onto his braids. Like most of the other shiplords, he wore his wealth on his person, where he could keep both eyes on it. His gold and his ship—those were his most valuable assets. In Jagger's world, the sand and rock, trees and flowers and olive trees of Carthis were worthless—they served only to divide one sea from another.

"We worry when you disappear like this," Roshan Sangway said, licking his lips nervously. Despite the breeze from the harbor, his forehead shone with sweat.

"Worry sharpens the mind," Evan said. "You worry about me when I disappear, and I worry about you while I'm gone."

"You should have an escort," Jagger said. "The empress's ships are everywhere. If anything should happen to you, we would all be . . ."

"Ruined," Riggs grumbled. He was gray-headed and creaking, always talking about leaving the sea for good after his next voyage.

"Then you'd better make sure nothing happens to me," Evan said.

"How can we do that if we don't know when you're leaving or where you go?" the Mongrel whined.

"An entire fleet of ships would offer little protection against Celestine. My best protection is to escape her notice."

"We are not afraid of a fight," Jasmina said. She was the youngest and hungriest of the shiplords, tough and muscular, with the personality of a badger. When she looked to the other shiplords for support, it was late in coming and less than enthusiastic.

"Then, by all means, sail out and fight her," Evan said. "If you kill her, I'll give you free use of the port of Tarvos in perpetuity." He said this knowing that, without Celestine, they would have no need of the port of Tarvos. And without him, they had no chance of defeating the empress.

"At least allow one of us to sail with you," Jagger said.

"Who's going to nanny him—you?" Jasmina said, showing her teeth in a sharkish smile. This was likely a quick preventive strike in case the other shiplords thought she should be on stormlord-sitting duty.

"I'm thinking of more of a lieutenant," Jagger said, "or a first mate." The pirate gripped Evan's arm, his long nails digging deeply into his flesh.

"Let go of me, Jagger," Evan said, his voice deadly calm, "or look for another bolt-hole." Evan had been a stripling when he'd arrived in Tarvos. It was easier to stare the shiplord down now that he was tall enough to look him straight in his dark, hooded eyes. After a moment's hesitation, Jagger let go, though his nails left red half-moon welts along Evan's arm.

You'll pay for that, Evan thought. Out loud, he said, "I don't need a nanny. That doesn't put money in my pocket. I need you prowling the wetland coast, taking ships and bringing the profits back to our port."

Unbuckling a bulging pouch from his belt, Evan distributed the contents among the steaming pots. Immediately, the air was filled with the seductive scent of the steeping leaf. When he was home, Evan always handled the ritual himself. It kept his options open.

When he was gone, he depended on Kel and Helesa to handle the ceremony for the bound crews. One dose was enough to bind a person; after that, they had an unquenchable thirst for more.

As Evan served each shiplord a small cup of tay, he or she murmured the expected pledge of homage. Those were about as honest as a fancy's kiss, but it was a lovely ceremony, anyway.

When everyone was served, Evan took his accustomed seat, cross-legged on the cushion with the best view of the water and the best access to the breeze coming in the window. That was one of the few privileges he claimed.

He waited until they had all emptied their cups, then set his cup down without touching it and rested his hands on his knees. "So," he said, "what are the numbers?"

Helesa had, in fact, already given him the numbers. Nothing came into the harbor that wasn't inventoried by his stormborn harbor crew. Evan took a fifth of whatever came in or out—that was the price of dockage.

Two ships had been taken in the past month; both off the southern coast of the wetlands—one by Jagger, the other by Jasmina, who had been captaining her own ship for three years. It was no wonder she had no interest in signing on as first mate to him.

"The empress is on the move," Sangway said, wrapping his thick fingers around his cup as if someone might try and take it away. "I ranged up the wetland coast toward Middlesea, and her ships were thicker than ever before."

"Were they?" Evan said, pretending ignorance. He wasn't going to offer any clues as to where he'd been or what he'd been up to. "Were they hunting wetland ships or spying on the wetlanders or taking a much-needed holiday?"

Sangway shook his head. "I don't know, but they seemed to be concentrated in the west, away from Carthis."

"Ah," Evan said, raising his cup. "My friends, we have finally succeeded in driving Celestine from the islands."

Some of them laughed.

"If she's hugging the wetland coast, it will make it risky to take prizes in the western Indio," Sangway persisted. "That has been the one hunting ground still open to us. Couldn't you send a gale their way and either capsize them or force them back toward home?" The shiplords had little understanding of Evan's stormlord gift, and they were always looking to him to solve problems with it.

"If I could do that, I would have no need of the rest of you," Evan said. "The Indio is a large ocean—I cannot police all of it. Would you rather I relinquish our stronghold on the Desert Coast and find a port in the wetlands?"

Two or three seemed to be seriously considering that idea.

"Of course, that will plunge us into a land war with the kings and queens in the Realms." He shook his head. "What about Southgate or Sand Harbor?"

"Too many gunships and not enough prizes," the Mongrel said.

"It's too windy in Invaders Bay, and there's too many mosquitoes in the Southern Islands," Jasmina said, rolling her eyes. "What's wrong with you?" She freed her hair from its cloth wrapping and shook it down around her shoulders. "Do you expect the stormlord to do your fighting for you? The next thing we know, you'll want him to wipe your lazy asses. He promised you a harbor. He did not promise to make the entire ocean safe for pirates."

This was not well received.

"It's easy for him," Blazon said, gesturing toward Evan. "The empress's ships steer clear of him because they know he can founder them with a wave of his hand. The rest of us have to fight."

"If the empress has taken her ships west, then perhaps we should pay a call there, or in the Northern Islands," Jasmina said. "I'm tired of tiptoeing around Celestine."

Evan watched their faces. Jasmina was the only one who seemed genuinely on board. One or two grinned and nudged each other, imagining what it would be like to give Celestine a poke in the backside and spending the treasure they would share. Most shifted nervously on their pillows, looking down at their hands.

Except for Jagger. Jagger was watching him like he was a ship about to hit a reef. The back of Evan's neck prickled and gooseflesh rose on his arms.

Besides, he was tired. His eyelids were heavy, and his arm tingled and throbbed where Jagger had gripped him. Despite the breeze from the gallery window, he'd broken into a sweat.

*I must be hungrier than I thought.*

"It's growing late," Evan said, "and we're not going to settle anything tonight. Tomorrow, after the midday, I invite anyone interested in planning an attack on Deep Harbor to meet me in the library." He levered to his feet, then nearly toppled over.

*Scummer.*

"My lord?" Helesa said. "Are you well?" She took his arm, supporting him, but he was watching the shiplords. Though by now, he was having trouble focusing his eyes, he thought he'd picked out the culprits.

"Poison," he said. "Jagger and Sangway, at least. It must have been under Jagger's nails. Run. Get help." He sagged to his knees, then slumped backward on the floor next to her feet. Helesa did not run. Instead, she sprang toward the shiplords, a blade in each hand.

Why doesn't anyone ever follow orders? Evan thought. Blood spattered Evan's face and the floor around him. He lay on his back, helpless, though fully conscious, while the fighting went on around him. He was stepped on at least once. It seemed to go on for a very long time. Eventually, Helesa went down, taking the Mongrel with her, and the fighting stopped.

Fair winds and following seas, Helesa, Evan thought. I'm sorry.

That was when the shouting began. It seemed that not everyone had been in on the plan.

"Are you crazy?" Blazon said. "With the Stormlord dead, what are you going to do when Celestine sails into the harbor?"

"That won't be a problem," Sangway said, with the confidence of a co-conspirator.

"Anyway, he's not dead," Jagger said, nudging Evan with his boot. "He's just immobilized."

"What if Strangward calls up a wave and washes us all away?" Jasmina said. "Or founders our ships? What if—?"

"That won't happen," Jagger said.

Blazon spat on the floor. "How do you know? What do you know about stormlord magic?" The shiplord eyed Evan with apprehension. Evan did his best, but it's hard to look threatening when you're flat on your back on the floor.

"What are you planning to do when it wears off?" Jasmina said. "Apologize?"

"We're going to make sure it doesn't wear off," Jagger said.

"*We* are?" Blazon shook his head. "If you wanted our help, we should have been in on the plan from the beginning."

"I don't care if you help or not," Jagger said. Grinning down into Evan's face, the shiplord ran his nails down Evan's other arm, gouging through skin, leaving a deep scratch behind. Evan's breath hissed out from the pain of it, but he couldn't even flinch away.

Now, Jagger drew on a pair of heavy leather gloves.

Wouldn't want to accidentally scratch your gutter-swiving self, Evan thought.

"There's no going back from this," Blazon persisted. "When the stormborn find out what happened, they'll tear us to pieces."

"We're going to blame it on the wetlanders," Jagger said. "Though if you keep on whining, I'll blame it on you."

Blazon shrank back a little, glancing toward the archway that led to the rest of the palace.

Evan wished he could somehow warn Ash and Talbot. That was your job, Helesa, he thought, regret sluicing through him. She still lay on the stone floor in a puddle of congealing blood.

"Look," Jagger said, "Strangward's been gone for months, and now he says he's leaving again. Meanwhile, we're all hurting, because the empress is sucking up everything worth having. There's less to go around than before. We need access to both coasts. We need the freedom to go wherever we like. We need to be on an equal footing with Celestine, but that'll never happen as long as this boy's in charge. If a port master isn't doing his job, it's our right to choose a new one. So. This is my harbor now. If you don't like it, leave."

"So you think you can do better?" Blazon said. "What can you do that the boy can't? You can't make weather."

"I can give the empress what she wants." He pointed at Evan. "Him."

Jasmina stared down at Evan, chewing her lower lip. Then looked up at Jagger. "You should have discussed this with us," she said.

"I didn't have to," Jagger said. "I've already discussed it with Celestine. In return for the stormlord and his two friends alive, she will give us control of the entire Desert Coast."

This was met by a stunned silence.

"Why would she do that?" Jasmina said.

"Celestine is shifting her focus to the wetlands," Jagger said. "She'll keep her capital in the Northern Islands, but she needs someone to manage her holdings in Carthis." He planted a thumb in his chest. "That will be me."

I knew it would end this way, Evan thought. Like everyone else, Jagger thinks he can make a deal with the empress and come out ahead.

If you believe that, you're in for a rude awakening. That didn't help much, because he knew that he would not be around to see it.

# 18

# BLOOD IN THE WATER

Ash slammed back into his body, acutely aware of his surroundings—the scent of the sea below the gallery, the sound of water lapping against the shore, the pain in his knees and spine informing him that he'd been lying in the same position for too long.

And yet—if a person can be giddy with joy and flattened by grief and worry at the same time, Ash was there. Spending even an hour with his father reminded him of what they'd lost, and what they stood to lose.

And just when it seemed that they were making progress in solving the puzzle of Darian, the demon himself had launched an attack that ended with Darian trying to worm his way into Ash's head. He'd nearly succeeded. What would have happened had his father not been there?

Ash shuddered. Is this what had happened to Finn? If so, how did it happen, and when? Was he aware of what was going on? If so, how horrible would that be?

Ash remembered what Finn had said on board *Sea Wolf.*

*It's like I have these spells when I miss things. I just blank out.*

And then, moments later, that cold stranger's voice.

*Do not presume to heal me, Adrian. I am not broken.*

Had Finn really tried to murder Lyss in the streets of Fells-march? The little sister who'd tagged after them on their boyhood adventures, gazing at Finn like he was a Solstice cake?

Not Finn. Darian. It was oddly comforting to know that his childhood friend wasn't himself when he tried to burn him and Talbot alive.

Had Finn survived his own attack on the *Sea Wolf*? Was Darian back in control, and on his way back to court to finish what he'd started?

The thought gutted him.

At least the demon priest hadn't succeeded in possessing Ash. And it seemed that he'd temporarily lost his connection to the living.

Was he talking about Finn? Could an Aediion shade possess more than one person at a time?

So many more questions he wanted to ask his father.

Finn had been at court when his mother was poisoned. But it hadn't been thirteen-year-old Finn who'd grabbed him on the streets the day his father was murdered. It hadn't been Finn who'd murdered Hana. Then who? Even now, was someone else at court scheming against the Gray Wolf line?

Ash needed to get word to his mother, to warn her.

He was startled by a knock at the door.

"Come!" he said, glad he was back in his body in time to answer.

A bloodsworn servant entered, carrying clean clothes, lin-ens, and bathing supplies. "Wetlander," he said. "Come with me. Lord Strangward said to take you to the baths."

Ash shook his head. "Not now. I need to send a message to the wetlands. How can I do that?"

The servant blinked at him. "Perhaps Lord Strangward can help you."

"Where's Strangward now?" Ash demanded.

"He's meeting with his shiplords," the servant said.

"I need to speak with him."

"And you will. After you've been to the baths."

He led Ash down some steps and onto another gallery on the floor below. Most of the gallery floor was taken up by a large, steaming pool lined with rocks, so that it resembled a grotto or a desert oasis.

Ash stared at it, trying to remember the last time he'd had a proper bath. "How— This is amazing," he said.

The servant nodded. "Lord Strangward called the water up from deep underneath the ground," he said. "It's constantly replenished, so it's always clean. Just be careful. It's quite hot."

Ash nodded, eyes fixed hungrily on the water, waiting until the servant left. Then stripped off his clothes and eased into the bath.

Despite his worries, despite everything that had happened, it felt like heaven. If I die now, he thought, I can't complain.

Picking up a large, rough sponge, he scrubbed himself off and worked soap into his hair, lying back to rinse it. Just then, he heard a sound, a door opening and closing, two voices approaching. He swam to the edge of the pool, where he was partly hidden by the ledge above, and waited.

It was another servant, with Talbot in tow.

"I'll be back to fetch you in about an hour, when the sun reaches the sea," the servant was saying. Then he left.

Talbot was beginning to strip down, and Ash knew he should alert her to his presence.

"Talbot," he said, and she nearly hit the gallery ceiling. "It's all right. It's me."

She glared at him, her robe clutched around her. "It is not all right," she hissed. "The least you could've done is warn me."

"That is what this is," Ash said. "The warning."

Talbot chewed her lower lip, looking longingly at the hot water. Then she sighed, droopy with disappointment. "No harm done. Maybe there'll be time for me to come back after dinner."

"It's all right," Ash said again. "Come on in. I won't look."

"What if I look at you?" she said. "Accidentally, I mean. It's not right."

"Don't worry about it."

"Worrying happens, Your Highness, whether you like it or not."

"I'm a healer. Not only did I get over nakedness a long time ago, I believe in the importance of bathing. Especially if we survive tonight and end up in a small boat together." Ash sank into the water, then emerged again, flinging his wet hair out of his eyes. "Trust me, Talbot, you don't want to miss out."

"Well . . ." Talbot said, wavering.

"There's one condition," Ash said.

"Condition?" Talbot took a quick step back, as if she'd known there was a catch.

"Call me Ash. Not Your Highness. It will make things a whole lot easier."

She debated, shifting from one foot to the other. "But you're a prince."

"I haven't been a prince in so long, I've forgotten how. What do you call Lyss?"

Talbot studied this for tricks. "Lyss."

"Not Your Highness?"

"Well, there's times I call her 'Your Highness.'"

"This is not one of those times. And, if it's all right, I'd like to call you Sasha," he said. "It's safer, anyway, if we don't use titles."

And so it was agreed.

When they'd both scrubbed off thoroughly and had a few minutes to soak, Sasha said, "This thing about Finn," she said. "I know you saw what you saw, and Strangward saw what he saw, but I still can't believe it."

Well, Ash thought, here's your chance to try out an explanation.

"I mainly saw him on the battlefield, when I was looking after Lyss," Sasha went on, "because, you know, I'm not—I don't move in his circles. I never saw anything that would make me think that he's capable of treason. And I know that Lyss would have trusted him with her life—and did, several times."

Ash leaned his arms on the side of the pool. "She had a bit of a crush on him when she was younger," he said.

Sasha slid a look at him. "She still did—sort of. Don't get me wrong—it wasn't like she was mooning over him all the time— it was just that nobody else had come along to nudge him out of the way. So when he announced his engagement to Princess Julianna, that came as a bit of a blow." She flushed. "I don't mean to be telling tales. I think she just felt kind of ambushed. You know how it is, with your first love and all that."

"I didn't have crushes when I was little," Ash said. "I was always in the library. Or the garden." There had been girls at

Oden's Ford, but nothing serious. Lila Barrowhill, of all people, had gotten after him for his fickle ways.

I was too busy hunting down King Gerard's minions. It's hard for an assassin to meet people.

Jenna Bandelow had been his first love. Wild, fierce Jenna, who'd scented the wolf in healer's clothes.

The way things were going, she might be his last love, too.

Wherever you are, Jenna, stay alive.

Now Sasha broke into his thoughts again. "I think one reason Lyss liked Finn was that he reminded her of you. Serious. Thoughtful. Purposeful. Not full of sly talk and scummer like so many at court."

"I was surprised that he ended up with Julianna," Ash said. "But a lot can happen in a few years." That being the understatement of the year.

"Especially in wartime. He's different, since he was wounded. That's when he decided that he would go into healing. I guess you could say he got more interested in religion."

"Well, that doesn't fit with blowing us to bits," Ash said. Taking a quick breath, he plunged on. "Listen, I think we can recognize the fact that Finn tried to kill us without necessarily blaming him."

Sasha stared at him, eyes narrowed. "You mean . . . he wasn't in his right mind?"

"That's a good way of putting it," Ash said. "I think someone is using him, forcing him to do things."

"Like . . . blackmail?"

"Like magic."

Sasha raised her eyebrows. "He's under a spell?"

Ash nodded. "That doesn't mean he isn't dangerous. He still

needs to be stopped, but maybe we can find a way to help him. And forgive him."

By now, the sun had dropped below the horizon, and still nobody had come to fetch them. Ash was beginning to get that prickly feeling between his shoulder blades that said that something was wrong. In his experience, it was always best to meet trouble fully clothed.

"Let's get dressed," he said, reaching for his robe. "It's getting late."

Sasha carried her clothes around to the other side of a sandstone outcropping. Ash hurriedly pulled on a linen shirt and loose trousers—the clothes his hosts had provided him with. He was strapping on his sandals when he heard the sound of running feet.

He looked up to see a crowd of bloodsworn swarming toward him. "There he is," they shouted. "He's the one."

Ash reached for his amulet, then realized it was lying beside his old clothes. It lit up like Solstice, sending light and shadow swimming across the walls and ceiling of the bathing chamber. He dove for it, but was intercepted by the bloodsworn, who pitched him down on his back, punching and kicking him.

"Stop that!" Sasha waded in, then, dragging them off Ash and getting in some punches and kicks of her own. But there were too many of them—fearless, and incredibly strong. Soon, both of them were fighting for their lives.

I'm glad I got that bath in, Ash thought, before getting beaten to death by a mob.

"Stop!" somebody called. "Lord Strangward wants them alive and unhurt."

The frenzy of punching and kicking stopped, and Ash and

Sasha were hauled roughly to their feet, their arms pinioned. Ash sent flash racing through his hands and arms, but it seemed to have no effect on their bloodsworn captors.

They were facing a man and a woman, the only two pirates in the room who were not bloodsworn. They were arrayed in layers of glitterbits, as Ash's da would have called them. These must be two of the shiplords Strangward had spoken of.

"What's this all about?" Ash said.

"You know what it's about," the man said. "Lord Strangward has been nothing but kind to you, and this is how you repay him."

The bloodsworn murmured and tightened the cordon around them.

"I don't know what you're talking about," Ash said. "Strangward was supposed to meet us for dinner and hasn't shown. We were just going to go look for him."

"You poisoned him," the shiplord said.

"*Poisoned* him?" Fear and despair rippled through Ash. "You mean he's dead?"

"He's not dead, but he's very ill." He thrust a stoppered bottle into Ash's face. "We found this in your room."

"What's that?"

"Poison."

"How do you know? Is there a label on it?"

He seemed stumped for a moment. "What else could it be?"

"If it's poison, what kind is it?"

"The kind that poisoned Strangward," he snarled. "You would know better than me."

"I never saw that before," Ash said. "I came here with nothing more than the stinking clothes on my back. And if I had just poisoned somebody, would I come down here and jump into a hot bath?"

"You hoped to cover your tracks so that we wouldn't figure it out."

While they were talking, the other shiplord was methodically searching the room. Ash watched as she scooped up his amulet. She weighed it in her palm, then bit down on the chain to test the metal. Sliding the chain over her head, she tucked the amulet under her shirt. Clearly, she meant to add it to her collection.

Her companion saw. "Jasmina! Give me that."

"It's mine by rights, Jagger," Jasmina said, clutching it more tightly.

It's *mine* by rights, Ash thought, but he doubted he would prevail in a three-way.

Jagger grabbed Jasmina's arm and yanked her in close so that the bloodsworn couldn't hear. "I'll need that as a token for the empress," he hissed.

"Find something else," Jasmina hissed back. "And you're a fool if you trust Celestine. Like I said, you should have discussed this with me before you—"

"I know what I'm doing," Jagger growled, "and I don't need to be lectured by you, of all people."

"Why me, of all people?"

"You need to shut up and do as you're told. There'll be plenty of shares to go around once I'm lord of the Desert Coast."

"That's not going to happen," Jasmina said, "so I'll take my share now."

With that, Jagger backhanded her across the face so hard that she landed flat on her back on the floor, her head slamming against the stones. While she lay there, momentarily dazed, Jagger ripped the amulet away and tucked it into his coat.

As he turned away, Jasmina's hand crept to her blade, then slid away again. Ash swallowed down disappointment.

"Listen," Sasha said, "if Strangward's been poisoned, Freeman here may be able to help. He's a healer. If you give him his pendant back—"

"So he can finish him? I don't think so," Jagger said.

A murmur ran through the bloodsworn. "Is it true the wetlander is a healer?" one of them said.

"Please," Ash said. "If you'll let me see him, I might be able to treat the illness or counteract the poison." Seeing hope kindle in their faces, he hurried on. "Lord Strangward is my friend. I wouldn't harm him."

"Don't be stupid," Jagger said. "He tried to murder the Stormlord. Why would he help him?"

The bloodsworn wavered. "But if he's a healer . . . ?"

"He's not a healer," Jagger said. "He's a liar. Now. Put the wetlanders in the cage."

Well, Ash thought, as they were hustled away, we've all learned something here today. I just hope we live long enough to use it. Meanwhile, any hope of going after Lyss seemed as remote as any one of the stars overhead.

# 19

# SUMMONS TO COURT

Lila reined in just outside the walls of the castle close, her eyes following the imposing granite to the crenellations at the top, the arrow slots an arm's length below. Familiar and yet alien. These walls had kept her at a distance all of her life.

After all that buildup back at Fortress Rocks, the information they had from Dancer and Willo was sketchy at best. The Gray Wolf line and the queendom were in danger, and Lila and Shadow were needed in the capital.

Same old, same old, Lila thought.

Shadow nudged his horse up next to hers. They both stared at the tower, poking above the wall walks, the windows illuminated as the sun dropped behind the Spirit Mountains, the Gray Wolf banner fluttering from the top.

"He probably wants to retire and make me captain," Lila grumbled.

"I don't think that's a job you can retire from," Shadow said.

"Everything else is changing—why not that?" Lila said. Everything *was* changing—including the rules of their friendship. It had been Lila's job to try to shine a light into the dark places in Shadow's soul. Now their roles were reversed, and

Lila felt like she was trapped in the wrong skin, and reading the wrong lines.

"Look at it this way," Shadow said. "If you're captain, you can change the uniforms, right? You've always said that blue isn't your color."

"I'll make everybody wear bunghole brown," Lila said. "And a red feather in their caps."

Shadow laughed. Lila sat on her horse, her mind in turmoil. What did her father want, and what would her answer be?

"Stalling won't make it any easier," Shadow said finally.

"Maybe not, but it *will* make it further away," Lila said. Still, she sighed and rode on, toward the gate.

The sentries seemed to have been notified about their arrival, because they were allowed through with little ceremony. Lila, reluctant to leave off her carefully honed identity, gave her name as Barrowhill.

"Captain Byrne wanted to see us right away," Shadow said. "Do you know where he is?"

"Likely he's with the queen," the sentry said. "He's there nearly all the time these days."

That's nothing new, Lila thought. "Let him know we've arrived," she said. "We'll be in the guard barracks."

For years, Lila had moved like a chameleon between habitats, sliding from the sheltered student life at Oden's Ford to the cutthroat Ardenine capital to the port cities of the empire. In each setting, she assumed protective coloration, playing whatever role suited her schemes and her surroundings. Except for the smugglers' enclaves along the east coast, where she could be herself. And the northern capital, where she was nobody.

In Fellsmarch, she'd always kept to the periphery, avoiding

engagement in the life she'd been shut out of. She traveled through the city like a cloud shadow, leaving no impression behind. She preferred that to being shoehorned into a life she never wanted.

And now that it suited her father to claim her, she'd come running like an eager dog whistled in from the field. True, she'd not come as quickly as he'd probably expected. She'd insisted on accompanying her southern guests as far as Hunter's Camp, and getting them settled there. Since they'd been raised on stories about demons in the north, some of the lýtlings were having nightmares about being eaten alive or sacrificed to the northern gods. The Matelons, mother and daughter, were a big help in soothing them. No doubt, for them, memories of the monsters in the south overshadowed any worries about monsters in the north.

The barracks were all but empty, since most of the Highlanders had been sent east to Delphi, to prepare to meet the empress in the field. With the army so thin, Lila sent up a prayer that Destin Karn was successful in convincing King Jarat that the real danger lay on the coast and not in the northern capital.

Her father must have meant it when he said that the matter was urgent, because they had scarcely stowed their belongings when the summons came—to report to the queen's apartments as soon as they were able. Lila wasn't able until after she'd bathed and changed into a uniform of her own choosing—a long wool jacket over a white linen shirt, narrow breeches, and tall boots, all in a color that might be described as "bunghole brown." All sourced from the palace laundry, where there were no red feathers to be had.

Shadow pressed his lips together and rolled his eyes when he saw her, but said nothing.

The corridors leading to the queen's apartments were quiet, all but deserted, reinforcing the impression that the capital had been abandoned, with every able body sent east. Was that why Byrne had warned them not to bring the hostages here? Because it was vulnerable to attack? There should at least be courtiers and officials coming and going from the queen's chambers.

Unless she was too ill to receive anyone.

Lila tried to sort out what the mission might be. What would Queen Raisa want with them? What were they good at? And why would the orders come directly from her?

Maybe she wanted them to smuggle the crown jewels out of the queendom.

When they reached the queen's wing, it seemed crowded by comparison to the rest of the palace. Blue-clad guards were stationed at the entrance to the suite, and they had to run an entire gauntlet of unsmiling wolves before they reached the doors to her reception chamber. There they were unceremoniously searched and all of their weapons seized.

Finally, they were admitted to the sitting room. Queen Raisa and Captain Byrne sat together on a settee close to the fire—a fire that seemed scarcely needed on this warm spring day. Byrne's uniform jacket was slung across the back of the seat, but a wool blanket was draped across their knees, and there was something domestic—even intimate—about the scene.

Except that they were chaperoned by an older woman with a long white braid. She sat under the window, reading a book, her somber garb resembling that of a dedicate. As they entered, she stood and rested her hand on the hilt of a massive sword that leaned against the windowsill beside her.

When Lila looked again, she saw that Byrne, too, had his

sword close at hand. Maybe *intimate* wasn't the right word. It was more like they looked . . . besieged.

"Captain Byrne," Lila said, with a stiff bow. "Shadow and I are here, as you"—Insisted? Ordered? Demanded?— "commanded," she said.

Her father looked up at her, then pushed the blanket aside and stood. The expression on his face was mingled relief and surprise.

It had only been a matter of weeks since she'd seen him, but Lila was shocked at how he'd aged. He stood, erect as always, but his hair had grayed to the point that it almost matched his eyes. Lila had heard of that kind of thing happening overnight, but didn't really believe it. Until now.

Still, her father looked hale and hearty next to the queen. She'd always been small, but now she appeared frail. The bones in her face stood out like never before, and there were hollows next to her collarbones. They both looked like the sole survivors of a disaster—or an epidemic.

Lila shifted her weight, put off balance by this peculiar, private meeting. She was used to meeting her father in taverns, barracks, and back hallways, while her encounters with the queen were always insulated by squads of bluejackets, herds of courtiers, and her own anonymity. Had they ever actually spoken to each other? Lila couldn't remember.

Should she salute, or curtsy, or what? Byrne answered that question by embracing her. "I am so very glad to see you, Lila," he murmured, before he let her go.

"Thank you for coming, both of you," Queen Raisa said softly. "I wasn't sure that you would."

"Well. It seemed urgent, so—we did." Lila paused. When

the queen didn't follow up, she said, "I— We heard you've been sick. I hope you're feeling better."

"I have been sick," Queen Raisa said, exchanging a look with Byrne. "I suppose you could say I've been to death's door. And back again."

Byrne smiled, in a strained sort of way.

"Please," the queen said. "Sit down." She gestured to the woman with the braid and the sword. "Magret, could you bring some of that tea Master Gryphon keeps pouring into me? I imagine the rest of you would prefer something more—"

"We won't be staying long," Lila said. "We don't need anything."

"Perhaps we could tempt you with some sugar cakes, child," Magret said, her jaw set disapprovingly. "They might sweeten your disposition."

"I love sugar cakes," Shadow said, shooting a quelling look at Lila, "and I'll drink anything but tea."

"Fine," Lila said, sitting down and pressing her sweating hands against her brown trousers. "If you insist, I'll have bingo. Or blue ruin."

She couldn't seem to open her mouth without bitterness pouring out. It made her feel like a small, mean person.

Magret rolled her eyes and stalked into the butler's pantry, muttering something that would likely *not* sweeten Lila's disposition if she'd been able to make it out.

"We heard about what happened along the Smuggler's Coast," the queen said.

"Really?" Lila said, hackles rising. She'd hoped to skate through this interview without discussing that topic.

"Is it true what we heard—that all of the settlements along

the shoreline have come under attack?" Byrne said.

"They're gone," Lila said, hoping that would end it.

Byrne and the queen looked at each other. Byrne cleared his throat. "Has there been any news about Chas and Leah, or—"

"No," Lila said curtly. "We saw a lot of bodies, but we couldn't get close enough to identify anyone. I assume they're dead, or carried off to Carthis. As soon as we're done here, I'll go find out for certain. And then I'll decide what to do."

"I'm so sorry," the queen said, leaning forward a little, attempting to meet Lila's eyes. "This damnable war has stolen so much from us—not just one generation, but two."

"That's war for you," Lila said, looking up at the ceiling. It was decorated with plaster roses and thorns. "People die."

"Yes," Queen Raisa said. "They do."

Stop being so damned sympathetic, Lila thought, eyes burning and throat aching. I am not going to cry in front of you.

Blessedly, about that time Magret returned with the refreshments. Lila felt much better after she'd knocked back a mug of bingo. Better in a dangerous sort of way.

"I look forward to hearing how you managed to abscond with King Jarat's hostages," the queen said. "I would love to have seen his face when he found out."

"It was a team effort," Lila said. Eager to change the subject, she said, "Speaking of families, I'd hoped to catch up with Prince Adrian while I'm here." She looked around. "Where is he?"

"A lot has happened," Queen Raisa said, pouring more bingo into Lila's mug. "Which is why we need your help."

# A DIFFERENCE OF OPINION

The next morning, Shadow looked up from a pile of papers he was sorting through to scowl at Lila. "Would you *sit*, Lila? It's hard to concentrate with you careening around the room."

"You're not supposed to concentrate on that," Lila said. "You're supposed to be thinking of a way to get us out of this."

"Get *you* out of this, you mean," Shadow said. "That's easy. Walk away. Or, better yet, ride. Go bury your dead on the coast, or go back to Ardenscourt and scheme with your friend Karn, or sail to Carthis or whatever it is you want to do. Just do it quietly, because I'm trying to work."

Their barracks residency had ended right after their audience with the queen. They'd been moved to Kendall House, a stately home within the castle close that was often used to house visitors and diplomats.

"Why are you doing this?" she demanded, planting her hands on her hips.

"Why am I doing what?"

"Why did you agree to sit on the queen's council?"

"Because the queen asked me to?" Shadow said. "Because she said it was important? Because she said the future of the queendom might depend on it?"

Yeah, but other than that? Lila thought, rolling her eyes. Shadow's sudden bout of patriotism felt like a betrayal. She'd always been able to count on him to be a fellow cynic.

"Even if everything she said was true," Lila said, "this job is all wrong for us—you know it is. Why would she ask us?"

"I don't know—maybe she wants to drive the queendom into the ground sooner rather than later."

"Be serious."

"If I had to guess, I'd say she's desperate," Shadow said. "She's scraping the bottom of the barrel. The princess heir is in Carthis—"

"The *queen* is in Carthis," Lila said. "Remember? Queen Raisa claims that Alyssa is the queen now. Only we're not supposed to tell anyone. It's some kind of Gray Wolf magical technicality."

"Queen *Lyss* is in Carthis," Shadow amended, "and Prince Adrian is off trying to rescue her, and everyone else is in Delphi, preparing to fight the empress, so . . ." He shrugged. "Lyss is my friend. I want her to have a queendom to come home to. I want Aspen's sisters to have a place to live."

"There are plenty of other people to choose from," Lila said. "Anyway, it sounds like the council's big enough. There's Princess Mellony, and Princess Julianna, or whatever her title is, and for wizards you have Bayar, and Vega and—"

"You *have* been studying up, haven't you?" Shadow said, raising an eyebrow. "They are already on the council, and someone on the council tried to murder her, remember? She doesn't trust them."

"She doesn't trust her own sister?" Lila said, thinking, It's pretty bad when you're making arguments you don't believe in yourself.

"Should King Gerard's brothers have trusted *him*?"

"Why should she trust us?" Lila said. "I'm unreliable—ask anyone." The last thing she wanted was to be held accountable for failing at a job she didn't want in the first place.

"You saved her son's life at Oden's Ford. Then you managed to bring him back from Ardenscourt. That must count for something."

"That was totally different," Lila said. "To be honest, Adrian got himself into trouble in Ardenscourt. Then got himself out of it."

"Hmm." Shadow studied a document, brow furrowed, obviously trying to ignore her.

Lila refused to be ignored. "So the only reason she picked us is that we weren't on the council before?"

Shadow grunted, put the papers aside, and opened a book.

"Your father could do it," Lila said. "Or your grandmother."

"My father is on his way to the Alyssa Plateau to help with the war effort. Willo Cennestre never leaves the uplands these days."

"They shouldn't have sent everybody out of the capital, then," Lila said. "She'd have more people to pick from." She knew she was being unreasonable, but being reasonable had never been her strong suit.

"Lila, she said she wanted some younger people on the council. People in our generation, who have the most to lose if the queendom is destroyed."

"Maybe she just wants somebody to blame if it goes wrong," Lila said, trying to ignore the voice in her head that said, Is that the problem? That you don't want the blame for the collapse of the queendom?

Shadow finally gave up and slammed his book shut. "Look, why are you so determined to persuade me to leave with you? I can understand if you have hard feelings against your father and the queen. If you don't want to stay, then leave."

"What's that supposed to mean?" Lila said, eager to wade in.

"I can understand why you resent the fact that your father abandoned you and your mother to be with Queen Raisa—"

Lila didn't remember drawing her knife, but the next thing she knew it was at Shadow's throat and he was gripping her wrist with both hands, their noses inches apart. His hands were warm and sinewy, the palms calloused.

"Don't be stupid," he said. "Don't forget, my mother was the best knife fighter in Ragmarket."

"Then why is she dead?" Lila shot back unforgivably.

"I don't know," Shadow said. "But she is, and your mother's dead, too, and we both have to deal with disappointed fathers."

"Don't put words in my mouth. Anyway, Dancer isn't disappointed in you," Lila said. "Not like—"

"Not like Captain Byrne? Do you really think he's disappointed in you?"

"Of course he is. I'm not like Simon. He was the one who inherited that Byrne self-sacrificial trait. Simon should have been the one to live. I have never fit into this family, and I don't know why I have to be shoehorned in now."

"Be honest. You're disappointed in your father, too."

"My father's a saint," Lila said, rolling her eyes. "Why

would I be disappointed in him?"

"Parents and children always disappoint each other," Shadow said, "because we don't get to choose. We're stuck with who we get. No matter who our parents are, we can always think of some way they don't measure up. It's even worse for them. They feel guilty about a child's shortcomings because they're responsible—partly, anyway." He let go of Lila's arm and sat back. "You feel guilty because you survived and Simon didn't."

Lila stowed her knife away. "Who the hell are you, and what have you done with my friend Shadow?"

"It's always easier to tell other people what to do than to fix yourself. Would you have been better off, after your mother died, being neglected at court?"

"It seems like he could have—"

"Remarried? Would you have liked that? So you could live with your stepmother and both complain about being ignored?"

"Like I said. Don't put words in my mouth," Lila snapped.

"If anyone puts words in your mouth, it should be me."

What the hell does that mean? Lila thought. "He didn't have to neglect us. Other people find a way to balance what they—"

"Or were you better off living with your aunt and uncle?"

Lila gathered her thoughts. "I loved my aunt and uncle, and now they're gone, too. I should have been there, instead of baby-sitting a runaway prince. I should have saved them, or died with them, or—"

"We're more alike than you realize. I'm of mixed blood, like you. It's always harder for us, because we're always choosing one tradition over another, one point of view over another, one parent over another. I may not be a mage, but I'm an uplander. So I believe in magic. It's built into me, so that I feel the connection with this land every single day. So, I thought, that's who I am. All I wanted was to climb up high—to leave the flatlands behind. I thought I could escape to the uplands with Aspen and ignore my Southern Island blood, the fight with Arden—all of that. Instead, I was fighting at Queen Court—with Lyss— when Aspen was murdered."

Lila sat on the edge of the cold hearth, her rage leaking out of her like wine from a punctured skin. "You had no way of knowing what would happen," she said.

Shadow ignored this platitude. "After Aspen was killed, I wanted to ride straight to Ardenscourt, track down the king and the general, and cut their throats. I didn't care if I died doing it." He looked up at Lila. "Do you know who kept getting in the way? You. And Lyss. You kept thinking up things I needed to do before I died like a martyr. It was really annoying. By the time I extricated myself, Speaks to Horses—Ash—got to King Gerard ahead of me. He managed to do the deed and survive."

There's still the empress, Lila thought. You could help me kill the empress.

"To be honest, I was lying to myself," Shadow said.

"What do you mean?"

"The thing is, I could have gone after King Gerard. It wasn't like you were keeping me prisoner. I really think I could have gotten to him, too. It's easy to kill a person if you're willing to die for the privilege. But if I killed the king of Arden, and died, I wouldn't be there for Aspen's family, either. That would be like a double betrayal." He looked sideways at Lila. "Anyway, it's hard to plan anything when you're drunk all the time."

"Ah," Lila said. "Well, I suppose . . ."

"When I found out Gerard was dead, I spent some time with Speaker Jemson. It was either that or drink myself to death. I couldn't understand how Aspen could be dead, and Gerard could be dead, and there seemed to be nothing to show for it. The war goes on, and Jarat hasn't been much of an improvement over Gerard, and now we have the empress to contend with. I felt like life was a massive joke on us."

"So he told you to accept it, that it must be the will of the Maker, right?"

"No, he didn't say that." Shadow thought a moment. "He said that all we can do is make the best decision possible in that moment. Then move on. Because we can't know how a different choice would play out, it makes no sense to beat ourselves up over what looks like a bad choice in retrospect."

"A speaker said that?"

Shadow nodded.

Lila had heard a lot about the speaker of the Old Church, but she'd never spoken directly to him. In her experience, the church was in the business of guilting people.

"He also said that it's easier to predict the benefits of intervening to save something than the consequences of destroying something you perceive as evil."

"You lost me there."

"Let's say you don't like snakes, and you decide to exterminate them, only to find that you are overrun by rats. Or you assassinate a king, to find out that the new king is even worse. Only the Maker can follow each path out to the end, so we should be cautious when we do things—like killing—that cannot be undone."

"What's your point?"

"So instead of feeling guilty about what I've lost, I've decided to focus on what I want to save. When I looked around, I decided it was this queendom, and its people. And I couldn't do that if I was drunk all the time. So I quit."

"What if you have to kill a few people to save the queendom—is it okay as long as the goal isn't the killing but the saving?" That came out more bitterly than Lila intended.

"You asked what happened, and I'm trying to answer you. We've all had losses in this war—including your father. So—what do you want, Lila? What do you want to save?"

"It's too late," Lila said. To her mortification, her eyes were filling with tears.

"What do you mean?"

"Every time I try to hold on to something, it slips through my fingers. I wanted to save my mother. She died anyway. I wanted my father to pay attention to me. He ignored me. I wanted to take over my aunt and uncle's business. It's destroyed, and they're dead."

"Your father's still alive," Shadow said. "And he's reached out to you."

"The only reason he's interested in me now is because I might be useful to the queen."

"Haven't you been listening?" Lila had managed to get Shadow to raise his voice, which was something.

"I've been listening," Lila said. "I just haven't heard anything to change my mind."

"You were the one trying to change my mind, remember?" He raked his hand through his hair. "Look," he said, "I don't know exactly how the binding ceremony works, but I know enough about it to tell you that Captain Byrne doesn't have a choice. The queen will always come first, because that's how the magic works."

"Why are you defending him?"

"Is that what I'm doing?" Shadow shook his head. "No. I'm trying to give you permission to forgive him, because he's the one you have left."

# FLEDGLINGS

Despite the cold, Lyss was sweating and breathing hard by the time she made it to the top of the mountain. The backpack full of supplies she was carrying didn't help. She'd brought more than usual, because it had been two weeks since she'd been able to slip away long enough to visit the mountain aerie.

Weapons, armament, and other ordnance flowed in from all down the Desert Coast. Every few days, ships arrived with more captives, more fodder for the bloodsworn army. Reprovisioned, the ships returned to the Seven Realms packed with Lyss's half-trained soldiers.

Lyss tried to persuade the empress to let her hold on to them a little longer. It was not in her nature to spend soldiers recklessly—even enemy soldiers.

"They're not ready," she argued. "They need more time, more conditioning, more practice with weapons."

"They are unflaggingly loyal and fearless," Celestine said. "That, with the training you've given them, will have to be enough."

Was that to be her role—to train soldiers and send them off to slaughter and be slaughtered? She found herself begging for a command that would take her home.

"Let me lead them, at least," she said. "Officers shouldn't send soldiers into battles they are not willing to fight themselves."

"Ah, Captain Gray," the empress said. "That time will come. Right now, you are too valuable to me here."

Lyss was learning that being valuable was a double-edged sword. It kept her alive, but it also kept her away from home. Either that, or the empress suspected that her commander would find a way to betray her if she went back to the wetlands.

When she arrived at the high ledge that housed the dragons, there was no sign of life. The sulfurous scent that Lyss had come to associate with their home had all but dissipated. The cleft the dragons used as a latrine had not been visited lately, and the bones of previous meals had been picked clean by scavengers who wouldn't have dared to venture into the dragons' lair had they been present.

Scalp prickling with worry, Lyss forced her way around the rockfall, past the brush obscuring the mouth of the cave. There was no sign of life, no evidence that the dragons had been there in the past few days. They'd left the stones behind—the stones Cas was using to teach the hatchlings to carry extra weight.

"Jenna!" Lyss called, stepping over bones as she made her way to the back of the cave. "Cas? Slayer?"

The only answer was the echo of her voice returning to her. Had something happened to the flight of young dragons? Had they moved to the ledge Lyss now thought of as Bosley's Leap? Had they been discovered and killed? Had they finally broken through the Boil and winged away to the Dragonback Mountains on the mainland? Had Jenna given up on her mission to kill the empress?

Had they abandoned her?

Lyss's backpack hit the floor of the cave with a dull *thud* as she fought down despair. She shouldn't have stayed away so long. Her interactions with Jenna and the dragons had given her hope during a dark season. Now she felt more alone than ever.

"Scummer!" she shouted, and, again, her voice echoed back. Scummer, scummer, scummer, scummer . . . gradually dwindling until it faded away. Lyss considered leaving a few items in the cave, in case they came back. In the end, she hefted the backpack over her shoulder and emerged into the fresh air.

She heard a faint cry, as if from far away, that made her skin prickle again. Some instinct caused her to look skyward in time to see a speck hurtling toward her that was rapidly growing larger. She stared at it for one heartbeat, two, then dove to one side as a dragon landed with a clatter of scale and claw on rock.

She'd thought it was Cas, but when she rolled to her feet, she saw that it was Slayer—significantly bigger than the last time she'd seen him. Not only that, he was wearing the leather fittings and tack that belonged to Cas.

"Where are the others?" she asked. "Is everything all right?"

He extended his head toward her, displaying his toothy dragon smile, then spread his wings, scales on edge—an invitation for Lyss to climb aboard.

"Are you sure?" Lyss said. She'd never seen Slayer carry a passenger before.

Slayer slapped his wings on the ground. The message was clear. *Quit stalling.*

Backing up a little to gain momentum, Lyss ran up the dragon's wing, using the raised scales for better footing. She managed to plant a hand on the saddle before she lost speed. Pulling herself up, she swung her leg over the dragon's back and settled into place. Slayer's back was narrower than Cas's, so easier to grip with her knees. She worried, though, about her inability to communicate with the dragon in the same way as Jenna did.

Slayer looked back over his shoulder at Lyss, to make sure she was seated, then launched himself from the edge of the cliff.

"Blood and bones!" Lyss shouted, followed by, "Hanalea the warrior!"

They soared out over the sea, almost to the margins of the Boil, where the winds buffeted and tumbled them. Then Slayer turned inland, over one shoulder of the dormant volcano. She could see other, smaller islands surrounding Celesgarde, most shrouded in a murk of sulfurous fume and mist.

Lyss could feel Slayer's shoulder muscles working beneath her arms as he accelerated, gaining altitude, before he swept out over the harbor itself.

Below, she could see two tall ships at the quays. One was disgorging dazed and stumbling captives into holding pens. Some still wore the uniforms of the Fells, torn and bloodied. Others had been fitted out with random replacements.

"Damn," Lyss muttered.

The other ship was onboarding bloodsworn soldiers in the uniforms Lyss had devised and insisted they wear.

Hopefully, that will make you better targets, she thought. Then was horrified at herself, which aptly illustrated the split within her.

That was when Slayer folded his wings and plunged toward the harbor below.

"Slayer! No! Stop!" There were no reins, of course, but Lyss wrapped her arms around the young dragon's neck and pulled, making a futile attempt to aim him skyward. Looking down, she could see tiny figures on the deck of one of the ships, pointing, their faint shouts reaching her ears. With that, Slayer thrust out his wings to slow their descent, all but flinging Lyss off his back. He closed his claws on the top of the mainmast and ripped it free, snapping lines and sending the crew down on their stomachs, covering their heads with their hands. Lyss flattened herself along the dragon's back, trying to blend in.

Wings beating frantically, Slayer struggled skyward, still clutching the mast, trailing lines and canvas behind them like an awkward sort of bird that intended to build a nest from ships' rigging. Arrows clattered against Slayer's sides, reminding Lyss that she wasn't as well armored as he was. Heart pounding, she pressed herself against the dragon's hot scales, praying she hadn't been spotted. Attacks by dragons weren't unusual; attacks by dragons carrying passengers—that would draw unwelcome notice. Fortunately, it wasn't easy to get a clear view or take a clear shot through the trailing rigging.

Lyss guessed that the mainmast was not only heavy, but it required the young dragon to gain altitude quickly in order to avoid tangling it in the equipment and rigging at dockside. He tried once, then circled around again, exposing the two of them to more fire from the ground.

"Let it go," Lyss said. "Please, Slayer. There'll be other ships."

Finally, Slayer decided to give up his prize. He circled over the second ship and let go. It plunged straight through the deck, and ended standing upright, like a fourth mast. Relieved of the weight of the mast, they rocketed skyward, out of range.

Lyss, clinging like a tick, felt Slayer's exhilaration pounding into her. Saw the ground through the dragon's eyes—incredibly sharp and seemingly close enough to touch. Images bled into her, vivid and packed with emotion. She ricocheted between her own terror and the dragon's joy.

Was this what Jenna meant when she described listening to dragons?

Soon, they had the flank of the mountain between them and the harbor, and Lyss quit anticipating the arrow point penetrating her flesh, striking against bone.

Speaking of bone . . . "That was a boneheaded move!" she shouted. "What were you thinking? Are you trying to get us both killed?"

*Slayer fast flyer. Good fighter. Lyss see.*

The message came through as clear as could be.

"So you were just showing off," Lyss said, trying to be stern but not quite succeeding. Now that it was over, she had to admit that she'd much rather stomp on the empress than tiptoe around her.

Slayer executed a fine barrel roll and arrowed straight for a cleft in the rocks. Turning nearly sideways, he slid through it at full speed with inches to spare. Then plunged earthward again, waiting until the last possible moment to put the brakes on so that he landed like a feather on a rocky ledge. It was on the other side of the mountain from their previous camp.

Politely, he thrust out his wings again, an invitation for Lyss to dismount. In the process, he nearly knocked over his brothers and sisters, who were swarming toward them.

Lyss all but rolled down his wing to the ground. Propping up on hands and knees, she hurled what remained of her supper into the dust. Emptied out, she flipped over onto her back and lay there, reliving the flight as images streamed through her mind. Slayer was sharing his adventures with his siblings, preening and striking poses. It was no wonder that he'd hoped to bring the mast back for a show-and-tell. Cas and Jenna were nowhere to be seen.

Commanding a salvo of human soldiers was hard enough. Dragon wrangling was a whole other challenge.

Soon the fledglings were scrapping with each other, rolling and tumbling across the ledge, taking short flights to gain a vantage point, and then stooping down on their littermates, spewing small gouts of flame. Lyss was beginning to realize that she was in danger of being trampled or charred if she stayed where she was. So she clambered up to a safe vantage point, wrapped her arms around her knees, and fell asleep.

Lyss awoke to a clatter of claws, human voices, and dragon greetings. She crept forward to see that Jenna and Cas had returned and appeared to be interrogating the fledglings about something. That was when Lyss realized that her backpack was lying out in plain sight, the contents scattered all around it. Clearly, the young dragons had been digging through, looking for treats. Just as obviously, Cas and Jenna were demanding to know the whereabouts of its owner.

"I'm here!" Lyss shouted, startling several of the fledglings into taking flight, circling around, and landing again.

Jenna stood, hands on hips, looking up at her. "Are you all right? What happened?"

Lyss slid a look at Slayer, who was crouched down, trying to be as inconspicuous as possible. If it was possible for a dragon to look sheepish, that was it.

Well, she wasn't going to give him away. The flight over the harbor was the most fun she'd had in a long time.

"I'm—uh—fine," Lyss said, scrambling down from her perch. "I was just taking a nap while I was waiting."

Jenna looked her up and down, frowning, then turned and confronted the fledglings. "*You* said the backpack fell out of the sky."

Now all of the dragons were trying to hide behind each other. Cas swung his tail, sweeping them all from the ledge. They tumbled, fluttering frantically until they landed back on the rocks. Dragon discipline.

Lyss cleared her throat. "I came to the cave looking for you. When I saw you were gone, I worried that something had happened."

"You hadn't been up for quite a while, and the dragons were getting too nosy about the harbor," Jenna said. "I think they were looking for you. As their range expanded, they were encountering the empress's people nearly every day. I was afraid Celestine would send a battalion up here to clear the heights. So we moved over here so they could hunt and practice flying without being seen. I didn't want to leave a note for somebody else to find." She paused. "So. How did you find us?"

"Slayer found me at the old den," Lyss said. "He brought me here."

Jenna turned and glared at the young dragon. "Slayer!"

Slayer hung his head in shame.

"It was supposed to be a surprise," Jenna said. "We were trying out different flying techniques, and all of the fledglings were practicing maneuvering with a rider on board. We were going to put on a little show when you came back."

After weeks of walking on eggs, Lyss could relate to the young dragon's desire to cut loose. She didn't want to see him get into trouble because of it.

"It's my fault," Lyss said quickly. "I begged Slayer for a ride when I saw he was wearing that gear."

You owe me, Slayer, she thought.

"Hmm." From the skeptical look on her face, Lyss knew Jenna wasn't buying it. But she didn't insist on gripping her hands to verify the truth. Instead, she looked from Lyss to Slayer and shrugged. "Well, no harm done. Let's sit and eat, and then we'll show you what we've learned."

# 22

# MUSTER AT TEMPLE CHURCH

Hal had greeted his newly recruited officers—Mercier, Lereaux, LeFevre, and Remy—with mingled gratitude and guilt. They were grown men, and able to make their own decisions, but still—the Montaigne family was not known for showing mercy to any it viewed as its enemy. Especially former allies who could be labeled as traitors.

That they understood the gravity of the decision they'd made, Hal had no doubt. He could see it in their faces, in the way they presented their arms. There was none of the usual saber-rattling bravado, or predictions of valor on the battlefield. There weren't even any complaints about previous manage-ment, or explanations for why they were here. They knew they might be going up against men they'd led or served beside. They were the kind of soldiers who would remain loyal to their king until the king made it impossible to carry on.

Having served the king himself, Hal knew that his for-mer comrades weren't exactly choosing risk over safety. And at least anyone who'd reported to him knew that he wouldn't needlessly send them into harm's way, or sabotage them to score a political point.

The sun was just breaking over the Heartfangs as Hal, Robert, and Thad Mercier rode east from Temple Church to the muster point off the North Road. Mercier had fought beside Hal or under his command in three different campaigns in the borderlands. In fact, Mercier had been in camp near Swansea when word had come that his farm at Bittersweet Springs had been overrun by raiders from the Wastes and his entire family killed. Mercier was from the downrealms, where mourning was a visceral, vocal, cathartic process. Thirteen-year-old Hal had given Mercier the use of his tent for three days, where he could conduct his rituals in private. Mercier had emerged from his tent cleansed, and gone straight back to fighting. Ever since, his loyalty to Hal had been fierce and unwavering.

Hal could tell they were nearing the encampment when he began to smell woodsmoke and horses, the scents that accompanied an army on the move. Here, the land sloped gradually upward to the foothills of the eastern mountains. They emerged from thick woods to where they could overlook the valley of the north fork of Ardenswater. Hal stared down at the camp, swarming with early morning activity.

"Saints and martyrs," Robert breathed. It had to be close to a thousand men, all wearing the buff of Arden.

"Are you sure this isn't some sort of a trap?" Hal said. "Or the advance guard of Jarat's army?"

Mercier smiled grimly. "You'll see a lot of familiar faces here, sir. The first rule of warfare is you have to feed your army. The second rule is that you have to pay it. King Jarat doesn't seem to understand that. Nobody believes his promises of estates in the north anymore. The only thing left to fight for is the True Faith and a place in heaven, but you have to be dead to collect."

Hal recalled what he'd said to his father. *I don't need an exorcism. I need an army.* Well, he had his army now, and these were experienced soldiers, not the tenant militias he'd expected to be leading. Now he had to figure out what to do with it and how to feed it, pay it, and equip it.

What he wanted to do was leave the thanes on their own and march this army north. But he'd promised his father he'd take Ardenscourt first.

*Protect your rear.*

"Here come Remy and LeFevre," Mercier said, pointing. Two more of his renegade officers were galloping toward him.

"We had a bit of a problem, sir," Remy said, saluting. "Everyone wanted to come. Had to draw straws to see who had to stay behind."

LeFevre nodded. "There's a rumor going around that you died at Delphi but the witch queen brought you back to life because she fell in love with your dead body."

*"What?"* Hal stared at him, horrified, while Robert stifled laughter.

"No worries, sir," LeFevre said hastily. "I don't think too many believed it."

"If anything, it enhanced your reputation," Remy said, which set Robert off again.

"Are there any mages down there?" Hal said, eager to change the subject.

"Aye, sir, I believe we have four or five," LeFevre said. He hesitated, then added, "All collared."

They'd been spotted now, because a roar went up from below.

"I think we'd best ride down," LeFevre said, "and let them know you're flesh and blood and not a ghost."

Five days later, flesh-and-blood Hal found himself in yet another meeting with the rebel thanes, discussing battle strategy. He'd had Rives on the run for weeks, trying to inventory the cannon and siege engines on hand, while the thanes guarded them like badgers, bent on keeping them for their personal use. It was the same with horses, wagons, and other gear. Even his own father was resistant when Hal begged for a few small cannon to send with his own secret army.

Hal was beginning to think that if Jarat had elected to send his army against the thanes instead of into the north, there was a really good chance he would have won.

Let's hope he doesn't figure that out before this is over, he thought.

"Matelon!" Rafe Heresford's voice brought Hal back to the present.

"I'm sorry, what?"

"So you don't think we should engage Jarat's army on its way north?" Heresford said, raising an eyebrow.

"Exactly," Hal said. "Let them march on by, and spend their blood and fortune in the north. Once they're well away, you'll march south on the capital. By the time they return—if they return—they'll find that we hold their city."

"Why would Jarat march north, leaving his capital at risk?" Heresford persisted.

Hal liked Heresford, who was somewhat younger than the other thanes. He'd spent time in exile in the north, after Gerard executed his father and seized his estates. He'd come south again, to join the fight, when the rebellion began. He had fewer bannermen, and less to lose than the other thanes. That made him bolder.

"Now that General Karn has been named a traitor," Hal said, "the king seems to believe that the late general was the cause of years of failure. He has a new general and new hope in his heart."

"Someone named Bellamy, I hear," DeLacroix said. "I don't know that name. He must have come up through the ranks." The subtext was, *How good could he be?*

"Bellamy did come up through the ranks, and is probably the best leader and tactician in the king's army," Hal said. "Jarat is lucky to have him. I wish that we did."

"I know that we agreed to give you overall command of this operation," Thane Henri Tourant said, "and I understand that you've persuaded some officers from the king's army to come over to us. However, I prefer to lead my own liegemen in the field."

There was a murmur of agreement from the other thanes, as if to say, First you want our cannon. Next thing we know, you'll want to be taking over our armies and our fiefdoms as well.

"That's why we're having this conversation," Hal said. "You'll all be leading your own bannermen in the attack on the city."

This was met with more approval, followed by suspicion. "Where will you be, then?" DeLacroix said, squinting at Hal. "I thought you were the military expert."

"By now, everyone in Ardenscourt has heard that I'm leading the rebel army," Hal said. "In addition to the officers, we've had some soldiers come over to us, too. So I'm going to keep a small, maneuverable force here as a diversionary tactic, to keep Jarat honest. We'll follow after him a little ways to make sure he keeps going north before we come south and join you."

This received a mixed reaction. Some, Hal knew, were just as glad to have the Matelon prodigal son out of the way while they staked their claims to the kingdom. Others seemed afraid that he was either up to something or getting out of something.

"You're going to lead from the *rear*?" DeLacroix said, his voice rich with disdain.

"I would much rather be marching into Ardenscourt," Hal said. "I took this duty because no one else seemed to want it, and because my father will lead the Matelon bannermen to the gates. If there is anyone who would like to volunteer to stay behind in my place, I would—"

That earned a resounding no. None of the thanes wanted to give any of their competitors a head start.

"Do you think Jarat will take his mages north?" Tourant said, "or will they be waiting for us in the capital?"

"That we don't know," Hal said. "I imagine he'll take some, to counter the mages in the north. He may not leave many in Ardenscourt. He'll know we only have a few, if any at all, and he may rely on his perimeter walls to keep us out."

"Is there any way we can get some mages before we march on the city?" Tourant said, as if Hal could procure them like any other ordnance.

"Not unless any of you have some socked away," Hal said, looking around the circle.

If any did, none would admit to it.

"Do we know when Jarat will march?" Heresford said.

"We know that preparations are under way," Hal said. "We'll have plenty of notice. You cannot move an army like that in secret. From what I'm hearing, they'll march within the week."

# 23

# THE QUEEN'S COUNCIL

"It seems to me," Lila said, "that this is a risky business." She stood in front of the looking glass in her quarters in Kendall House, trying to put her unruly hair into some kind of order.

"Says the girl who spent three years spying on the king of Arden?" Shadow raised an eyebrow. "Says the girl who saved the prince of the realm from a pack of assassins? Says the girl who—"

"I know how to spy on somebody," Lila said crossly. "I don't know how to represent a queen I've only met once."

"Pretend you're spying on the queen's council," Shadow said.

There came a knock on the door. Their bluejacket guard poked her head out, then turned back to them. "Captain Byrne wants to know if you're ready," she said.

Lila smoothed down her curls one more time. "Let's get this over with," she said.

Four bluejackets trailed them down the hall. It made Lila edgy.

"If it's not risky, then why do we have an escort?" Lila said.

"Maybe your father is afraid we'll bolt," Shadow said.

Captain Byrne was waiting for them outside the council chamber.

"I have the writs for your appointments, signed by the queen," Byrne said. "No one else on the council knows that Prince Adrian has gone to retrieve his sister. As far as they know, he's tending his mother day and night. I don't know how you'll be received, but I suspect there'll be some resistance—to you, especially, Lila, because they don't know you. Just be firm and pleasant, and stick to your guns."

Guns, Lila thought. That's what we need.

"The membership of the council has shifted since the fall of Chalk Cliffs," Byrne said. "General Dunedain, Shilo Trail-blazer, and, of course, your father, Fire Dancer, are not here. They have been some of the queen's most reliable allies."

Does a queen need allies on her own council? Lila thought. Can't she just boot off the ones who don't cooperate?

"Also, the High Wizard, Lord Bayar, is sitting in, though he's not been attending regularly this year. He was wounded near Chalk Cliffs, and is home for the moment."

Lila scanned the list of council members for the thousandth time. *Princess Mellony, sister to the queen. Lady Barrett, niece to the queen. Miranda Mander, representing wizards, also mother of Finn sul'Mander and soon-to-be mother-in-law of Julianna. Dimitri Fen-waeter, representing the Waterwalkers. Roff Jemson, speaker of the Cathedral Temple. Harriman Vega, commander over the health service. Randolph Howard, for the nobility.*

Maybe it would help to put them in alphabetical order, Lila thought. Shadow, at least, knew a few of them via his comings and goings at court.

"The queen is in fragile health, remember," Byrne said, "but you'll carry any actionable items back to her. Avoid making commitments on your own."

"Got it," Lila said. Just sit there and look pretty, she thought. Truth be told, it was kind of a relief to know she'd be on a short leash.

"Let's go," Byrne said.

The council no longer met in the royal wing of the castle, but had moved to what had been a library in the Cathedral Temple.

When the door opened to the council chamber, Lila saw that it was a room with a high gallery running around the perimeter, and lined to the ceiling with books. Work desks had been moved to the side and replaced by a massive oak table. As Lila entered behind Shadow and Byrne, all conversation stopped.

Byrne motioned them to the two empty chairs. All eyes followed them as they took their seats. Byrne remained standing, signaling that he didn't mean to stay long. Noticing that everyone was still staring at the newcomers, Byrne said, "We can speak freely. Once we get started, I'll deliver a message from the queen that will explain their presence."

Only one of the other council members was close to Lila's age. She was a young woman with a scarf embossed with wolves. She seemed to recognize Shadow, because she smiled at him.

"Captain Byrne," said a pretty blond woman with a circlet of gold in her hair. Princess Mellony, Lila thought. The queen's sister. "I'm glad you could join us. How is Raisa?"

"She remains fragile," Byrne said, back straight, chin up, as if at attention. He was always at attention.

"I'm sorry to hear that," Lord Bayar said. He was sitting next to Princess Mellony. Lila recognized him by his High Wizard stoles. One of his arms was wrapped in white linen bandages, and it appeared that one side of his face was healing from a bad burn.

"Just when we think she's improving, there's a setback," Byrne said. "She's not been able to keep her food down these past three days."

Mellony frowned. "I wish that you would allow me to go and see her," she said. "It would put my mind at ease."

"That's Prince Adrian's call," Byrne said. From the weary way he said it, Lila had a sense that this ground was well trodden. "Though I'm sure Her Majesty would love to see you, Lord Gryphon and His Highness both worry that visitors would tire her, and might bring in infection. Prince Adrian is concerned that the room might still be contaminated with the poison that sickened her. Since we haven't identified the source—"

"If the queen still hasn't recovered after weeks of convalescence," a tall, pinched-faced wizard said, "then doesn't it make sense to get a second opinion from a more senior practitioner?"

Byrne's lips tightened. "Lord Vega, we appreciate your repeated offers of assistance," he said, "but Prince Adrian was very specific about restricting access of caregivers to Lady Magret, Master Gryphon, and himself. Given that he is next of kin to the queen in the absence of Princess Alyssa, and that Prince Adrian is an academy-trained healer himself—"

"Who never graduated," Lord Vega sneered. "If Prince Adrian wants to defend his decisions with regard to care of the queen, he should come here in person to do so."

"Since both he and the queen agree on this course of action, he did not believe that it needed defending," Byrne said, his voice hardening.

Lord Bayar cleared his throat. "While I cannot speak to Prince Adrian's skills," the High Wizard said, "I've seen Master Gryphon's work on the battlefield. The queen could not be in better hands."

That was a definite poke at Vega, who turned to Princess Mellony. "Really, Your Highness, I beg of you to overrule Captain Byrne in the interest of—"

"This is the queen's decision, not mine," Byrne said. "Do you propose to overrule your blooded queen?"

"Lord Vega, let's not begin this meeting with an argument." It was the young woman who'd recognized Shadow. Her sober and businesslike clothing reminded Lila of the way she herself used to dress as a scribe at King Gerard's court. It looked better on her than it ever had on Lila. Her black hair was pulled back in a low twist that accentuated her high cheekbones and narrow, smoky eyes.

As for nonsense, she was not having it.

"Lady Barrett, with all due respect—"

"With all due respect, Lord Vega, I would like to move ahead with our agenda. You are welcome at any time to submit a motion to select another interim chairperson until the queen is well enough to resume that role." Lady Barrett waited, but Vega shook his head and settled back in his chair.

So, Lila thought, that must be Lady Barrett, cousin to Adrian and Lyss, daughter to Princess Mellony. Hence the wolf scarf.

"Now, Captain Byrne," Barrett said, "you said that you have a message from Queen Raisa?"

Byrne nodded. "Prince Adrian has decided that the queen

might benefit from some time in the Spirits, since they have always connected so closely with the queens of the Line."

"Pardon me, Captain, but aren't we *in* the Spirit Mountains?" This was a handsome woman with red-streaked pale hair wearing the Mander fellscats on her stoles. Lila snuck a look at her notes. This must be Miranda Mander.

"Specifically, time on Hanalea Peak," Captain Byrne said. "Speaker Jemson has offered the use of one of the temple's retreat houses there. The queen intends to spend a month or two in seclusion in the hopes that it will restore her usual good health."

This announcement was met with mingled dismay, confusion, and consternation.

"This is very bad news," Lady Mander said. "This is a disastrous time for the queen to be absent. The next two months may decide the future of the queendom."

Byrne's jaw tightened. "Her Majesty recognizes that the timing is poor, but she has confidence in her team on the council. To further strengthen it, she has appointed two new members."

Now the eyes of the council turned to Shadow and Lila. Lila read their expressions as *Them? You can't be serious.*

Byrne continued on doggedly. "Since Fire Dancer left for the war in the east, we've not had a clan representative on the queen's council, and Queen Raisa has been eager to remedy that. She has appointed Dancer's son, Shadow Dancer, to the council on a temporary basis."

"Shadow!" Lady Barrett said, smiling. "How did you get talked into this?"

"Captain Byrne said that it was the only way to lower the average age on the council," Shadow said. He scanned the empty sideboard and scowled. "He also promised refreshments."

Lila laughed, and Barrett smiled, but nobody else seemed amused.

"Was it really necessary to bring on a substitute for this relatively short time period?" This was an older man in a slashed velvet coat. "By the time he learns how things work, he'll be leaving us."

"It's been months already, Lord Howard," Byrne said. "And there's no telling how much longer we'll be in this situation."

"I, for one, am glad he's here," another council member said. He was middle-aged, with fine, almost translucent white hair and blue eyes. "Shadow owes me money."

"You promised I'd get a chance to win it back, Mitri," Shadow said. "I'm still waiting."

That must be Dimitri Fenwaeter, representing the Waterwalkers, Lila thought, checking him off her list.

"I intend to accompany the queen and Prince Adrian to her temporary quarters on Hanalea," Byrne said. He dropped a hand on Lila's shoulder, startling her. "I would like to introduce my daughter, Lila Byrne. The queen has asked her to sit in for me in my absence."

Barrowhill, Lila thought fiercely, as jaws dropped around the room. A person would think that Byrne had brought his faerie chance child to the garden club.

"I had . . . forgotten that you had a daughter, Captain Byrne," Princess Mellony said, looking from Byrne to Lila. "We all remember Simon, of course. . . ." Her voice trailed off.

Yes. We all remember Simon.

"I'm the one who's not Simon," Lila said.

Bayar studied her, rubbing his chin. "It seems that you take after your mother," he said. Which might have been a polite way to say, Are you sure Captain Byrne is really your father?

"Lila grew up on the east coast, splitting her time between my sister Lydia's and her mother's family," Byrne said, "which is why she's not well known at court."

"Forgive me," Lord Howard said. "I cannot imagine how a person who has never been at court could make a meaningful contribution to our discussions and decisions."

"Lila has been working with me for several years," Byrne said, "elsewhere in the Realms."

The expression on every face said, *Huh. Really? Where? Doing what?*

"Still, it smacks of nepotism," Lord Howard persisted.

"It seems to me that nepotism is the linchpin of an aristocracy," Fenwaeter said. "Lady Barrett, didn't you assume your mother's post on council at one time?"

Barrett nodded. "That's true."

"With all due respect, Captain Byrne, in a time of war, do we really want this kind of inexperience on the queen's council?" Lord Vega said.

Isn't it interesting how often the phrase "with all due respect" is the prelude to disrespect? Lila thought.

"Sometimes a new voice can offer a new perspective." From his cleric's robes, Lila assumed that this was the famous Speaker Jemson. "Unbound by habit or tradition."

"Speaker Jemson can attest to the fact that I am blood-bound to serve both the queen and the queendom," Byrne said, his shoulders even stiffer than usual. "I would not speak for these appointments to council if I did not believe they were the best choice for the good of the realm."

"I wonder if it is time to discuss the possibility of a proxy for the queen," Lady Mander said.

Lord Bayar straightened in his chair, eyes narrowed. "What exactly do you mean, Miranda?" he said in the kind of voice that would signal most people to take cover.

"Like I said before, we're in a crisis. We have a war on two fronts, a missing princess heir, a here-today-and-gone-tomorrow prince, and a queen in ill health. There are many decisions to be made in the near term. Wouldn't it make sense to appoint someone—a regent, perhaps—to stand in for the queen until she can resume her usual duties?"

"Did you have a candidate in mind?" Bayar raised an eyebrow.

"It would make sense if it was someone in the royal family," Lady Mander said. "Someone close to the queen. Princess Mellony, perhaps, or Lady Barrett."

Your in-laws-to-be? Lila thought, feeling like a first-time player in a street game, the ball whizzing back and forth over her head.

Mander paused, as if dithering whether to make that final leap. "We haven't seen the queen in weeks," she said. "How do we know that she's still alive?"

This was met with a quick intake of breath, followed by a storm of protest.

"We haven't seen her since she was poisoned," Mander went on, raising her voice to be heard over the hubbub. "For all we know, Captain Byrne has been lying to us, unable to admit that his mistress is—"

"Captain Byrne is not a liar."

Everyone flinched and looked around, wide-eyed. The

queen's voice seemed to echo from every corner of the library.

"I may have been poisoned, and my strength and stamina are limited, but I assure you, Lady Mander, that I am very much alive."

That definitely came from overhead. Lila looked up, scanning the gallery. The queen stood at the railing in a sumptuous robe, the jewels in her tiara glittering in the light from the sconces. She leaned on the railing for support, and Lila could see Gryphon hovering behind her, to catch her if she fell. There was a chair next to her, suggesting she'd been sitting there listening for some time.

"Raisa," Mellony whispered, chin quivering, her cheeks streaked with tears.

"Thank the Maker," Bayar said, closing his eyes, as if sending a silent prayer after the spoken one.

Lady Mander appeared totally ambushed. "Your Majesty, I never meant—I didn't realize—"

"I also assure you that I am in complete control of my faculties, and so have no need of a regent. Although I recognize the inconvenience of communicating with me over a distance, I am confident it can be done."

Mander resembled a flamboyant potted plant, rapidly wilting in the midday sun.

The queen's gaze found Lord Vega, who appeared thunderstruck. "Now, as to these new appointees to council, Lord Vega, before you pass judgment on my choice of representative, you should know that Lila Byrne has contributed more to our war effort than many of us on the council. Despite her youth, she has engaged in critical espionage and sabotage operations on behalf of our queendom—often at great risk to herself. Lila was the one who brought Prince Adrian safely home. She has done this without rank, title, or recognition. Both she and Shadow Dancer have suffered great personal losses during this time of war. I don't know how I can ever repay them.

"I have demanded much of them, yet they've never faltered when it comes to loyalty and service. Anyone, and I mean *anyone* who questions their suitability to serve on this council will answer to me."

Lila and Shadow looked at each other. Well, Lila thought, maybe we've faltered a time or two. Yet the queen was getting to her. The pain in her heart and the burn of tears in her eyes said so.

Gryphon leaned toward the queen and murmured something in her ear. She nodded and turned back to the counselors below. "Now, is there anything else to discuss with me before I return to my bed?" She gazed down at the council for a moment. "Good. Then I suggest that you all get seated and do business." With that, she eased herself back into her chair and Gryphon wheeled her away.

So, Lila thought, that's how she does it.

# 24

# A MATTER OF TACTICS

Lyss's days in Celesgarde were long and physically strenuous. She would fall into bed, exhausted, only to find that her mind continued to work all night. At first, she spent that time second-guessing herself, wondering if she was doing the right thing. If staying alive justified her contributions to Celestine's war machine. Wondering how long she could continue this charade.

I'm just not that good at lying, she thought.

If Lyss had hoped that her Gray Wolf ancestors would return regularly to advise her, she was disappointed. Having delivered their message about her accession to the throne, they seemed to have returned to the uplands, leaving her on her own.

Gradually, she left off dithering.

*You won't get what you don't go after.* Lyss's father, Han Alister, had drilled that into her. *So the first thing to do is to figure out what you want.*

The events of the past year had stripped away the self-doubt and ambivalence that had dogged Lyss since her sister, Hanalea, died. She might not be the queen everyone planned on, or maybe hoped for, but she was the queen they had. She was the survivor. Everyone would just have to deal with it.

So. First and foremost, she was determined to survive and return to the Fells and take her place in the line of Gray Wolf queens.

In order to achieve that goal, she had to succeed in a job she didn't want. The more time she spent with Empress Celestine, the clearer the consequences of failure. The Desert Coast was littered with the bones of those who had disappointed her. Her armies were swollen with her blood-bound slaves.

If Lyss wanted to remain free of the empress's blood magic, she had to hone Celestine's land army into a viable fighting force. Or at least do well enough to sell the appearance of success. If she could forge clan warriors, wizards, and Valefolk into an army, then surely she could hone the bloodsworn into something resembling that. Probably. Maybe.

She still had to deal with the voice in her head that said she might be building an army capable of taking her birthright away.

So the second prong of her strategy was to persuade the empress that Arden would prove a much more valuable target than the queendom in the north. It was a delicate dance for Lyss, who preferred to do her dancing on the battlefield. The empress was moody, arbitrary, quick to anger, slow to forgive, and capricious as hell. She loved flattery but resented unsolicited advice, and even *solicited* advice that didn't dovetail with her own opinion, which seemed to change daily.

Lyss, Celestine, Captain Samara, and Breon often dined together, when Samara was in port. Lyss came to dread these stomach-churning ordeals, as she picked her way through conversational land mines.

Breon, of course, said nothing, only picked at his food and dreamed through dinner, his pipe in a little dish by his plate. Sometimes Celestine scolded him for not eating more. He would dutifully take another bite, then put his fork down. The empress was unfailingly affectionate toward him, solicitous of his well-being, doing everything she could to improve his quality of life without actually giving him his voice back.

Sometimes, Lyss caught Breon watching the empress with unblinking intensity, as if he was storing something away for later. She didn't know whether to be hopeful or worried about that.

At these dinners, Celestine often included some handsome young man for Lyss, and a lovely young woman for Breon, or vice versa. She seemed determined to distract the erstwhile lovers with new options. These guests were heartbreakingly beautiful, talented on the jafasa or basilka, and thoroughly trained in flattery and meaningless conversation. Maybe they were interesting people in real life, but in this setting Lyss found them irredeemably boring.

The empress seemed puzzled by Lyss's lack of response to the young courtesans put before her. "They are not to your liking, Captain Gray?" she said. "You could take either one or both to your bed. If there is a different . . . need you have, I will do my best to—"

"They are fine," Lyss said hastily. "They are lovely and charming. I'm just . . . not in the mood."

Celestine's eyes narrowed. "I hope you are not harboring any hopes regarding a relationship with my brother. He is not for you."

What *is* he for? Lyss wanted to say. Instead, she said, "I understand that, Your Eminence."

"If you are inexperienced, don't worry. They are very good teachers," she said. "In fact, that can be a good way to——"

"No!" Lyss said. She was tempted to add, *If I go to bed with someone, I want it to mean something.* Her face heated as an image of a shirtless Matelon came to mind—those broad shoulders, his muscled arms, the odd silver thimble on a chain around his neck. The way he paused to collect his thoughts before he spoke. The way he challenged her day after day. The way she challenged him. There was always something to learn from Matelon.

*Blood and bones.* Clearly, she hadn't buried *that* deeply enough.

"Captain?"

The empress was still looking at her, frowning a little, as if waiting for an answer, so she said, "I find that when going into battle, celibacy sharpens my mental skills and improves my performance."

Samara's eyes widened, and he went a little pale.

"Oh!" Celestine said, shooting a smirk at Samara. "If that's true, shall we order our soldiers to abstain until such time as——"

"No!" Lyss said, trying not to shout and only partly succeeding. "I'm speaking just for myself. Everyone is different."

With that, the look of alarm faded from Samara's face. "I agree, Your Eminence," he said. "I find that a bout between the sheets stirs my blood and prepares me to shed the blood of others."

See? Lyss thought, struggling not to roll her eyes. Everyone's different.

Tully Samara continued to be a thorn in Lyss's side. Though he had little to no experience at fighting on land, that did not prevent him from having an opinion on nearly everything—usually the direct opposite of Lyss's. He must have suspected that Lyss was trying to redirect any attack on the Seven Realms toward Arden, because he did his best to undermine everything she said.

"I'm impressed by how the cavalry is coming along," Lyss would say. "I've never seen horses like those. They are completely different from our military mounts at home."

"Our bloodlines are pure," Samara said. "We refuse to mount an inferior beast. That is why we have off-loaded several hundred of our horses at Chalk Cliffs, so that we can ride down the soldiers of the northern queen." Having thrown down that verbal gauntlet, he waited for her response.

"That might work well on the Alyssa Plateau," Lyss said, wishing that geographic feature were named anything else. "But once we get to Fortress Rocks, we're in the mountains, where everything changes."

"I have no doubt that our horses—and our soldiers—are up to the task," the empress said.

"I am doing my very best to make it so," Lyss said. "However, having fought in the north for so long, I am choosy about where I spend soldiers' lives. It's a matter of tactics."

"Our soldiers do not go down easily," Samara said. "You've seen that for yourself."

Lyss nodded. "I have. But our horses go down, just like wetland horses. They are built for racing across the desert, not climbing the narrow, steep trails in the uplands. And even the bloodsworn can be stopped where geography makes it difficult for them to engage." She paused, hesitating about whether to go on. "It's not enough to have the best soldiers, and the best horses. You have to have the right soldiers, and the right horses, in the right place."

"It sounds to me like you are making excuses in case you are not successful in the north," Samara said.

"Oh, I have no doubt we'll be successful," Lyss said, skin prickling under Celestine's gaze. "But at what cost, in terms of time and treasure? And what will we have, at the end of it? A mountainous queendom whose people are its greatest asset. They know how to make a living off an unforgiving land, and how to keep their enemies out. If you enslave them, their value is lost." She realized that her voice was shaking, so she stopped with that.

"I can understand why you would want to protect your homeland, Captain Gray," Samara said, with a serpent's smile, "but right now your loyalty is to the empress—or it should be." He turned his cup between his hands.

The empress pressed her lips together, her eyes shifting to a frosty blue. Lyss suspected that part of this was playacting. Celestine seemed to feast on whatever discord and competition she could foment between Lyss and Samara, just as she reveled in watching the bloody tournaments among the bloodsworn.

"Your Eminence, I am giving you the very best advice that I can," Lyss said. She searched for an argument that would make sense to these seafarers. "Tell me this—do you sail straight into a storm or do you try to avoid it?"

"I sail into a storm if it's necessary," Celestine said.

"But what if it's not necessary?" Lyss said. "What if you can go another way, or wait a day until it passes?"

"I would avoid it, of course," the empress said grudgingly,

"if, in the end, I'd still get where I wanted to go."

"Do you spend much time in the Dragonback Mountains?"

Samara and Celestine looked at each other, perplexed by the apparent change of subject.

"Why would we?" Samara said finally. "It's infested with dragons, and there's nothing to steal but sheep."

"That's my point. Marching into the Heartfangs is like sailing into the worst storm ever—and that's in summer. In winter, it's impassable. Once you're through: more mountains, and nothing to live on. Why would you do that, when you can land in Baston Bay and march straight down the fertile valley of the Arden to the capital, with plenty of forage along the way?"

"But we're already in Chalk Cliffs," Celestine said. "We've landed soldiers, horses, and supplies."

"I'm not saying we should give up Chalk Cliffs." *Though if you want to, I won't stand in your way.* "As long as we hold it, we can keep the northerners bottled up with no deepwater port to the east. If we take Baston Bay, and then Ardenscourt, you'll have control of the empire, for all intents and purposes. You can march west across the flatlands for hundreds of miles. Everything you win in the south makes you richer. The north will make you poor, I guarantee it."

Celestine and Samara looked at each other as if Lyss was dropping the names of places they'd never heard of. She hoped that would reinforce her value to the operation.

"Your Eminence," Lyss said, "at first, I could not understand why you would put a wetland captain at the head of your blood-sworn army. Now I see that it was a stroke of genius. You are wise enough to know that the tactics that have been successful in Carthis may not work as well in the Realms. So you chose a commander who's fought there before, who knows the terrain, the climate, and the people."

By now, Celestine was smiling, basking in the tripe Lyss was shoveling.

"That may be true," Samara said, "but putting a foreigner at the helm of our army carries with it the risk of betrayal."

"As does promoting an ambitious local," Lyss said. "That causes jealousy among those who were overlooked and a sense of entitlement among the chosen. Tell me, Your Eminence, who has betrayed you in the past?"

Celestine blinked at her. "Friends and family, I suppose," she said.

"That's my point. It's not always strangers we have to worry about—often it's our closest allies."

"Perhaps, Your Eminence," Samara said, eager to change the subject, "we should capture a commander from the Ardenine army and have him argue for an invasion in the north. It would be a deadly dull tournament of words. In the Nazari empire, we do our fighting on the seas and in the field, not at the din-ner table."

Lyss shrugged. "In the Fells, we have been making our arguments on the battlefield for more than a quarter century. I would challenge your Ardenine commander to explain why they have failed, year after year, to win that debate."

Celestine had been looking back and forth between them. "Perhaps," she said, "I should hold a tournament between the two of you, and see who wins."

"Perhaps it will come to that," Samara said, leaning back, lacing his fingers behind his head, his jewelry reflecting the dying sun.

"I'm in," Lyss said, "as long as we hold the contest on dry land. I also suggest we wait until after we win the wetlands. Captain Samara will be needed to ferry us back across the sea."

Celestine laughed, banging her cup on the table and wiping tears from her eyes while Samara scowled. Lyss knew it was dangerous to taunt the naval commander, but he was the sort to keep pushing until someone pushed back.

Also, it occurred to her that, with practice, she was getting better at fighting in the arena of words.

"I'm curious, Your Eminence," Lyss said, to change the subject more than anything else. "Why did you choose Chalk Cliffs as a target in the first place? Was it the element of surprise, or—"

"There's someone that I'm looking for," Celestine said. "The last time I saw her was off the northern coast. That is why we took Chalk Cliffs."

Ah, Lyss thought. Someone marked like Breon? "Does she know you're hunting her?"

Celestine hesitated. "Yes," she said. "She does now."

"So she's on the run?"

Celestine nodded. "I suppose so."

"Do you really think she's still there?" Lyss said. "I mean, she couldn't have missed the attack on Chalk Cliffs. She knows you're coming. It's easier to hide in the south. More people, better weather, friendlier terrain. Though Arden and the Fells are enemies, the borders are more porous than you think for one person traveling. If I were her, I'd be in Bruinswallow by now, on my knees in a desert temple, disguised as a flatland priest."

Celestine laughed. "I would very much like to see that."

Lyss could tell the empress was wavering, and moved to press her advantage. "If you're in no hurry, of course, we can fight in the north for however long it takes, and then go south. But I recommend that you gain control of the south before you go north. The Fells had only one deepwater port. Arden has a half a dozen. That will enable us to use our strength at sea. It may be that realms like We'enhaven, Bruinswallow, and the Southern Islands will throw in with us. That enables us to build our numbers and march on the Fells in force."

The empress rose from the table, flinging her napkin down. She crossed to a large map on the wall that showed the Desert Coast and Northern Islands in great detail, but only the coastline of the Seven Realms. "If it were up to you, where would you land our armies in the south?"

Lyss joined her at the wall. "If we act quickly, we'll have the element of surprise. King Jarat knows by now that you've taken Chalk Cliffs. He'll look for you to continue inland there. If it were up to me, I'd suggest Baston Bay, which gives you a good road all the way to Ardenscourt." She traced it on the map. "That allows us to use our long-legged horses and be there inside of a week."

Knowing that it was important to Celestine to make strategic decisions, she said, "If you want to keep marching to a minimum, I'd sail around the claw all the way to Southgate." She ran her finger along the sea route, even though she dreaded the notion of spending so much time aboard ship. "That gives us a shorter road to Ardenscourt. We can bite them in the ass before they know what's happening."

It also put the empress's army as far as possible from the queendom.

The empress stood, hands on hips, studying the options.

Then touched the spot on the map that was Spiritgate. "Here, I think. That way, if we need to change our plans and go north, we can." Celestine slid a look at Samara, who was trying to rearrange his scowl into something resembling agreement.

To Lyss, the message was clear: the empress was keeping her options open. Spiritgate was a gateway to both Arden and the Fells.

Celestine turned then and smiled crookedly at Lyss. "When you came here, Captain Gray, I accused you of being a poor sailor. I asked if you were better on land. I believe you are."

Don't give me too much credit, Lyss thought. I've been planning an invasion of Arden ever since my father was murdered. I just never thought I would do it leading a Carthian army.

# MAGE MISCHIEF

After the meeting with the thanes, Hal rode back to the valley camp to meet with one of the mages he had socked away.

He was wary of mages, after his experience at Queen Court, and they were wary of him, too, so that made them even.

The mage's name was Marc DeJardin. Unlike most mages in Arden, he'd been a blackbird—a member of the King's Guard, and not the regular army—so Hal's contacts had little information about him. He had little to say, and the other mages kept their distance, possibly because of his history in the feared King's Guard. There was a chance he was here as a spy for the king. If that was the case, better to find out sooner rather than later. But there was something about him that drew Hal's trust. Maybe it was the ring of scar tissue around his collar that suggested he had not always been as steady and docile as he seemed. Hal also hoped that, having been a member of the king's elite guard, he might know more about how the collars worked than most captive mages.

Hal was in the command tent with LeFevre when DeJardin was shown in. He offered a perfunctory salute, either because he wasn't military, or because that was just what he thought Hal deserved.

"That will be all, Captain," Hal said to LeFevre. "We'll talk later." The officer saluted and left.

"Sit down," he said to the mage, gesturing toward a camp chair.

DeJardin sat, as if it was a pleasure to take a load off. He was decades older than Hal, with steel-gray hair and the sturdy, broad-shouldered build of someone who'd been physically active all of his life.

"I'm General Matelon," Hal said, the word *general* all but sticking in his throat. In the Ardenine army, there was so much bribery, politics, and skulduggery involved in getting to the point of being a general that a man was used to the title by the time he claimed it.

"I know," DeJardin said. "Congratulations on your promotion, and your recent resurrection." He paused. "Assuming you were in favor of it."

"I haven't decided yet," Hal said. "So you can hold the congratulations for now."

DeJardin did a kind of double take, as if not expecting humor from an officer in the Ardenine army. He then smiled crookedly. "Consider them held."

"You are most welcome to join our forces," Hal said, "but I'm wondering how much freedom you'll have to fight with us, given that you're collared by the king."

"It's a risk," DeJardin said, "for you and for us. It's a risk I'm willing to take, because this is the first viable challenge to the empire since Gerard killed off his brothers and took over. I can't sit by if I might be able to help."

"I've commanded mages on the battlefield," Hal said, "but, to be honest, I don't know that much about how the collars work. What can you tell me?"

DeJardin reached up and ran his fingers over the collar. "Do you want the long or the short of it?"

"You choose," Hal said.

"They were invented by the copperheads in the north to control captured mages during their civil war."

"Is there a way to get them off?"

"Short of cutting off my head?" DeJardin snorted. "They can only be opened using a magical key. It used to be that each collar had a unique key. If the key was lost, too bad. It was a major design flaw, but the copperheads never much cared, because captive mages never lived very long anyway."

It was Hal's turn to be surprised. DeJardin spoke like a scholar who'd finally been asked to discuss his life's work. "You've made a study of this, haven't you?"

DeJardin templed his fingers. "I spent the first ten years of my captivity studying the collars, trying to figure out how to get rid of mine. In the process, I've become something of an expert." He waited, as if expecting Hal to argue that mages were better off being enslaved. When he didn't, the mage continued on. "During the Ardenine civil war, when Gerard was killing off his brothers to get to the throne, it was General Karn, a mage himself, who realized the value of mages on the battlefield. But he had to have a way to remind the mages whose side they were on and to reassure the church that their demonic energy was under control. So he began collecting collars and amulets to outfit the mages he kidnapped in the countryside. To this day, that's been the bottleneck in increasing the size of the mage division."

Something DeJardin had said caught Hal's attention. "You said that it used to be that each collar had a unique key. Has that changed?"

DeJardin nodded. "Recently, Karn found a supplier who could provide new collars in quantity that could be controlled with a single key. Not only that, they combine the function of amulets and collars. They can be removed from a dead mage and applied to a live one. The perfect solution. So the king has been buying every one he can get his hands on. He's refitted as many mages as he could with the new gear."

Hal thought about this. "Do you have any idea who's been selling them the gear?"

"I don't know who's making it, but the intermediary is someone named Lila Barrowhill."

Lila Barrowhill, Hal thought, his heart beating a little faster. Everybody's girl. And nobody's girl. Who'd sent the message that the flash used by the Ardenine army was "special issue."

"Is that one of the newer collars?" he said. "The one you're wearing?"

DeJardin nodded. "The King's Guard mages were the first to be fitted out."

Hal pulled out the pouch that had been "delivered" to Robert in Ardenscourt. "I want to show you something," he said. Untying the cord, he shook the pendant out onto his palm.

The mage stared at it. He reached out a finger, and it lit up in response. "That appears to be the kind of key used to open collars," he said. "Where did you get that?"

"From someone working for Barrowhill," Hal said. "The thing is, I don't know exactly how it works, or what will happen if it's used. The only message we have is that most of the collars in the king's armory are 'special issue,' but I don't know what that means. I assume the collar has been working as expected up to now?"

DeJardin nodded, his eyes still fixed on the key.

"Consider the fact that these new collars—and this key—were made by the copperheads in the north. Mortal enemies of the empire. Now, those involved might be traitors, selling out the northern queendom for a price. Or this could be part of a plan to sabotage the empire's military efforts."

"How so?" DeJardin said, cocking his head.

"One key opens all of the collars. One key controls all of the collars. Nearly all the mages fighting for the Ardenine king are wearing them now. What if this one key"—Hal hefted it in his hand—"could kill all of the mages wearing them in one stroke?"

DeJardin's eyes widened marginally. "I'd say that would be very, very clever on their part."

"So. If we try this, it could kill you. It could kill you and all of your fellow collared mages. It could allow me to take control of the collared mages. Or it could open the collar." As Hal said this, he thought, Why do you have to be so damnably honest?

"Go ahead," DeJardin said, lifting his chin to allow clearer access to the collar. "Give it a try."

"Hang on," Hal said, taken aback by the mage's willingness to trust to luck. "Let me show you something. The key seems to have settings. If you turn the head, like so . . ." He manipulated the joint, demonstrating how the shank clicked into place in four different spots. "So what it does may depend on the setting."

"Are any of them marked with K for *kill*, or O for *open*?" DeJardin said drily.

Hal couldn't help laughing. "No," he said. "They're not marked at all. But we understand that it takes a mage to use it."

"May I see it?" DeJardin reached out his hand, and Hal dropped the key into it. In the mage's hand, it glowed more brightly than before, and eventually symbols appeared next to the notches, shining against the metal around them.

Hal leaned in, his head nearly touching DeJardin's. "I'm going to guess that the skull means 'kill,'" he said.

"Here's an open lock, and a closed one," DeJardin said. "I'm thinking that's 'lock' and 'unlock.' And this one is a symbol I'm not familiar with."

It looked like a stick with a zigzag across it. It looked vaguely familiar to Hal, like he'd seen it somewhere before. Had it been somewhere in the north, when he was being held prisoner?

Then he remembered. It had been during one of the tournaments at Delphi, when Lyssa Gray's Highlanders were going up against Hal's fellow prisoners. One of Hal's men had caught his rebated sword in the hem of Captain Gray's shirt, ripping it all the way to her collarbone. She'd continued fighting in her chemise until she won her bout. When Hal brought her another shirt to put on, he couldn't help noticing a tattoo just above her collarbone. It was a stick with a zigzag across it.

"What's that?" he'd asked, trying not to stare too hard at her collarbone.

"That's the staff and flash," she'd said. "Symbol of the Demon King."

"Didn't he nearly destroy the world?" Hal said.

"Don't believe everything you hear in your flatland temple schools," Gray had said. "He's my ancestor."

"Well, that explains a lot," Hal had said. She'd punched him in the shoulder, and that had ended it.

"General?" DeJardin was watching Hal, looking puzzled.

"I think it's a symbol for the Demon King," he said. "For magery."

"So that might relate to the collar's function as an amulet," DeJardin said.

They sat there for an awkward moment.

"I think the 'lock' symbol is clear enough," DeJardin said, handing back the pendant. "Let's try it."

Hal shook his head. "I think a mage has to use the key," he said. "You do it, if you choose to." He dropped the key into the mage's hand.

DeJardin gazed down at it for a moment. Then, gripping it by the shank, he turned the bow so it lined up with the open lock. Steadying the collar with one hand, he slid the business end of the key into the collar and turned it. With a soft *click*, the collar separated into two halves and clattered onto the floor.

DeJardin raised both hands and fingered the place on his neck, puckered with scar tissue, where the collar had rested. He cleared his throat, his eyes unnaturally bright. "I can die a happy man now," he said.

"Hopefully not any time soon." Hal leaned down and picked up the collar, fitting the two pieces back together, then took the key from DeJardin. "I'd like to try something else, if you don't mind." Using the key, he locked the collar again, and turned the setting to the Demon King symbol. Fortunately, it didn't burn him to a cinder.

"Next question. Can you tell by touching this if it can function as an amulet?"

"I think so," DeJardin said. "Are you sure that you want me

to unleash my mage-ish powers in here?"

"Just don't set fire to the tent," Hal said.

The mage reached for the collar, and it lit up in greeting. He took it in his hands and spoke a charm. For a moment, it seemed that nothing had happened. Then the center tentpole burst forth with leaves and buds that opened into flowers.

DeJardin grinned, plucking one of the flowers and handing it to Hal. "I was a damned good farmer. Before," he said.

Hal grinned back, relieved that nobody was dead, and nothing was burnt, and it seemed that they had ferreted out the secrets of the key and the "special-issue" collars.

DeJardin took a deep breath and let it out slowly, as if breathing free air for the first time in a long time. "I don't know how to thank you," he said, "but I think you'll tell me."

Hal laughed. This was a man he could work with. Then, sobering, he said, "You came to us because you said that you wanted to help us against the Montaignes," he said. "We can really use your help, and that of the other mages who have defected. I would like you to lead our gifted division. If we win this war, I pledge on my honor that no mage will wear a collar in this kingdom again, except as an amulet."

# 26

# A MIXED BLESSING

If Destin had thought that his troubles would end with the general's death, he was wrong, of course. With the removal of that major scourge from his life, all of the other threats and obstacles that had been waiting in the wings elbowed forward to claim his attention.

The blackbirds had finally taken his father's corpse down from the battlements and buried it in Potter's Field. Yet he still loomed over Destin like an avenging demon, tainting him in the king's eyes. Though Destin had created the case against the general (*created* being the operative word) and served as prosecutor and executioner, the king did not like to be reminded of past mistakes.

Destin savored the irony. Though the general had been a vicious, cruel, despicable bastard, he'd served the Montaigne line more faithfully than any of the survivors on Jarat's council. Including Destin.

Destin had only peripheral involvement in preparations for the march north, which suited him fine. He had no interest in being associated with a project that seemed likely to end in disaster. He worked with the quartermasters to make sure that all of the army's gifted soldiers had the new-style collars. He provided updates to the king's new general about conditions between Ardenscourt and Delphi and beyond.

The intelligence reports he was getting from the capital of Fellsmarch were confusing. It seemed that Queen Raisa had taken ill and hadn't been seen in public in weeks. A large contingent of Highlanders remained in Delphi, but they seemed to be preparing to march east against the empress.

Meanwhile, the garrison in the northern capital seemed to be getting smaller by the day.

What did that mean? They have to know we're coming, Destin thought. The queen's intelligence service was run by her niece, Julianna Barrett, and Barrett was better than that. Had the queen and her court secretly abandoned the capital to lead her troops in the field?

Where were the hostages? If they were in Fellsmarch, surely he'd have received word by now. Where would Lila stash them? It was as if they'd disappeared into some black hole in the north. Destin didn't like being outsmarted and outmaneuvered, and Lila had definitely done that when it came to that operation.

In the absence of hard information, Destin's creative imagination took over. Maybe Lila had been working for Celestine all along. Maybe Queen Marina and the others were on their way to Celesgarde. Maybe the empress planned to hold them hostage, contingent on delivery of Evan Strangward.

Where was Evan? The last time they'd spoken, Evan had been on his way to the northern court to try to convince the queen of the danger posed by Celestine. Did this mean he'd succeeded, that they were pouring all of their troops and treasure into the threat in the east while neglecting the threat from the south?

In the years they'd been apart, it wasn't unusual to go a long time without communicating—especially because each contact had the potential of catching the attention of their enemies. But, given the current political and military landscape, Destin couldn't help worrying.

I can't think about that right now, he thought. He had to prepare for one of Jarat's war councils. King Jarat had taken to holding meetings in the duty room in the barracks, where he could survey activity on the parade ground. He loved to sit, resplendent in his uniform, and hold forth on military strategy. Generally, Destin was spared attendance at these meetings, but he'd been commanded to attend this one.

The war council was a mingle of new and old: Jarat's remaining loyal thanes, including Lord Botetort, Beauchamp, and LaRue; Barbeau, captain of the King's Guard; and Eric Bellamy, the son of the king's Master of Horse and the new commander of the Ardenine army.

The barracks had never been Destin's favorite place, given its association with the general, but he'd hoped that would fade now that his father was gone. It hadn't, at least not so far.

When Destin arrived, Jarat and Bellamy were on the gallery, watching a platoon of soldiers drill in the sun. Jarat was talking, gesturing at Bellamy, who was listening politely. Jarat's uniform was spit-and-polish new, while Bellamy's looked to have seen hard use.

Destin had never spent much time with Eric Bellamy prior to his appointment as general of the armies. Though Bellamy occasionally appeared at the winter court, he was fighting in the north the other three seasons of the year. Bellamy had a good reputation, however. Nothing would make Destin happier than to see him succeed where his father had failed. That might put the final nail in the coffin of his father's reputation.

Still, Destin worried that they were fighting the wrong battle against the wrong opponent. Once the king marched his armies north, Destin planned to return to Tamron for the rest of the summer, so that he could settle his mother's estate and work his sources and try to locate Evan. He preferred to be elsewhere when Ardenscourt fell to the rebels, which seemed likely.

Jarat called the meeting to order around a large, battered table in the duty room. "Thank you for coming, gentlemen," the king said. "Let's keep this meeting brief, shall we, since I know that we all have much to do. General Bellamy, what can you tell us about the readiness of the troops?"

"To be honest, Your Majesty, the sooner we go, the better," Bellamy said. "I had hoped to march three weeks ago. While we're waiting, we're eating through our food supplies. We've also seen considerable loss of manpower."

"Loss of manpower?" LaRue said. "Are you talking about desertion?"

"Aye, my lord," Bellamy said.

"Are soldiers simply leaving our service, or are they going over to the rebels?" LaRue persisted.

Bellamy hesitated. "In some cases, yes, they are going over to the rebels."

Here, Destin had something to contribute. "I've had confirmation that the thanes have put Halston Matelon at the head of their army."

"I thought he was dead," LaRue said.

"Apparently not," Destin said. "He's very well thought of among his fellow officers as well as the rank and file. If soldiers are leaving to join the rebels, that might have something to do with it." Destin could tell from Bellamy's expression that the officer already knew about Matelon.

Botetort laughed. "Not even Captain Matelon can turn a peasant militia into an army," he said. "It seems to me that what we need to do is make the consequences of desertion clear. In wartime, desertion constitutes treason and should be dealt with harshly."

"With all due respect, Lord Botetort, we've been at war for as long as I can remember," Bellamy said. He stopped, cleared his throat. "It would really help, Your Majesty, if we could offer a payroll before we march. It would improve morale considerably, and I believe it might stem the desertion problem."

"It seems to me that paying soldiers while they are still here in the city will only lead to problems," Jarat said. "They'll be roaming the streets with money in their pockets and time on their hands. It would be better to wait until after the marching season."

"They haven't been paid in months, Your Majesty," Bellamy said. "Most have families to support, who can't wait until after the marching season."

"Do they really believe that they are more likely to be paid by Lord Matelon and his fellow traitors?" Jarat said.

"I don't know, Your Majesty, but it seems that some have opted to take that chance. With the shrinkage we've seen, there will soon be a question as to whether we can continue to adequately garrison the city while sending a sufficient force north to achieve a decisive victory. In particular, we seem to have lost a large percentage of our magical assets."

With that, all eyes turned to Destin, the only mage in the room.

"How can that be, Lieutenant?" LaRue said. "Why haven't the collars kept them in line?"

"I don't know," Destin said. "That's not really my area of expertise. Perhaps General Bellamy could—"

"General Karn was always in charge of that," Bellamy said, deflecting that missile with military precision, "being a mage himself."

A thick silence descended, while Destin waited for the other shoe to drop. Such was the life of the token mage at the Ardenine court—always suspect, blamed for everything, credited with nothing.

As usual, Jarat did not disappoint.

"Lieutenant Karn, congratulations. You will assume command of our mage forces with the rank of colonel. In that role, you will report to General Bellamy. You will, of course, continue as head of the intelligence service, reporting to me."

Destin's visions of a summer at his uncle's estate in Tamron quickly evaporated. Now he would be embedded in the thick of this debacle, and in line to take the blame if it went wrong.

But he could tell from the look on the king's face that there was no use arguing.

"Yes, Your Majesty," he said, forcing a smile. "Thank you, Your Majesty."

Having disposed of that problem, Jarat turned back to Bellamy. "The rebels are still at Temple Church, are they not?"

"Yes, Your Majesty," Bellamy said, "based on our most recent dispatches."

"Have they shown any sign that they intend to march on the city?"

"I have not heard anything specific in that regard, sir," Bellamy said, shooting a look at Destin.

"With the hostages gone, isn't it more likely that they will engage us on our way north, outside the protection of the city walls?"

"That's one possibility, Your Majesty, but it's also possible that, in our absence, they will opt to attack here."

"With the delays we've had, it is absolutely critical that we make good time on our way to the border," Jarat said. "Therefore, if a choice is to be made, I opt to take an overwhelming force north in order to make quick work of the rebels at Temple Church—if they engage us—and the garrison at Delphi. We'll leave the city lightly garrisoned, relying on our walls to keep the rebels honest. We can conclude our business in the north and return before any damage is done."

Bellamy made one more try. "Your Majesty, if our mages have joined the rebel forces, it may be that—"

"Do you understand, General?"

Bellamy had been in the army long enough to know a command when he heard one. "I understand, Your Majesty."

Jarat smiled, having schooled this veteran soldier on battle strategy, then added generously, "Colonel Karn will address the attrition in our mage division."

And I will pull mages out of my ass, Destin thought.

King Jarat had a habit of leaping over the hard part to get to the reward, but this time he was taking it to the extreme. Never mind the rebel army waiting on the road north. Never mind the garrison in Delphi, the shortage of mages, the dangerous path through the mountains, and a possible battle under the city walls.

We should be talking about what happens *if* we get to the Fells, not *when*.

Something was going on to bolster the king's confidence, something Destin couldn't divine, at least not yet. King Jarat was hot to get to Fellsmarch, over and above everything else. Did it have to do with the spies and contacts the king had mentioned, spies and contacts that Destin knew nothing about? What was he missing?

"Now, as to timing, I understand your impatience, General," the king said. "I'm as anxious as anyone to get on the road. Unfortunately, it has taken Pettyman longer than expected to assemble the goods that we will need in the north."

"Pettyman?" Bellamy said, obviously puzzled. "Who is that?"

"Percival Pettyman," Botetort said. "The royal steward."

"The steward?" Obviously, that didn't help. "What is it that he is assembling, Your Majesty?"

"Once we reach Fellsmarch, we'll need suitable clothing for court, gifts, and so on," Jarat said. "We must arrive like conquerors, not like poor relations."

"Clothing . . . for court?" Spots of color had appeared on Bellamy's cheeks. "That's what we're waiting for?"

"And other things," Jarat said hastily. "If we want the people in the north to bend the knee, we'll need to show them what royalty looks like."

This was met with an awkward silence.

"Have you ever been in the north, Your Majesty?" Bellamy said. "I doubt you'll see anyone bending the knee."

"Not right away, of course," Jarat said breezily. "First we'll wield the stick, and then we'll offer the carrot. Unfortunately, given current demands on the royal treasury, and the difficulty of collecting taxes in the disputed territories, we'll be unable to make a military payroll until after we conquer the north."

Welcome to court, Bellamy, Destin thought. The land of broken promises. He felt genuinely sorry for the young general, and more than a little alarmed. The last thing they needed was for his father's replacement to end up in gaol. He resolved to meet with Bellamy sooner rather than later and give him some guidance before he took his army north.

Destin had no interest in returning to Delphi, even in summer, when the weather was just barely tolerable. If things didn't go as well as the king anticipated, Destin didn't want to be around to catch any of the blame.

He needed to get busy. He still had bodies to bury here in Ardenscourt before the thanes arrived, as he was fairly sure they would.

# 27

# ATTACK PLAN

Jenna's time with the growing dragons on the mountain was a combination of intense training and magical roughhousing. She and the dragons flew everywhere the Boil allowed—on the far side of the mountain from the capital, at least.

These days, they tested the weather boundaries, poking through the wall of wind a short distance, training themselves to counter the turbulence, preparing for an escape in the not-too-distant future.

Lyss joined them as often as she could, bringing treats and gear and updates about what was happening in the capital. They made an odd sort of family, but it worked. Here, there was an illusion of safety, a sense of being high above the dangers below.

Jenna had noticed the growing bond between Lyss and Slayer. Dragons might be prone to holding grudges, but they never forgot a favor, either. From the moment that Lyss covered for Slayer in the backpack incident, the young dragon was hers, body and soul. He was always showing off for her, demonstrating his best aerobatic moves whenever she was around, stealing looks to see if she was watching. He brought her gifts ranging from sheep's carcasses to bits of quartz. When days passed without a visit from Lyss, he'd be trying to convince Cas that a reconnaissance flight over the harbor was in order.

At times Jenna actually felt jealous. She was used to having the dragons to herself. Bonds with dragons were high-maintenance relationships, but both dragons and humans seemed to benefit.

Lyss would arrive, tense and snappish from the tightrope she walked in the empress's presence, her spirits ragged with worry. Gradually, her fists would unclench, her muscles uncoil until she was laughing at dragon humor and feasting on the results of the day's hunt.

Lyss's ability to hear and communicate with the dragons was improving, but they were perplexed by her fragility, by her inability to grow scales when needed. They had to be careful that she wasn't in the line of fire during their increasingly physical mock battles.

Jenna, on the other hand, seemed to grow more impervious to flame every day. Now, even her bare skin was resistant enough to protect her temporarily against flame and blade until her scales surfaced to provide sturdier armor.

Jenna had not really had friends since Maggi and Riley. Friendships were all but impossible for a girl who was keeping so many secrets. Then Adam Wolf had come along, with his lupine scent, solemn face, and grieving eyes, wearing armor of his own. It wasn't until she'd broken through that armor that she realized how lonely she had been. Then he was taken away, too.

Cas had filled the void in a different way, with shared mind and joined hearts. At times, though, when she was alone with the dragon, she worried that she was forgetting how to be human. Instinct often overwhelmed whatever veneer of civilization remained.

And now, Lyss. Lyss was so different from her brother, and yet she reminded Jenna of Adam in so many ways. They smelled the same—of wolf, stone, heather, and the fresh air of high places. They shared the same iron-willed capability. They reminded Jenna of the heroes in the stories she'd read, holed up in her attic in Delphi. Stories full of farm boys who turned out to be princes, and warriors who slew the evil king and won the day.

Lyss kept Jenna's head and heart in the world of people.

But she sometimes wondered—would she ever be fully human again? Did she want to be?

Lyss was a constant reminder of what Jenna had lost, of what, even now, she might be losing. The sands of time were sliding through the glass; she couldn't help feeling that she was running out of time.

Was Adam Wolf dead? Was he alive? If he was alive, how long would that last, with the empress landing an army in the wetlands? Jenna knew from experience that if Celestine wanted to find you, she eventually would.

Meanwhile, the dragons were busy conferring, wrestling with their own problem. Cas came to Jenna with their idea.

*Make armor for Wolf.* He looked at her brightly, as if to say, *See? Problem solved.*

"How would I do that?" Jenna said. "I don't have a foundry. Anyway, a suit of armor would be awfully heavy for flying."

Cas's excitement waned, and he sloped back to join his companions.

The dragons went back to plotting and planning. One day, when Lyss was visiting, her jacket went missing. She and Jenna looked high and low for it, but it was nowhere to be found. The dragons pretended to help in the search, but they were working so hard to look innocent that Jenna knew they were the culprits. Dragons were great at playing tricks on each other.

Lyss finally gave up, said her good-byes, and took the trail down the mountain.

Once Lyss had left, Jenna confronted the dragons, hands on hips. "What did you do with the wolf's jacket?"

Cas pulled the jacket down from a niche in the rocks high above their heads, then dropped a pile of glittering scales next to it, a collage of brilliant colors. It appeared that they'd all contributed.

*Make armor for Wolf.*

Jenna studied the materials they'd gathered. She knew from experience how difficult it was to penetrate dragon scales. They weren't the kind of thing you could poke a needle through, else they'd be useless as armor. But when she looked closer, she could see tiny holes around the perimeter. The dragons had already done that tedious work for her with tooth and claw. But what could she use to stitch them on that wouldn't disintegrate in flying weather or burn away during a battle?

She'd have to think of something. The dragons had done their part.

By now, the fledglings were three-quarters the size of Cas, and becoming strong flyers. They were growing restless, less willing to abide by arbitrary human rules. Cas's wing seemed to be nearly healed, though it still stiffened up every night while he slept. Jenna was getting too comfortable, living here with her dragon family, with events at home out of sight and out of her control.

It was easy to blame her inaction on Cas's injured wing, the fledglings' inexperience, the challenge of the Boil. True, two dragons had flown through it, and both had ended up injured. But if the empress and her ships could come and go, then surely they could find a way. Maybe, with the empress gone, the Boil would subside.

The time for waiting was over. The time for action had come. Or, as Cas put it, *burn the nest, kill the hatchlings, claim the hoard.*

So, one night, until long after dark, Jenna and Lyss sat and schemed. The plan was simple—destroy the city, burn the ships in the harbor, then break through the Boil and wing it for the Seven Realms. If they encountered any Carthian ships along the way, they would burn those, too.

Lyss wanted to take her Fellsian officers with them, but Jenna doubted they could be persuaded to climb aboard a dragon, not even to escape the empress and fly home.

And so it was decided. Lyss would make one more trip down the mountain. The next day, she would return, bringing the supplies they would need. She'd spend the night at the camp on the mountain, and they would attack at dawn.

# 28

# DEVIL'S BARGAIN

By the time Lyss made her way back down to the city from the mountain camp, it was close to dawn. It would be another long day tomorrow after a short night's sleep, but she still felt wide awake, her mind seething with plans. She had little to pack—the fleece-lined leather jacket she wore to fly in, the knit cap she used to confine her hair, the locket Adrian had given her, with images of her family inside. It was tempting to gather some of the supplies she needed before the sun rose. There was less chance of being spotted, but fewer excuses if she was caught. In the end, she decided to go back to her chamber and steal as much sleep as she could before the day began.

To her surprise, the harbor front was awash with activity. Barrels of goods were being rolled up the gangway to the empress's flagship, the *Siren*. Horses were corralled at the wharf, ready to be led aboard. It appeared that Celestine herself was preparing to set sail. Lyss debated whether this was good news or bad news. If Celestine sailed away, she would escape an attack on the city. Once under way, however, she would be a sitting duck on the Indio. And an attack on Celesgarde would be a lot less risky in her absence.

Lyss was so focused on redrawing plans in her head that she didn't notice the lamplight leaking from beneath the door to her rooms. She entered, closed and locked the door, then turned and saw that somebody was sitting in the chair by the hearth, the light from the flames reflecting off the goblet in her hand and the ropes of gemstones around her neck.

"Empress!" Lyss said, tasting fear like rust on her tongue. "I— You're up early."

"And you're out late, General Gray," Celestine said. "Or, should I say, 'Your Highness'?"

Lyss's heart stuttered, then began to hammer so hard that it seemed it would crack her ribs. "I—I don't know what you mean, Your Eminence. I couldn't sleep, so I—"

"Sit down, Princess," the empress said, gesturing to the opposite chair. "The time for games is over."

For a moment, Lyss stood frozen, as a dozen frantic schemes slid through her mind, each pushed aside by common sense. Then she swallowed hard and sat, chin up, her hands on her knees, and waited.

Celestine studied her with her unnerving amethyst eyes. "Before we begin, I am dying to know—what did you do with poor Bosley?"

"Bosley?" Lyss waited one heartbeat, two, while the implications of that question sank in. "I pushed him off a cliff," she said. Wetting her finger, she rubbed blood from a scratch on her arm.

This empress feasts on fear, she thought. Don't give her that satisfaction.

Celestine laughed. "He was an insufferable prick," she said, "but an excellent source of information. We talked for hours. I learned so much before he went missing."

"I should have cut his throat the night he arrived," Lyss said.

"Why didn't you?"

"Because I preferred to push him off a cliff," Lyss said. "And now, every night, I return to that spot and piss off the edge."

"I wondered where you went every night," Celestine said. "I thought maybe you had a secret lover."

Use your anger, Lyss thought. You won't get home if the empress sees you quake and sweat.

Show no fear.

Lyss conjured up a memory of Bosley rising into the air in Cas's grip, arms and legs flailing, spilling shit and spittle, an expression of absolute terror on his face. She imagined killing him again in other, even more creative ways.

"Ah," the empress said, with a grudging nod. "I can see the wolf in you now."

"How long have you known?"

"From the day your wetland officers arrived," Celestine said. "Bosley was so pitifully eager to get into my good graces, especially when it meant destroying you." She paused. "Why did he hate you so much?"

Lyss thought of what she'd said to Jenna the night they met. *Because he has the talent of a turd floating in an ego the size of the ocean.* "It's a long story," she said. "Not worth the time it would take to tell it." She decided to leave it at that. "So. You've known who I am for quite a while. Why didn't you confront me before now?"

"To be honest, I hadn't decided what to do with you. By

the time Bosley came, I already knew what an asset you'd be to our military efforts. I decided to let you continue to train the bloodsworn, with the idea of using you as leverage when we sailed to the wetlands. Now we're ready to sail, and my officers still don't have the capacity to lead a major military operation."

"Well," Lyss said, "training takes time. Give me another six months to a year, and I think you'll see progress."

"Unfortunately, I don't have six months to a year," the empress said.

"That's too bad," Lyss said. "Does this mean that you'll lead your armies yourself?"

Celestine shook her head. "At sea, perhaps, and on land, from time to time. But my empire requires tending, and I have important business to take care of here in the islands at midsummer. That's why I recruited you. As I said, I needed a commander with experience in land battles."

Lyss's usual impatience was surfacing. Get to the point, you sadistic, gutter-swiving crow.

Celestine poured herself some more wine, then thrust the decanter toward Lyss. "Would you care for some?"

"No, thank you," Lyss said.

The empress laughed. "Are you afraid I will poison you? Or add you to the bloodsworn?"

"Why don't you tell me what you plan to do with me and save us both some time?" Lyss said. "I'm not going to sit here and guess."

"Not even if it means you will live a little longer?" The steel was back in the empress's voice.

Lyss lifted her chin. "I'll do what it takes to survive. Why don't you tell me what that is."

"I'll add you to the bloodsworn if I have no other choice," the empress said. "I could hold you hostage to force the Fells to submit, but it seems that no one is left to redeem you."

Lyss tried to maintain an expression of indifference. "Is that so?"

"Your mother the queen is dead," Celestine said. She seemed to be watching for a reaction.

Lyss tightened her hands on the arms of the chair, hardening her face into a blank mask. "Really," she said through stiff lips. "I'd not heard that. What happened?"

"She was poisoned," Celestine said.

Once again, Lyss stood waist-deep in a sea of wolves on that terrace overlooking the sea. Hanalea and Althea were telling her that her mother had been poisoned, that the Line was broken, that she was now queen.

If her mother was dead, that meant that she was the last survivor of her family, the only one left in the true line. The last of the star-crossed Alisters. Her father, her sister, her brother, and now her mother had been taken from her by this damnable war.

But the wolf queens had also said that her mother was alive. Had they lied in order to prevent her from succumbing to grief? Or had her mother died since their conversation on the terrace?

Was Celestine trying to trick her into leading a fight against her own people?

That last theory seemed most likely.

"Alyssa."

Startled, Lyss looked up to find the empress gazing at her with an expression of deep sympathy, her eyes brimming with tears. "I'm so sorry about your mother," she said, reaching out and touching her arm. "There is no bond like that between mother and daughter."

Any conversation with the empress was like a series of zigzag ambushes.

Playing for time, Lyss said, "Your sources—did they say who poisoned her?"

Celestine shook her head. "The last I heard, there was a proposal to put your aunt or your cousin on the throne."

"Who?" Lyss's mind went blank.

"Your mother's sister, Mellony. And your cousin, Julianna. She would be the heir after your aunt."

Aunt Mellony, who hadn't displayed an ounce of ambition in Lyss's lifetime? Still, people said that she had conspired with Micah Bayar to claim the Gray Wolf throne years ago. Julianna? Sweet, clever, agile Julianna, who'd put the last nail in the coffin of Lyss's crush on Finn? Who, perhaps by now, had married him?

"However, her rule might be short-lived. King Jarat is marching north with his army, meaning to add the final jewel to his emperor's crown."

Lyss's stubborn defiance was crumbling, eroding into despair. Maybe she would be better off staying here and letting the jackals fight over the carcass of the Seven Realms.

She looked up, startled, as Celestine gripped both her hands. "They killed my mother, too. That's what drives me. They killed my mother and stole my legacy, and I'm determined to get it back."

"The queendom is not your legacy," Lyss blurted. "It's mine."

"And so it can be," Celestine said. "It depends on you. You see, it's not all bad news."

It took a moment for that to register. "What—what do you mean?"

"It's about your brother."

"My brother?" By now, Lyss's mind was circling like a kettle of vultures.

"Here." Celestine pushed a velvet pouch across the table toward Lyss.

Lyss rested her hand on it. "What's this?"

"Open it up and see."

Lyss undid the cord at the neck of the pouch and dumped the contents into her hand.

She stared, speechless. It was her father's serpent amulet. She hadn't seen it since the day he'd died in the street and it disappeared, along with her brother.

It lit up, illuminating the entire room.

"My agents met with your brother in Tarvos a few weeks ago."

"I—I don't understand," Lyss said, running her fingers over the elaborate carving. "What would . . ." She stopped, gathered her thoughts, realizing that the empress might be fishing for information. "What makes you think I have a brother?"

Celestine's face hardened. "Don't waste my time, Alyssa," she said. "Your brother's name is Adrian: he's a wetland mage, two years older than you, and he came to Tarvos looking for you." She paused, then said impatiently, "I thought this news would please you."

"I—it does," Lyss said. "Or . . . it would. But—my brother is dead. What makes you think this—this person you found is my brother?"

"He told us all about you," Celestine said. "He wanted to

strike a deal. He offered a ransom in return for your freedom. He sent this pendant as a token. He said that you would recognize it."

"Why didn't he come himself?"

"I've sent Captain Samara to fetch him."

Lyss closed her fingers over the amulet. "Adrian . . . is coming here?"

Celestine nodded, smiling. "He is."

Hope rose in Lyss like a full-moon tide. She tried to ignore the voice that said, That's how they get you—hope. That's how they break your heart.

Ash had come to the Desert Coast to find her. And now—he was walking into a trap set by Celestine with Lyss as bait. Lyss pressed her fingers into her forehead. "When—when do you expect him to arrive?"

"It should be within the week," Celestine said. Then drove the blade home. "Unfortunately, we're leaving before he arrives."

Lyss looked up and met the empress's eyes. "What do you mean?"

"So here is the offer I make to you. You lead my army to the wetlands, and you drive the southerners into the sea. Retake your legacy, and you and your brother can rule the northern queendom on my behalf." She paused, having offered the carrot, then followed with the stick. "Disappoint me, and I will burn your brother alive before your eyes. Then I will add you to my bloodsworn army."

# 29

# NIGHT VISITOR

For hours, Evan had lain flat on his back, unable to twitch a finger. The only thing that continued to work was his mind—racing from one implausible escape scheme to another, segueing to one horrible fate after another.

If I escape this, I'll never, never, never trust a shiplord.

The shiplords had carried him from the gallery into a plain stone chamber with windows overlooking the sea. He listened as they fed his stormborn a story that his wetland guests had poisoned him. After that, the blood-bound came and went, bathing him and turning him under the watchful eyes of the shiplords. First Jagger, then Riggs, and now, tonight, it was Jasmina. Evan wondered what had happened to Sangway, the other mastermind.

Destin's amulet still rested, hot against his skin, primed with power, but it might as well have been at the bottom of the sea. Amulets were not recognized on this side of the Indio, else they'd never have left it with him.

He made a mental note—if you survive this, always carry poison. Though the simple act of getting it to his mouth would be as impossible as reaching his amulet. He managed to occupy himself for some time with devising ways around that problem should he survive long enough to try to kill himself again. For instance, he'd heard of assassins and spies who wore hollow teeth full of poison they could bite down on in a pinch.

He'd be constantly worried that he'd bite down on it by accident. It might be worth the risk if it meant that he could slip through the empress's fingers.

Where were Prince Adrian and Talbot? Dead, probably, unless, for some reason, the empress had given orders to keep them alive. Poor Helesa was dead, and he assumed Kel was, too.

The stormborn wept to see him so helpless, massaged his limbs, stroked his face, changed his linens, cursed the wetlanders for their betrayal. There were times that Evan felt like he would burst, the truth spattering over them like pus from a ruptured boil. But, of course, that didn't happen, and they finally left when they could find no more excuses to stay.

For a time after the bloodsworn left, Jasmina stood, staring out of the window, hands clasped behind her back, like a figurehead on a ship. Finally, she turned away from the window, crossed the room, and sat on the edge of his bed.

What now? Evan thought.

She leaned down toward him so that their noses were inches apart. "Listen to me, Stormlord. You know, and I know, that Jagger is a fool to trust Celestine. Once she gets hold of you, we are done." She drew her blade and touched it to the tip of his nose. "I could kill you, and that would keep you out of Celestine's hands, but then you'd be gone, and with you our protection, and she would be looking for revenge and so would Jagger. I'd probably have to kill him if the empress doesn't get to us first."

She paused, as if waiting for a reply, but of course that didn't come.

"So, as you can see, it's a problem."

Try as he might, Evan couldn't conjure much sympathy for Jasmina and her problem. Especially since her blade was still pricking his skin.

Evan heard footsteps in the corridor outside, rapidly approaching. Jasmina must have heard them, too, because she swore softly and put the blade up. Sliding her hands under his neck, she lifted the chain holding Destin's amulet over his head, leaving behind the pendant his father had given him. She tucked the amulet into her pocket and stood, crossing to the window and sitting on the sill.

Jagger banged the door open and then stood in the entrance, looking from Evan to Jasmina. "Is everything all right?" he said.

"I hope that you're here to relieve me before I die of boredom," Jasmina said. "It's like babysitting a corpse." She slid from the sill, her boots hitting the stone floor with a *thump*. "Are the wetlanders more entertaining? I'm going to go find out."

"Leave them alone, Jasmina," Jagger said. "The empress made it clear that she wants them alive and untouched."

"Don't worry," Jasmina said, her hand caressing the hilt of her knife. "I won't damage them very much."

"I mean it," Jagger said. "Find something else to do. Everything is riding on this."

"Fine. I'll call in my crew and sail on the evening tide tomorrow."

"No," Jagger said. "I don't want anyone leaving the harbor until we receive instructions from the empress."

"And when will that be?"

"Sangway set sail early yesterday. It might be a few days or a week."

"Already kissing the empress's ass, are you? Well, I'm not going to sit around here for another week. I've got to make up for lost time. You're not the harbormaster yet, and neither is she. I'll do as I please." Jasmina strode past him, but Jagger gripped her arm and yanked her toward him. The next thing Evan knew they were wrestling on the floor, punching and kicking.

He wished he could turn his head so he could get a better view. Eventually, the fight ended, apparently badly for Jasmina. She stood, her eye rapidly purpling, sucking in her breath in ragged sobs. They sounded like the angry kind, not the sorry kind.

That was confirmed by her parting words. "I get it now. You're hoping to be Celestine's new favorite. Wait until you find out what happens to her favorites when she tires of them."

She banged out the door.

"That girl is going to be the death of me," Jagger muttered.

God willing, Evan thought.

The cage could have been worse, Ash thought, based on the name. It was small—probably eight by eight, with a straw pallet and a chamber pot. It had one barred window, not large enough to climb through, and too high to reach anyway. The heavy iron door let out onto a gallery overlooking a small exercise yard. It wasn't a dank, wet dungeon, deep underground, like the kind he'd experienced in Ardenscourt. Maybe because there weren't many dank, wet places in Carthis.

At the base of the door was a small slot through which meals were served, and dishes and chamber pots returned. Ash didn't even get a good look at the person or persons who were coming and going. He tried calling to them when he heard movement in the corridors, but there was no answer. The shiplords were taking no chances.

Sasha was locked up next door. Though the walls were thick, they could converse by speaking out their windows, but of course there was no way of knowing who else was listening.

That first night, Sasha said, "Do you think Strangward is dead?"

"I doubt it. His stormborn would have torn us to pieces if he were."

"Maybe the shiplords intend to turn him over to the empress, and tell the stormborn he died, and blame us. *Then* they'll tear us to pieces."

"Anything's possible, but I don't think so. They would have just killed us right away."

"I think you're right," Sasha said quickly. "Remember, Jagger took your amulet and said that he needed it as a token for the empress." She paused. "Do you think he took it because it was fancy, or do you think the empress is looking for us, specifically?"

In other words, did she know all along they were coming? Had they been betrayed?

That was Sasha—always walking the dark alley of despair.

Speaking of despair, Ash mourned the loss of his father's amulet with a visceral kind of grief. He'd worn it almost continuously since that day in Ragmarket when Han's death had launched him south, into enemy territory. At first, it had been his only legacy from his father. Since they'd connected in

Aediion, it had become so much more.

And, of course, it was an heirloom—it had been made for his many-greats-grandfather Alger Waterlow, notorious through the generations as the Demon King, who broke the world.

He'd held history in his hands, perhaps the key to the survival of the Gray Wolf line, and he'd let it slip through his fingers.

After that, Ash and Sasha mostly restricted their conversations to "Are you awake?" and "What did you get for breakfast?" The last question was unnecessary, really, because it was always flatbread, fruit, and tay for breakfast, and flatbread, fruit, fish, and tay for other meals. Plus olives sometimes.

Still, the questions kept coming, whether spoken aloud or not. Why would Celestine want them alive? They'd never met—he'd been in Arden for years, and most people in the Fells still thought he was dead. Did she think he and Strangward were friends, and intend to use that connection somehow?

You might be disappointed, he thought. *Friend* is a strong word for what's between us.

And yet—their present predicament proved that much of what Strangward had said was true. That he wasn't working for the empress, that he was doing everything he could to stop her, that he'd come to Fellsmarch for that purpose.

That when he'd said he'd come to Ardenscourt to help Jenna, he was telling the truth. If Jenna was still alive, he'd succeeded. Awkwardly, badly, maybe—but still.

Maybe you need to find a way to save Strangward, thought Ash, so he can save Lyss.

Or maybe they needed to learn to work together.

How long did they have? How soon would Celestine come? Or would she come at all?

Where was Strangward? Was he already on his way to the empress?

One night, when Ash had just rolled up in his blanket for sleep, he heard movement in the corridor that was more stealthy than usual. It was long past time for supper, and their dishes had already been collected.

Was it the stormborn, there to avenge the stormlord? Celestine's minions, there to drag them into the presence of the empress?

The steps paused outside his cell. Moments later, he heard someone fitting a key into the lock, the *click* of the tumblers. The door eased open.

It was Jasmina, looking like she'd just come from a vicious street fight. One eye was all but swollen shut, her lip was fat, and a trickle of blood had dried at the corner of her mouth. She scanned the tiny cell with her good eye. "Where's the other wetlander?" she hissed.

"Next door." Ash eyed the shiplord, measuring the distance between them. Even without an amulet, if he could get his hands on her—

"Stop giving me the side eye," she snapped. "I earned these bruises getting hold of the keys to your cells. Show a little appreciation and gather your things."

"Where are we going?"

"I'm going to help you escape."

Ash hesitated. Was this going to be one of those killed-while-escaping schemes? It didn't make sense, though. It was not as if the shiplords answered to anyone, now that Strangward was down.

"Here," she said, pulling something out of her breeches

pocket and tossing it at him so that he reflexively caught it with both hands. It was Strangward's odd-looking amulet, the one that looked like a small mechanical device. It greeted him, lighting up in his hands. Did that mean that Strangward had died, or—?

"Will that work for you?"

"I think so, but—"

"Try it out. I'm going to go free your giant friend." Jasmina was out the door again.

She must be serious, Ash thought. Otherwise she wouldn't have handed me an amulet. Assuming it actually works.

Hinges squealed outside as Sasha's door swung open, and he could hear their low voices in the corridor.

He needed to test Strangward's amulet in a non-flashy, non-noisy way. He gripped the device, feeling the welcome current of flash. Would the stormlord's magic be different from his own? For instance, would he be able to make weather now?

It appeared to be clan-made, like any other flashcraft. It must have come from the Realms originally.

Best to start with something familiar. Working quickly, Ash draped a translucent barrier over the doorway. Just as he finished, Sasha came barreling around the corner and all but bounced off it.

"Scummer in the gutter," she swore, just managing to keep her feet.

"Sorry." Ash quickly dismantled his magical wall. "It works," he said to Jasmina.

"Good. You're going to have to fetch the stormlord while I ready the ships."

Hope kindled within Ash. "Strangward is still alive?"

"He's alive, but Jagger's kept him drugged up so he can't move a muscle. Sangway's sailed for the Northern Islands to notify the empress. She could be here in a few days." The shiplord handed Sasha a rough sketch of the palace. "Strangward's being kept here." She pointed. "One of the shiplords will be guarding him—I don't know who. You'll need to kill the guard and carry Strangward down to that little ketch of his. Kel should be down there waiting. He'll be able to get you out of the harbor."

"Where will you be?"

"I'm going to create a bit of a distraction," Jasmina said.

Ash knew time was wasting, but he couldn't help himself. "Why are you doing this?"

"Because I don't like taking orders from fools, and Jagger is a fool if he thinks he can trust Celestine. Strangward may be a will-o'-the-wisp, but he's always kept his word to us. Jagger's the one breaking the bargain. I'm the one keeping it."

# BEARERS OF BAD NEWS

Since it seemed that Lila and Shadow had been sentenced to serve an indefinite term in the capital of Fellsmarch, Shadow set up his foundry in the courtyard of Kendall House, so that he could continue to make flashcraft and weapons for the army in the east. It was probably the first flashcraft made outside the camps in the uplands. Clan technique was a closely guarded secret.

Lila had been dealing Shadow's work to the Ardenine Empire for more than a year, but she'd never seen much of the actual process. It was a mingle of blacksmithing, ironworking, leatherwork, and jewelry-making. Along with a dash of upland magic.

Lila began helping Shadow to keep her mind off what might be going on to the east and down to the south. There was nothing like hammering iron and stone to work off frustration. It also kept her out of the taverns and gambling halls.

To begin with, Shadow allowed her to do only the simplest jobs—the ones that cost the least in time and materials if they went wrong. Gradually, though, he gave her more and more complicated tasks.

Even here in the north, it was hot work. At day's end, they both stank of charcoal, sweat, and metal. Then it was into the bath, a quick supper, and to bed, where Lila, at least, slept like a corpse.

It was strange to be doing such physical work in such a fancy setting. It was as if Shadow had set up a blacksmith's forge in somebody's elegant dining room.

The smell and heat and noise of metalworking at all hours served to discourage other palace guests from lodging at Kendall House. So, most of the time, Lila and Shadow had the guesthouse to themselves.

Shadow worked at a relentless pace, producing racks of blades of all sizes, dozens of the special collars he'd devised, along with the serviceable talismans they provided to soldiers in the field. At least, in the foundry, they could count up what they'd accomplished at the end of the day. In that, it was a refreshing change from their other job, which was politics.

Late one afternoon, Lila slid the tray of flasks into the kiln and shut the heavy door, turning her face away from the searing heat. Her skin already stung like she'd been out in the sun too long. Hot as it was, it would take just a few minutes for the burnout. When the molds were clear of wax, she'd set them on the rack by the centrifuge so they would cool slowly. Meanwhile, Shadow would melt gold, silver, copper—whatever material he was using that day—in a crucible. When it reached the right temperature and fluidity, he poured it into the centrifuge, which flung the metal into the molds, filling every nook and crevice.

Shadow had stripped to his waist, but sweat still gilded every rugged hill and valley of his back and shoulders, running down his face and between his shoulder blades. Sometimes Lila simply stood and watched as he swung his hammer, bending metal and magic to his will.

He was well worth watching.

Lila had tied her mass of curls back with a scarf, and guessed she probably looked like her aunt Jazz after a day at sea.

Lila couldn't help wondering if they were wasting their time. Arden was one thing. But she'd seen what had happened in the villages of the coast. What good would a talisman do against an enemy that used brute, fearless, relentless force instead of magic?

Speaking of Arden, Lila wondered if the Matelons had received her message about the collars. This project had begun in an effort to free Gerard Montaigne's collared mages. Now that the empress was their most dangerous enemy, she hoped that helping the rebels in Arden's civil war would lead to a quicker cease-fire.

Lila lifted a mold from the cooling rack and plunged it into the quenching trough. Steam hissed up into her face as the investment crumbled away.

She had swiveled to set it on Shadow's worktable when she noticed that he'd stopped working to watch Lieutenant Ruby Greenholt sprinting toward them across the courtyard. Since the departure of Queen Raisa and Byrne, Greenholt had become their liaison with the queen's Gray Wolf guard.

Sprinting bluejackets never bring good news, Lila thought. Good news tiptoes in sheepishly, while bad news charges at you, howling.

"Pardon me," Greenholt said breathlessly. "Lady Barrett sent me to fetch you, to tell you that there's an emergency meeting of the queen's council. There is news about Captain Gray."

Lila and Shadow looked at each other. "When is the meeting?"

"It's happening right now," Ruby said. "In the library."

They were sweaty and dirty from hours at the foundry, but they followed Ruby across the close to the coachmen's entrance of the palace.

It was bedlam inside the library, with council members milling around, firing questions at two travel-worn newcomers they had backed up against the wall.

Shadow leaned in close to Lila's ear. "Finn sul'Mander and Hadley DeVilliers," he whispered. "Both wizards. Finn fought with the Highlanders for several years. DeVilliers is commander of our navy. They were on the team that went to rescue the princess heir."

Sul'Mander was handsome in an ethereal sort of way. He looked like the next of kin at a wake, someone who intended to follow the deceased to the other side. DeVilliers resembled the chance child of a street busker and a pirate.

Lady Mander was planted next to her son, practically showing her teeth in an attempt to drive away the wolves. Lady Barrett was on his other side, holding his hand. Lord Vega hovered, as if ready to step into the breach. DeVilliers stood to one side, unattended. Her expression said that she wished she could be anywhere else. She didn't seem the sort who'd be easily flustered or intimidated, but she looked to be both of those things right now.

Scummer, Lila thought. Couldn't we get some good news for a change?

Finally, Barrett interposed herself between the council and

the besieged. "I would ask you to hold your questions until Queen Raisa arrives, so that they only have to tell this story once."

"Queen Raisa isn't coming," Greenholt said.

That landed like a cannonball in the duck pond.

"The queen's not coming?" DeVilliers's expression shifted from distressed to alarmed.

Mellony looked as unhappy as the naval commander. "What do you mean? She *has* to be here."

That hit Lila's ear wrong. It was as if Mellony had planned a party and Raisa stayed home.

"Captain Byrne is afraid that bad news might undermine the progress Her Majesty has made over these weeks. He has asked me to take careful notes and report back to him."

"That is unacceptable," Princess Mellony said. "Captain Byrne should not be making these decisions, excluding the queen's family and chosen council. Raisa should not be going through this alone."

"Captain Byrne is bound to serve the queendom and the Line, Your Highness," Speaker Jemson said. "He cannot do otherwise. If that is his decision, we can assume that it's an honest one, and in the queen's best interest."

Princess Mellony opened her mouth to respond, but Lady Barrett held up her hand. "Please, Mother. Everyone else is here. Could we sit down and hear what Finn and Hadley have to say?" She was usually pale, but right now she looked positively ashen.

"Lady Barrett is right," Micah Bayar said. "This is getting us nowhere." He pulled out a chair and sat.

Everyone else followed suit.

"First, let me emphasize that anything said in this room must be kept confidential, for the good of the queendom and the safety of the Line," Barrett said. "Some of you already know that Her Highness Alyssa Gray was in Chalk Cliffs when it fell to Empress Celestine. We have evidence that she may have been carried off to the Northern Islands as a prisoner of the empress. A small team was organized to attempt a rescue. Members included Captain DeVilliers, Finn sul'Mander, Captain Sasha Talbot, and Prince Adrian sul'Han."

This was met with a storm of consternation.

"You sent Prince Adrian to Carthis?" Lord Fenwaeter said. "After he'd just come back from the dead?"

"I didn't send Prince Adrian anywhere," Barrett said, a little testily. "This was Prince Adrian's mission from the beginning. Everyone else volunteered."

"Why wasn't the council consulted?" Lord Howard said. "It seems to me that in a matter this important, we should have been involved."

Because this council leaks like a sieve, Lila thought. Because someone on this council poisoned the queen.

"It was critical that the operation be kept a secret," Barrett said. "It's very possible that the empress does not know Alyssa's identity, and we wanted to keep it that way. The only people who knew were those who were directly involved."

And you, Lila guessed.

Barrett paused, as if waiting for further argument, but there was none. "Now," she said, "who wants to begin?"

Finn shook his head, looking down at his hands.

"I'll tell you the short of it," DeVilliers said. "We were sailing off Deepwater Court, when—"

"Deepwater Court?" Lord Howard said. "Where is that?"

"The northern coast of Carthis. We were on our way to the Northern Islands, where we thought Lyss was being held—"

"But you didn't know for sure?" Lord Bayar said, glancing at Finn sul'Mander. The young wizard avoided his uncle's gaze.

"No," DeVilliers said. "We didn't know for sure. We came under attack by a Carthian vessel, and took a direct hit to the stern." DeVilliers stopped, cleared her throat. "Finn and I launched one of the jolly boats when it was clear we couldn't save her. She went down in a matter of minutes."

"What about Adrian and Sasha?" Barrett looked from Finn to DeVilliers.

DeVilliers shook her head. "Ash and Sasha were aft when *Sea Wolf* was hit. There was no sign of them after. As far as we know, we were the only survivors."

*The princeling is gone?* Lila thought, stunned. *After I spent all that time nannying him?* It hit her unexpectedly hard. As she looked around the table, expressions ranged from dismay to horror.

"What about the pirates?" Fenwaeter said. "Didn't they come after you?"

"We'd already taken out their mainmast," DeVilliers said. "We were pulling away under full canvas when we were hit. By the time we went down, they were nowhere in sight."

Lila didn't know DeVilliers, not really, but the story seemed incomplete, somehow, or maybe skeletal, like she'd left out important details. She glanced over at Shadow, and he was gazing at the ship's master, frowning, rubbing his chin.

"How did you get back?" Barrett kept looking at Finn, as if she expected him to contribute, but he said nothing.

"We swam to shore in a cove near Deepwater Court," DeVilliers said. "We stole a fishing boat, a two-master that I figured wouldn't draw too much attention. We hugged the coast nearly all the way to Endru before we turned west." She paused. "We were lucky, if you can call any part of this lucky."

"And so—we are no closer to rescuing Princess Alyssa," Bayar said, looking even gloomier than usual.

DeVilliers shook her head. "We'd hoped that Sasha could help us locate her. Now Sasha's gone, and we don't know where she is, or if she's even still alive."

"Captain Byrne says she's still alive," Shadow said. "He says that he would know if she were dead."

"It would be wonderful if Captain Byrne were here to speak for himself," Lord Vega said. "We keep hearing about this mysterious bond between the Byrnes and the Gray Wolf line. I can't help thinking that the nature of the bond is more of the flesh and less of the spirit."

It was as if some rogue demon gripped Lila by the scruff of her neck and dragged her to her feet. "It would be wonderful if you would shut up about things you know nothing about," she said. "Not only wonderful, but wise."

Vega stared at Lila as if she were a gnat buzzing around his head that had suddenly drawn blood.

Before he could respond, Barrett intervened. "Your comment was inappropriate, Lord Vega," she said. "Tempers are running hot, but I'll ask you to keep a civil tongue and leave rumor and innuendo outside this chamber." She turned to Lila. "Sit down, please, Lady Byrne."

Not until he takes it back, Lila wanted to say, like it was a schoolyard squabble. But she sat down, aware that Shadow was looking at her with mingled astonishment and awe.

"My point is that we have a queen in very ill health, and a missing princess heir," Vega said. "The queen's other children are already dead."

"That is an incredible streak of bad luck," Bayar said. "I can't help but think of our neighbors to the south—the Montaignes. Poor Prince Gerard lost his brothers, one by one, until there was only him."

"Explain yourself, Bayar," Vega said, bristling.

"Merely an observation," Bayar said. "You were saying?"

"We need to do something quickly to secure the royal succession," Vega said.

"I agree," Lady Mander said. "We are a heartbeat away from chaos, and we are fighting a war on two fronts."

"Shall we assume that you have a proposal?" Lord Fenwaeter said.

"Princess Mellony is next in line for the throne, after Alyssa," Lady Mander said. "Wouldn't it make sense to name her officially as the successor to Alyssa, in the event that—that, heaven forbid, Alyssa is dead?"

Mellony held up both hands, palms out. "I appreciate your confidence in me, but I've never been well suited for politics, especially as it's practiced today. It's premature to be moving forward with this as long as there is a possibility that Alyssa is alive. The succession is, understandably, a sensitive subject for Raisa."

What's that supposed to mean? Lila thought.

"Sensitive or not, it must be addressed," Lady Mander said. "In the meantime, it would be sensible for you to step in as regent while our queen is incapacitated. I believe the queen is making decisions with her heart and not her head."

"The queen is not incapacitated!" Bayar practically shouted. "She was here, in this chamber, a scant few days ago. I have learned over the years to believe in our queen, and not to count her out too quickly."

"It's not a matter of counting her out," Lord Vega said. "It's a matter of—"

"I would also say that it's too soon to count out Meadowlark," Shadow said. "I have known the princess heir since we were children together. I have fought beside her on the battlefield, and I can tell you this—against all odds, she will find a way to win. If she is held captive, she will escape, and she will return to us if she has to swim across the Indio."

"Which will be supremely difficult if she's dead," Lady Mander said.

Shadow ignored this. "If General Dunedain and Shilo Trailblazer and others were here instead of fighting for the queendom, they would say the same. I mean no disrespect to Princess Mellony, but Lyss is the queen we need right now."

"I would agree, if she were here," Lady Mander said. "I move that we name Princess Mellony as regent for Queen Raisa until she is able to return to her regular duties, or until Princess Alyssa returns home."

"I second that motion," Lord Vega said.

Again, the council dissolved into an uproar.

Lila had a nose for conspiracy, and she'd caught the scent of it now. How had they so quickly segued into a vote about appointing a regent?

"That's not our decision to make, while the queen still lives," Barrett protested, "especially when the queen has made her position clear." But when the vote was taken, she voted for it. The motion passed, six to four.

Mellony shoved back her chair and stood. "I will serve as regent for Raisa in her absence," she said, "since that is the decision of the council. But when it comes to the succession, my daughter, Julianna, would be a much better choice than me."

Now all eyes turned to Barrett, who flushed under the scrutiny.

Vega nodded. "I see your point. One could argue that Julianna has broader experience than Princess Alyssa, given that she has been presiding over this council since the queen's illness and has served this government in both intelligence and diplomatic roles. Princess Alyssa has demonstrated considerable talents as a military commander, but she has spent little time in any official capacity at court."

"That's just wrong," Barrett said. "It's unfair to compare me with Alyssa. It's not like we're competing for the job. She is the heir to the Gray Wolf throne, not me. We have much more important issues to consider."

"We do have important issues to consider," Lord Howard said, "which is why we need leadership. Lady Barrett has been leading us in the absence of those in the direct line. Why not make it official?"

"It seems to me," Lord Fenwaeter said, "that we should address the issue of the succession as well as the regency. If Princess Mellony wants to step aside for Princess Julianna, why not formalize that now, so that there is no confusion if the worst happens?"

"In essence," Bayar said, "Lady Barrett would be next in the succession *after* Princess Alyssa? Replacing Princess Mellony?"

"Precisely," Lady Mander said.

"The queen should be involved in decisions about the succession," Bayar said.

"The queen appointed two representatives," Vega said, gesturing toward Lila and Shadow. "Isn't that why they're here? Because she is not?"

Everyone looked at Lila and Shadow.

I knew this would happen, Lila thought.

"I don't see why we have to make a decision right now," Shadow said. He turned to Jemson. "Speaker Jemson, does this even fit with canon law?"

"Canon law does not speak to this specifically," Jemson said. "However, bear in mind that Lady Barrett would also stand behind any blood issue of Queen Raisa or Alyssa ana'Raisa, heirs to the Gray Wolf line."

"So the only thing that changes is that Lady Barrett steps in front of Princess Mellony when it comes to the succession," Vega said.

"Is that a motion?" Lady Mander said. "If so, I second it."

That motion passed, six to four. Shadow, Lila, Bayar, and Jemson voted against it. Lila's vote sprang less from principle and more because she didn't like the smell of it.

Lila caught Shadow's eye. *What is going on?* It was like they were actors in a play, and everyone had a script but them.

"In light of these decisions," Lady Mander said, "I suggest that we move forward with the marriage between Princess Julianna and Finn as soon as possible. We had hoped that Princess Alyssa and Prince Adrian could attend, but it seems that cannot happen. In these uncertain times, I don't believe it is wise to wait. Their children will strengthen and protect the succession."

Hang on, Lila thought. We've already added Finn and Julianna's unborn children to the Line?

Finn's head came up, and he gazed at Julianna with a kind of mournful longing, as if she were a bauble on a high shelf that he could never reach. Meanwhile, Captain DeVilliers was staring at Finn as if he were a fortress, and she was trying to devise a plan of attack.

"Lady Mander," Princess Mellony said, "I, too, look forward to seeing our children married, but I think circumstances dictate that we wait until Raisa is well enough to attend the wedding. A lavish celebration at this time seems . . . inappropriate."

We need to talk, Lila thought, meeting Shadow's eyes. We definitely need to talk. And the sooner the better.

# 31

# UP FROM UNDER

Dawn came early this time of year, but Hal was up long before the sun. He and his handpicked crew had been on the move for most of the night. Now they were hunkered down just south of the city walls of Ardenscourt. Just behind them, two companies of his most seasoned soldiers waited to be called forward. The rest of his little army was gathered at Brightstone Keep, awaiting marching orders.

The sky to the east was brightening, so Hal could now make out the silhouettes of sentries on the walls. He could hear their voices, and the soft splatter onto leaves as somebody pissed off the wall. These moments before a battle always got his blood moving.

Stop it, he thought. With any luck, this wouldn't be a battle at all. His mentor, Jan Rives, used to say that the best battles are the ones that never happen.

Hal was glad Bellamy wasn't there, both because they were friends and because Bellamy, with his soldier's sixth sense, might have somehow detected their plan. He knew where Bellamy was—they'd just received word that Delphi had fallen to Jarat's army. The thanes and their armies should be traveling south on the North Road, heading for the capital. Hal meant to have the city secured before they arrived.

Marc DeJardin materialized out of the trees, more a ghost than a mage.

"How'd it go?" Hal whispered, trying to hide his relief. In many ways, DeJardin's mission was the riskiest of all—to seek out collared mages in the city and offer them freedom in exchange for betraying their masters.

DeJardin smiled his crooked smile. "I never saw a more treasonous bunch in my life," he said, holding up the collar key. "After everything the empire has done for them. Shameful."

"Did anyone say no?"

"No," DeJardin said. "They'll make sure the gate is open, too. And here." He pressed a folded paper into Hal's hand. "Here's an up-to-date map of the city, with key locations marked."

Hal grinned. "Have you ever considered a military career, DeJardin?"

The mage shook his head. "Like I said, all I ever wanted was to be a farmer."

Hal called his dozen men together. He'd chosen those who already knew the city well. Some had been serving in the garrison here a scant few weeks ago. They went over the map, and Hal handed each man an assignment and a scarf in Matelon colors, some blazoned with the spreading tree. He hoped that would minimize confusion, since most of his men still wore the dirtback brown of the regular army. As soon as all of the gates were open, his two companies would pour in, followed by the rest of the army.

"I'd like to keep bloodshed to a minimum," Hal said. "Our

mages will barricade the barracks and keep anyone who's still in bed out of the fighting. If you need to lock anyone up, bring them to Newgate. Lock the blackbirds in separate cells, away from the civilians." Based on the intelligence they'd had, the city was garrisoned primarily by the King's Guard. Most regular army members had marched north with Bellamy.

They entered by the postern gate, fanning out across the sleeping city. To the palace, to the barracks, to the walls. Taking out sentries, unlocking some doors and locking others. Hal ran past the ruins of the armory and the Cathedral Temple, both destroyed during the escape with the hostages. Neither had been repaired.

In less than fifteen minutes, the first waves of soldiers were pouring into the city. Hal himself led a company over the drawbridge and into the palace. They went room to room, routing people out of bed and herding them into the great hall on the ground floor. Children were crying, officials were blustering, servants were praying, and many of the citizens were trembling in fear.

Tensions eased somewhat when they realized that they were not under attack by the queen in the north. But only a little.

Hal could hear people whispering to each other. "That's young Matelon, isn't it?"

"It couldn't be. Matelon's dead!"

"Well, he's back from the dead, then. I should know—I danced with him at a party last Solstice."

"Where are *our* mages?"

"It looks like they've all gone over to the rebels."

And so on.

The city was secure in a space of two hours. Hal knew there

might be pockets of loyalists in hiding, but he wasn't interested in ferreting out every last one of them. From what he'd seen, most of the king's supporters were flexible when it came to allegiance. They would see the value of joining the winning side.

Hal went looking for Destin Karn. He still couldn't fathom the spymaster's endgame, but, like it or not, he had saved Hal and Robert—and the hostages—from the king's prisons. Yet Karn was uniformly hated and feared by the rebel thanes, and his life would be forfeit when Hal's father and the others arrived. Karn knew it, too—he'd said as much after the rescue of the hostages. Hal wanted to come up with a plan to protect him, or at least to get him out of town.

Hal headed straight for Newgate, Karn's stronghold in the city, guessing he might be there if he hadn't already fled the city. He found Remy and LeFevre processing prisoners, releasing some and locking up others.

"Has anyone seen Lieutenant Karn?" Hal asked. "Does anyone know where he is?"

Reflexively, LeFevre made the sign of Malthus. "No, I haven't seen him, and I hope I never do."

"If you see him, take away his amulet and keep him secure, but don't harm him," Hal said. "I need to talk to him."

The two officers looked dubious that the spymaster mage could be captured and held by anyone.

"Where are the other blackbirds being held?"

Remy pointed down a corridor. "Their captain's name is Barbeau. He's in the first cell on the left."

Barbeau must have replaced Granger after Harper killed him, Hal thought. It couldn't help but be an improvement. Possibly. Maybe.

Barbeau was another young up-and-comer, from the looks of him. He appeared to be just a few years older than Hal, with thin hair and a permanent shadow of beard.

"Captain Barbeau?" Hal said.

"That's right," Barbeau said. He looked Hal up and down. "You must be young Matelon. I heard you were back from the dead."

"Congratulations on your recent promotion," Hal said, his lady mother's training kicking in. "I'm looking for a colleague of yours. Destin Karn."

"He's not my colleague," Barbeau said quickly. "He doesn't report to me. I don't really have anything to do with him or what he does." Before long, Barbeau would be denying they'd ever met.

"Whatever your relationship," Hal said, gritting his teeth, "do you know where he is?"

"He's gone north," Barbeau said, "to Delphi, I presume. Two days ago."

Hal did not have fond memories of Delphi, scene of his humiliation at the hands of Captain Alyssa Gray. From everything he'd heard, it wasn't a favorite of Lieutenant Karn's, either. "Why would he go there?"

"The king seemed to think that his services would be needed there," Barbeau said. "Either that, or the bastard found out you were coming."

That's Karn, Hal thought. Always two days ahead of any army.

Hal found Robert and Mercier in the great hall. His brother's cheeks were flushed with excitement. "Just think, Hal—the last time we were here we were prisoners! Now we come as conquerors!"

Hal wasn't nearly so excited to be a conqueror. At this point, he saw the capital as an obstacle he had to overcome to reach the more important fight in the north.

"You should speak to these people, Captain," Mercier said, waving at the assemblage, "and put their minds at ease."

"I'm not very good at speeches," Hal said.

"If you tell them you're not going to execute them or imprison them, that will be enough," Mercier said. "That will make you the most popular person in the room, if not the city."

I don't want to be popular, Hal thought. I want to march my army north.

Reluctantly, Hal mounted the dais at the front of the room and stood next to the throne. The last time he'd been there, King Gerard had been sitting on it. It seemed like a lifetime ago.

"Good morning!" he said. "I know it must be frightening to be roused from your bed by an army. But we are not strangers or invaders—we are your countrymen. Many of us were protecting this city just a few weeks ago."

"Then you're traitors!" someone shouted, but was quickly hushed by his neighbors.

"We are not traitors," Hal said. "We are soldiers who know firsthand the cost of war in flesh and blood. We are not afraid to fight to protect our homeland, but we are tired of fighting this endless war in the north in order to avenge a king's wounded pride."

"Liar!" A tall, spare figure forced his way through the crowd into the relatively empty space in front of the dais. "We fight for the True Faith! We fight for the great saint against the demons in the north."

Hal recognized the newcomer as the principia of the Church of Malthus, Cedric Fosnaught.

"We will never stop fighting," Fosnaught shouted, turning and waving his arms to egg on the crowd. This was met with scattered cheers, mingled with a few catcalls.

"Is that so, Father?" Hal said. "I've been fighting this war since I was eleven years old. How much fighting have you personally done?"

The churchman pressed his lips together, then said, "We all fight this war against evil in different ways, my son," he said.

"And you're doing your fighting from a luxurious suite in the Cathedral Temple, and in the gilded rooms in the palace, while eating three full meals a day, am I right?"

"Precisely," Fosnaught retorted, without a trace of shame. "This church needs strong leadership that can speak directly to power in order to keep this empire on a righteous path. We have all made sacrifices to support this holy war."

"Sacrifices that did not include paying the soldiers who are doing the fighting," Hal said. "Soldiers whose families are starving, their fields gone fallow while they risk their lives in the north."

This was met with a rumble of agreement from the gathered citizens and soldiers, and a few shouts of "Hail, Matelon!"

Fosnaught drew himself up. "You must have faith that the Maker will provide, Captain Matelon. Truly, you have been tainted by your time in the north. You'd best repent and look to the fate of your immortal soul. The time will come, in a matter of days or weeks, when you will see what befalls the enemies of the church. You will see the hand of the great saint at work, for the greater glory of King Jarat, the church, and the empire."

Hal had never been impressed by the churchman, but there was something about the threat that sent a shiver down his spine. It was as if Fosnaught had some private knowledge that emboldened him.

Others were not so impressed.

"It's going to be a pretty small empire, seems to me," Robert muttered.

Now there came a chorus of shouts. "Hail, Matelon!" and "King Hal!"

Fosnaught pointed a trembling finger toward where DeJardin was standing with a small group of mages. "Behold the traitor mages!" he thundered. "We gave them a chance to earn a place in the empire and grace in the eyes of the Maker, and you see how we are repaid. You will burn for this, I promise you. We will wipe the scourge of magic from every corner of the Seven Realms."

# DESTINY

At least Evan's prison was open to the sea. The cooling of the air and the changing of the light marked the sliding of one day into another, while the sound of water against stone was constant. Three days he had been lying on his back, awaiting the arrival of Celestine. At first, every tiny sound had yanked him unceremoniously into the present, cold sweat beading on his exposed skin. Now dreams and reality mingled together, and he traveled seamlessly between.

Any hopes of support from one of the other shiplords was dwindling, especially since he was silenced by the poison. They were all committed to this scheme now—they'd cast their lot with Jagger, and there was no going back. His current gaoler, Maig, didn't seem particularly happy about it, but she was the kind of person who expected the worst and was usually right. She sat in one corner, playing nicks and bones with herself.

The sun was setting on the third day, bloodying the walls and ceiling over Evan's head, when something or someone blocked the light that poured in from the terrace. He heard Maig's cry of alarm, cut off abruptly. He smelled the scent of magic, sharp in his nose. He'd never realized that magic had a scent before.

Then the healer's lean face came into view, scowling as usual. His brilliant eyes narrowed as he looked Evan over. "Can you move at all, Strangward?" he whispered.

Evan didn't move, didn't speak, and the healer got the point. Sul'Han leaned closer, and his amulet swung forward into Evan's face, all but hitting him in the nose. Only it was Evan's amulet—the one Destin had given him. The prince was wearing it on a chain around his neck. It seemed that the poison had slowed Evan's mind down, too, because he couldn't puzzle that out—how the healer had come to be wearing Evan's amulet in place of his own.

Sul'Han pressed his hand against Evan's bare chest, gripping the hammer-and-tongs amulet with the other. Evan could feel flash seeping into him like a sweet tonic that left behind a faint euphoria but little else.

"Blood and bones," the healer growled, looking disappointed but not surprised. This time, he closed his warm hands on Evan's shoulders, gritted his teeth, and closed his eyes.

Evan was conscious of the pull of magic, like suction that threatened to turn him inside out. At first, his skin prickled, and then began to burn as if he'd been set on fire. The muscles in his arms and legs jumped and twitched as his brain reconnected to them.

At one point, he developed an excruciating cramp in his calf, but the healer soothed it away, rubbing down his legs from knee to toe. He then massaged his arms and shoulders, using a combination of pressure and magic to quiet his damaged nerves. It was an exquisite kind of exorcism that left his body at peace.

*I have died and gone to heaven*, Evan thought. He licked his lips. He'd never appreciated the ability to lick his lips before.

"Can you hurry it up, Ash? We've got to go." It was Talbot, from the direction of the door.

No, Evan thought. Don't hurry it up. Take all the time you need.

But Prince Adrian moved back to the head of the bed and looked down into Evan's face. "How are you doing?" he said. "If you can manage to stand, we've got to get out of here." The healer was pale, sweating, trembling a little. He looked for all the world like he had a bad hangover.

I guess it was better for me than it was for you, Evan thought. "According to custom here in the drylands," he said, in a nearly normal voice, "we are married now, and you are bound to perform this service every day."

The healer's lips quirked into a rare smile. "Dream on, pirate," he said. Lifting the chain over his head, he restored Destin's amulet to its usual place over Evan's heart.

Talbot took one arm, and the healer the other, and they managed to tip Evan onto his feet. With his arms draped over their shoulders, they hobbled out into the corridor to find a crowd of stormborn milling about, awaiting their next opportunity to visit their ailing master. Evan was happy to see that Kel and Maslin were with them—his two free crew members.

When they saw Evan with the wetlanders, they drew their swords, practically in unison. "Let him go!" Kel said, taking a step toward them.

"The wetlanders are helping me," Evan said, his voice raspy and strange from lack of use. "It was the shiplords who poisoned and betrayed me. They intend to surrender the port of Tarvos to the empress."

"That will never happen," Maslin said grimly. She waved the gathered stormborn forward. "Together, we can kill them all."

"That won't be necessary," Evan said. "I am leaving with the wetlanders. Make sure the shiplords don't follow, that's all. The empress will be here soon. They'll have their own problems when Celestine finds out they have nothing to trade."

Kel looked downcast. "You are leaving, my lord? But . . . you only just came."

"I am leaving," Evan said. "And you should leave, too, before the empress comes."

"We want to go with you," Kel said.

Evan sighed. "You can't go where I'm going," he said.

"But if the empress takes Tarvos, where will we go?" Maslin said. "If we cannot go with you, then why can't we stay here?"

"If Celestine thinks I'm here, she will find a way in," Evan said.

"She will not," Kel said grimly.

"All right," Evan said. "Maslin, I'm putting you in charge of the port. Do you still have the mirror that I gave you the last time?"

The harbormaster nodded.

"Tell the shiplords they can go, or stay and fight with you. But we have to leave. Every minute that passes increases the chance that she'll intercept me." Impulsively, he embraced Kel, and then Maslin. "I'll return to Tarvos if I survive."

"We'll come down with you and open the straits," Kel said.

They took the back stairs to the ground floor of the palace. At first, Maslin and Kel half carried Evan, while Sasha helped the healer. The descent down the hill to the docks seemed to take forever. As they reached the water's edge, Evan heard shouting to the south, along the shoreline.

Jagger and two of his crew stood on the shore, hurling orders at the occupants of a jolly boat that was halfway between the quay and the tall ships anchored in the harbor.

"Get back here, Jasmina," Jagger shouted. "I told you— nobody leaves until the empress arrives."

"And I told you I was leaving," Jasmina shouted back, making a rude gesture. "Say hello to Celestine for me."

Jasmina's crew was already swarming over the decks of the *Scorpion*, making ready to sail.

She's creating a distraction, Evan thought, and we need to take advantage of it.

Kel all but dropped Evan onto the deck of *Destiny*, then leapt after him. He and Maslin dragged Evan aft, propping him between the binnacle and the wheel.

Jasmina had kept her promise to prepare the ketch for sailing, releasing the gaskets from the sails on the masts, replacing broken lines, reefing everything but the mizzen to start. It suited their skeletal crew very well.

"Cast off," Evan said quietly. "I'll give you the wind you need and a bit of a following sea. Maslin, I'll signal you to open the straits. Let Jasmina through, too. Then close the straits and run back to Cliff House. Don't let the shiplords see you if you can help it. They won't be happy."

Maslin nodded, clutching the mirror in her right hand.

*Destiny* eased away from the quay, Sasha and the healer manning the sails, with Evan on the tiller. They still hadn't been spotted, given the spectacle elsewhere in the harbor. Several of Jagger's crew launched their own longboat, pulling hard in an effort to catch up to Jasmina. But she had too much of a head start. As soon as the jolly boat came alongside *Scorpion*, Jasmina scrambled aboard and her crew winched the boat up after.

As Jagger's boarding party approached, *Scorpion*'s gun ports slid open. The message was clear. The jolly boat quickly reversed course. Jagger shouted curses from the quay. Everyone on shore was still focused on that drama.

"Now," Evan said, "shake out the sails and let's see if we can slide through the channel ahead of *Scorpion*."

They picked up speed, making for the straits, keeping *Scorpion* between them and the spectators on shore. Evan closed his eyes, enjoying the snapping of canvas, the rattle of the rigging, the kiss of the sea air on his skin.

"You won't get through the cut, Jasmina!" Jagger shouted. Something glittered in his hand. Evan's heart sank as he realized that Jagger must have taken his mirror while he was incapacitated. "I'm warning you. I'll founder you if I have to."

"Suck scummer in the gutter, Jagger!" Jasmina shouted back. *Scorpion* came about, showing Jagger her stern, and raised more sail.

Blood and bones, Evan thought. We'll have Jagger and Maslin competing for control of the Guardians. This can't end well.

There was no going back. They had to go forward, and hope for the best.

"Shake out the mizzen!" he shouted to his crew. "And hurry, if you don't want to get run over."

*Destiny* leapt forward, spray clearing the gunwales and spattering the varnished deck.

Evan heard shouting from the quay. They'd been spotted. If Jagger hadn't figured it out already, he soon would, given the fact that *Destiny* hadn't stirred from her berth in years. Evan hoped Jagger wouldn't remember the four twenty-four-pound cannon mounted to either side of the channel. With any luck, Jagger would rely on the Guardians to keep them out of the straits.

"More sail!" Evan shouted as *Scorpion* bore down on them. As long as he could keep the bigger ship between *Destiny* and the quay, Jagger couldn't get a clear shot at them. But *Scorpion* was gaining speed, and the straits would not accommodate more than one ship at a time.

Ahead, in the cut, Evan could see the shimmer in the air, the Boil on the surface of the water that said the barriers were in place. Hopefully, Maslin would wait until the very last minute to catch the light with her mirror to open the magical gates so that Jagger couldn't counter it. Timing was everything.

Looking astern, Evan saw that *Scorpion* was gaining on them and would be on top of them before they made the straits. They had no more sail to deploy. Not only that, ships entering the straits always lost momentum when the high cliffs cut off the wind. Being bigger, *Scorpion* had more momentum than they did. They had to give way.

"Hard to starboard!" Evan shouted, pushing the tiller and hoping that by now his novice crew knew what to do with the sails. They leaned, leaned, until the light chop in the harbor was spilling over the gunwales, then righted slightly. They were all but capsized again when *Scorpion* swept by and into the cut.

Coming about, Evan gripped his amulet and pushed wind into the sails of their little ship, driving her forward, eating *Scorpion*'s wake. The bigger ship shuddered, and for a panicked moment Evan thought his worst fears were coming true. Then the waters calmed, the air cleared, and *Scorpion* plowed on, headed for open water.

Their own ship pitched and shook, spinning as the sea began to boil around them. Jagger must be closing the straits. Walls of water rose around them and they plunged down until Evan was sure his keel would hit the sea bottom.

"Hold on!" he shouted. Somehow, he managed to get his feet under him and stood, leaning against the mizzen. Raising both arms, he swept them counter to the whirlpool sucking *Destiny* down. Water dumped onto the decking from all sides as the spinning slowed, then reversed. They were rising again, until they popped above the surface like a cork, landing with a sickening *thwack*. Evan drove wind into the sails, relying on his companions to manage the canvas. As *Destiny* lunged forward, Evan fell backward, cracking his head on the rail. And that was all he remembered.

# BURN THE NEST

At the dying of the day, slanting rays of the sun gilded the top of the volcano, leaving the valleys and ravines shrouded in darkness. And still, Captain Gray did not come.

Jenna had put the finishing touches on Lyssa's armored jacket, and they meant to present it to her on the eve of battle. The dragons had planned a feast to celebrate. They'd carried two goats and a wild boar to the mountaintop and grudgingly consented to roasting one of the goats for Jenna and Lyssa in view of their strange preference for "burnt" meat.

Jenna passed the time by calling up flame from under the ground. On Weeping Sister, flame seethed close to the surface, sometimes spilling forth as lava, steam, and superheated water. She'd discovered she could call it forth, sending pinwheels flying from the cliffs for the dragons to chase. Red, orange, yellow flames, splitting into smaller and smaller orbs. It was like their own private Solstice fireworks display.

That distracted them for a while, but they always came back to who was missing.

Cas kept bulling his way into Jenna's mind, always asking the same question. *Where is she?*

"She'll come, Cas," Jenna said for the hundredth time. "She said she would, and she will."

The days were getting longer as they approached the summer solstice. So it was late when full darkness fell, and still, there was no sign of Lyssa Wolf.

All of the dragons were restless, abruptly rolling off the ledge, unfurling their wings, and soaring off the mountain, their scales glittering in the remnants of sunlight, creating pinwheels of their own. Slayer was the worst. He'd never been known for his patience. Now he resembled an immense terrier, somersaulting off the edge, circling around, stooping down on them from high above, changing direction at the last minute to avoid smashing them into the rock. Cas finally lost his patience and chased the young dragon nearly all the way to the Boil before he turned back.

Jenna knew that hunger was making the dragons cranky. She gestured to the food, laid out on the ledge like an offering to neglectful gods. "Go ahead and eat. I know you're hungry."

And so they did, but the festive atmosphere had dissipated, replaced by worry.

Slayer returned, landing cautiously in the farthest corner of the ledge. He edged closer. *Go find Wolf,* he said.

"We need to wait for her here," Jenna said. "We don't want to alert the empress before the attack." The plan had been to destroy Celesgarde, and then to break through the Boil and fly to the Dragonback Mountains on the mainland. After resting there for a few days, they planned to cross the Indio to the wetlands. If Lyss was still in the capital city, they needed to find her before they destroyed it.

*Will we go tomorrow without Lyssa Wolf?* Cas asked, when Jenna curled up next to him to sleep.

"We will go tomorrow," Jenna said, "and we will see what we can find out."

After a fitful night's sleep, Jenna rose before dawn to find Slayer crouched on the edge of the cliff, still wearing the saddle, as if preparing to launch. He'd fallen asleep in that position, waiting for Lyssa Wolf, who had not come.

The dragons, who had been so excited about the prospect of "burning the nest," were subdued as they ate a breakfast of half-frozen goat from the planned feast the night before. It was a serious matter when a dragon lost enthusiasm for food.

*We go in high,* Cas told the fledglings. *We'll see what we see, then decide. Do not attack the city until we know where the Wolf is.*

"Bring everything you want to save," Jenna said. "We probably won't be coming back." Carefully, she folded Lyssa's jacket and stowed it in one of her panniers. Then she slid into her own battle armor and helmet, and the leather-framed goggles that protected her eyes.

Over time, the young dragons had each gathered together small hoards of shiny objects—mostly bits of quartz and stones smoothed by ancient oceans. Lyss had brought each of them a leather carry bag, and she and Jenna had sewn on long straps that could be fastened across their chests and over their backs. Jenna had helped them pack them the night before.

Slayer nudged his hoard sack with his nose. *But what if Lyssa Wolf comes back, and we aren't here? Like before, when we moved to the back side of the mountain.*

"Let's see what we find at the harbor," Jenna said. She had

a bad feeling that Lyssa Wolf would not be returning to their mountain aerie. An image was swimming in the sea of her mind—a tall ship, moving away from them under full sail.

Cas broke into her thoughts. *Jenna see Lyss on ship?*

"No," Jenna said. "I just— Let's go."

Jenna mounted Cas and settled her own panniers across the dragon's shoulders, wishing that they did not have to leave this place, which had become a refuge and a sanctuary.

You did not come here to hide, she thought. You came here to kill the empress and then return to the wetlands to find Adam Wolf. She'd delayed too long already.

She was seized with a sudden urgency, a need to get moving.

One by one, they launched from the ledge, with Cas in the lead. His shoulders moved smoothly under her hands, neck extended toward the sky, his wing strokes sure and strong, with no sign of the injuries he'd sustained in the Boil.

"Impressive," she said, rubbing the bare spots behind his ears, itchy places he couldn't reach.

*I know.*

"Arrogant dragon."

*Best dragon.*

Jenna laughed. They often needled each other this way. It somehow took the edge off the vulnerability of their connection, their immense reliance on each other. If she ever found Adam Wolf, would there be room for him to elbow in?

Memories of incendiary kisses rippled through her.

Yes.

Would he want to?

*Rabbit in Jenna's head.*

That was Cas's term for incessant worrying.

Cas kept climbing, until they could view the entire southern side of the island. A little higher, and they could see over the island's spine to the more populated north side.

The air was lean up here, and Jenna focused on wringing every bit of oxygen from it.

*Jenna all right?*

"I need dragon lungs."

Jenna looked over her shoulder, and saw the fledglings arranged in a V formation behind them, struggling to maintain it in the air currents over the mountains.

I've got to stop calling them fledglings, she thought. They are growing so fast.

Once they'd crossed the mountains, Celesgarde came into view. To Jenna's surprise, the harbor lacked its usual forest of masts. It was all but empty of ships.

"Where is everyone?" she murmured.

The town appeared deserted as well. Even its usual stench of burning peat was fainter than usual. Only a handful of horses remained in the corrals by the waterside.

*Trap?*

"I don't know, Cas," Jenna said. "We're going to have to go lower."

Cas lacked the patience required for a slow, circling descent. Instead, he folded his wings and plunged earthward, extending them again to slow down a few thousand feet above the ground.

The rest of the flight tried to follow suit, with varying degrees of success. One of the young dragons miscalculated and landed in the harbor with a tremendous splash.

"Don't teach them bad habits," Jenna said.

*Need practice.*

"Not right now they don't."

*Learn to swim, too.*

The young dragon floundered in shallow water, vocalizing her dismay. That drew a bloodsworn soldier from the building next to the corral. He carried a loaded crossbow.

Seeing the dragon in the water, he charged down to the pier and raised his crossbow.

"Cas!"

But Cas was already plummeting toward the pier, claws extended. He struck the bloodsworn, hard, just as he took his shot. The shot went wild and the soldier ended up pinned to the ground, screaming, bleeding from a dozen wounds.

A handful of bloodsworn had spilled from the building after the first man. When they saw what was happening, they fled back inside.

*Look for Lyssa*, Cas told the fledglings. They spread out through the town, searching for her scent, peering into windows, ripping off roofs and looking inside, which must have been heart-stopping for any occupants.

Right away, Jenna noticed the scent. It seemed to cling to everything here at the harbor. The smell of home. Of family. Of death.

Of rebirth.

Was this the scent of the empress? Or was it something else?

*Jenna.* Cas extended his wing, a staircase for Jenna. *Ask man about Lyssa.*

Jenna clambered down to the ground, jumping the last few feet to avoid the injured soldier, still pinned to the ground. His eyes all but bulged out of his ashen face when he saw Jenna.

"Please," he said in Common. "Please. Let me go."

To Jenna's eyes, he looked to be mortally injured. Then she remembered what Lyss had said about the bloodsworn—that they were all but impossible to kill. That they could live on with the worst kind of injuries. They weren't very bright, but they would not knowingly betray the empress.

So it was unlikely that threats or torture would work.

"Let go of him, Cas, but keep an eye on him."

Reluctantly, Cas released his grip and moved aside.

"I'm sorry you got hurt," Jenna said, to the pirate, improvising. "This is an unfortunate misunderstanding. You see, we were coming to join the empress's forces."

The soldier blinked, once, twice, like an owl exposed to sudden sunlight. "Dreki? In the empress's army?"

"It's very secret." Jenna lowered her voice, as if someone might be listening. "We've been training in the mountains so that nobody knows. We were supposed to join the empress before she . . . left." Jenna took one more look around. "Where is she? Are we too late?"

"She is not here," the soldier said.

Stifling her impatience, Jenna tried a different question. "When did she leave?"

"Many ships left in the past three days. She is not here."

"Where was she going?"

"I don't know. Most sailed for the wetlands. Some for the Desert Coast."

The young dragons were returning to the quay. *No Lyssa*, they said.

"There was someone we were working with. A wetlander with hair the color of wet sand. Do you know where she went?"

"Captain Gray?" the soldier said, and Jenna's heart leapt.

"Yes! We were working with her."

"I don't know where she went," he said, shaking his head. "She sailed with the others. She might have gone to the wetlands; she might have gone to Carthis."

Motioning her closer, he said, "There's something you should know."

Jenna dropped to her knees and leaned toward him.

When the bloodsworn made his move, it was only Jenna's dragon-quick reflexes and her clan-made armor that saved her. His curved Carthian blade came up, and would have opened her from her navel to her collarbone, but Jenna saw it coming and slammed the soldier's elbow with her gloved fist, diverting the blow enough that it glanced off the hardened leather. Jenna threw herself backward out of harm's way, landing hard on the quay.

Cas screamed, a bloodcurdling challenge. After that, it was all a blur of glittering scales and teeth and claws and flame. At the end of it, the bloodsworn pirate was reduced to an unrecognizable pile of charred flesh and ash.

*Dead now*, Cas said.

And so he was. But now Jenna had no idea where to start looking for Lyss—or if she still lived.

# 34

# HOMELAND

Lyss said good-bye to Breon at dawn on the day she sailed, waking him from a sound sleep. He'd been groggy and disoriented, and it took her a while to get through to him that she was leaving.

Once he understood, he tore up his bed, hunting through the bedclothes, then finally reached under his bed and retrieved the little tablet that he used to communicate. His reading and writing skills were rudimentary, but it was better than nothing.

*WHERE?* he wrote.

"I'm going home," Lyss said. "The empress knows who I am. She is coming, too."

His face fell. *SORRY*, he wrote. He handed her the tablet, scooped up his pipe, and threw it across the room so that it slammed into the wall, shattering into pieces.

Lyss gaped at Breon. He mopped at his eyes with his sleeve.

"It's not your fault," Lyss said. "You can beat this. If not the first time, then the second, or the third. We will win—I swear it."

For a long moment, he stood, head down, fists clenched.

Then took back the tablet and wrote, *BE CAREFUL.*

"You be careful," Lyss said. Impulsively, she hugged him. "My brother may be coming here," she said, her tears dampening his shoulder. "Look after each other until I come back. Stay alive. Escape if you can. If you can't, I'll come back for you."

Now Lyss stood on the deck of the *Siren*, peering through the glass to catch a first look at the white cliffs that would signal that she was nearly home. The ship was packed with bloodsworn, yet she had never felt more alone.

She glanced over her shoulder at the empress who stood on the quarterdeck, shouting orders to her crew, her mane of silver hair flying in the wind.

Lyss missed Breon. She missed Jenna, Cas, Slayer, and the others. They had provided much-needed relief from the relentless and deadly dance with the empress.

Even the wolves seemed to have abandoned her. She hadn't seen them since the ultimatum from the empress. You told me I was the Gray Wolf queen, she thought. I thought you were supposed to offer counsel and advice.

Her Highlander officers were with her, but after the Bosley incident, she resisted confiding in them. She didn't want to put them in more danger than they were already in.

On this, her second trip across the Indio, Lyss had at last made peace with the sea. Or at least an uneasy armistice, broken by a few bouts of seasickness when the weather got rough. It was one of those things she needed to conquer to get where she needed to go. And so she would. Present disasters had elbowed ahead of childhood fears.

During the crossing, she watched the skies, hoping to see a

formation of six dragons passing overhead. She was probably the only sailor, anywhere, who had ever wished that.

She was keenly aware that she was on her way to kill somebody—several somebodies, in fact. Time would tell who'd be on her list. Every night, as she passed into sleep, she imagined the new capital of Celesgarde charred into ash. She imagined sweeping King Jarat's smirking head from his shoulders. Confronting Julianna and Aunt Mellony and demanding answers.

Those dreams, dark and bloody, sustained her.

She touched her father's amulet, swearing an oath on Han Alister's grave. On the grave of her mother, of her sister, Hana—of the thousands who had died for the Gray Wolf line. She would win back her queendom, save her brother, and put their father's amulet into his hands, or die trying.

You may think you're winning, Celestine, she thought. But this story isn't over. I'm going to find Jenna and the dragons and burn every one of your ships to the waterline. I'll save Breon from the leaf and find Hal Matelon and finish whatever it was we started. How that story would end was anyone's guess.

Jada Long Foot came up next to her, and Lyss silently handed over the glass. Long Foot was one of Lyss's Highlander officers—one of the few clan members of the regular army.

Jada looked through the glass, then lowered it, slapping it against her hand, her face unreadable. "Are you glad to be almost home, General Gray?"

To be honest, Lyss didn't know how to answer that.

"I'll be glad to see some forests again," she said finally. "I'll never get used to the drylands."

"Me neither," Jada said. "It's been especially hard on Farrow." She nodded toward the Waterwalker, who was practicing his sticking on an open stretch of deck with an avid audience of bloodsworn.

Lyss looked north, to where the rising sun was burning cloud from the flanks of Alyssa Peak.

Jada leaned in close. "Is it true the bloodsworn are getting their asses kicked in the uplands?"

Lyss nodded, careful to keep her opinions to herself. "The empress has decided to take the southern route."

When they'd arrived offshore, fresh dispatches had confirmed Lyss's prediction. The invasion had stalled out in the mountains to the west of the Alyssa Plateau. Even as spring turned to summer, the high passes were filled with snow and clan war parties. The empress's armies suffered staggering losses as they foundered on the slopes of the northern Heartfangs. The bloodsworn might be difficult to kill, but the northerners found a hundred ways.

"Where are they getting all these soldiers?" the empress had grumbled.

Lyss suspected but didn't say that if Char Dunedain still commanded the army, she had probably abandoned the war in the south to focus on this one. The Fellsian general was used to making these kinds of difficult decisions. She was smart enough to know that what happened in Delphi wouldn't matter if the empress conquered the north.

This theory was confirmed when word came that Delphi had fallen to King Jarat's army.

But who was giving Dunedain her orders? Mellony? Julianna? If Jarat's army marched all the way to Fellsmarch, the wolf in Lyss hoped that the traitors would end up hanging from the walls.

Words from her battle anthem echoed in her head.

*From mountain camp to upland vale*
*You'll hear our battle cry:*
*You think you've come to conquer.*
*Instead, prepare to die.*

"I'd better go bring up my gear," Long Foot said. She saluted and turned away.

They rounded the point with the tide behind them and sluiced into the harbor at Spiritgate.

It had been a long time since Lyss had been to this port. Even then, she'd generally seen it from a distance, being in enemy territory. But even someone unfamiliar with the seaport could tell that the waterfront had been all but destroyed.

The empress's forces had taken out the artillery on the heights to either side of the harbor entrance a week ago. Since then, they'd been firing on the city itself. Most of the buildings along the harbor front had been burned or cleared away—the taverns, clicket-houses, warehouses, chandleries and the like.

The keep was still there, of course, and the fortifications along the cliff face. But soon it would be the empress's flag that snapped in the onshore breeze.

Batalions of Carthian cavalry were crossing the Alyssa Plateau from the beachhead at Chalk Cliffs. Thus far, they'd met with little resistance. The plan was that the land force would open the way to land troops, artillery, and supplies directly from the harbor.

Lyss would have preferred to be in the fighting on land than to be watching it from a distance. Then again, she did not intend to die for the empress of Carthis, even if it meant that she could take a few Ardenine soldiers with her.

She watched the bombardment for a while, trying not to think of everyone who might be in the path of this war. Where was Hadley, now that the Fells had lost its one deepwater port on the east coast? Where was Hal Matelon? Had he made it home, or had he died near Chalk Cliffs? Her mind kept turning to Sasha Talbot, to that image of her kneeling, presenting her sword. Sometimes it seemed as if Sasha was inside her head. Other times, it was as if she were calling to her from a distance, a distance that grew with every passing day.

Spiritgate was in flames, now, sending sparks rising into the night sky. Guns thundered from landward. The horselords had arrived. Soon, she would be bringing her army ashore, on Ardenine soil. It was what she had wanted for a long time. It wasn't quite the way she'd anticipated it, and it wasn't the army she would have chosen, but she would make it work.

Soon, she thought. I'm coming for you, Jarat.

# BURNING THE BURNABLE

The dragons weren't finished with Celesgarde. They were already in a bad mood, after Lyssa's disappearance, the empress's escape, and the less-than-satisfying interview with the bloodsworn pirate. The attack on Jenna sent them into a frenzy of destruction. They burned everything that was burnable, from the quays to the houses that were tucked into the terraces on the hillside to the small fishing boats that were all that remained in the harbor. Every now and then, a small pocket of bloodsworn emerged from cover. The dragons showed no mercy. They took "burn the nest" very seriously.

Jenna's dragon nature warred with the part of her that deplored the massacre.

It's necessary, she thought. This is what you came for. But it would mean a lot more if the empress had been there to share the fate of her garrison. Only her scent remained, taunting them.

It was odd. Celestine's scent reminded her—a little—of Evan Strangward. What did that mean? Were they all connected?

Were they all—somehow—related?

Did Celestine have a magemark, too?

The dragons were frustrated by the palace, raining flame down on it and charring every wooden part, but it still stood like a marble monument to the empress's power. Finally, they began slamming into it, trying to knock off pieces.

"Stop that!" Jenna cried. "You'll hurt yourselves. Your armor is hard, but stone is harder than you."

The young dragon that had splashed into the harbor came up with the idea to lift loose boulders from the volcano and drop them onto the palace. They kept it up, lifting larger and larger boulders until the palace was a pile of glittering rubble.

*Rocks harder than palace*, she said, with great satisfaction.

Each attack flushed a few more bloodsworn from their hiding places in the palace. The dragons dispatched them as soon as they ran from the shattered structure like moles from a burrow. Eventually, they quit coming.

"The dragon that splashed into the harbor" was an awkward name for humans, though it made total sense for dragons, who communicated through images. Slayer's mind would conjure a dragon falling into the water, and that would tell him all he needed to know.

In fact, when they'd finished reducing Celesgarde to a charred ruin, the young dragons began to reenact her humiliating landing by fluttering a short distance into the air, then pretending to fall into the bay, changing direction at the last minute to escape their nestmate's fate.

She seemed unperturbed. She was no longer wet, either. She was literally steaming as the heat from her body evaporated the water.

"I need a shorter name for you," Jenna said. "Can I call you 'Splash'?"

*Good name*, she replied gravely. *Water snuffs fire.* She looked sidelong at her brothers and sisters. And so another one of the young dragons acquired a name.

After so much work and play, of course, the fledglings were famished, and three of them flew off hunting, promising to bring back meat. Slayer and Cas were among those who stayed behind.

Slayer was morose. He'd participated in the destruction of Celesgarde with ruthless efficiency. Now it was as if every part of him drooped.

*Find Lyssa Wolf*, he said.

"I know, Slayer," Jenna said, soothing and raveling his tangled mind. "I think she's aboard one of the ships that sailed yesterday, but we don't know which one, and we don't know which way she went."

Slayer nudged the pool of metal that had once been the pirate's sword. *Lyssa needs armor.*

"Lyssa is smarter than me," Jenna said, thinking of her close call. "She'll be careful."

Cas, though, kept returning to the ruined palace, nudging stones out of the way, trying to poke his nose into the rubble at the entrance.

"What's the matter?" Jenna came up beside him.

*Something still alive in there.*

Jenna caught the scent. Very faint. Familiar, and, yet—not. It struck a chord deep inside her. It wasn't Strangward's scent, but it reminded her of him. It wasn't Celestine's scent—not quite— but it conjured up the same vexing mix of emotions. Home.

Family. Danger. It kindled in her the hope that somewhere inside, she might uncover the truth.

Slayer nudged his way in. *Not Lyss*, he said with an air of finality. *Let's dig it out and kill it.* He slammed his tail against the nearest wall, knocking it down.

"Wait," Jenna said. "I need to find out who's in there."

*Nobody good*, Cas said, then added, as if Jenna had forgotten their mission, *Kill the hatchlings.*

*Burn the nest*, Slayer said and poured flame over the broken facade of the building.

"No!" Jenna said, thrusting herself between the dragon and the palace, her scales surfacing as skin met flame. "I'm going in to see."

This produced a cascade of dragon unhappiness.

"I have to go," Jenna said, taking a sword from a dead soldier. "You won't fit. Now stay away from the building so it doesn't come down on top of me."

Over strenuous objections, Jenna threaded her way into what was left of the marble palace. Bits of shattered rock pelted down on her from above, and the walls that remained standing threatened to fall at any moment. The scent grew stronger, though, so she pressed on, knowing that she must be getting close.

As she passed a ruined staircase, she realized that the scent was coming from the floor above. Certain that at any moment, the building would come down around her ears, Jenna began to scramble up the remains of the staircase, hearing the clatter behind her as rocks hit the tiled floor below.

Eventually, she heaved herself over the top step, where she rested a moment, her blade beside her, breathing hard. That was when she heard it—music unlike any she'd ever experienced before. It washed over her, so full of melancholy and desire and pain that she all but wept. It sounded like a stringed instrument, but not the basilkas she was used to.

For a long moment, she lay there, flattened. But she knew she couldn't linger long, or the dragons would come in after her and probably bury her in the process. She rose to her knees, then to her feet, and followed the sound and the scent back toward the front of the palace, picking her way around obstacles, leaping over chasms. Along the way, she passed more bodies—a crowd of bloodsworn crushed under debris, all holding weapons, as if ready to fend off intruders.

The scent grew stronger until she reached a large, arched doorway. Across the threshold lay one of Celestine's bloodsworn, broken but barely alive. When Jenna came into view, he lifted his sword and attempted to slash at her ankles, but she easily evaded him and leapt over his prone body, slicing off his sword arm along the way. He was like the last guardian of what lay beyond.

And there, perched on what remained of a terrace overlooking the ocean, Jenna found the most beautiful boy she'd ever seen. His clothes had once been fine, but now were covered in dust and grit and soaked in blood. His hair was of an indeterminate color, powdered white by marble dust. In addition to his own distinctive scent, another scent clung to his hair, his clothes, his skin. A familiar, charred, smoky scent. There was something about him, a delicate, pampered quality, despite the dirt and disarray.

Then Jenna noticed something else that set him apart. He had no aura. He was free, not bloodsworn.

He was so focused on his playing that he didn't notice Jenna until she said, "Who are you?"

He looked up at her, smiled, and shook his head without missing a note.

"What are you doing here?" she persisted. "Do you work for the empress? Are you her . . . musician?" She almost said *favorite*, but changed it to *musician* at the last moment.

With that the music faltered just a bit. He hugged his instrument closer, as if she might try to take it from him. He looked at her mutely as if he wasn't sure how to answer that question.

"Can't you speak?"

He pointed at the pipe, and then at his throat, and shook his head. He stroked the strings, and they spoke more beautifully than any human voice.

Jenna eased closer. She couldn't help herself. The music was so enchanting that it drove caution from her mind. The boy rested his instrument on his lap, one leg bent. The other leg was pinned under a block of marble.

"You're hurt!" she said, throwing caution to the winds and kneeling down beside him.

The boy looked sadly at his leg, and half-shrugged, as if he hadn't noticed his predicament until now. Up close, the smoky scent was even stronger. When she saw the pipe lying next to him, she realized what it was. Leaf. She'd known people in Delphi who'd smoked it, in an attempt to make misery less miserable.

"You can't stay here," Jenna said. "This building is going to collapse before long."

The boy mimicked pushing at the stone, then shook his head, his expression resigned. Then, raising both hands, palms flat, he pushed toward her, clearly telling her to go.

Jenna tried putting her shoulder to the block of marble.

Though it seemed like it didn't budge an inch, the boy's breath hissed out as if the attempt was painful. He closed his eyes and played some more, as if the music eased his pain.

Pebbles and sand pelted them from above as something large and heavy landed on the broken palace wall behind them. The light dimmed as a massive head intruded between the terrace and the sun.

*Jenna?*

It was Cas.

Jenna scrambled to her feet. "Cas! No!" she said, standing over the musician, spreading her arms to shelter him. "That wall can't hold your weight."

If being crushed to death didn't seem to worry the musician, the arrival of the massive dragon did. His eyes went wide and round and the music ended abruptly as he raised both hands to protect his face.

*Music?* Cas said, leaning down toward the boy, looking plaintively into his eyes, which only terrified him further. *Music?*

"You're scaring him, Cas," Jenna said. "Help me lift this rock off his leg. Careful not to put your weight on the—"

It was too late. With an earsplitting crack, the terrace broke free from the ruined palace, dumping all three of them into space. At least two of them would have ended up in the harbor, except that Slayer and Splash hurtled past, intercepting them in midair with such bone-rattling force that Jenna thought her legs and arms might be shaken free from her body.

All three dragons spiraled toward the ground, gently depositing their human cargo at the water's edge. Jenna rolled to her feet, but it was clear the musician wasn't going anywhere on his damaged leg for a while. He wrapped his arms around his instrument as if to protect it at all costs.

Cas thrust his head in closer. *Music?*

The dragon was trying to be charming, but it wasn't working. When no music was forthcoming, the other dragons
crowded in. They closed in on the boy from all sides, nudging
him with their noses to see what he'd do, hitting the strings so
that they sounded discordantly.

"Stop it!" Jenna said. "He's hurt, so he won't be playing any
music now. If you behave, maybe he'll play again when he's
feeling better."

*Hurt?* Slayer said. *Need Lyss.*

We do, Jenna thought, but I'll have to do. Fortunately, she'd
packed up their medical supplies along with everything else.
Using her belt dagger, she cut away his breeches below the
knee, exposing the injured leg. Miraculously, the bones didn't
seem to be broken, though the leg was bruised and bleeding. It
didn't help that the dragons wanted in on every move she made.

She sent the dragons in search of fresh water to wash out the
boy's wounds, which got them out of her hair for a bit. She was
wrapping his leg with linen when the fledglings returned with
meat, prompting a dragon break for dinner.

As Jenna was finishing up, the boy abruptly took hold of her
hands. At first, she thought maybe she was hurting him, but
then information flowed between them. His mind was cloudy,
but the effects of the leaf seemed to be wearing off.

An image came to Jenna's mind—of a small boy with reddish hair streaked with gold. Familiar. Just like his scent.

He cocked his head, eyes closed, as if listening, then reached
for his instrument and struck a few tentative notes that pierced
like a knife to her core.

Startled, Jenna jerked her hands back. What had he taken from her that he could strike so close to the bone? She was the one who gleaned information, not the target.

The promise of music drew the dragons away from their bloody feast. They crowded around like an audience impatient for the concert to begin.

The boy flinched back, eyes wide.

"This is your fault," Jenna said to the musician. "You started it. They want to hear more music."

The boy half-smiled and played three songs in quick succession while the dragons listened raptly.

I need to interrogate him, Jenna thought, but that won't be easy. He seems to be able to hear well enough, but he can't or won't speak. Was he naturally mute, or had something been done to him to prevent him telling tales?

Maybe Celestine cut out his tongue, Jenna thought with a shudder. Or his vocal cords.

She put her hand on his shoulder. "Open your mouth."

Looking mystified, he complied. She slid one hand behind his head to tilt his head back. And froze.

He froze, too. They stared at each other as her fingers explored the magemark on the back of his neck. Looking frightened, he reached up and tried to dislodge her hand.

The dragons were growing restless. *More music*, Cas said.

Jenna ignored him. Taking hold of the musician's wrist, she lifted his hand and placed it on her own neck.

His eyes widened, and his muddled mind reacted slowly. With a hoarse cry, he pulled her into a rough embrace, his shoulders shaking with sobs.

# 36

# HOME IS THE SAILOR

After the council meeting ended, Lila followed Shadow out into the hallway to find Captain DeVilliers waiting for them. For Shadow, rather.

"Shadow!" the sea captain hissed. "We need to talk."

"We do," Shadow said. "We're staying in Kendall House. Why don't you come back with us?"

DeVilliers looked at Lila and raised an eyebrow, as if to say, *And you are . . . ?*

"This is Lila Byrne," Shadow said quickly. "Captain Byrne's daughter."

DeVilliers did a double take. "*Byrne?* I heard Julianna call you by that name in the meeting, but—"

"I'm Captain Byrne's chance child by a nixie," Lila said. "He barely escaped with his life."

"Is that so?" DeVilliers drew her pierced eyebrows together in a skeptical frown.

Maybe, Lila thought, I should get a sash embroidered with that story so I don't have to repeat it.

"You can trust Lila to hear whatever you have to say,"

Shadow said. "Just don't believe anything that comes out of her mouth." He looked up and down the corridor. "But let's not talk here. Let's go back to Kendall House."

"Only if a girl can get something to drink at Kendall House," DeVilliers said.

"A girl can," Shadow said.

And so they walked to Kendall House, Shadow and DeVilliers reminiscing about past bad behavior, and Lila trailing behind, like a scowling chaperone.

What's wrong with you? Lila gave herself a mental shake.

Back at Kendall House, Shadow pulled glasses down from the shelf while DeVilliers circled the room, her hand on her amulet, putting up barriers to eavesdroppers.

As soon as she'd finished, she poured herself some cider, took a long pull, and sat on the edge of the cold hearth. Lila poured bingo for herself and sat in Shadow's most comfortable chair. Shadow drank water.

"What the hell is going on, Shadow?" DeVilliers said. "That was by far the strangest meeting I've ever been in. I came in expecting to be pilloried for a massive scummer-storm. Instead, they've moved right on to a new succession plan." She drank again. "Where's Byrne? Where's the queen? Is Julianna in charge now?"

Shadow explained what had been happening in the captain's absence.

"So the queen is hiding out in the woods?" DeVilliers shook her head. "That's not like her. And what's Bayar doing sitting on council? They could use him in the east."

"I think he's going back soon," Shadow said. "As for the

queen, Captain Byrne is taking no chances with her health."

Now DeVilliers looked at Lila, almost accusingly. "Your father."

Lila shrugged. "Not my fault."

"What exactly happened, Hadley?" Shadow said. "You had four wizards aboard *Sea Wolf*. How did the pirates manage to sink your ship? I noticed you never mentioned Strangward in council. Did he betray you or what?"

DeVilliers slumped against the fireplace. "I don't think so," she said glumly.

"You don't think so?" Shadow poured more cider.

"It was partly my fault," DeVilliers said. "I didn't trust Strangward, and that made me question everything he said. As things turned out, I think I should have listened to him." She paused long enough to take a drink. "He warned us not to sail to the Northern Islands in *Sea Wolf*. He wanted to stop in Tarvos and switch to a different ship. We were afraid of a double cross, so we elected to sail straight to Celesgarde.

"Strangward refused. He asked us to drop him off on the nearest point of land if we insisted on sailing north in *Sea Wolf*. I refused. I was afraid he was going to alert Celestine. So he took the wind away."

"He really can do that?" Lila blurted.

"Aye," DeVilliers said. "He can. So it was a standoff, until one of the empress's ships showed up. Strangward recognized the ship and her captain. He said that there'd be no wizards on board, so we should use conventional weapons so as not to tip the empress off. I told Finn to raise a barricade, Strangward was handling the wind, and Prince Adrian and Talbot went aft to stall the enemy while I readied the guns. They refused to stand down, so I loosed a broadside at the other ship. It was so badly damaged that when we got under way, it couldn't follow. We were pulling away, and I thought we were in the clear. And then, as I said in the meeting, we took a direct hit to the stern, where Prince Adrian and Talbot were standing."

"I thought you said that Finn had put up barricades," Shadow said.

"He did," DeVilliers said, "but they were down when we were hit." She paused. "Not only that," she continued in a low voice, "it was wizard flame that hit us. Not cannon fire."

"So . . . Strangward was mistaken when he said there would be no wizards on board?" Shadow said.

Getting this story out of DeVilliers is like prying a barnacle off a pier, Lila thought crossly.

DeVilliers shook her head. "I guess it was what you might call 'friendly fire,'" she said.

"Strangward?" Lila guessed.

"Much as I would like to think that," DeVilliers said, staring at her boots, "it was Finn sul'Mander who sank my ship."

Shadow broke into the stunned silence. "Finn!" He shook his head. "That doesn't make sense."

"I know," DeVilliers said, nodding miserably. "I've known Finn since we were lýtlings. He and Prince Adrian were very close, too, before the prince went away. And Finn was one of our best war wizards, fighting against Arden, until he was wounded. He's changed since then."

"War changes a person," Shadow said, sliding his betrothal ring up and down his finger. "Some of us get stronger, and some . . . anyway." He cleared his throat. "I knew Finn was struggling, but he seemed to have turned a corner. He was planning a wedding."

"Did you confront Finn?" Lila said. "After—you know, when you got back to land? Does he know that you know?"

DeVilliers shook her head. "It just— I didn't want to have to kill him, and I didn't want him to kill me, either. I wanted to bring him back with me, and I didn't want to have to fight him every step of the way. I decided I'd tell Queen Raisa and Captain Byrne about it and let them decide what to do. I was going to recommend that a healer evaluate him. Someone like my brother, Ty. I planned to ask for mercy for Finn. But when I got back here . . ." DeVilliers trailed off.

"When you got back here," Lila said, "you find the queen and Captain Byrne gone, and Finn's fiancée, Julianna, is running the council. And Finn's mother and mentor are on the council, too."

DeVilliers blinked at Lila, as if she hadn't expected insight from that quarter. "Exactly. I meant to talk to the queen privately before we released that news to the full council. And now I hear that Queen Raisa cannot deal with any trauma." DeVilliers blotted at her eyes.

"I'm so sorry, Hadley," Shadow whispered. "And I'm sorry about your ship. I know how much you loved *Sea Wolf.*"

Hadley brushed that aside. "Ships can be replaced, but people can't."

That's generous of her, Lila thought. Having been raised on the coast, she knew how much masters prized their ships.

"See, I feel like I've failed everyone," DeVilliers continued. "And when I looked around that council table, the only friendly face I saw was yours."

Shadow embraced DeVilliers, patting her back and whispering in her ear.

"So who do you think is in on this?" Lila said, to break up the lovefest.

They both looked up at her. "In on what?" DeVilliers said.

"This whole thing stinks," Lila said. "I've been around long enough to know a conspiracy when I catch a whiff of it. Finn is engaged to Julianna. He sabotages a mission to rescue the princess heir, and eliminates her brother. It's not looking good for Princess Alyssa, and Julianna is suddenly next in line to the throne. Does Finn fancy being consort to the queen?"

DeVilliers frowned. "I don't know," she said. "It's hard to imagine Finn coldheartedly planning the murder of his childhood friend."

"Like you said, war changes people," Lila said briskly. "Maybe it's an advantage that I don't know and love any of your friends here at court. I do know that Prince Adrian never trusted the Bayars, and the High Wizard has taken a special interest in his nephew. Do you think they're conspiring together, or do you think Bayar is using Finn to get what he wants?"

"I'm more inclined to think that Finn's war experiences have traumatized him," DeVilliers said a little stiffly.

"Couldn't wartime experiences make a person more vulnerable to being used by someone, especially someone as strong-willed as the High Wizard?" Lila said.

"Possibly," DeVilliers said, frowning. "Ty said Lord Bayar strongly opposed Finn's decision to enter the healing service. He wanted him to continue to train at the academy. It was a real bone of contention between them. I've heard that, years ago, Bayar was involved in a conspiracy to seize the throne."

"Look," Shadow said, "we can sit here and speculate, but Captain Byrne and Queen Raisa know more than anyone about that history. I think it's important that we seek direction from them."

"But—I didn't think—I was told that—" DeVilliers sputtered, looking confused.

"The truth is that the queen is healthier than the council has been led to believe," Shadow said. "Captain Byrne has the same nose for conspiracy that Lila does. He no longer believes that the palace is safe for the queen. We've been sending messages back and forth. Ty is attending her. We should go talk to her, and you can also ask Ty what he thinks about Finn."

"You want *me* to tell the queen what happened?" DeVilliers looked even more miserable than before. "Why do I always have to be the bearer of bad news? First it was Oden's Ford, and now this. I may as well dress up as the Breaker's messenger."

Lila understood. The only upside to the queen's illness was that DeVilliers could avoid confessing her failure to the queen. But Lila felt that prickle on the back of her neck—a warning that Death was pausing at the gate, deciding whether to pay a call.

"We should go tonight," Lila said. "Something is going on, and I'm afraid it's going to get ahead of us if we don't act quickly."

# 37

# BLOOD BROTHERS

That night, Lila and Shadow rose after midnight and slipped out of the castle close. They met DeVilliers at the livery a few blocks away from the palace, where they kept their horses. By mutual agreement, they spoke no unnecessary word until they were well on their way up Hanalea Peak.

DeVilliers was glum, lips moving silently, probably practicing what she might say.

Queen Raisa, I have bad news and bad news, Lila thought of suggesting.

They passed the ruins of a cabin—little more than rotting boards and a stone chimney. Shadow explained that it had been occupied by a hermit moonshiner years ago, who'd been cursed to live forever. If he was cursed to live forever, Lila reasoned, then why isn't he still here?

Gooseflesh rose on Lila's neck again. There are so many ghosts in this place, she thought, so many forgotten stories. Too much magic for her taste.

It was a good night for ghost stories. The air was thick and warm, unusual in these mountains, especially before the summer solstice. Branches clattered overhead as the wind rose, and last year's leaves eddied around their horses' feet. The moon and stars were obscured by thick clouds. It will storm before morning, Lila thought. She hoped they would be under a roof when it did. Storms on Hanalea could be heart-stoppingly fierce.

Her stallion, Swiver, seemed to sense the tension in the air, or in his rider, anyway. He plunged and danced and shied at every imagined threat. He was a terrible horse to begin with—cranky, unreliable, cagey as hell. That's why Lila liked him. They were kindred spirits.

Lila always felt out of place in the Spirits. She was a city girl and a smuggler, a fair hand with a boat, but no mountain scout. To her, woods were what you traveled through to get someplace with a warm bed, a roof, and ale on offer. She continually twisted in her saddle to scan their back trail, convinced that she heard footsteps following and felt the pressure of hungry eyes.

Wolves, she thought, and that theory was confirmed when she heard their lonely howling echoing from peak to peak. Swiver didn't like that one bit.

What am I doing here? Lila thought, for the umpteenth time. Somewhere to the east, her family lay dead, gulls and ravens picking at their bones. Somewhere, hidden by that wall of mountains, the queen's army was fighting a desperate battle against the forces of Empress Celestine. Lila had never been the military type, but a dark, vengeful part of her longed to be engaged in a fight that involved the hacking off of heads.

Thunder rumbled to the northwest, suggesting the rain would be here sooner rather than later. The howling continued. It seemed to be coming from farther up the mountain, from the direction of the temple house.

Ahead, Shadow had reined in. He looked about, as if perplexed.

"What is it?" DeVilliers said, coming abreast of him on the narrow trail, glancing back over her shoulder at Lila.

"We should have been challenged by now," Shadow said. "The Demonai have been keeping a wide perimeter around the temple house to prevent anyone from getting too close."

"Maybe they didn't want to get wet," Lila suggested as the first fat drops of rain came down.

This earned an eye roll from Shadow. Lila got the message. *Demonai warriors aren't afraid of a little rain.*

He seemed to be crafting a retort when a nearby tree exploded, a bolt of lightning cleaving it in half. Lila fought to control Swiver, breathing in burning wood and the metallic smell of death, feeling the tingling in her fingers and toes that signified a close call. The skies opened and the rain poured down.

That's when she heard DeVilliers shout for help.

Lila wheeled her horse, looking for the others, and saw dark shadows swarming through the trees. Had the wolves come for them? She blinked rainwater from her lashes and looked again. Now one of the shadows was in her face, swinging at her with a very real blade, apparently attempting to take off her leg. She twisted Swiver's head around, trying to back away, and the blade bit into the stallion's shoulder.

Swiver had had enough. He reared, his hooves smashing down on the blade man's head.

Lila leaned down from her saddle, sword in a two-handed grip, but the man was obviously dead, given that his skull was crushed in. He was dressed in a black robe, like a priest or dedicate, maybe. This pinged a memory, but Lila had no time to dwell on it.

She looked around. Shadow was on his way to dispatching one of the blade men, but DeVilliers was surrounded, fighting for her life, six on one.

"What the hell?" Lila said to herself, heeling Swiver forward. "Why pick on *her*? What's wrong with *us*?"

Swiver was more than happy to contribute by smashing into one of DeVilliers's attackers. Lila leaned down from her saddle and finished him by severing his head from his shoulders. Well, she thought. You're hacking off heads. What you wanted, right?

Shadow had finished his blade man and also came to DeVilliers's aid. Her assailants were so fixed on her that they scarcely noticed Shadow was there until he began cutting them down. DeVilliers was bleeding from a dozen wounds, but she kept fighting, and they kept coming, with Lila and Shadow circling like snarling, biting dogs.

Finally, the assassins were all down, if not dead. There were eight of them, all dressed in those dark robes. Lila dismounted and moved to intercept one of them, who was dragging himself forward on his belly. As she raised her sword for the killing blow, she saw that he was lapping at a puddle of mingled rainwater and blood.

"Scummer," she growled, taking an involuntary step back, remembering another posse of assassins with a taste for wizard's blood. She rolled the man over. The blood smeared around his mouth and the telltale silver cup pendant confirmed her suspicion. She narrowly avoided spewing all over him.

Why do all the bad, creepy things always come around again, while the good things are one-offs?

With that, the assassin took his last breath and expired.

Well, Lila thought, nudging him with her foot, at least he died happy.

*This* time, Lila searched the man thoroughly, finding three more blades hidden in various places on his body. In a cloth bag, she found a familiar, crystalline stone. What was it he'd called it?

Lord Darian's stone.

Lila tried to swallow down the dread boiling up in her throat. There was a pattern here that she wasn't seeing, an unseen puppetmaster working the strings.

Lord Darian. The image that came to her mind looked a lot like Micah Bayar.

You don't even know the man, Lila scolded herself. Can a person inherit mistrust?

More importantly, had the assassins been on their way to the temple house, or on their way back to the city, their mission accomplished?

What would she, Shadow, and DeVilliers find at the temple house? A scene of carnage? More assassins? Should they go on or hurry back to town to raise the alarm?

She knew the answer as soon as the question surfaced. They had to go on.

Shadow's voice broke into her morbid thoughts. "Lila. Are you all right?"

She looked up. DeVilliers was off her horse, and Shadow was supporting her with an arm around her shoulders. She stood dripping in the rain, the streaks of blue in her hair vivid against a face as pale as new snow.

"I'm all right," she said. "You?"

"I'm good," Shadow said. "Hadley's lost a lot of blood."

"I'm fine," DeVilliers said, trying to shake off his arm and all but losing her balance. "Who the hell were they?"

"They're called Darian Brothers," Lila said. "Another bunch of them tried to assassinate Prince Adrian at Oden's Ford. It's a radical sect in the Church of Malthus. They serve somebody they call Lord Darian." Lila hesitated, rubbing her chin. "Oh, and they're addicted to wizards' blood." She held up the assassin's silver cup pendant. "Hence the cup."

DeVilliers looked a bit nauseous.

Here's a question, Lila thought. Why is it that some people think bloodlust is normal, but blood drinking is disgusting?

Pocketing the stone and the pendant, Lila searched the rest of the dead, collecting more knives and enough stones to build her own rock garden. Shadow rounded up the horses and led them back to the scene of the attack.

"Can you ride?" Shadow said to DeVilliers. "If so, we should get moving. There may be more of them."

DeVilliers insisted she could, so Shadow helped boost her up into the saddle.

"I'll ride in front," Lila said, "and Shadow can bring up the rear and keep an eye on our back trail."

They moved more slowly after the encounter with the Darian Brothers, for fear of blundering into another trap. But they encountered nobody else, and finally the trees thinned, the trail leveled, and the clearing around the temple house came into view. It was more of a cabin than a temple, in the rustic style of the Old Church shrines. They sat their horses just on the edge of the woods and watched for signs of life. With the rain still pouring down, it was unlikely anyone would be taking the air.

A wisp of smoke leaked from the chimney, so somebody was there, or had been recently.

"Stay here and cover me," Lila said.

"I'll go," Shadow said quickly, angling his horse across her path.

"Look, you're a deadeye with a bow," Lila said. "I'm useless at a distance, so there's no way I can cover you."

Shadow knew she was telling the truth, so he stayed with DeVilliers, while Lila nudged Swiver forward. As she crossed the clearing, every nerve was tingling, anticipating pain.

She reached the temple house without incident, dismounted, and tied the stallion to the porch in front. At the side of the house, she saw what appeared to be a pile of bloody, sodden clothing, but never is.

Lila approached warily and nudged it with her foot, rolling it over. It was what was left of one of the Darian Brothers, blood spattered all around. A knife lay in the mud nearby. He looked like he'd been torn apart by wolves. In fact, he was surrounded by wolf prints.

Lila turned back toward where Shadow and DeVilliers were watching from the trees and shook her head. Nobody we know.

She climbed the steps to the porch, where she found another body, similarly clad, similarly dead. This one looked like he'd been trying to get in the door when he was attacked. The latch was smeared with blood.

She tried the door. It was unlocked, and she pushed it open with her foot, standing to one side to give Shadow a clear shot if somebody rushed out.

When no such thing happened, she craned her neck around the doorframe and peered inside.

As she'd suspected, a fire was still smoldering on the hearth. Dirty plates and cups littered the table, as if a meal had been interrupted. There were no signs of a struggle, and no more bodies, and no more blood inside. It appeared that the queen, her captain, and their Demonai bodyguards had fled in a hurry, leaving most of their belongings behind.

If they had been there at all.

"Hello?" she said, quietly at first, and then more loudly. "Is anyone here?"

There was no answer.

Lila breathed out slowly, seriously relieved that she wouldn't have to clean up after another Darian bloodbath.

She loped silently up the stairs. On one side of the staircase was a dormitory, usually occupied by dedicates, but recently by the Demonai warriors, who'd been guarding the Gray Wolf queen. On the other side, three small bedrooms; all looked recently occupied but were now empty of people.

Lila emerged from the last of the bedrooms, turned toward the stairs, and found herself eye to eye with a massive silver wolf. There was no way to get past it—it practically filled the gallery, blocking the way back to the stairs. She looked over the railing to the floor below, debating whether she'd break her legs if she jumped. Then she'd be in an even worse fix.

She considered and discarded the idea of barricading herself in one of the bedrooms. The wolf would be on top of her long before she got that far.

With a sigh, Lila pulled her knife and broadened her stance, knowing that this was not the kind of close-up fight she could win.

The wolf seemed more amused than anything else. "Put

away the knife," she said. "You cannot slay the dead."

Not just a wolf. An undead wolf. A talking undead wolf.

"I know you fear the worst, but the queen regent is safe," the wolf said.

Lila licked her lips. "The queen regent?"

Now I am having a conversation with a talking undead wolf.

"She and your father are traveling east. The queen is on her way back to the Realms, but she is alone and in grave danger," the wolf said.

"Hang on. I thought you just said—"

"Your mission at court is not over," the wolf said. "Your father was right—it is a very dangerous place—but you must go back."

"More dangerous than here?" Lila said.

"Unfortunately, yes," the wolf said.

"Were you the one who killed the priests outside?"

"My daughters and I did," the wolf said. "That and our warning gave the queen regent time to get away." She shook her great head in the manner of an elder deploring what the world was coming to. "At one time, that kind of interference would have been unthinkable. Once the wall between the living and the dead is breached, it becomes more and more tempting to intervene."

"So. You're . . . uh . . . dead," Lila said. "Who are you?"

"I am Hanalea ana'Maria, the founder of the New Line of queens."

"I thought that was just a story," Lila said.

"It is a story," Hanalea said, "but some stories are true."

So, Lila thought of saying, what is the Demon King like?

But the great wolf had a presence that made Lila want to be on her best behavior.

"I thought you just appeared to the Gray Wolf queens," Lila said.

"To the queens, of course," Hanalea said, "and occasionally to the queen's family, and to the Line of guardians."

"The guardians?"

"Guardians like your father," Hanalea said.

"Oh." Lila cleared her throat, feeling like the worst kind of shirker. "I'm not really in the family business. In fact, Princess Alyssa has—"

"*Queen* Alyssa," Hanalea corrected her gently.

"Queen Alyssa already has a bound captain," Lila said. Unless—did this mean that Captain Talbot was dead?

"Captain Talbot is alive, and the queen is alive. For now. In these times, many guardians are needed."

So now I'm being ganged into the Gray Wolf guard? No, thank you.

"You are called, Lila Byrne," Hanalea said. "It is in your nature to serve."

Lila was thoroughly unsettled by the wolf's seeming ability to dip into her mind.

However, one does not argue with a giant wolf, dead or not, that has just ripped a pack of Darian Brothers to pieces.

"What do you want me to do?"

"You and the others must return to court and protect the queen's interests as best you can. Identify who the traitors are and eliminate them. The queen must have a throne to return to."

Sure, Lila thought, and what about the day after tomorrow? She couldn't seem to rein in her mocking mind. But the wolf didn't seem to be offended.

"Young one," Hanalea said gently, "you have already sacrificed much in service to the Line, and more will be demanded of you. The life of the guardians is not an easy one. Your grandfather gave his life, and your father gave up his family."

All at once, inexplicably, Lila was crying, tears running down her cheeks, her chest heaving with silent sobs.

"I'm sorry," she gasped. "I'm sorry. I never meant— I didn't understand."

Hanalea nudged in next to her, her broad back at Lila's chest level, and Lila leaned on the ancient queen, burying her face in her fur.

Lila heard a door open and close, the sound of footsteps below.

"Lila?" It was Shadow.

Lila straightened, her hands still clutching Hanalea's fur.

"Now," Hanalea said softly, "I think it's best if the council continues to believe that the queen regent is here at the temple house. If they think she's here, they will not look for her elsewhere." Her shape shimmered, became indistinct, and was gone.

Lila looked down into the hearth room. DeVilliers leaned against the wall by the door in case she had to make a quick getaway. Shadow stood at the bottom of the steps, and was looking up toward the gallery.

"I'm up here," Lila called over the railing.

Shadow trudged up the steps and joined Lila at the railing, and leaned a little sideways to look into her face. "Are you all right? I saw the bodies outside. Is there any sign of . . ." He trailed off. "You're crying." Gently, he wiped tears from her face with the edge of his thumb and looked toward the bedrooms. "Are you—are we too late?"

"No," Lila said, clearing her throat and scrubbing at her face with her sleeve. "Nobody's home. I don't think the Darian Brothers ever got inside. It looks like the wolves held them off until the queen, Byrne, and the others got away."

"The wolves . . . held them off?" Shadow looked around. "What wolves?"

"Didn't you see the tracks outside?" she said. Not allowing him time to ask any more questions, she turned toward the stairs. "Let's go down and see if we can get DeVilliers patched up. We shouldn't stay here long. Whoever sent those assassins knew where the queen's party was staying. They may drop by to count the bodies."

"We should wait for them, then," Shadow said grimly.

There's the self-destructive, foolhardy Shadow I know and love, Lila thought. It also brought back memories of trying to convince Prince Adrian to leave Oden's Ford after the attack on the dormitory.

"There are only three of us," Lila said, "and our only wizard is injured. We don't know who'd be coming, or how many. We're the only ones who can speak to what happened here."

"We could go after the queen and see if they need help," Shadow said. "They couldn't be too far away."

Lila shook her head. "I think we should go back to Fellsmarch and do the job we were asked to do. That's the best way to help the queen."

Shadow cocked his head, drawing his eyebrows together.

"*What?*" Lyss said irritably.

"It's just that I thought you'd jump at any excuse to leave court," Shadow said. "Now you want to go back?"

"Sometimes you don't get to do what you want," Lila said.

# 38

# DARK DAYS IN DELPHI

Destin rode into Delphi with a company of mages the day after the city surrendered to Bellamy's army. He was surprised to find that the city had improved since his last visit. The air was cleaner, for one thing, and the river that ran through the city was no longer an open sewer. The water still wasn't safe to drink, but even now, in late spring, the stench no longer soured his stomach.

There were schools now, for the children who had once worked in the mines. Some of the worst slums had been torn down, and that housing relocated up the mountain and closer to the mines, so that travel to and from was easier.

True, parts of the city had been reduced to rubble in the battle for the city. It was still a cluster of mines and factories, with a town attached like a boil on an ironworker's ass.

The citizens were no more willing to take the yoke of Arden than they had when Destin was last there. In fact, having been given their first taste of freedom in a long time, they'd fought like demons, block by block, street by street, and house by house. Every inch of land was gained with blood and sweat.

Though the townspeople fought tooth and nail, the regular Highlander army seemed to be absent.

They made a choice, Destin thought. They're fighting Celestine in the east. If they lose there, they know that what happens in Delphi is meaningless.

There being no royal palace in Delphi, the king and his courtiers took over the opulent mayor's palace. The mayor had died under mysterious circumstances not long after Arden lost control of the city. During his time in Delphi, Destin had worked with Willett Peters, and whatever had happened to him, he deserved it.

Destin and Bellamy met with the king in the palace's great hall to brief him on the status of the city. Jarat was absolutely giddy about the "easy victory" they'd achieved in Delphi. "All I hear about is how great a commander young Matelon is," he crowed. "Well, he lost this city, and we won it back. It was prescient on our part to send an overwhelming force north to assure a quick and convincing victory."

Destin suspected that in this case the king was using the "royal" plural.

"I think we should be careful not to be overconfident, Your Majesty," Bellamy said. "We were fighting local militias and citizens with clubs, and we still suffered heavy losses. The outcome might have been different had we been facing the copperheads and the regular army."

"Well, then clearly we outfoxed them," King Jarat said. "We caught them with their breeches down. I think we must give some credit to Colonel Karn and the intelligence service." King Jarat was willing to raise a cup to just about anyone in his present mood. It was difficult to push praise away with both hands, but Destin knew how quickly that could change.

"My eyes and ears are telling me that the bulk of the High-lander army has been deployed to the east, where fierce fighting continues with Empress Celestine's forces," Destin said.

"Well, let's hope the pirates keep them occupied until we take Fellsmarch," King Jarat said. "*My* eyes and ears are telling me that the capital is similarly thinly garrisoned."

Every so often, the king drew blood in that way, reminding Destin that he had his own sources and knew secrets that the spymaster didn't.

"Let us hope for another easy victory, then," Destin said, glancing at Bellamy. A muscle was working in the general's jaw, but Bellamy kept his peace. He hadn't survived for so long under General Karn's command without learning when to keep his mouth shut.

"How is the pacification of the population coming?" Jarat poured himself another cup of wine.

"I think we can safely say that they are not pacified," Destin said, "judging by three instances of sabotage in the past twenty-four hours." The population hadn't lost any skill when it came to blowing things up.

"Isn't this your second posting to Delphi?"

"Yes, Your Majesty," Destin said. My third, actually, if you count my term as the general's aide-de-camp, he thought.

"Then you should know how to handle them by now," Jarat said. "How many mages are here?"

He asked this as if all mages must know each other and stay in touch.

"I don't know, Your Majesty," Destin said. "Not many,

I would guess, because most of the mages in the north have joined the war in the east. I believe that we only encountered two of them in the recent battle for the city."

"Where are they now?" Jarat said.

Destin looked to Bellamy for answers.

"One is dead, Your Majesty, and the other is a prisoner," Bellamy said.

"Colonel, I want you to locate all of the mages in this province," Jarat said. "It may be that many of them are in hiding. I understand that, being a mage yourself, you are able to spot them. The first step will be to get collars on them."

"The first step, Your Majesty?" Dread collected in Destin's gut.

"This will prevent them from joining the war effort on the northern side, or leading insurrections in this city," Jarat said, as if explaining to the slow-witted. "Eventually, we will collect them and hold them in a secure facility."

No. This was not the job Destin wanted. He'd already had that job, the last time he'd been sentenced to Delphi—hunting down someone who did not want to be found.

Destin recalled the advice the general had given him, the day he'd met King Gerard in the garden to learn his fate after failing to kill the princeling, Adrian sul'Han.

*Whatever the king asks you to do, say yes.*

Simple advice that Destin was finding harder and harder to follow.

"Thank you, Your Majesty," Destin said. "With the help of General Bellamy, I will assemble a team that—"

"Colonel, rest assured, I would not assign you such an important task without offering you assistance," King Jarat said. He gestured to an aide, who left the room.

The aide returned, leading nine black-robed figures. Destin's heart sank.

"I believe that you have worked with these people before," Jarat said. "My contact Lord Darian has explained to me the role his dedicates played in the failed operation at Oden's Ford. Despite his losses, he has once again offered us his assistance in cleansing the north of the scourge of magic. Although they won't have a specific scent to follow this time, he assures me that they can track the stench of magery to wherever it is hiding." Jarat paused. "I do hope you will take better care of his faithful than you did the last time."

# 39

# FRIENDLY FIRE

In the days after Ardenscourt fell to Hal's little army, the rest of his recruited regulars arrived to reinforce their garrison. All told, he counted more than a thousand soldiers and fifteen freed mages under his command. He'd also done some hard thinking about where he wanted to go and how he would get there.

During his time in Delphi, he'd never moved beyond the role of the commander of an army of occupation. Delphi had never bent the knee to Arden, and Hal had avoided any meaningful engagement with the citizens. His immediate goal had been to return to what he saw as the real battlefield as soon as possible.

This should be different. This was *his* country—he'd grown up here and shed his blood in its service. He had a vested interest in its future.

But Hal wanted to live in a place where all voices were heard, where soldiers fought not for money, but for ideas they believed in, and to protect the realm. Where rulers put the good of their people first.

That was one of the reasons he'd promised to help Lyssa Gray defend her embattled realm from its enemies. He preferred to do it with an Ardenine army and the backing of the Ardenine king, but he'd do it on his own if need be. He hoped he could find his family, and the families of the other thanes, and send them home. That would fulfill his last great promise to the empire he had served for so long.

If he and Alyssa succeeded in preserving the queendom, he'd hoped he might one day live in the north and serve the Gray Wolf line in whatever way he could contribute. In whatever way she would allow.

But that would, of course, mean that he would likely be leaving his family behind.

Hal's father had promised that once he captured Ardenscourt, he would be free to take an army north. So he laid the groundwork by meeting with his officers and enlisted men. Soldiers rarely get choices, but Hal made an exception in this case. He made plans for military governance of captured territory and asked for volunteers to come north with him. Again, there were so many that he had to turn some away. He assembled the ordnance and supplies they would need for the march north.

In just a few days' time, word came that the advance scouts of the rebel army had come into sight north of the city. Hal raised the Matelon spreading oak banner over the ramparts and waited.

Eventually, a handful of horsemen spurred toward the gates, the soldier in the lead waving the flag of parley. Every rebel thane was there, and each brought a contingent of horsemen carrying the banners of their houses—Tourant wearing the sword and crown, Pascal and Rolande DeLacroix in the shield and cross, his father and Jan Rives for the spreading oak, and

Rafe Heresford with the tower on the water.

The horsemen halted a short distance away as the thanes continued forward. They didn't come too close to the walls, though. They were far too familiar with Ardenine tactics to take that risk until they knew who was in charge.

Hal, Robert, and Mercier rode out to meet them, backed by a dozen of his Ardenine regulars, the spreading oak plastered over their red hawk signia. The eyes of the rebel thanes grew wider as they recognized the Matelon brothers.

Sergeant Rives looked at Hal, then up at the Matelon flag flying over the walls, back to Hal. "Little H— General, sir, ah—what the hell is going on?"

"A very good question," Lord DeLacroix said. "What *is* going on? Have you betrayed us? Are you fighting for Jarat after all?"

"The battle is over, and we have won the city," Hal said. "It's as simple as that."

"Who is *we*?" Tourant demanded.

"Me and my army," Hal said, gesturing back toward the walls. A roar went up from the battlements—"Matelon!"

"I thought you were marching north!" Rolande protested. "What are you doing *here*?"

"We saw an opportunity," Hal said, "and we took it."

"But—you had a salvo at best!" Heresford said, a note of admiration in his voice.

"It's not the size of your army," Mercier said, "it's the skill of the commander."

Again a shout went up from the walls.

"It looks like there's more than a salvo on the walls," Heresford said drily. "Where did the rest come from?"

"What's the matter, gentlemen?" Lord Matelon said, his voice ringing out over the delegation. "Are we moving too fast for you?"

As Hal looked over the posse of thanes, his father was the only one smiling, his face alight with triumph.

"What are you waiting for, General?" DeLacroix said. "Open the gates." He turned to wave his platoon forward.

"To be honest, Lord DeLacroix, we've no need of more soldiers inside the walls," Hal said. "Things are well in hand, and I want to minimize contact between our militias and civilians."

"You're not going to let us *in*?" Tourant practically shouted.

"*You* are welcome to come in," Hal said, "but leave your armies outside."

This was met by a rumble of discontent.

"You expect us to enter the city without protection?" DeLacroix drew himself up. "You expect us to put ourselves at your mercy? What's to prevent you Matelons from taking advantage of this situation to eliminate your rivals?"

Hal put on a perplexed expression. "I thought we were allies," he said, "not rivals."

"So said King Gerard as he plucked us, one by one," Tourant snarled.

This was the last thing Hal wanted. He'd never meant for it to turn into a power struggle among the thanes, though he'd known that was a possibility, if not a probability.

"We need to convene a council of thanes," Hal said, "to discuss our next move. I assume that, whatever happens in the north, Jarat and his army will eventually come back. Perhaps sooner rather than later, once word reaches him about the fall of the city. We need to plan for that, as well as to prepare to—"

He broke off as a flicker of movement amid the mixed militias caught Hal's eye. A brace of bowmen stood tall in their stirrups, raised their crossbows, and—

"Look out, Hal!" Robert spurred his horse into Hal's stallion, causing him to lurch sideways so that the bolts hissed past Hal, though one ripped through Robert's shoulder before it pinged against the city walls.

Mercier urged his horse forward so that he stood between Hal and Robert and the thanes. Above, Hal heard the rattle of wood against stone as the bowmen on the walls nocked arrows and raised their weapons.

"Robert!" Hal cried, gripping his brother's horse's bridle and leaning down to look into his brother's face.

Robert managed to keep his seat, though his face was deathly pale. "I'm all right," he said. "Just—just get me inside so I don't fall off my horse in front of everyone."

Some of Hal's regulars hustled Robert through the city gates and out of danger. Hal's father and his bannermen surged forward and formed a prickly wall between the militias and Hal's party. The other thanes and their bannermen dissolved into a melee as they put more distance between themselves and Hal's archers.

Hal thrust his fist into the air. "Hold!" he shouted to his men. Then turned toward the thanes, struggling to control the rage welling up inside him. "This is exactly why we don't need more soldiers inside the walls," he said. "I am, however, assembling an army to march north to free our families and fight the empress in the east. If any of you are willing to contribute to that effort, send word to me. If you are willing to come into the city under a flag of truce for a thane council, you are welcome.

If not, I suggest you take your men and horses back to the fields you've been so worried about so that we can look forward to a good harvest this season."

The thanes looked at each other, their hands on their swords. Their horses snorted and stamped and banners snapped in the wind. But nobody moved. The thanes who had been so reluctant to fight were equally reluctant to leave the spoils in the hands of those who had done the bloody work.

"But—in the absence of a council, who's in charge, then?" Tourant demanded.

"I suppose I am," Hal said.

# HIDDEN BAY

Evan woke to a bad case of the all-over itches. Also, the smell of grilled fish.

He opened his eyes, blinked once, twice, until his eyes focused.

He was propped against the winch housing at midships. They were at anchor in quiet waters, the stars a glittering vault overhead, the dark shapes of cliffs looming all around. Hearing quiet conversation, he looked forward, to where Prince Adrian and Sasha were sitting, their backs against the collar of the mainmast, a feast spread before them.

"Well," he said loudly, "it seems we are not drowned after all."

They stopped talking abruptly, their heads turning his way.

Evan breathed in sharply. "And I smell something worth waking up for." He slid his hips backward until he was sitting up, then fingered the lump on the back of his head. His hair was sticky with blood, but the bleeding seemed to have stopped.

"I know I'm not in heaven because I have the mother of all headaches."

"You know you're not in heaven because they'd never let you in," Sasha said, whacking a large fish into pieces with her knife.

"And I itch all over."

"That's the residue of the nerve poison," Adrian said. "A parting gift from your shiplords. Be glad that you missed the worst of it."

"I'll take your word for it," Evan said.

When he groped for his amulet, the healer said, "I took your amulet back. I needed it to—"

"I'm sure you put it to good use."

"Are you hungry?" The healer gestured toward the food spread out on the decking.

"Ravenous." Evan carefully stood, gripping the mizzen shroud for balance, then made his way forward like a drylander on his first blue-water crossing.

They were in a small cove. Evan could hear the slap of waves against stone along the shore.

"Where are we?" he asked, sitting next to Sasha and pouring himself some cider.

"Somewhere between Tarvos and Deepwater Court," Sasha said, pushing a platter toward him.

"*How* did we get *here*?" Strangward looked from the healer to Sasha, pretending bafflement but unable to keep a straight face.

"We sailed here," Adrian said. He and Sasha clinked their cups, looking smug.

Strangward grinned and stretched, put his cup down, and carefully laced his fingers behind his head. "My work is done," he said. "Carry on."

"*You* carry on, Strangward," Sasha said, licking her fingers.

"Call me Evan," Evan said. Then he added, "*Captain* Evan."

"We've been sailing all night, Captain Evan. Then we netted the fish and cooked it. Now we're eating, and you're on watch."

Evan laughed and helped himself to fish. "I hereby proclaim you able-bodied seamen," he said. "Adrian and—"

"Call me Ash," the healer said.

"Ash?"

"Stands for 'Adrian sul-Han,'" the healer said.

"Call me Sasha," Talbot said, "terror of the high seas."

Evan got the impression that they'd been at the cider for a while.

"How come your maps are different from the ones we brought from home?" Sasha said. "None of this . . ." She raised her hands, gesturing at the small bay around them. "None of this is on our maps."

"Mine are smugglers' maps," Evan said. "They offer a little more detail. I started out as a smuggler, sailing from Tarvos." He fell silent, ambushed by memory of all he'd lost since then. It was especially poignant to be aboard *Destiny* once again. That had been such a hopeful time—making plans with Destin for a future that now seemed out of reach.

"So now you've lost your home port," Ash said, reading his mood. "I'm sorry."

Evan half-shrugged. "Maybe. Kel and Maslin seemed determined to stand and fight. We'll see how it plays out."

"What do you think the shiplords will do?" Sasha said.

"Right now I'd rather be me than them. Celestine is not a forgiving sort of person. It's soothing to know that their betrayal of me may cost them their lives or their freedom."

"Still," Ash said.

"It just means that it's more important than ever that we succeed," Evan said. "Tomorrow, we'll sail for the Northern Islands."

The next morning, they left the hidden bay behind and continued on north, hugging the shore, hoping they would pass for a coastal smuggler and not attract the attention of Celestine's shiplords. In particular, Evan did not want to meet Celestine on her way south to Tarvos to claim her prize. He ran Endruvian colors up the mast, explaining to the others that Endru was so impoverished that its vessels never made an attractive target for a pirate.

They sailed past Deepwater Court without stopping. Evan warned Ash and Sasha that the port was a routine stopping-off point for Celestine's captains, who preferred to come and go from that northernmost port than to brave the Boil with a heavy cargo. Besides, they'd been delayed too long in Tarvos. His wetland crew grew edgier as the days went by.

Especially Sasha. The closer they came to the narrows between the mainland and the Northern Islands, the more restless she became. Evan wondered if it was just worry about the crossing, though she hadn't shown any particular nervousness about sailing before.

Maybe "terror of the high seas" had a totally different meaning.

Ash noticed it, too. "What's the matter?" the healer said finally.

"Something's wrong," she said. "It seems—it's almost like we're getting farther away from Lyss rather than closer."

"What do you mean?"

"I don't know. But I feel like we're going in the wrong direction."

"What's the right direction, then?" Evan said.

She shook her head. "I don't know," she said, her voice nearly inaudible.

Ash put his hand on her shoulder. "Are you sure you're not just losing confidence because you're the first bound captain of the Gray Wolf line who wasn't a Byrne?"

"That's the thing," Sasha said, with a bit of her usual spirit. "I *am* confident. I'm confident that we're going in the wrong direction."

"We've come this far," Evan said. "We can't turn back now. If we don't find your queen at Celesgarde, we'll go wherever you suggest. But in order to do that, we'll need a seaworthy ship. So I want to go over some strategies for getting through the stormwall without losing our rigging."

Evan knew from the charts he'd collected over the years that as soon as they rounded the head north of Deepwater Court, the westerly currents around the storm head of Carthis would drive them straight into the Boil. However, he hoped to control their entrance into the storms by leaving only the mizzen deployed and driving air into it in order to slow and control their forward movement.

He wished he could practice this strategy with his novice crew, but he had no idea how to predict the conditions inside the storm and account for them. Riding out a storm was one thing—he'd encountered typhoons several times around the Southern Islands. In this case, they couldn't wait for better weather. They had to deal with the weather they had.

All he could do was practice both hand signals and verbal orders in the hopes that they could change the running rigging on the fly. A dozen times he second-guessed his decision to sail with these wetlanders instead of his trusted crew.

No, he thought. This is the crew I'll need on land.

Based on Evan's reading of the tides, they planned the crossing for just after dawn the day they rounded the head. Evan handled the tiller, and Sasha and Ash served as sail crew to port and starboard. Even in the semidarkness, Evan could see the rips that signified the rogue currents beyond the headland.

"We're in for it," Evan said. "Make sure everything movable is lashed to the deck, hatches battened, lines stowed. We're going to have a following sea—at first, anyway. We'll be sailing close-hauled, but I'm guessing it'll be a beam reach once we're into it."

The wind freshened as they came about, into the wind, where, he hoped, he could balance the forces of air and water. *Destiny* shivered as the currents struck her, then all but stood still in the water, her masts creaking and leaning rakish against the night sky as wind and water fought for dominance.

All at once, she surged forward as the mainsail ripped free and the seas caught her. Evan had to cling to the binnacle to remain upright. Ahead, the stormwall was a dark blot against the brightening sky.

Evan struggled to tease the winds around, but his efforts seemed to have little if any effect. This was weather birthed in magic—not the kind he was accustomed to managing. He gripped the hammer-and-tongs amulet and wrung power from it. It seemed to take everything he had to keep his ship from shaking into splinters.

He shouted out his orders, hoping his crew of two remembered some of what they'd been practicing.

"Drop the mizzen. We're going to go in on the jib only."

Ash and Sasha scrambled to comply. As they struck the storm-wall, the crossbeam winds drove rain and ice and salt water into Evan's face. All at once, they were running before the wind, caught in the funneling weather that surrounded the island. But they couldn't just circle the Sisters, they had to cross through.

Evan eased the rudder over, and they turned until they were sailing on a broad reach. Though the jib was closely reefed, he still heard lines snapping overhead. Their little ship heeled over until seawater slopped over the gunwales. Once again, Evan pushed back against the gale with all his might, nearly wringing his amulet dry, and *Destiny* righted herself enough to avoid foundering.

The tiller went loose in his hand, and he knew that the rudder had broken free. The sails were all he had left to control her. Racing forward, he pushed air into the jib in a desperate effort to keep their momentum so as to push through the inner stormwall. And then, all at once, the countervailing winds were gone. Under pressure of Evan's weathermaking, the mizzen gave way with a heart-rending crack and fell forward, all but taking out the mainmast as well. By now, the deck was awash with rigging and sails.

"Ash? Sasha? Are you all right?"

His voice seemed to echo in the sudden silence as the ketch slid forward on calm seas. He looked over his shoulder, all the way to the bloody orb of the sun as it cleared the horizon.

The stormwall was gone.

# PORT IN A STORM

Jenna and the dragons continued to search the islands but found no sign of Celestine or Lyss.

*You waited too long.* That message resonated in her head, driving regret deep into her bones. *You're too late.*

For weeks, Celestine had been within reach, and Jenna had spent her time hiding out on the mountaintop, using Cas's damaged wing and the raising of the hatchlings as an excuse for inaction.

Jenna had been fighting her personal war of vengeance since she was eleven years old. She was skilled with fire and explosives. She did not need the help of her dragon brethren to burn the nests of her enemies. The next time, she would not hesitate. The next time, she would not fail.

But now, overcome with urgency, she didn't know where to go.

The day after Jenna and the dragons freed the musician from the empress's ruined palace, Jenna sat down with him to try to get some answers. The musician's lack of voice made the interview an awkward and laborious process.

"What is your name?" Jenna said, gesturing toward the tablet on the musician's lap.

In careful block letters, he wrote *BREON*. After a moment's hesitation, he added, *D'TARVOS*.

"So you're from Tarvos?" Jenna said.

He shrugged, as if to say, *Maybe.*

Jenna wasn't entirely sure where Tarvos was, but it seemed like she'd seen it on a map somewhere. "That's in Carthis? On the coast?"

Breon nodded. Laboriously, he drew a squirmy vertical line. His hand shook, and it seemed to take forever. Still, Jenna recognized it as the coast of Carthis from their aerial views. He added a dot near the lower end and labeled it *TARVOS*.

"It's on the southern coast of Carthis?"

He nodded, looking pleased that she'd deciphered his map.

"Did you know your parents?" By now, Jenna wasn't hopeful, but she had to ask.

He shook his head.

"How old are you?"

He rocked his hand, then wrote *16*.

"What is your gift?" Jenna said, feeling like she was asking the wrong questions somehow. That she was missing something important.

He pointed at his throat, then at his instrument.

"Music?"

He nodded.

"Do you know any other magemarked people?"

He shook his head, pointing to Jenna, and then back at himself.

"Have you met a pirate named Evan Strangward?"

*NO*

Well, you smell like him, Jenna thought of saying. But didn't. But he was writing again, unprompted. He held up the tablet.

*CELESTINE SAYS SHE IS MY SISTER.*

*"What?"*

Breon nodded. Then squeezed his eyes shut, massaging his forehead with the heels of his hands, as if he had a headache.

Jenna studied Breon, seeking telltales of kinship with Celestine. She breathed in his scent, tantalizingly familiar.

If Breon was Celestine's brother, and the empress was hunting him, and hunting Jenna, and hunting Strangward, then—

"Cas."

The dragon had been sleeping off breakfast in a patch of sun. He opened one eye.

"Does Breon's scent remind you of anyone else?"

Jenna scrambled away from the musician as Cas lifted his massive head and swung it toward him. The closer it got, the paler Breon became. The dragon breathed in sharply. Breon closed his eyes, his lips moving in silent prayer.

*Musician smells like Jenna*, Cas said. Then rested his head on his forelegs and returned to his nap.

Jenna's mind raced. If Celestine, Strangward, Jenna, and Breon shared the same scent, then they must share the same blood. Was it possible that they were all siblings?

Though this news hit her like a slate fall, it was almost as if she'd always known it, under the skin. It was as if they shared a long-buried history.

Scent is the seat of memory.

She looked up. The musician was sitting, eyes closed, his face gleaming with sweat, as if enduring some private pain.

"Do you know where the empress is now?" Jenna said.

*THE REALMS.*

"Do you know where? What city?"

Breon shook his head, then wrote:

*SHE WILL COME BACK. MUST LEAVE NOW.*

"Do you know why the empress is hunting us?" Jenna said. "Is it because of the magemark?"

Breon lifted his hands, palms up, as if to demonstrate that he was all out of answers. Then he leaned forward, looking into Jenna's eyes as if to give the letters on the page greater emphasis. He was pale, trembling.

"Are you all right?" Jenna said.

He waved off the question, running his finger under the words *MUST LEAVE NOW.*

"We're getting ready to leave," Jenna said. "But there's someone else we're looking for. A Captain Gray. Do you know where she is?"

Breon hesitated, eyeing Jenna suspiciously as if unsure of her intentions, then picked up his tablet and wrote, *WHY?*

"Why do we want to find her?"

He nodded.

"Because . . . because we're friends. We're worried about her."

The spellsinger gazed at her for a long moment, as if he might look through her skin and read her heart. Finally, he wrote, *LYSS LEFT WITH THE EMPRESS.*

*Lyss?* "You know Lyss?"

He nodded. *FRIENDS.*

"So she is on her way back to the Realms?"

Breon nodded.

"We'll leave tomorrow, then," Jenna said, her mind racing. By now, Celestine's ships could be anywhere on the broad ocean between here and the Realms. She knew that Lyssa Wolf had been trying to persuade Celestine to take her forces south, but there was no guarantee the empress would listen. The entire wetland coast was a lot of territory to cover.

Jenna told the dragons what she'd learned, and they packed up again, preparing for departure. For safety's sake, they left the remains of the harbor town and moved back into the mountains.

But the young, magemarked musician had a bad night. He shivered and sweated, as if he were running a fever, but his skin was cold and clammy. He doubled up, like he had belly pain. The only thing that seemed to soothe him somewhat was playing the jafasa, but the music was harder and harder to listen to, it was so infused with pain.

The dragons were beside themselves with concern. They brought choice chunks of raw goat meat and water from a spring high in the mountains, but he ate next to nothing. They put on aerobatic displays to divert him. They carried glittering bits of quartz from the mountains and intricate shells from the sea.

Finally, Jenna took hold of his hands again, hoping to get a clue to what ailed him, and his pain and despair all but overwhelmed her. His mind was clearer than before, though, and she could make out the shape of a curved pipe and some crinkled brown leaves.

That's when Jenna finally understood. *He's addicted to razorleaf*, she thought. *He's in withdrawal.*

*Spellsinger sick?* Splash asked, for the fiftieth time.

As soon as Jenna mentioned leaf, the dragons were off to

all parts of the island, returning with their claws filled with every kind of leaf, dropping them in front of the boy for his inspection. He just kept shaking his head. Finally, he jerked upright, his limbs twisting as he went into a seizure. That made the fledglings so nervous that they kept taking off and landing again, unable to control their agitation.

Finally, Splash curved her body around the boy in a tight embrace, holding him close until the seizures eased and he fell asleep.

Once again, they were being held back by the weakest in the flight.

That night, they held a council. "We can't stay here," Jenna said. "We've burned the nest, but Celestine still lives. We need to find her."

*Find Lyssa Wolf*, Slayer said.

*Stay with Spellsinger*, Splash said, adjusting her coils around the musician with an air of finality.

"I don't want to leave the spellsinger behind," Jenna said. "He's marked like me. He might be my littermate." At the very least, she hoped he might know pieces of her own story.

*You stay. We go find Lyssa Wolf*, Slayer said.

*No*, Cas said. *We all go or we all stay.*

A dragon argument erupted, punctuated by brief launches and landings, eruptions of flame, tail slapping, and aggressive posturing. At the end of it, they came to a decision: they would leave the island in two days. If the spellsinger hadn't recovered by then, they would have to carry him along and hope that he survived the journey.

The next morning, Jenna was awakened by the keening of a dragon. She'd been leaning against Cas, but he rolled away, dumping her unceremoniously on the ground.

Now fully awakened, Jenna scrambled to her feet. The young dragon who called himself Goat Toes was the one raising the alarm. He'd been on the dawn watch. Finally, Jenna could make out what he was shouting.

*Ship!*

*One ship or many ships?* Cas said.

*One ship*, Goat said. *Where Splash fell.* To the dragons, Celesgarde would forever be "Where Splash Fell."

Jenna's heart clenched like a fist in her chest. Was it Celestine? It seemed unlikely that the empress would return so soon, if she had been heading for the Realms. Unless she'd made a quick trip to the Carthian mainland and come back again.

"Is it a big ship?" Jenna asked, even though she wasn't all that confident about Goat's ability to judge the relative size of ships. "The empress's ship?"

*Not big ship*, Goat said. *Little ship.*

It could be just another one of Celestine's captains arriving at an inopportune time. The dragons were whipping themselves into a fiery frenzy, anticipating revenge.

Then Jenna noticed something else. It was eerily quiet, save for the sounds of seagulls, the hiss of steam from the fissures, and the battle cries of dragons. The continuous roar of the wind was gone. The light had changed, too. The sun had cleared the horizon, sharp and bright, no longer muffled by cloud and ice.

The stormwall was down.

What did that mean?

Fear quivered through her. It had to be the empress. Who else would have the power to put up a stormwall or bring it down?

"Cas," Jenna said, fetching her armor from their campsite and buckling it on. "I think it must be Celestine. If it is, we'll have to be smart and careful. We don't want to scare her off." She knew that would be better received than *She might kill us.*

*Dragons sneak*, Cas said. *Splash and Pricker, stay with Spellsinger. Slayer and Goat, come with us, find ship. Splinter, stay high, watch for more ships.* There was a certain amount of grumbling about these assignments, but the young dragons deferred to Cas in the end.

One by one, the dragons launched from the side of the mountain, circling to gain altitude, losing themselves in the glare of the sunrise, something Jenna hadn't seen since her arrival on Weeping Sister. Jenna and Cas were the last to fly. When all were so high as to be barely visible from the ground, they flew west, to the harbor side of the island.

Jenna leaned down over Cas's shoulder, straining to see. There was the ruined city, the rubble that had been the palace, and the remains of the quay. And there—one small ship at anchor in the harbor.

*Not the empress ship*, Cas said. *Too small.*

Jenna squinted. "Can you see anyone aboard?"

*Something moving*, Cas said. He circled lower, followed by his dragon honor guard.

Soon, even Jenna could pick out details on the boat. It looked to be badly damaged, its masts and rigging mangled and broken. The empress's fleet included a broad variety of ships, given that she often put into service the vessels she'd captured. Still, this was smaller than most she'd crewed. Jenna didn't recognize the tattered flag they flew; it was not the empress's siren signia.

Jenna could make out three people moving on deck,

attempting to clear away the mess, oblivious of death coming at them from the skies.

*Prey.*

Had they been damaged going through the Boil?

Had they damaged the Boil going through it?

*Burn the nest?* Cas said hopefully. Jenna could hear the fledglings behind them, their excited chorus.

*Burn the nest! Kill the hatchlings! Claim the hoard!*

Jenna fingered her magemark. It wasn't responding the way it usually did in proximity to the empress. It did not burn, or seethe, or even prickle. Instead, images sluiced through her mind, so quickly that it was difficult to grab hold of any one of them.

"Not yet," she said. "Go lower."

*Have guns,* Cas warned. *Tricky maybe.*

Still, the dragon continued to lose altitude. Now Jenna could mark out the enemy individually. All three of them were wearing watch caps pulled down over their ears. Two of them shone like pale dawn stars against the horizon. Wizards—but not the kind that Celestine fielded in her army. One of the wizards was slender and agile, scrambling up the single remaining mast and down the standing rigging like a spider. The other was tall, rangy, more deliberate in his movements. Something about him struck a chord of memory in Jenna.

The third—a female—was not gifted, except in size and strength. She went at the work with a will. The spider seemed to be the one in charge. Jenna saw no sign of the empress.

*Burn ship and go?* Cas said.

*Burn ship!* the fledglings chorused.

Jenna was about to agree, but then a new sound rose from the

broken ship. The spider was singing, in Common. He seemed
to be trying to cheer up his companions.

*The mate was drunk, and he went below*
*To take a swig of his bottle, oh*
*A bottle of belch and a clank of stingo*
*The sailor loves his bottle, OH!*

*The laddies, oh, the lassies, oh*
*The sailor loves the clicket, so*
*A romp in the Midden and a dock in the bow*
*The sailor loves the clicket, OH!*

It seems wrong to burn somebody alive when he's singing
a bawdy song, Jenna thought. They hovered, indecisive, Cas
keeping them aloft with broad sweeps of his wings.

*Let pirate finish song,* Cas suggested. *Then burn ship and go.*

Jenna was beginning to think they should just return to the
aerie and hide until the crew of the little ship made its repairs
and left.

She remembered her vow. *I will not hesitate. I will not fail.*
This ship had to be part of the empress's fleet. No enemy or
rival would be foolish enough to sail this little gunship into the
siren's lair.

Whatever she might have decided, it was too late. Goat
had continued to circle, each round bringing him closer to
the water's surface. Now he folded his wings and plummeted
toward the sea, screaming a challenge. Just before he hit the
surface, he shot forward, skimming the deck, obviously meaning to rake the ship bow to stern with dragon flame. He was

so focused on his target that he neglected to notice the lines
spreading like a net from the single standing mast. He plowed
into them at high speed, then landed heavily on the deck, the
rigging that remained coming down on top of him. The more
he flailed, the more ensnared he became.

The singing stopped abruptly. The female shouted and
pointed skyward, at Cas and Slayer, then sprinted toward the
guns that spiked both sides of the ship. Cas plunged toward
the deck, too, but the spider mage, quick as thought, swept his
hands toward them, and they were buffeted by a blast of wind,
sending them tumbling head over tail. The tall mage followed
with a bolt of flame that would have burned anyone else to a
crisp.

Slayer began his own sortie, screaming out of the blinding
dawn like an avenging banshee. But the tall, rangy wizard held
his ground on deck, one hand on his amulet, the other casting
skeins of glittering netting over the ship with each flick of his
wrist. Slayer had to turn away at the last minute to avoid being
entangled himself. His torrents of dragon flame didn't penetrate
the barricade, either.

In his struggles to free himself, Goat managed to set fire to
some of the debris on the deck. The spider gestured, and a large
wave crested over the deck and quenched it, quenching Goat in
the process.

A weathermaking mage, Jenna thought. There was something she should be remembering.

The cannon boomed, one by one, as the female lit the match
and projectiles screamed past them. All in all, it was an impressive defensive display. Ships' cannons make a satisfactory noise,
but they are not good at hitting any target that moves as fast as

a dragon. Once all the cannon had fired, it would take time to reload. Meanwhile, Goat was reducing what remained of the ship's rigging to splinters and line, screaming all the while.

Both wizards seemed weary, though, wrung out, their auras as pale as the winter sun. Jenna suspected that they couldn't keep up a defense for too much longer.

Who were they? She breathed in sharply, but couldn't catch a scent other than woodsmoke.

Meanwhile, they couldn't get through the wizard's magical barricade and free the hopelessly entangled young dragon.

As Jenna watched, the taller wizard fought his way through the tangled debris to reach Goat's side. He crowded in as close as he dared to the floundering dragon, staying just behind the dragon's front legs, where Goat couldn't see him. Even if he had, he couldn't reach him with his tail, his flame, or his teeth.

Cas dropped as low as he dared, while still avoiding the magical barrier, the force of his wings driving ripples across the water's surface.

"Goat!" Jenna shouted. "Look out!"

The wizard heard. He stopped and looked up, shading his eyes with his hand. Then he shook his head and went back to business. He pressed one hand against the dragon's side and leaned in close, his forehead all but touching Goat's scales. The wizard murmured a charm. His voice—and the words—seemed familiar. Gradually, Goat quieted, stopped struggling, lowered his head to the deck, and closed his eyes, all but purring.

The tall mage reached under his coat, and something new glittered in his hand. A knife.

*Goat!* Cas screamed a warning. But Goat, mesmerized, did not respond.

*Mage trick attack!* Slayer roared his frustration, sweeping back and forth over the ship, repeatedly flaming the mage's barricade. It seemed to be fading, weakening in places, and now and then the flame penetrated. As if aware of the danger, the spider repeatedly wet down the decks and drove the dragons back with gusts of wind while the female beat out any flames that caught.

But the wizard did not attack. Instead of trying to stab into Goat's underbelly, or creeping forward to cut his throat, he began methodically slicing away at the rigging pinning the young dragon's limbs. He worked his way around the dragon's body, even hoisting himself onto the dragon's back so as to cut away the lines that had threatened to strangle him when he struggled. He spoke to Goat, and the dragon rolled onto his back so the mage could get at the rigging underneath him.

The mage was skilled with a knife. It wasn't long before Goat was free of his bindings.

That was when the heat rising from Goat finally brought Jenna the wizard's scent—wild, intoxicating, wolfish. An image came back to Jenna—a scene in the dungeon at Ardenscourt, the red-haired healer, Adam Wolf, carefully cutting away the bandages over her magically festering wound.

"Wolf!" Jenna cried.

*Where?* Cas said, pinning his ears and scanning the ship and the shoreline.

"There!" Jenna said, and vaulted from the dragon's back. That wasn't a smart move, because they were higher off the deck than she'd expected. She plunged right through the failing magical barricade and hit the decking hard. She lay there trying to drag breath back into her body.

Moments later, the entire ship shook and listed as Cas landed between her and the healer. She found herself peering out between the dragon's legs. The healer stood, legs braced apart, his little knife extended in front of him, chin up, ready to do battle. She could see the copper hair peeking out from under his watch cap, the long, lupine face, the stubborn resolve in the blue-green eyes. Then his female companion pushed in front of him, brandishing her larger sword. Still, it was ludicrous, these two tiny humans with one big sword, confronting a nearly full-grown dragon.

Cas's muscles bunched, his head came forward, and Jenna knew he was seconds away from bathing them in flame.

"No!" Jenna leapt between Cas and his targets, planting her hand firmly on the dragon's snout. "The male is Lyssa Wolf's littermate."

Cas inhaled sharply. *Smells like wolf,* he conceded. He cocked his head, grinning charmingly, exposing teeth the size of rock slabs. *Flame female?*

Jenna knew this was dragon humor, but she still scowled at him and said, "No."

She turned back to Adam Wolf and his companion. The tip of the female's sword had dropped so that it pointed at the deck. Adam Wolf stood frozen, unblinking. His knife slid from his hand and pinged on the planks by his feet. "Jenna?" he said hoarsely, taking one step forward, his body canted warily as if expecting disappointment.

Jenna flew at the healer, slamming into him so hard that they both nearly toppled over backward. She pulled him close, feeling his heart pounding through those odd sailor's clothes and her own leather armor. She traced his broad back with her

ng them down to the base of his spine, squeezing
ss, pulling him tightly into her body. He seemed
more weathered than before.

ed her nose into his shoulder, breathing him in,
recent history. Back in Ardenscourt, he'd always
tly of herbs, medicines, blood, and teas. Now, the
water, sea air, and sweat overlay his wolfish base.
r face up and found that their lips were inches apart.
s stubbled face between her hands, she kissed him
savagely.

Faintly, Jenna heard the beating of dragon wings overhead, felt the wind stirring her hair. She heard Cas's voice in her head. *Slayer! Splinter! Wait on shore. Jenna maybe mating with wolf.*

Cheeks flaming, Jenna stepped back, suddenly aware of being surrounded by an audience. Goat had crept forward on his belly until his head was practically touching them. Adam Wolf's female companion was staring, openmouthed. Cas was hovering behind her, his hot, slightly sulfurous breath on the back of her neck. He resembled a scaled chaperone, ready to intervene.

And then, finally, the spider leapt down from the rigging, both boots hitting the deck. It wasn't until he doffed his watch cap and bowed that Jenna realized that it was the pirate Evan Strangward.

"I told you she was alive," he said to Adam Wolf.

# BORDERLANDS

Destin had been repulsed by the Darian Brothers during their brief partnership at Oden's Ford. Repulsed and disappointed, since they'd failed to assassinate the Fellsian prince. He'd never dug too deeply into their history, because he intended it to be a one-off. He'd only used them because King Gerard had made it clear that he wanted the blame for violating the centuries-old Peace of Oden's Ford to be deflected elsewhere.

After that debacle, Destin had made a mental note—never, ever work with fanatics again.

Easier said than done, it turned out. When Jarat assigned this murder of crows to Destin, he'd done some research in the cathedral library before he took the road north. There was plenty of information about Saint Darian, one of the patriarchs of the Church of Malthus a thousand years ago, and his followers, known as Darian Brothers, who were bent on eliminating the gifted from the Realms. But Darian and his henchmen seemed to have died out. Nothing had been written about them for centuries.

Now, it seemed, the Darian brotherhood had been revived,

with a new leader. Destin could find little on o
modern Lord Darian. The two bits of intellige
glean suggested that he was a mage himself, and
somewhere in the north.

*I guess that makes him a wizard, not a mage, Des*
*And he might be hard to find in a place where* p
*throw a rock without hitting a wizard.* Which was
because Destin was more than happy to give the new
his discipline book.

In the meantime, he served as the unwilling captain of an
entire company of bloodthirsty priests. Literally bloodthirsty.

"Your job is to collar the mages," Destin told them, "not to
suck them dry. Understood?" But threats made little impression
to those with their eyes on paradise.

Fortunately, aside from the few unlucky mages in the Delphian garrison, Destin found no gifted among the general
population. After all, mages could live wherever they chose.
That being the case, why would they choose Delphi? He had no
doubt, however, that when Jarat's army crossed into the Fells,
they would find mages aplenty.

While the Darians sniffed around, hunting for mages in hiding, Destin sniffed around, trying to learn what he could about
the military situation in the north and the location of the missing thane families and the queen mother and princess of Arden.

He also made inquiries about possible sightings of fugitive
pirates along the wetland coast. There were plenty of pirate
sightings, but they all seemed to be the ships belonging to the
empress in the east. The fighting was reported to be fierce from
Invaders Bay to the border town of Spiritgate, and as far west as
the Alyssa Plateau.

It was almost a blessing when the king sent word that they would march north on the morrow, and that Destin and his minions were ordered to march along.

The day of marching dawned cold and nasty, like every other day in Delphi. Destin chose to ride, not march. For someone who'd gathered a great deal of intelligence about the Fells and its people, he'd spent little time north of the border once he was old enough to avoid the general's grip.

Though the Ardenine army had suffered losses in Delphi, it still numbered in the thousands as it climbed into Marisa Pines Pass, graveyard of so many southerners in the past. Mercenaries, marked by their striped scarves, comprised close to half of the soldiers. Destin wondered if his king was better at paying his mercenaries than at paying the regular troops. He hoped so.

King Jarat was in high spirits, despite the weather, prancing about on a fine horse, his personal guard of collared mages struggling to keep up. He was dressed to kill—quite literally, in a general's uniform with his father's well-used sword in his saddle boot. At the end of the columns of infantry, trundled wagons carried whatever it was Jarat needed to feel at home in the Fellsian Court. There was one bright note—Destin's friend and sometime operative, the seamstress Jocelyn Fournier, came along in the wagon train, in case Jarat needed some emergency alterations on the long road north.

Destin positioned himself between the wagon train and the van of the army. He'd made an exception to his usual rule and had worn standard-issue military garb. Thanks to the general, he knew his way around a battlefield. It was best not to stand out in a country famous for hit-and-run ambushes. If you were a clan archer on the hillside, who would you aim at—a general, a despised spymaster, or an ordinary line soldier? If there were wizards on the heights, of course, he would be picked out as gifted and picked off for sure.

If he had to die for a cause, so be it, but, given a choice, he preferred not to die for the young king of Arden.

Their slow climb into the pass was eerily uneventful. The veterans rode, shoulders hunched, faces grim, eyes scanning the hillsides and the trail ahead. New recruits and stripers nudged each other, nervously joking that the northerners must have slept in. General Bellamy and his officers seemed to be every-where, tightening up formations, consulting with the scouts, directing the excavation of wagons that had become stuck in the mud. When they were nearly to Marisa Pines Camp, they came upon a huge rockfall in the road that made it impossible to go farther until it was cleared away.

I have a bad feeling about this, Destin thought. He dis-mounted and helped in the effort to clear it, organizing the mages into a team to blast the barrier away. When they sleep-walked through that, Destin rigged up a makeshift block and tackle to lift debris from the path.

Well, he thought, you always wanted to be an engineer.

The road was still mostly blocked when he heard the first snap of bowstrings. Soldiers and officers alike dove for cover as arrows rained down on them from the heights on both sides of the trail. They were effectively pinned down by volleys of cop-perhead arrows, and prevented from moving forward and out of range by the blockage of the road.

Their mages encircled the king, repeatedly sweeping the heights with flame. They charred the shrubbery and set trees on fire, but the copperheads seemed impervious to it.

A contingent of soldiers had begun the climb up the slope, meaning to clear out the bowmen, but they would be lucky if any of them made it to the top.

Destin approached Bellamy. "The copperheads must be wearing talismans, which makes direct magical attacks ineffective. If we can withdraw our forces a few hundred yards south of the pass, we can blast away the cliff face and dislodge them."

Bellamy studied Destin, hands on hips, then looked up at the cliff face. "We'd be running the risk of closing the pass completely," he said.

"It's closed now," Destin said, "and we can't clear it under constant fire from above. You'll lose the mages you have."

"It'll be all but impossible to turn these wagons around," Bellamy said. Which was true. The Ardenine army was like a giant Bruinswallow constrictor sliding through a rabbit burrow. It could not circle back on itself, but the segments could swivel and march back the way they'd come.

"Leave the wagons for now. Move the men."

Bellamy shot a look at Jarat, enclosed in his magical bunker. He rubbed his chin, then turned away and sounded the order for retreat. The columns marched back the way they came, parting like a river around Jarat's wagons, and flowing together beyond them.

The king of Arden spurred toward them. "General Bellamy! What are you doing? We need to go forward, not back! We have a schedule to keep."

"This was my idea, Your Majesty," Destin said, in an unusual act of gallantry. He expected that it would be beneficial to have the rising young star of the Ardenine military on his side.

Also, he liked Bellamy. Also, it was true. "We need to clear the archers from the heights before we can go forward, or we'll be lucky to have enough men left to form a brigade."

The king scowled. "You'd better hope this works," he said. He stood in his stirrups and seethed, keeping a tight rein on his horse, while the fall zone was cleared of soldiers, leaving only the wagons behind. Destin lined up his mages behind a magical shield and ordered them to target the rock face just below the vantage point of the enemy archers.

The mages blasted the cliffs to either side, sending shattered rock, gravel, and flailing bowmen cascading into the roadway. It didn't take long for the archers to recognize the danger and withdraw.

Unfortunately, a massive boulder made a direct hit on one of the king's precious wagons, reducing it to mingled splinters, silks, and satins, all soaked in red Tamron wine.

While Destin and the mages worked to clear away the debris and open the road, Jarat's steward and servants salvaged what was salvageable from the mess. Four hours later, with the pass already in the shadow of the mountain, they were on their way again, determined to emerge on the other side before they had to camp for the night.

The next morning they marched into a deserted Marisa Pines Camp. The camp had been raided, conquered, and burnt numerous times over the centuries. It just never stayed conquered. *The residents probably have the evacuation thing down to a science,* Destin thought. Hunching his shoulders, scanning the surrounding peaks, he imagined hundreds of pairs of eyes looking down at them.

Seasoned soldiers met this disappointment stoically. Marisa

Pines had been the scene of the shedding of vast quantities of southern blood in repeated assaults through the pass.

On the other hand, Jarat's frisky young underlords were crestfallen that there was no one to kill and little to plunder. They were in favor of burning everything to the ground, but Jarat took an almost proprietary interest in preserving the territory they'd "won." The entire army camped overnight in the Vale north of the deserted village.

Destin never once closed his eyes.

The next day, they marched northward, unmolested, through the relatively flat Vale. Fields were planted, and orchards were in bloom, but the farmers were nowhere to be seen, nor was there fresh food or livestock to fill an army's empty bellies. They'd brought provisions with them, but an extended siege could deplete them quickly.

The way this "invasion" is going, Destin thought, the witch queen may throw open the gates and host a welcome party with the missing Ardenine hostages in attendance.

Unless this is a massive trap and we are walking right into it.

# KINGMAKER

Fortunately, the bolt that had pierced Robert's shoulder had passed through, leaving a clean wound behind. Though few mages in the south had much experience in healing, Marc DeJardin had spent some time in the healing halls at Ardenscourt. He treated Robert's shoulder under strict instructions from his patient to be sure and leave a flashy scar.

Hal was relieved, but his anger and disappointment had not abated. Robert could have been the first casualty in the battle for the crown.

He fought down the urge to find the guilty archers and hang them from the walls. Soldiers are not the problem, he thought. No doubt they were acting under orders.

Hal had hoped to rise in the military through his performance in the field, and he had—up to a point. Then he'd run straight into General Marin Karn, and realized that valor and skill and strategy would never win against Arden's venomous politics.

For more than three decades, the empire had been pinned under the boot of a ruthless king. After decades of war, and its cost in blood and treasure, Hal wanted more than an even swap—one despot for another. He'd seen a better system in the north, and he'd planned to support it by defending the Fells against the empress and whoever else threatened its survival.

Yet, despite everything that had happened, he retained a loyalty to his homeland, if not the empire. Arden's traditions, its language, and its customs were all engraved on his bones. As things stood, Arden seemed destined to descend into another civil war, which would mean easy pickings for Celestine. Somehow, he had to bring better government to his homeland, though he had no idea how to accomplish that in a realm that hadn't known freedom in hundreds of years. But he knew it wouldn't happen if he didn't step up.

Hal's father was the only thane who accepted Hal's invitation to come into the palace for a thane council. Most of the other thanes had already departed to their home keeps to seethe and plot vengeance.

So it was that the Matelon men found themselves drinking the king's wine and dining at the king's table. Hal's father was giddy with joy over the way that Hal had outmaneuvered their unsuspecting allies.

Well, perhaps *giddy* was too strong a word. Lord Matelon was still grumbling about the fact that Hal insisted that he leave the White Oaks bannermen outside the gates, along with everyone else's. His mood was rapidly improving with the help of the finest wine in the empire.

"I understand that there was a need to keep up the appearance of impartiality," Lord Matelon said, "but now there's nothing wrong with driving it home that we've won."

"I came here to end a civil war," Hal said, "not to launch another one."

"Exactly," his father said. "How many times have I told you that in a civil war, nobody wins? The key to preventing a war is to let the rebels know from the outset that it's hopeless. Overwhelming power will discourage any thoughts of toppling us. You saw how unwilling they were to sign on to go north after our families. They probably think it's another trick to make them vulnerable to an attack from us."

Hal hadn't really expected the other thanes to contribute to his venture in the north, but he was open to being pleasantly surprised. The only one who'd sent word was young Rafe Heresford, who likely knew that he hadn't a chance to prevail in any contest for the throne. Not only that, the only family he had left was the family who'd been carried off north.

"I'll go with you, Hal," Robert said, his cheeks flushed with triumph and a little too much wine. "I'm almost as good as new."

"Neither of you are going north," Matelon said. "You're needed here."

Hal and Robert stared at their father.

For once, Hal spoke first. "When I agreed to lead the combined thane army, I told you that I meant to march north once we succeeded in taking Ardenscourt." He paused, then forged ahead. "I kept *my* promise."

Lord Matelon tossed a bone to the dogs under the table, then tossed a bone to Hal. "I'm not saying that you can't send an army north, Son," he said. "I'm saying that someone else should take command of it. Heresford, maybe, since he seems willing to go."

"I am not sending Heresford to do the job that I swore to do," Hal said. "If he wants to come with me, that's fine."

"Look," Lord Matelon said, "armies don't keep. We need to press the advantage we have. We hold the city, and we have—what—more than a thousand seasoned soldiers at our disposal, in addition to the bannermen I brought with me. A show of strength now will prevent further bloodshed. We'll hold the coronation within the week."

"The coronation?" Hal's stomach sank into his boots.

"Aye," his father said. "Once I'm crowned emperor, we'll reach out to the downrealms and offer them more autonomy—at least temporarily—in exchange for their support. If Jarat survives his invasion of the north, he'll come back to find that his throne is occupied. The other thanes will know that Jarat will never forgive them for taking up arms against him, so they'll have to throw in with us. Especially if they want to reclaim the properties they've lost."

"What about Mother and Harper?" Robert said, voice rising. "Are they anywhere on your list?"

"You forget yourself, boy," Lord Matelon snapped. "If Heresford doesn't get them back, we will negotiate for their release, once we have consolidated power here in the south."

"Who'll we negotiate with?" Hal said. "If the empress overruns the northern queendom, she'll be the one setting the terms for any negotiation."

"I cannot understand this obsession you have with the empress," Lord Matelon growled.

Hal couldn't help thinking of what Lieutenant Karn had said after the rescue of the hostages. *Maybe your father will be crowned king. King Arschel. Meanwhile, the empress is marching. As things stand, I suspect whoever wins will have a very short reign.*

Hal was a Matelon, and he'd been raised to be a good soldier, a dutiful son, a faithful subject of the king. Now, perhaps, he was none of those things.

He took a deep breath. "You're wrong, Father."

The big head came up, the heavy brows drew together. "Wrong? What do you mean?"

Hal met his father's eyes, and held his gaze, conscious of the pressure of Robert's eyes. "You said that we have a thousand seasoned soldiers at our disposal. In fact, *I* have two thousand seasoned soldiers. *You* have your bannermen. Maybe."

"What are you saying, Halston?" His father employed that bass rumble that had been so intimidating when Hal was a boy. But Hal wasn't a boy—not anymore.

"I am saying that I keep my promises," Hal said, "and you will keep your promises to me."

Lord Matelon slammed his hands down on the table. "You are not seeing the big picture. For more than twenty-five years, we have suffered under Gerard Montaigne. This is our chance to change that. We come from a line of kings. We have ruled in the past. There is no reason we shouldn't rule now."

"You are the one who's not seeing the big picture," Hal said. "You are so blinded by local squabbles that you haven't noticed the storms gathering in the north. I've tried to tell you, and you haven't listened. While we jockey for position, the empress will conquer the north, and then she will conquer us, too."

His father's jaw worked, and beads of sweat glistened on his forehead. He wasn't used to resistance from this quarter. Hal could tell that he was sorting through arguments, trying to come up with the one that would work.

"If this is about the succession, Son, rest assured, you will rule after me. I am old, and you are young, so you won't have to wait long. In the meantime, I'll put you in command of our armies. We'll negotiate a suitable marriage—perhaps to a princess of the downrealms. There's no reason not to aim high. You'll rule an empire, and your children after you, and bring a lasting peace to the Realms. I think that you'll find that it's worth the wait." Matelon pushed to his feet. "Think about it, Son, and you will see that I am right." With that, his father stalked out of the hall.

After their father departed, Hal and Robert remained at the table. Robert poured more wine.

"He has never once listened to me," Hal said, running his finger over the rim of his glass.

"That's because he's used to riding over the both of us," Robert said.

"I've learned a lot from him," Hal said.

"And he hasn't learned a thing from either of us," Robert said. He looked sideways at Hal. "You're going to have to take the throne, you know."

"You take it," Hal growled. "Jarat isn't much older than you, and you'd do a better job than he has. I'll put the crown on your head myself."

"I can't take the throne," Robert said. "Your army wouldn't stand for it. I'd be dead within the week." He paused. "If you stay and rule, I'll go north with the army."

Hal shook his head. "I need to lead. I'm the one who asked for volunteers. No offense meant, but I'm the one with the experience. I'm not going to sit home and send them—and you—into harm's way."

"That's what politicians do," Robert said.

"That's proof positive that I'm not suited for the throne."

"If you leave the throne vacant and go north, someone will claim it. Father, probably, until somebody else pushes him off. The bloodshed continues, and the empress waltzes in and claims what remains."

Hal eyed his brother. "I might win, you know."

Robert raised both hands. "I'm not saying you won't. If you do, you'll come back to a mess, if not a ruin. If DeLacroix or Tourant gains the throne, they'll be sending assassins after you or colluding with the empress to defeat you. Just like old times."

"When did you get to be a politician?"

"Somebody has to be, since you don't seem to have inherited Father's ambition."

Hal laughed. "It's not that I don't have aspirations," he said. "I do." Aspirations that involved Lyssa Gray, if she still lived. If he survived. He was like any soldier who marched away to war with a miniature of his sweetheart in his duty bag. The symbol of a life after the fighting is over.

"My money's on you."

"You might be backing the wrong horse."

"I'll take my chances," Robert said. "My point is, if Father takes the throne, you'll never get your way. He'll always have reasons for you to stay and support his agenda, until the empress comes knocking on the door. If you don't cooperate, he'll discard you, the way he's discarded Mother and Harper."

"That's harsh," Hal said. "This has always been his policy, not to negotiate with—"

"It's time to stop making excuses for him," Robert said. "That's what we always do. Father looks good, compared with what we've had for twenty-five years. But is he good enough?" He paused, and when Hal said nothing, he continued on. "It's time to figure out what your policy is, and go after what you want."

"That's enough wine," Hal said, plunking his glass down. "You're beginning to sound like the voice of reason." He cocked his head. "Why is it that you believe in me, when nobody else does?"

"I've always believed in you, Hal," Robert said.

Hal rested his elbows on the table, his chin on his clasped hands, thinking furiously. Was there any way to march north without leaving the crown up for grabs?

He'd promised the mages their freedom if they supported him. He had a feeling that if his father ascended the throne, that would turn out to be inconvenient also. Another promise broken, leaving mages with a grudge. Mages no longer imprisoned by their collars.

"All right," Hal said. "Here's what I'm thinking."

Early the next morning, Hal met with the officers who had been so eager to proclaim him king and gained their support for his plans. He realized that it might be unfair for him to use his history with these men to further his own agenda, but he liked to think that their trust in him was honestly earned. Thad Mercier agreed to serve as military commander of the city in Hal's absence. Mercier was well respected by his fellow officers and soldiers. Then he and Mercier met with DeJardin and the mages. During this time, Hal and Robert ignored several messages from their father, demanding a meeting.

Hal asked Jan Rives to serve as quartermaster and steward

for the city, alongside Robert as administrator. He didn't really expect Rives to agree, given the old sergeant's loyalty to his father, but he did.

"It's time," Rives said. "We've made a fair mess of things. If we want change, we need to make room for the young ones."

Hal's coronation took place two days later, in Jarat's small hall. Hal hadn't been present at Jarat's coronation, but he had to think that it must have been similar to his own. Small, hurried, and secretive, as befitted a ruler under siege.

They'd searched the royal vault for a suitable crown, but Jarat seemed to have carried most of the royal regalia along with him. They finally found a small crown, more of a circlet, really, but it suited Hal.

By custom, the principia of the church would have presided over the ceremony, but Hal didn't need another rant from Fosnaught. Instead, they found a flexible priest of the Church of Malthus who was willing to stand in. Most of the attendees were Hal's officers, including Marc DeJardin, representing the mages. It was an entirely male event that smelled too much like a military coup.

The women who might have attended were somewhere in the north. The noblewomen who were still in the capital hid in their houses, not wanting to come to the attention of the rebel forces, especially after the way the hostage families had been treated.

Hal recalled something Captain Gray had said. *Oh. Right. You don't have women in your army. No wonder you're losing.*

One step at a time, he thought.

Hal's thane "allies" were huddled in their keeps, laying plans and no doubt plotting his destruction. Only Rafe Heresford was there to toast the embattled new king.

After some debate, he invited his father, and, to Hal's surprise, Lord Matelon came. Perhaps he wanted to minimize the appearance of division in the family. Perhaps he had hopes that he could exert more influence in the new regime if he sanctioned it. Perhaps he was hoping for some more of that excellent Tamron wine.

On impulse, Hal invited the children from the Cathedral Temple school, too, on the theory that change begins with the young. The students were from all over the empire, many of them girls, since an arts-and-religion-focused temple education was considered suitable for them. They watched, wide-eyed and apprehensive, as Robert carefully set the crown on Hal's head. The crown might have been modest, but it still weighed him down.

In Arden, death was the only way out from under the crown.

The temple chorus sang, their voices high and true.

Then the children came forward, one by one, to be blessed by the new king. Hal gave each of them a token, a pewter button with the Matelon tree on it.

"Thank you for coming," Hal said to the children. "I will do my best to be a good ruler. If you ever want to come and see me and tell me how I'm doing, show your token at the palace gate, and I will see that they let you in."

One older girl, who looked to be from the downrealms, weighed the token on her palm, and said, "How do you get to be an emperor? Is there a school for that?"

"Well," Hal said, "rulers need to know a lot of different things. So we learn as much as we can, and then we find good helpers who know other things." He paused. "Any other questions?"

"If we come and see you," a little boy said, "will there be pie?"

Hal laughed. "I cannot guarantee future pie, but there is food on the back tables now, so help yourselves."

A modest feast had been laid out in the back of the hall, and the temple children swarmed toward it.

Hal's officers gathered around him, congratulated him, offering flamboyant curtsies to their new emperor, swearing elaborate oaths, proposing preposterous toasts. Until a cry from the dining tables caught their attention.

A little girl had collapsed onto the floor, and was writhing in pain, a few of her schoolmates clustered around her. A teacher knelt next to her, leaned in close to ask questions, then rolled the girl onto her side as she vomited. Across the table, an older boy stood staring, a turkey leg halfway to his mouth.

No. Oh, no.

"Stop!" Hal shouted, charging toward the feast table. "Don't touch anything. Don't eat anything. Stand back. Now."

The boy eyed the turkey leg wistfully, unwilling to let go of it until Hal snatched it out of his hand and pitched it back onto the table.

He turned toward his officers, who'd followed him. "Call for a healer. On the double, now." He paused, then added softly, "One of ours."

"It's already done," Robert said.

Hal turned back toward the children, who stood, pale-faced, clearly frightened. "Who's eaten from the table?" he demanded. "Tell the truth, now."

Hunching their shoulders as if anticipating a blow, three of the children timidly raised their hands.

"Sit over there and wait for the healer," Hal said, motioning them toward the hearth.

"But . . . you said we could go ahead and eat," the turkey leg boy said plaintively.

"I did," Hal said. "It's not your fault. It's just . . . I'm worried there is something wrong with the food."

With that, two more children raised their hands and went to sit with the others. One girl dug a sugar cake out of her skirt pocket and set it back on the table.

"General Mat—Your Majesty," DeJardin said. "I may be able to help." He nodded toward the ailing girl.

"Go ahead," Hal said. "See what you can do."

In the end, the combined efforts of DeJardin and Georges Tomasson, Hal's field surgeon, prevailed, and it seemed the girl would recover. Apparently, none of the other children had eaten enough of the wrong thing to become ill. DeJardin and Tomasson met with Hal's command circle to render their verdict—gedden weed, the go-to poison in the empire. Easy to come by, treatable if identified in time.

"Do you think it was a warning?" Hal asked. "Or were they trying to lop off the head of the new regime?"

"Oh, most definitely the latter," DeJardin said drily. "If all of your officers had bellied up to the table, it would have sickened or killed a great many of them. A poor beginning to the new order." He paused. "Don't forget—the Montaignes always used a taster."

Instead, in effect, Hal had used children for that office.

You've got to do better, Matelon, if you're going to survive this, Hal thought. Nobody plays by the rules when the stakes are this high.

Gods, he thought. What have I gotten myself into?

# 44

# SACRED AND PROFANE

Destin had to admit, the witch queens in the north had built a fine road through the Vale from Marisa Pines Pass north to the capital. Prior to the war, clan traders traveled freely between north and south, selling goods to willing buyers in the empire.

The Ardenine army made good progress through the empty countryside, with little risk of ambush, since the view across the fertile valley was clear all the way to the mountains. Having studied the geography, Destin knew that those to the left were the Spirit Mountains, the homes of the Gray Wolf queens. On the right stood the Heartfangs, the resting place of many a southern commander who thought he'd found a shortcut into the belly of the north. And, looming ahead, the moody face of Gray Lady, stronghold of the northern mages.

Somewhere, on the other side of the Heartfangs, Celestine had landed her army.

Was Evan here in the north somewhere? When they'd parted, the pirate had said that he was sailing north, to convince the Gray Wolf queen to take heed of the danger to the east.

Destin's eyes and ears continued to report that the city was lightly garrisoned, that the bulk of the Highlander army was fighting the empress in the east. They could tell him little about conditions inside the castle close. As far as anyone knew, the queen was seriously ill; some said she was dead. No one knew the whereabouts of what was left of the royal family or the queen's council. If they had any sense, they would be high in the mountains in some inaccessible crevice, with mages guarding the door.

Still, Destin thought, this war is far from over. Long before I was born, King Gerard marched his army all the way to the gates of Fellsmarch. Then was chased and harried all the way back to the flatlands.

Destin was tasked with chasing and harrying his bloodsucking Darian Brothers back into line. All the way north, they ranged far and wide into the countryside, hoping to ferret out mages in hiding. They rarely found any. As a result, the brothers were sullen and ill-tempered, like guests who thought they'd been invited to a feast and were then presented with bread and water. Despite Destin's aversion to the military, he was finding he preferred the company of his mage division to his mage-hunting crows.

Several times, they were delayed by skirmishes with local militias, but these were less effective in the relative flatlands of the Vale than they were in the mountains. Eventually, Jarat's thousands forced their way to the city walls. The king sent a demand for surrender. The city refused. Thus Arden's second siege of the city began.

Destin had read volumes on King Gerard's previous assault on the city. That history was hard to come by in Arden, but he enjoyed reading about his father's humiliation in the north.

Now that they were in camp, the Darians were constantly at Destin's heels. Either they'd been assigned to spy on him, or it was because they were drawn to the only available mage. The pressure of their hungry eyes made his skin crawl.

Now I know how Evan feels sometimes, he thought.

Finally, one night, Destin was summoned to King Jarat's command tent just as he was debating whether he was ready to face another night on the ground.

Destin walked through camp, trailing dark-robed fanatics like a bright comet with a black tail.

"Stay outside," he told them when they'd reached the command tent. "Better yet, go back to your quarters." He entered the tent, knowing that his entourage would stay put.

Generally, the king's tent was boisterous until late into the night, crowded with newly minted nobility, up-and-coming young officers, and camp followers, lubricated with ale and blue ruin. Tonight was different. The tent was lit only by three hooded lanterns and two tall, spare mages in black cloaks.

In addition to King Jarat and the mages, there was a flock of the king's blackbirds. Jarat, in his dress uniform, was the only one not clad in black. Destin felt like he was wading through the black-muck swamp in the Shivering Fens.

"Karn," King Jarat said, "I have someone I want you to meet." He gestured toward the taller of the two mages. "Valentin is an official at the Fellsian court, but he is also, secretly, a priest of the true church, and an agent of the empire."

"Really?" Destin said. "You must be a remarkable man. There are not many mages serving as celebrants in the Church of Malthus. In fact, I believe you're the first I've heard of."

"There are not many uncollared mages in the south," Valentin said. "You must be remarkable as well."

Jarat seemed amused by this sparring between mages. "Valentin has provided much useful support to us through the years, beginning in my late father's reign. He and his acolyte . . ." The king looked at the other priest expectantly.

"Fabian," Valentin put in.

"Fabian—have agreed to help us win the city in order to extend the grace of Malthus into the sinful north." Maybe it was his imagination, but Destin always detected a note of sardonic excess when Jarat spoke about the "true church."

"We've hit a snag, however," Jarat continued. "I'd been assured that the witch queen would be dead and buried prior to our arrival, but now I hear that she is widely believed to be alive."

"The queen is dead, Your Majesty," Valentin said, biting off each word. "I was there. I saw her die. The poison I used has never been known to fail."

"There is always a first time, isn't there?" Jarat snapped, petulant as a child whose Solstice gift has gone missing.

This exchange drew Destin's full attention. This Valentin had poisoned Queen Raisa? Useful support, indeed, if it was true.

"If the queen is dead, then why have there not been a state funeral, wailing in the streets, or . . ." Jarat paused, then added delicately, "the coronation of a new monarch?"

"They refuse to acknowledge her death, Your Majesty," Valentin said. "They have used glamours and conjury to convince the council that she is alive."

"Who is 'they'?"

"The queen's faction is reluctant to surrender power, Your Majesty. That is all."

"Factions usually are," Jarat said drily. "Where is she supposed to be, then, if she's not been seen at court functions?"

"Her attendants claim that she's been relocated to a lodge in the mountains to rest and recover, but I sent a team there and it was empty."

While Jarat sparred with Valentin, Destin fixed his attention on Fabian, who'd said nothing so far. Destin leaned in to get a glimpse of the priest's face within the shadow of his hood. He was much younger than his partner, in his late teens, maybe. He was gaunt, yet heartbreakingly beautiful, with smoky, haunted eyes and silver hair.

He also looked familiar. Suddenly aware of Destin's scrutiny, Fabian's eyes widened, and he tried to turn away, but Destin gripped his shoulder.

"Have we met?" Destin said.

"No, Lieutenant." The young mage pulled his head in like a turtle, as if he could disappear into his robe.

"It's colonel, actually," Destin said. So they *had* met before— when he was still a lieutenant.

Odd that he thought of the young priest as a boy, since he was close to Destin's age. But Destin was good at reading the scars of emotional trauma. Again, Fabian tried to pull away. This time, Destin gripped his hand.

"I'm Destin Karn," he said, his voice and his grip warm and full of persuasion. "What's your real name?" He caught a brief glimpse of a blood-soaked battlefield, bodies charred and blown to bits, dank stone walls reflecting candlelight, robed figures chanting prayers, and—something else. Something foreign—a very old and evil soul.

With that, the walls came down. Flame crackled between

them, and Destin yanked his hand away to avoid being burned.

Destin met the boy's eyes, and it was like looking into one of the fissures in the north where the seething blood of the earth comes to the surface. Fabian ducked his head and charged out of the tent.

Jarat and Valentin swung around, staring after the young priest.

Destin shook his head, shrugging as if baffled. "I was just trying to be friendly," he said.

"How *dare* you?" Valentin snarled. "How dare you lay your profane hands on him?"

He gripped the front of Destin's uniform tunic and dragged him in close, which gave Destin a fine opportunity to press the tip of his dagger through the priest's robes. He hit metal several times before he found soft and yielding flesh.

The mage's eyes widened as he felt the prick of the blade.

"Let go of me," Destin said, his voice audible only to Valentin.

The mage's hand dropped away.

"I know something about poisons, too," Destin breathed. "Next time, I'll share that knowledge with you directly. Whatever you're doing to that boy, I want you to stop."

Destin took a step back and stowed his blade.

Destin Karn—making friends wherever he went.

King Jarat was watching the two of them. Destin knew the young king was familiar enough with the verbal knifework at court to know that something had happened. But, happily, he must have chosen to ignore it for now.

"Valentin has conceived a plan to breach the city walls and get into the castle close without an extended siege," Jarat said. He paused. "I do hope that the three of you can work together."

"Of course," Valentin said. "It is all for the glory of God and the great saint."

Of course, Destin thought. Sieges are boring.

"Thank you for this opportunity, Your Majesty," Destin said out loud. "I am always delighted to work with men of the True Faith."

Per Valentin, the raid would coincide with a meeting of the queen's council. Both Valentin and Fabian would be at that meeting. The two priests would secure the royal family while Destin, the Darians, and the blackbirds cleared the castle and the close.

Destin had to admit, it was a good plan—for Valentin and Fabian. Destin's team would have the bloody work of clearing the castle, floor by floor and room by room, while the priests ended up in control of the royal family.

It might even be a trap. Traitors could be useful, but they tended to be untrustworthy. Traitorous, even. Hence Destin's personal rule—never trust a traitor. It went along with *never work with fanatics.*

By now, Destin wanted nothing to do with Valentin, Fabian, or the blood-drinking crows. Violence and bloodshed had been a part of his life for as long as he could remember. Yet this was different.

Jarat said that Valentin was an official at the Gray Wolf court. What official? By now, Destin knew a lot about the personnel at the Gray Wolf court. They wouldn't use their real names, of course. They both must be members of the council, since Valentin said they would be at the meeting.

So many questions, so few answers. So much to do.

When Destin left the king's tent, he was surprised to find no flock of crows waiting outside. Not that he missed them or anything. He threaded his way back across the camp, wondering if they had actually gone back to their tent as he'd told them to do.

When he reached the tent that the Darians shared, he noticed that it was brightly illuminated from within. He heard hushed voices, chanting prayers. Curious, Destin detoured toward the tent, put his ear against the canvas, and listened. By now the voices had fallen silent.

Just go, he told himself. There will be no way to unsee whatever it is you'll see if you look inside.

It was hopeless. Destin circled around to the entrance, eased back the flap, and peered inside.

The Darian Brothers sat in a circle on the ground, each with a hooded lantern. At the center of the circle stood the young priest, Fabian, now stripped to the waist. Without the robe, Destin could see how very thin he was, the ribs standing out, belly flat. His arms hung out from his sides, palms forward, and blood dripped from numerous cuts from elbow to wrist on both sides.

The lamps underlit the priests' faces, smeared with blood, their expressions of bliss. They seemed oblivious to Destin's presence, but Fabian opened his eyes and looked directly at Destin.

Once again, Destin sensed an alien presence looking out through the young mage's eyes.

"Don't look so distressed, *Colonel*," Fabian said. His voice sounded different, deeper, ancient, wistful all at once. Like a skein of voices spun together. "You cannot save me. I am beyond your reach." He gestured at the circle of Darian crows. "I cannot deny them access to this body I inhabit. They are, after all, my children."

# 45

# RED WEDDING

Lila lay awake in her fancy bed in Kendall House, berating herself for not having slipped free of this trap before it snapped shut. If there was one thing she'd always been good at, it was reading the weather and escaping before the storm broke. One of the benefits of being everybody's girl was that she was nobody's girl, too. There were no annoying bonds of loyalty to tie her to lost causes.

Well, except for her family at Wolf's Head. If she'd had her way, she would have died alongside them, but she'd arrived too late.

And now here she was—chained by circumstance to a cause she'd never believed in before. Trapped in a castle under siege in a war she'd never committed to. Bullied by a dead wolf and guilted by a boy who'd always played by the same rules as Lila. Until now.

Said boy was sleeping next door.

But now she heard movement in the corridor outside, and before she knew what was happening, someone *else* was knocking on Shadow's door. And she had a good idea of who that someone was. Hadley DeVilliers was staying at Kendall House, too.

That was enough to spur Lila to action. She jammed her feet into her boots and slammed open her door.

Hadley DeVilliers spun away from Shadow's door, her hand on the hilt of her sword. Odd. She had a sword belted on over a rather fancy dress.

"Hello, Captain," Lila said. "Are you lost?"

At that moment, Shadow's door opened and he poked his head out, his curls in a snarl. "What's going on?" he said, yawning, looking from Lila to DeVilliers. He certainly didn't look like he was expecting visitors.

"I heard an intruder in the hall," Lila said, nodding at DeVilliers. "So I came out to investigate."

DeVilliers shot an irritated look at Lila, then turned back to Shadow. "There's a situation, and I don't know what to do."

Um. Go back to bed in your own room? Lila thought. But she could see from the captain's expression that something was seriously wrong. "What's the matter?" she said, moving in closer.

"Finn and Julianna are getting married in the Cathedral Temple in half an hour," DeVilliers said. "Julianna wants Shadow and me to stand up with them."

Shadow had an uncanny way of transitioning from nearly asleep to instantly awake. He motioned both of them into his room and shut the door.

"They're getting married in the middle of the night?" he said.

DeVilliers nodded. "Julianna's mother is against it, so they thought they would elope. Except that, because of the siege, they have to do it without leaving the castle close."

"I thought Princess Mellony was all in favor of the match," Lila said.

"Well . . . she is, sort of," DeVilliers said. "I mean, she has been. But now Julianna says she's dragging her feet, that she thinks with the siege going on and all, they should wait."

Sounds like good advice, Lila thought. Especially since they'll probably have to serve barley and water at the reception.

"Do you think Princess Mellony found out about Finn's role in what happened to *Sea Wolf*?" Shadow said. "Is that why she's changed her mind?"

"Have you said anything to Julianna about Finn?" Lila said.

DeVilliers hung her head. "I couldn't. She was so excited and happy, and—it's awkward. I mean, when we were children—"

"Or do you think she already knows?" Lila said.

"What's that supposed to mean?" DeVilliers snapped.

"Maybe Julianna's the star of her own storybook romance. And the only person between her and the throne was Princess Alyssa. So Finn—"

"No," DeVilliers said flatly. "Julianna would never sanction that."

"You didn't think Finn would blow up your ship, either."

"Are you absolutely sure about what you saw?" Shadow said.

"There's always room for doubt," DeVilliers said, almost eagerly. "I mean, there was a lot going on at the time of the attack. Maybe I misinterpreted—"

"You were pretty sure of yourself until now," Lila said. "Is it possible that you're just, you know, wimping out?"

"I didn't think I'd have to decide in the middle of the night!" DeVilliers cried. "I'd rather attack a flotilla of pirates than tell Julianna at her wedding that her fiancé is a traitor and a murderer."

She's telling the truth, Lila thought. It's not that she's a coward.

Well. She'd always wanted to be that person who speaks up and stops the wedding.

"I'll do it," Lila said. "Just give me a minute to put on my armor." When they stared at her, she added, "Just joking, but they probably won't let me in wearing my nightshirt."

A few moments later, the three of them hurried down the corridors toward the Cathedral Temple. The palace was strangely deserted, though, to be fair, it *was* the middle of the night. Still, Lila thought, shouldn't there be sentries on the walls, what with the siege and all? DeVilliers was the most familiar with the palace, since her parents had been on council in the past. She took them along the wallwalks and over rooftops, cautioning them to avoid poking their heads above the parapets on the outside walls in case the southerners camped below were looking.

The Cathedral Temple was separate from the palace itself, but could be reached by walking across a courtyard or an overhead gallery. They opted for the gallery. They were nearly across it when they heard an alarm bell clamoring somewhere. Had the elopement been discovered?

Maybe somebody else would stop the wedding, and they wouldn't have to.

When they reached the temple, they tried the doors on the gallery level, but they were locked. Circling around, they tried the doors on the other side, with the same result.

"How does she expect us to *be* in her wedding if we can't *get* to her wedding?" Shadow growled.

Descending to the cellar level, DeVilliers finally found an

unlocked door that led from the castle close into the crypts. Passing among the tombs of long-dead royals, they raced up several flights of steps that finally led out into the choir. They could hear voices in one of the side chapels.

When they burst into the chapel, the celebrants looked up in surprise.

It was a small wedding, even by wartime standards. By now, Lila recognized participants who were members of the queen's council. Finn's parents, Lord and Lady Mander. Finn's mentor, Lord Vega. Finn's uncle, Lord Bayar. It was no wonder Lady Barrett had asked Shadow and DeVilliers to attend. There was no one to stand up for her, unless you counted Speaker Jemson, who seemed to stand up for everyone.

It was difficult to say who was more beautiful—the bride or the groom. Finn wore the stoles of his wizard house over a purple tunic that set off his silver hair. Julianna's gown was an emerald green, her sheer gray shawl embroidered with gray wolves and owls, her sleek dark hair done up into a twist.

"Oh!" Julianna said, her cheeks stained pink. "I am so sorry. We didn't want to wait any longer for fear we'd be interrupted, so you're a little late for the ceremony, but you're in plenty of time to drink a toast with us."

"Scummer!" Lila blurted. "So you're—you're already married?"

Bride and groom held up their joined hands, their wedding rings glittering in the torchlight.

"How long has it been, Finn?" Julianna said. "Five minutes?" With that, bride and groom kissed, long and slow, in a way that threatened to set the entire room on fire. They split apart only when the sound of running feet in the main church drew their attention. Booted feet.

Bluejackets poured from the main sanctuary into the chapel. They ripped Finn away from Julianna, pinioning his arms and stripping off his amulet. They handled Julianna more gently, mainly physically blocking her from sprinting to her husband's side.

"What is the meaning of this?" Lady Mander strode toward the bluejackets and their captives.

A voice rang down from the gallery above. "Stand down, Lady Mander, if you do not want to receive the same treatment."

Lila looked up, half-expecting to see maybe-dead Queen Raisa again, but it was Princess Mellony, backed by more blue-jackets, including Lieutenant Greenholt.

"Finn sul'Mander, I charge you with high treason and com-plicity in the murder of my sister, Queen Raisa ana'Marianna; her son, Prince Adrian sul'Han; and the princess heir, Alyssa ana'Raisa."

"No!" Once again, Julianna tried to force her way to Finn, but was blocked by the bluejackets who held him prisoner. "Finn is not a traitor, and he's not a murderer, either."

Lord Vega stared up at the queen regent, his face contorted into a mask of anger. "How dare you?" he shouted. "You lying, conniving, duplicitous witch." Gripping his amulet, he extended a shaking hand toward Mellony, releasing a torrent of flame. Lieutenant Greenholt launched herself into the prin-cess, shoving her sideways and down so that the lightning bolt missed.

Undeterred, Vega charged toward the steps to the gallery. He had made it halfway up the stairs when Micah Bayar tack-led him and the two wizards rolled all the way to the bottom, sending off sparks like a Solstice candle.

Finn screamed, a high, feral sound that was scarcely human. Despite his lack of amulet, despite the fact that he was surrounded by the Queen's Guard, he exploded into flame, driving back his captors. Lila thought he might try to reach Julianna, but instead he leapt toward the foot of the stairs, where Micah Bayar stood over a motionless Harriman Vega.

Bayar took two steps back, raising his arms to fend off his nephew. Again and again, Finn drove flame against the barrier the High Wizard had erected. Having no luck there, he turned and directed his fire at the wedding guests, who dove behind pews and fonts to escape.

Lila ended up squeezing into a niche with Lord and Lady Mander.

"Get out!" snarled Lord Mander, unsuccessfully trying to push her out. "There's not enough room."

"Why don't *you* go talk sense into your son?" Lila snapped back. "I'll wait here."

But they seemed to be leaving that up to Uncle Micah.

"Finn!" Bayar cried. "Blood and bones! Stop it!" When Finn continued his assault on the crowd, the High Wizard raised his hand and spoke a series of charms that seemed to have no effect. Finally, the High Wizard hit one of the temple pillars with a torrent of flame. It toppled, slamming into Finn. The impact should have ended it, but Finn pushed to his feet, resembling an effigy consumed in flame. He turned and threw himself down on top of Vega. In a few minutes' time, Finn's body was consumed in flame, leaving only scraps of wedding velvet and silk and bits of metal behind.

Vega's body appeared undamaged.

In the sudden, horrified silence, Lila heard bodies thudding against the locked temple doors, again and again. It could be reinforcements, Lila thought, but something about the way they repetitively hit the doors made her think that, whoever was outside, she didn't want them inside. One of the bluejackets left off gaping and stumbled out of the chapel and toward the nearest door.

"No!" Lila shouted, breaking out of her stunned stupor. "Don't open the—"

By then it was a moot point. The door crashed in and black-robed figures poured through, blades glittering in their hands.

Darians.

Why does this keep happening? Lila thought. Fanatics at Oden's Ford, fanatics on Hanalea, now fanatics in the palace itself. That was all the thinking she had time for before she snatched up a dropped sword and plunged into the fighting. The bluejackets were battling the dark priests, trying to hold them back from the gallery and from what remained of the wedding party.

Lila was not a particularly good swordswoman, especially in a dress, but she saw the advantage of a longer blade in keeping the Darians at a distance.

"Lila! Give us a hand." DeVilliers and Shadow bolted past her toward the altar, where Julianna stood frozen as a swarm of blood brothers closed in. She still clutched her wedding flowers, though her shawl lay crumpled at her feet and her hair hung in long strands around her face. Blood poured from a wound on her forearm. Lila, Shadow, and DeVilliers boosted themselves onto the altar, driving the Darians back from the recent bride.

Gone was the confident spymaster and court official; in her

place was a distraught young widow, blood soaking into her wedding dress. "Let them have me," she whispered, swaying, closing her eyes, raising her chin to provide better access to her neck.

"If you faint, I'll kill you," Lila growled, or something equally heroic.

Julianna remained conscious as they helped her toward the steps, but there was a major knife fight going on at the foot of them as Princess Mellony's bluejackets fought to prevent the Darians from climbing up to the gallery.

"Julianna!" Mellony screamed from the gallery. Lila could see her frightened face floating above the railing like a pale moon.

Bayar forced his way across the room to the foot of the stairs, incinerating Darians as he went. He looked like some avenging spirit, his face grim and stricken with sorrow. He turned, extended his arms, and Shadow and DeVilliers boosted Julianna up to him. The wizard carried her up the stairs to her mother, then descended again to rejoin the fighting.

The wizards—the Manders, Bayar, and DeVilliers—were killing the brothers at a furious pace. It helped that the Darians were more frenzied than strategic, though a frenzied person with a knife can do a lot of damage. Still, the northerners were vastly outnumbered. Just as it seemed that the battle might soon be over, more black-clad fighters poured into the room and filled the gallery. At first, Lila thought they were more Darian Brothers, but these wore tailored black uniform tunics instead of hooded black robes, and they carried crossbows and swords instead of knives. They deployed their weapons in a disciplined fashion.

Blackbirds, Lila thought. Smoking-hot scummer. Who let them in?

She looked toward the gallery, searching for Mellony and Julianna, but saw only a sea of black uniforms.

A tall officer stepped forward, rested his gloved hands on the gallery rail, and surveyed the scene in the sanctuary.

Recognition rippled through Lila. It was Destin Karn. Maybe it was her imagination, but he actually looked sickened by the carnage below.

"Shoot the swiving crows," he said. "All of them."

Crossbows sounded, and all around the chapel, Darians crumpled to the floor until not a one was standing.

Have I ever told you that I love you, Destin Karn? Lila thought. Who knew that the day would come that I'd be glad to see you?

# 46

# BEDTIME STORIES

That first night, Ash and the crew of the disabled ketch *Destiny* camped amid the ruins of Celestine's marble palace. They found stable shelters in the outbuildings in which to hang their hammocks and store the supplies that hadn't been damaged or destroyed coming through the stormwall.

Ash stumbled through these chores, panicking a little each time Jenna was out of sight. Some part of him was still afraid that he was dreaming and she would disappear if his attention wandered.

"Ash!" Sasha said, gripping his arm when he tripped over a coiled line. "Will you be careful? I can't tell if you're moonstruck or sunstruck."

"Lovestruck," Evan said, his lips twitching. "Incurable." The pirate seemed to be taking ownership of their reunion in an *I told you so* kind of way.

Ash didn't care. After what had seemed like a long series of failures and losses, there was *this*.

Jenna explained that their main camp was high in the mountains, away from possible traffic at the harbor. They'd left two more dragons and another human back at camp. Another mage-marked human.

Gripping Ash's shoulders with her hot hands, she pushed an image into his mind—of a cave and a ledge littered with bones. Laughing at his startled expression, she said, "Words are too slow."

Since Ardenscourt, she'd acquired—no, befriended—six dragons and a human. Ash couldn't help wondering how he fit into all of this.

The dragons went hunting and then joined them in feasting on dragon-roasted pork and wine from the empress's cellar. Sasha kept her own counsel, but Ash noticed that she'd moved in close to the pirate, as if for mutual defense. Her hand never strayed far from her dagger, her eyes shifting from dragon to dragon like she expected to be the dessert at this fireside feast.

Ash scarcely tasted the meal. He treasured up the details that would hold Jenna in his mind, tallied up the changes that had occurred since they'd parted in Ardenscourt.

Jenna's golden raptor's eyes glittered in a face burnished by firelight, dusted with copper and gold. She wore thick leather armor that exposed her muscled arms above her gauntlets, a divided leather skirt, riding boots. Her hair was woven into a knot low on her neck, and she ate without a scrap of self-consciousness, tearing off chunks of meat, chewing, swallowing, licking her fingers, throwing back her head and laughing at silent dragon jokes. Every so often she would lean toward Ash and kiss him. Her kisses were like incendiary promises, flavored with Celestine's wine.

There were many kisses but few words. His questions drew brief, vague answers, punctuated with the vivid images she delivered through touch. Since she and the dragons could speak mind-to-mind, human speech seemed to be a little too much trouble.

There were other changes. She was restless, in constant motion while awake. Maybe it was because, for much of her life, she'd been confined in a mine, only to end up imprisoned in a dungeon. It was as if she'd slipped free of the shackles that held her to the ground, shed the gossamer cloak of civilization, and opened her wings. Ash couldn't help feeling like an outsider. What if the gulf between them had become uncrossable?

Anyway, it was difficult to relax in the company of four dragons who grew merrier and rowdier as the night wore on. Eventually, Cas began poking his head between Jenna and Ash, eyeing the two of them, and then nudging Jenna with his nose until she all but toppled into Ash's lap. Jenna kept pushing him away, silently scolding. Finally, laughing, Jenna scrambled to her feet and extended her hand to help Ash up.

"What?" he said, blinking up at her. "Where are we going?"

"Cas says it's time to—to—twine our tails," Jenna said, scarcely able to speak for laughing.

"*What?*" Ash resisted the temptation to press his hands against the back of his breeches. Evan and Sasha were watching this back-and-forth like avid spectators at a match.

"Dragons often mate in flight, so they twine their tails in order to, you know, maintain their—"

Ash couldn't help laughing, though his face blazed with embarrassment. It was like having four enormous scaly relatives pushing a bedding ceremony at a wedding.

"Tell Cas to mind his own business," Ash said, glaring at the dragon who appeared to be grinning, though it was hard to tell with dragons. "Tell him that we will . . . we'll—ah—twine our tails when we're good and ready."

With that, Jenna took Ash's hands, looked him in the eyes, and murmured, "I'm ready, Wolf. Are you?"

Ash had chosen to hang his hammock in what seemed to be the tack room in the half-built, then half-demolished stables. Who builds a stable out of marble, anyway? he'd thought. But the dragons hadn't done as thorough a job wrecking the stable as they had the palace, so it had seemed safer to lodge there. It was close enough to the harbor that he could hear the water gently sloshing against the quay and sucking at the piers.

He stood awkwardly in the doorway as Jenna walked around the tiny room, then paused at the window. She stood in the pool of moonlight pouring through the one window, peering out to sea.

Ash shed his stormcoat, folded it carefully, and set it on his sea trunk. Then began unbuttoning his shirt. Jenna turned away from the window and leaned back on the sill, watching. She made no move to disrobe.

Ash stopped unbuttoning. "Is something wrong? If you want to wait, I understand. We haven't even spent that much time together, and most of that was in a dungeon." He couldn't seem to keep the words from tumbling out, words that unmade the case for going forward.

"I don't want to wait," Jenna said, her voice a throaty growl. "But—"

"If we need to find some maidenweed or—"

"Shut up, healer," Jenna said. "Look—you've already seen my body, in the scummery dungeon in Ardenscourt. I've never seen yours without clothes. I want to see."

Ash took a deep breath, released it. Bit his lip to keep from issuing a disclaimer. Resisted closing his eyes. He finished unbuttoning his shirt and slipped it off his shoulders, letting it fall to the floor. Then fumbled with the buckle on his breeches, managed to undo it, and stepped out of them. He followed with his smallclothes until he stood, totally naked, partly illuminated by the light through the window. It took everything he had to meet her eyes.

Jenna studied him, eyes unblinking, as if memorizing everything. Still looking, she carefully, methodically unlaced her leather armor and let it fall, pulled her thick knitted sweater over her head, following with her cotton undershirt. She stripped off her skirt, leggings, and smallclothes, kicked them aside, and purposefully walked toward him. When she stopped inches away, he could feel the constant heat she generated. She reached out both hands and ran her fingers over his chest, his collarbone, his shoulders, then lunged forward and pressed her chest against his, warming him skin to skin, until he thought he might explode. Carefully, hesitantly, he closed his hands around her hips, drawing her in close.

"Oh," she whispered into his neck, "you are a handsome wolf. Now show me how to get into this strange bed of yours."

Making love with Jenna Bandelow was a twining of minds as well as bodies, a mingling of imagery and sensation so complete that sometimes it was hard to tell who owned what—who was giving, who receiving.

Later, as they lay, still entangled with each other, Ash said, "I told my mother about you."

"You did?" Jenna said sleepily. "What did you say?"

Ash laughed, kissing her eyelids. "I told her you were dead."

"Huh!" Jenna snorted. "I guess that was the end of *that* conversation."

"No," Ash said. "It wasn't. I told her how we met. I asked her . . . I asked her if it's possible to fall in love with someone over such a short space of time, under those circumstances."

"What did she say?"

"She told me that love is not measured by the amount of time you spend together, it's how that time is spent."

"So you're saying that washing blood and scummer off a person in a dungeon is—"

"I'm saying that sometimes the patient heals the healer." Ash shut off further speech with kisses, then pulled back enough to say, "She told me that love moves fast in wartime—it has to."

"I told your sister about *you*," Jenna said, burrowing into his side, nipping and nibbling, and absolutely driving him to—

Hang on.

"What do you mean?"

"Your littermate was here," she said. "Lyssa Gray."

Ash reared up, sending the hammock swinging wildly. "*What?* My sister was here?"

"She was teaching the empress's horselords how to fight," Jenna said, forcing him flat again with kisses and biting his lower lip. "Breon may be able to tell you more when he gets his voice back."

"Mffblt," Ash said, attempting to talk around the kisses. Having no luck with that, he pressed his hands against her shoulders, putting enough distance between them to free his lips.

"When? What was she doing here? Is she all right? Where is

she now? Who's Breon? Why didn't you tell me?"

Jenna frowned, as if picking through the cascade of questions, looking for one she wanted to answer, then ended by answering most of them. "She left about a week ago, and I believe they've sailed for the Realms. I didn't tell you before because I would rather make love than talk. I knew that once I told you, lovemaking would be over." She wriggled under him in a very distracting way, then arched her back and flipped him over so that she was on top. "She was the empress's prisoner. It was either fight for the empress or join the bloodsworn."

"So . . . she's not . . . ?"

Jenna shook her head. "Lyssa said that the blood ritual makes people strong, but it makes them stupid. The empress wants smart officers."

Ash felt like he'd been clubbed. Again. In a good way. That seemed to be a constant with this girl. It took a while to get his mind moving again, grappling with this new information. Lyss had been here, just a week ago. Sometimes it seemed that he and his sister were cursed to follow each other around the globe, never quite connecting.

But she was alive—and, according to Jenna, on her way back to the Realms. It reminded him of what Sasha had said, when they were sailing for the Northern Islands—that it seemed they were going in the wrong direction.

"What is my sister like?" Ash said, hungry for information. "You could know her better than I do. I haven't seen her for five years." He tried to dismiss the thought that he might never see her again.

Jenna thought a moment. "She's not afraid of dragons," she said, as if that spoke volumes. "She's fierce and strong, in a way that's different from you. You smolder, and she burns hot." She paused, then said, "I know you're worried about her, Wolf, but she is a survivor. She's faced down death many times. She will find a way." Jenna's clipped, dragonish speech was like poetry—economical and yet vivid.

"Breon will be able to tell you more about her when he's feeling better," Jenna said.

"Right," Ash said. "Breon? Who is he?"

"He's the magemarked boy I told you about. He was a prisoner here with Lyss."

"He's sick? Hurt?"

"The empress was giving him leaf. He's in withdrawal right now."

"Maybe I can help him," Ash said.

"We can go see him tomorrow. Goat might be willing to carry you. Or you can ride with me."

"Goat?"

"The dragon you freed from the rigging. The dragon you charmed with your voice."

Ash took a breath. Now to the hard part. "Lyssa. Did she . . . did she tell you who she is?"

"She told me she was Captain Gray, and your sister," Jenna said. She took his face between her calloused hands again and said, "I've been waiting for you to tell me the rest."

# A SIT-DOWN WITH
# A KING

The road between Ardenscourt and Delphi was familiar, at least. Hal had marched up and down it at least once for every year he'd been in the army. North in the spring, fit and well fed, and south in the fall, licking their wounds. Except that one time when he'd been stationed at Delphi, and Lyssa Gray had kicked his southern ass.

His quartermaster, Rives, had done his best to provision their army, knowing they were unlikely to find much to forage on the way north. It would be a long time before another harvest, and they were following in the footsteps of Jarat's army. The countryside along the North Road appeared deserted. Hal imagined farmers and householders huddled in their cellars, lying flat in the fields, hoping to escape the attention of the second army to march through in a fortnight.

This should be the prosperous heart of the empire, Hal thought. People shouldn't have to hide in their cellars to protect what is theirs.

Hal was reminded of a song popular among the veterans of the army.

*I turned my sword into a walking cane,*
*To replace the leg I lost.*
*Kings propose and thanes dispose*
*But the soldier pays the cost.*

Where was Bellamy? Was he still in Delphi or had he marched on toward the northern capital? If he'd marched on, then who had been left in charge in the border town? How long would it take for Jarat to realize that someone was following along behind him, picking up bread crumbs?

Bellamy would have to turn back then. Hal needed to take Delphi before he did.

Hal knew this territory, this town, and its defenses intimately—no doubt better than Jarat's army of occupation. He was familiar with a whole range of mistakes that could be made, because he'd made them. The cannon on the heights had been his undoing the last time. Years ago, after Arden took control of the independent city, they'd neglected the cannon, which had been placed by the Delphians to keep Arden honest. The Ardenine military had assumed they were no longer needed, but they'd left them in place. The Fellsian army made good use of them once they'd won the heights.

He recalled Captain Gray's words after she won the day in Delphi. *Perhaps if this place were defended properly, it wouldn't be so easy to take.*

Hal had learned his lesson then, but he could hope that Jarat hadn't.

His army left the North Road, striking west across the coun-tryside, and then north to cross the Delphi Road. Hopefully the town garrison wouldn't be expecting trouble from that quarter. They camped in a spot north of the east–west road, one that he hoped would be outside scouting range from Delphi. Again, he sent Mercier and DeJardin into town to evaluate the enemy's assets and defenses, to see if the northerners had made changes during their tenure. He also gave them the names of two people to find, if they were still alive, and a verbal message to deliver.

His emissaries returned the next day with two guests in tow. Hal recognized them immediately—Brit Fletcher and Yorrie Cooper, Patriots of Delphi. Fletcher had one arm in a sling and severe burns down the side of his face that cracked and seeped when his expression changed. Cooper looked much the same as always, though somewhat better fed than before.

Hal sent up a grateful prayer. He hadn't been sure how—or even if—his offer would be received.

"Well, now," Fletcher said, "if it ain't Captain Matelon. Or should I call you King Hal?" He shot a look at Mercier and DeJardin.

"Matelon will do," Hal said. He knew Mercier and DeJar-din had used his new title as the carrot to entice the Patriots to come, but he half-wished they hadn't mentioned it.

"Good," Cooper said. "We're not that fond of kings—espe-cially southern kings."

"Which is why I appreciate your coming and your will-ingness to hear me out," Hal said. He gestured toward the command tent. "This way."

It was a lovely late-spring night. The tent flaps were tied back, and the scent of sweet bay and honeysuckle wafted in on the breeze. The Patriots accepted Hal's offer of refreshment, and he tapped the last barrel of autumn cider. They sat down on camp chairs and atop barrels of salted fish.

"You know, Matelon, I heard you was dead," Fletcher said, blotting cider from his lips with his sleeve. "Several times, I heard it."

"One day," Hal said. "Not today. I'm glad to see you're still alive. I hear that Jarat paid a steep blood price for every city block."

"That's what keeps us going," Cooper said. "Killing southerners."

Clearly, this wasn't going to be an easy sell.

"Is it true, what your people said—that you won the southern capital?" Fletcher said.

"It's true," Hal said.

"So you're the new top-dog thane?"

"Not exactly," Hal said.

"Then what's this about?" Fletcher said. "I know you didn't invite us here just to share your cider."

"I need your help," Hal said.

"That's the only time we have a sit-down with kings," Cooper said, sliding a look at Fletcher. "When they need our help."

"The thing is—you need my help, too," Hal said.

That got their attention.

Cooper clunked her mug down, hard. "What do you mean?"

"Your location is a blessing and a curse. As long as we're at war, you're a game piece in play. You may win free for a while, but sooner or later, the armies come back. A free Delphi doesn't suit the larger game."

"We're for the queen in the north," Cooper said. "She came

here and kicked your ass, as I recall."

"She did," Hal said, raising his glass. "To the ass-kicking queen in the north."

They mumbled back the toast, eyeing him suspiciously.

"Since then, she's let us run our own affairs," Fletcher said.

"Aye," Hal said. "She's one to keep her word. And yet, Jarat didn't sign on, and now he's here."

"And now you're here," Cooper countered.

"And now I'm here. I want to take Delphi back from King Jarat and return it to you."

"Return it to us," Fletcher said bitterly. "Beware of kings saying they're here to help you."

"The queen in the north was straight with us," Cooper said.

"But she's not here," Fletcher said.

"Aye, she's not here," Hal said. "The northern armies are fighting for their lives in the east. If they fail, you'll get to meet Empress Celestine."

Cooper and Fletcher looked at each other, then back at Hal. "The pirate?"

Hal nodded. "I saw what happened in Chalk Cliffs. I was there. If the empress wins, we're all in for it. Remember that saying? Things may be bad in Delphi, but they can always get worse."

The Patriots eyed him as if unsure whether they should be offended or not.

"If you're so concerned about the empress in the east," Cooper said, "then why aren't you helping the northern queen?"

"I am," Hal said, faintly surprised to hear that coming out of his mouth. "She doesn't need Jarat putting a knife in her back, so I'm going to handle him."

"For her," Cooper said, raising an eyebrow.

"For her," Hal said.

"Why would you do that?"

There was no simple answer to that, but Hal gave it a try. "The queen in the north was straight with me," he said. "The king in the south has never been."

"Well, if you want to help her, you better hurry up," Fletcher said. "Jarat's marching on Ardenscourt, if he ain't already there."

# INTERCEPTION

Lila stuffed her clothes into her saddlebags and strapped her money belt around her waist. She had to get out, even if it meant leaving Shadow and DeVilliers behind.

Those two had been rounded up on the day of the wedding, and she hadn't seen them since. She assumed that they were being held in the dungeon, but she didn't even know where the dungeon was. Had it been at Ardenscourt, she could have made discreet inquiries through her allies and sources to locate them. It was jolting to realize that she knew more about the secrets of Ardenscourt Castle than of the palace in her homeland.

Including potential escape routes.

King Jarat and his retinue had arrived yesterday, with salvos of soldiers, brigades of blackbirds, and crews of collared mages.

She had no idea why she'd been overlooked, but it couldn't last forever. If Karn hadn't spotted her amid the chaos in the Cathedral Temple, he'd find out she was here soon enough.

She had to get out. She'd delayed too long already, trying to find her friends (when had she come to regard DeVilliers as a friend?). She couldn't very well be introduced as Lila Byrne, daughter of the captain of the Queen's Guard, to people who knew her as Lila Barrowhill, smuggler, mercenary, and southern spy.

That's what you get for allowing Captain Amazing to pin his name on you, she thought.

You have to go. It's a matter of survival, she thought.

Then why are you wasting time arguing with yourself?

If she could just slip away before she came face-to-face with any representatives of the new regime, she might be able to return to the south and be Lila Barrowhill again.

For how long? a voice in her head whispered. How long will it take the empress to reach Ardenscourt? Anyway, I thought you wanted to avenge your family.

It was the kind of voice that could be drowned in a vat of blue ruin once she was far away from here. She might leave the wolves behind, too. After all, she'd never seen talking dead wolves in Arden.

Lila swung her bags over her shoulders and fastened her cloak over top so that she resembled an odd sort of hunchbacked crone. She hoped no one would question the cloak, despite the fair weather.

"You're not done here."

Lila swung around to find an immense gray wolf with green eyes planted in front of the door.

"Who are you?" Lila said. "Where's the gray-eyed wolf?"

"She's with the queen," the wolf said. "I'm filling in."

So now I have to deal with substitute talking dead wolves?

"Where's the queen?" Lila said. *And which queen is it?*

"She is coming. You need to stay and protect those who serve the Line."

"Look," Lila said, "I've already been here longer than I meant to be. I promise, I'll come back and help the queen once she's here."

With that, the door slammed open (hadn't she locked it?) and the wolf faded away.

It was Destin Karn, dressed to kill in his spymaster blacks.

He looked around the room. "Who's here? Who were you talking to?"

"A dead wolf," Lila said. "Listen, I'd love to catch up, but I was just leaving." She tried to dart around him, but he stuck out an arm to stop her.

"We need to talk," he said.

"I need to go," Lila said. She tried to slide past him once again, but he pushed her farther into the room, slammed the door, and put his back to it.

"We need to talk now," Karn said.

"The last time you tried to strong-arm me, I nearly put a knife in your gut," Lila said.

"That's the operative term," Karn said, "*nearly*. If we're giving credit for *nearly*, I've *nearly* killed you a dozen times. I've lost track of the times I've *nearly* maimed you."

Threaten or negotiate?

Threaten.

"Let me go, Karn," Lila said. "I'm warning you."

"And I'm warning *you*," Karn said. "You'll never get out of the castle close. It's locked up tight as the principia's ass."

What do you know about the principia's ass?

"I'd rather be killed trying to escape than be hung as a spy," Lila said.

"Actually, I think Jarat favors burning these days," Karn said.

"It costs more up front, for fuel and accelerant, but it's a crowd-pleaser and saves on disposals and burials."

Lila glared at him but said nothing. The spymaster must have smelled victory, because he planted himself in a side chair and gestured to the one opposite.

"Sit," he said. "Put your bags down. This will take a while."

Did that mean that he was going to let her go after he questioned her? Maybe, maybe not.

Lila dropped the cloak and the bags, stalked over to the proffered chair, and sat.

Negotiate.

"I'll answer all your questions if you let Rogan Shadow Dancer and Hadley DeVilliers go."

She'd surprised him, for once. The wheels turned behind Karn's eyes. "Your copperhead supplier and the naval commander?"

"Yes."

"Lila Barrowhill, looking out for someone else?" Karn shook his head. "I don't even *know* you."

"There's another thing. They call me Lila Byrne here." She sighed, then spit out the rest. "I'm the daughter of the captain of the Queen's Guard."

"I know that," he said impatiently. When Lila stared at him, openmouthed, he rolled his eyes. "*Spymaster?* I know a few things. But I've never held it against you, because I also know from personal experience that sometimes the apple falls far from the tree. As for DeVilliers and Dancer, we'll see, depending on whether your information is useful." He paused, leaned forward, and said, "Give me your hands."

"You don't really have to—"

The thin smile disappeared. "Give me your hands."

"Fine!" Lila said, scowling. She'd found that it was always best to resist the use of persuasion. Agree too readily, and wizards started looking for a talisman. And that wouldn't do at all.

Karn was stuffed full of questions—and persuasion. He asked about Queen Raisa and Captain Byrne, about the whereabouts of the Highlander army and General Dunedain, and about various members of the council. He had a list of the nobility that he went through, one by one. It was always hard to tell what Karn already knew, so, for the most part, Lila answered his questions honestly, though sometimes not completely.

"Tell me about the dead groom and his friend," Karn said, his eyes so clear of connivery that she knew they were getting to the meat of the matter. "What were their names?"

I bet you know damn well what their names were. "Harriman Vega and Finn sul'Mander."

"Vega," Karn repeated. "Are you sure?"

"Yes," Lila said, "I'm sure. I served on council with him. He's in charge of the healing halls here at court. Or was."

"Hmm." Karn reached into his uniform tunic, pulled out a pouch, and handed it to Lila. "These items were recovered from them. Some of it I recognize as church regalia, but the rest . . ."

Lila shook the contents out onto the table. Her breath caught in her throat. "Scummer," she muttered, poking the items around with her forefinger, sorting them into two nearly identical piles.

"What?" Karn said, leaning in. "What is it?"

There were two amulets, two of the rising sun pendants worn by priests of the southern church, two sets of the keys to the kingdom that Malthusian crows liked to wear at their waists. A handful of stones in caramel-colored quartz. And two tiny gold cups on chains.

A memory surfaced, like a corpse that Lila had tried to bury ever since. Ash interrogating Usepia, the bloodsucking priest who'd tried to murder him in his dormitory room. Ash had asked who had given the Darian Brothers his blood-soaked handkerchief and sent them after him like hounds on a hunt.

"A mage," the priest had said. "It seems that this mage is a man of faith."

Lila remembered thinking it was odd for a mage to be ordering around the self-styled Blades of Malthus, fanatics whose mission in life was murdering wizards and collecting their blood.

Lila looked up at Karn, who was fixed on her, waiting for her answer. No matter which way she turned it, she could see no harm in giving up dead Finn.

"The little cups are carried by Darian assassins so that they can drink the blood of their wizard prey," Lila said. "They use little rocks to immobilize wizards. So I'm guessing this means that both Finn and Vega were Darian Brothers." She paused. "But you should know that already. Aren't you the one who hired the crows to kill Adrian sul'Han at Oden's Ford?"

"Well, no," Karn said. "Not exactly."

"What do you mean, not exactly?"

"I was involved," Karn said. "My job was to keep you out of harm's way. But the plan—and the personnel—came directly from Ardenscourt. My contact with the Darians was the person you know as Finn sul'Mander."

"Finn?" Lila's head was spinning. "Finn sent the Darians to Oden's Ford?"

Karn nodded. "He was involved, but I think Vega was the mastermind. I think Vega's been working with Arden for a number of years, maybe as far back as the killing of the High Wizard, Han sul'Alger." Karn paused, as if choosing a path forward. "But there's something else going on. I can't help thinking Vega did something to Finn, something unholy. Something unforgivable." Lila was taken aback by the raw emotion in the spymaster's voice.

Well, Lila thought, recalling her interactions with Vega, sometimes when your gut tells you that a person is an arrogant sleazebag, it turns out to be true.

"Right before they died, Prin—the queen regent, Mellony, accused young sul'Mander of treason and the murder of the queen, the prince, and the princess. Do you know anything about that?"

"You mean, aside from the fact that it's true?"

Lila had thought Destin Karn was unshockable, but her response left the spymaster looking startled, at least.

She cocked her head. "Are you trying to tell me that you don't know any of this? That you didn't hire Finn to kill them?"

Karn shook his head. "But that doesn't mean that the empire wasn't involved." He paused, thinking, then looked up at Lila. "So they're all dead? And Finn killed them?"

"That, I don't know," Lila said. "If they're still alive, it's no thanks to Finn." She went on to detail the ill-fated mission to rescue the princess heir in Carthis. She assumed that she wasn't giving away critical secrets—the entire council knew about the mission, and its failure. And if they knew, the spymaster did, too.

"They didn't have any reason to suspect Finn of treachery before then?"

"Apparently not," Lila said, "else why would they have invited him along? Both Shadow and DeVilliers said that he hadn't been himself since being wounded in the war."

"Right," Destin murmured, brow furrowed. "When did he team up with Vega?"

"Vega cared for him after he was wounded, I guess," Lila said. "That's when Finn decided to join the healer's service."

"Was that when he got religion?"

Lila shrugged. "I'm the wrong person to ask," she said. And yet—the entire council did not know about Finn's role in its failure. One question had been aggravating Lila ever since the wedding—how did Mellony know what Finn had done, if DeVilliers didn't tell her?

Unless Finn—or his co-conspirators—did. Because she was a part of the conspiracy.

Lila looked up and met Karn's eyes. She and the spymaster were like card players, shoving cards toward each other while trying to keep their full hands hidden. It made sense that he'd wring as much information from her as possible. But why was he sharing so much with her?

"So Finn and DeVilliers were the only survivors from *Sea Wolf*," Karn said.

"Right," Lila said. "Adrian, Talbot, and Strangward were lost and presumed dead."

"Wait, what?" If Karn had looked startled before, now he looked absolutely ambushed. "*Evan Strangward* was with them?"

Lila nodded. "The Carthian pirate, remember?" she said, though clearly Karn did not need reminding. "Strangward had been here, trying to convince the queen and her council that Celestine meant to invade the Realms. It wasn't until she actually won Chalk Cliffs that they took him seriously. When the prince proposed a mission to rescue Princess Alyssa, Strangward volunteered to serve as pilot."

"And Finn killed them? He killed all of them?" Karn's voice had taken on a brittle tone. When she looked up into the spymaster's face, she saw no expression at all. It was like a frame with the picture ripped away.

"They could be alive, like I said. Talk to DeVilliers. She might be able to tell you more."

Karn said nothing. Didn't look at her. But his grip on her hands had become painfully tight. "Ow! Ease off, Karn, you're going to break my bones."

Karn let go completely then, dropping his hands to his sides. After a moment, he moved them to his lap, as if he couldn't decide what to do with them. The spymaster closed his eyes and swallowed, and a single tear leaked out from under his lashes.

What the hell? Lila felt like an intruder in the presence of loss too profound to name. She licked her lips. Tried and failed to think of something to say. Wished that she could tiptoe out, but it was, after all, her room.

"Well," Lila said finally, "it's too bad both Finn and Vega are dead. They're probably the only ones who can answer some of our questions."

"Vega's not dead." Karn spoke so softly that Lila wasn't sure she'd heard him right.

"What did you say?"

Karn opened his eyes. They resembled windows into dark and turbulent waters. "Vega's not dead. I have him safely locked away, along with DeVilliers and Shadow."

"Oh." Lila wasn't sure if this was good news for DeVilliers

and Shadow, but she suspected it was definitely bad news for Vega.

And then Karn said something completely unexpected. "That churchman who presided over the wedding—Jemson, I think his name was. Do you know him?"

"Not well," Lila said. "He's on the queen's council. But I've heard nothing but good about him." She hesitated. "He's not a celebrant in the Malthusian Church, but—"

"Good," Karn said.

"People talk about him like he's practically a saint of the Old Church."

"That might be exactly what I need," Karn said. "A saint."

"I think Jemson would be one to go to if you're looking for spiritual counseling," Lila said.

Karn blinked at her. "No doubt I'm in dire need of spiritual counseling," he said. "Right now I'm looking for someone who can handle an exorcism."

# 49

# PERSUASION

Roff Jemson had to be the steadiest churchman Destin had ever met. When Destin made the ask, he didn't blink, he didn't waver. Just rubbed his chin and said, "Can you tell me why you suspect that poor Finn was possessed? And, if he was, why this would be of concern to you?"

There was no judgment or derision in the speaker's voice, as if he took Destin's request at face value.

At this point, Destin didn't really care what Speaker Jemson thought of him. He just wanted him to agree to his plan.

They were sitting in Jemson's tiny office in the Cathedral Temple, surrounded by shelves of books. More books were stacked on the floor, on his desktop. Behind him, a child's drawing was pinned to a board on the wall.

"I'm told that Finn changed after he was wounded," Destin said. He went on to tell the prelate about using persuasion to dowse Finn's soul, finding something ancient and alien in residence there, and the ceremony he'd witnessed involving Finn and the Darian Brothers.

Jemson listened attentively, then sat back, folding his hands.

"So your theory is . . . ?"

"My theory is that Saint Darian, or someone like him, was controlling Finn's actions. Either through possession or through spellwork. I think Lord Vega facilitated it somehow."

"The concept of possession does not have a lot of support in the Old Church," Jemson said. "Demonic possession plays a larger role in the literature of the Church of Malthus."

"Maybe there's a reason," Destin said bluntly. "Setting aside the notion of possession, mages or wizards have a history of interacting with the dead in Aediion, the dream world. Mystwerk scholars warn about the dangers of a dead spirit riding back with a visiting mage into the real world."

Jemson grunted. "I have known Finn since he was a child. He is a very different boy than he was before the war." He paused for a heartbeat. "War leaves many wounds, some of them invisible. I would very much like to think that Finn was not responsible for the things he's done, but I worry that you're grasping at straws."

"I never knew Finn," Destin said, "and I have no reason to want to condemn or redeem him. What I don't want is for him to take the fall while the real culprits walk free." He paused, realized that his hands were shaking, and pressed them to the desktop.

"Are you all right, Colonel Karn?" Jemson said, brow furrowed with concern, dark eyes searching Destin's face.

No, Destin thought. I am not all right. I probably never will be. Which is why I need to do something about the hole in my heart.

Aloud, he snapped, "I'm *fine*. Why?"

"Forgive me, Colonel," Jemson said. "It's just that you seem so very sad."

Destin could not squeeze a denial past the lump in his throat. They sat looking at each other for what seemed like a very long time.

"Would it do any harm to try?" Destin said, his voice thick and strange.

"I still don't understand exactly what it is you want me to do. I cannot perform an exorcism on a corpse. Especially since, as I recall, Finn's body was almost entirely consumed by flame."

"I should have been clearer," Destin said. "I want you to perform an exorcism on Harriman Vega."

"Vega?" Jemson looked perplexed. "But I understood that Lord Vega was also . . . dead."

"Not exactly," Destin said. "He should be dead, but he isn't. He survived, and he's locked in a cell under my supervision. Since then, I've interrogated him several times and gotten nowhere. Torture produces nothing but threats and defiance. When I use persuasion, I run into a fierce pushback from the same presence that I sensed in Finn. Whatever it is, I think it jumped hosts."

Jemson seemed to be hunting for a way to say no to this odd request from the Ardenine spymaster without earning his enmity.

"Do you know anything about the accusations the queen regent made regarding Finn?" Destin said abruptly.

"No," Jemson said, looking relieved at the change in subject. "Princess Mellony—the queen regent, rather—did not confide in me. And, obviously, I would not have presided at the marriage had I known that he was accused of treason."

"So this was not discussed in the council," Destin said.

"No."

"And Julianna obviously knew nothing about it."

"I would like to think that she did not."

"Did you think Finn was capable of cold-blooded murder?"

Jemson hesitated. "I would have said no, before the wedding. He seemed to have turned a corner, with his new interest in healing and his betrothal to Julianna. I was optimistic that he was healing."

"Yet, after Princess Mellony challenged him, he tried to kill Lady Barrett along with the rest of the wedding party."

"I assumed that the regent's accusation awoke the demons inside him once again."

Literally, Destin thought.

After an awkward silence, Jemson said, "I am a speaker in the Old Church, and so I am comfortable with elements of magic. But, still—this seems like a complicated explanation for the tragic actions of a traumatized boy."

"There's someone else I want you to hear." Destin rose and went to the door to speak to the blackbird outside. Moments later, DeVilliers was ushered in.

"Hadley!" Jemson said, smiling for the first time, and rising to his feet. "Thank the Maker you are alive. When you were arrested, I feared the worst."

"It seems I'll be alive a little longer," DeVilliers said, glancing at Destin.

"As you probably know," Destin said, "Captain DeVilliers has known Finn since childhood."

"Speaker Jemson," DeVilliers said. "I held back information when I told the council about the attack off Carthis. I didn't know how to tell Julianna that her fiancé had killed Adrian and Sasha and fatally sabotaged the mission to rescue Lyss."

DeVilliers went on to share what had happened on the *Sea Wolf.*

"You're probably wondering why I would listen to anything Karn says. I can't quite believe it myself. I don't know Lord Vega very well, but Lyss despises him. She has always believed in her gut that Vega had a hand in her father's death."

Jemson nodded. "Queen Raisa shared that suspicion. She tried not to show it, because she had absolutely no proof."

"So," DeVilliers said. "It seems like we've been working with our enemies all along. Why not at least consider the fact that Karn may be right on this? I know the story he's pitching is difficult to believe, but I hope you'll consider what he's asking you to do. If his theory is wrong, then there's no harm done. If he is right, then"—she swallowed hard—"then I hope I might find a way to forgive Finn."

# 50

# EXORCISM

Whenever a monarch raises a wall, a castle, or a fortification, people immediately set out to find a way over, under, or through it. As in Ardenscourt, Fellsmarch Castle was riddled with hidden chambers and tunnels, some of which led out of the city entirely. Upon arrival, Destin had assigned one of his trusted agents to begin to map it, both to prevent comings and goings by the resistance in the occupied city and to reserve a small part of it for himself.

For his temporary lair, Destin had chosen a warren of empty storerooms that had been needed in more prosperous times, but now stood empty amid the privations of war. These storerooms were less trafficked than the dungeons, which were currently full of the king's prisoners, and marginally more comfortable.

Harriman Vega was locked up in a small room with thick stone walls, a bed, a basin, and a bucket in a remote area where no one would hear him. Still, it was dry and reasonably comfortable compared to the Pit in the palace at Ardenscourt.

Much more comfortable than Vega deserved. The wizard had survived this long only because Destin's desire to get at the truth exceeded his desire to kill him. Up to now, anyway.

For once, Destin wanted plenty of witnesses present, and at least one more wizard, for safety's sake. So the torch-lit, stone-walled room ended up fairly crowded—with Destin, Speaker Jemson, Lila, Shadow, and DeVilliers, in addition to the guest of honor.

In comparison to officials of the Church of Malthus, Jemson brought little in the way of regalia: a bottle of water from the Dyrnnewater, a river considered sacred in the north, and a stone basin of dirt. He was barefoot and wore a plain black wool robe. Vega was still dressed in his wedding clothes, though they were now streaked with blood and dirt. Destin had added a layer of hurt on top of the beating Vega had sustained at the wedding, but all signs of injury had faded away unnaturally quickly. If anything, he was more defiant than before.

Vega scowled when Destin's delegation crowded in, but he brightened considerably when he spotted Speaker Jemson.

"Jemson!" he said, coming to his feet. "Surely you can use your influence to put an end to this madness. I don't know what the colonel has told you, but if you could get word to Princess Mellony, or to King Jarat, we can quickly sort this out."

Princess Mellony? Destin thought. The one you tried to kill at the wedding? The one you called a lying, conniving, duplicitous witch?

"I'm afraid I have little influence with either the princess or the king," Jemson said. "We've had no communication from anyone save curfews and restrictions. I'm here because Colonel Karn asked me to talk to you."

"Since when does a member of the king of Arden's guard issue orders to speakers of the Old Church?" Vega turned on

Destin. "When the king finds out how I've been treated, Colonel, you will pay dearly."

"I never realized that you and King Jarat were so close," Destin said.

"And you call yourself a spymaster. In fact, you have no clue what—"

"The king thinks you're dead," Destin said, "and, to be honest, he is not losing any sleep over it. It seems that you are no longer useful."

"Well," Vega said, losing some of his bluster. "We'll see about that."

"Vega, the sooner you accept the fact that nobody is on your side, the sooner we'll get through this," Destin said.

"The colonel asked me to come because he is worried that perhaps you are not quite . . . yourself," Jemson said. "He thought you might benefit from some spiritual intervention."

"I am hardly in need of—"

"When, exactly, did you become a priest in the Church of Malthus?" Jemson said, finally losing patience.

"Is that what this is about?" Vega eyed the basin of soil and the pitcher of water. "My advice to you is that you carefully consider your way forward. We all worship the same god, but it is time to let go of the rituals and heresies of the Old Church. The great saint is ascendant, and you would be wise to acknowledge that."

"That may well be," Jemson said, "but I am an old man now, and the Old Church suits me." He turned and motioned to DeVilliers. "Captain?"

"Lord Vega," she said, "my father was on faculty at Mystwerk Academy at Oden's Ford. In his classes, he taught the concept of Aediion, the meeting place between life and death, past and present. He demonstrated how it could be used to communicate across time and distance."

Vega studied her for a long moment, as if trying to read her agenda in her face. "We've all heard stories about the so-called dream world. Everyone has heard about someone who's managed to cross over, but they never seem to be available for an interview. I've concluded that it is just another relic from the Old Church. At the point of death, we go to the Maker or the Breaker. There is no in-between."

"And yet many of my father's students were successful in accessing the hidden realms," DeVilliers persisted.

"Or said they were," Vega retorted.

"Still, having attended the academy, you are familiar with the technique," DeVilliers said.

Although it was chilly in the underground storeroom, a sheen of sweat had appeared on Vega's forehead. "That was a long time ago. I doubt they even teach it these days. Enrollment in Mystwerk has dwindled significantly as the empire has grown."

"As a churchman," Jemson said, "I can imagine how tempting it would be to be able to meet the saints and philosophers from the past and receive the truth directly from them."

"No doubt that is why those tales have persisted," Vega snapped.

"And if I were *both* a wizard and a priest," Jemson said, "it would be difficult to resist making an attempt to access the wisdom of the ages. Imagine, in the midst of a doctrinal dispute, being able to say, 'I spoke to Saint Darian, and you are wrong.' Imagine the power that would give you over the gospels. Over believers?"

When Jemson mentioned Darian, Vega stood, and paced back and forth. "I may be a prisoner, but I don't have to sit and listen to this superstitious nonsense."

"Even better," Jemson said relentlessly, "what if you could bring the saints back in person and send them out into the world to right the wrongs of the present?"

"Enough!" Vega snarled. "If you are here to harangue me and not to help me, then leave."

"That's just it," Destin said, "Speaker Jemson and I are here to help you." He pulled up a stool and gestured toward the bed. "Please. Sit and give me your hands."

"No. Don't touch me. Get out. I am done." Vega pointed toward the door.

"Please sit down," Jemson said. "We're not here to hurt you."

"Go to the Breaker, you black-robed heretic!" Vega spat.

It took everyone present to pin the wizard to the bed. Shadow had supplied them all with talismans, but Destin wasn't sure if that was adequate protection from whatever was coming.

Destin gripped Vega's hands, and DeVilliers placed her hands on top of his. He opened the channels of persuasion, and was hit with a stream of the vilest curses he'd ever heard. Even given that he'd served in the army and lived on the waterfront.

Jemson sprinkled Dyrnnewater over Vega's thrashing body, and he only thrashed harder. The speaker followed with a dusting of earth. By now, all of the celebrants were soaked with river water and caked with mud.

"Let us pray," Jemson said, raising his voice to be heard over Vega's objections. "The body and blood of the Realms is the purest manifestation of the Maker in the corporeal world. We ask that this man, Harriman Vega, be freed of any unclean spirits and wicked invaders and appear before us cleansed and perfect as he was born into this world."

Maybe it was Destin's imagination, but he could have sworn Vega's black eyes turned ruby red. Power jolted into his hands from Vega's, making a claim on him. Jemson had warned him that this might happen, but it was stronger than he'd anticipated. He pushed back, trying to contain the energy that was attempting to enter his body.

DeVilliers stood frozen, eyes wide with shock.

"DeVilliers!" Destin gasped. "A little help?"

She added her flash to his. It took both of them to keep the spirit contained in the intersection of their joined hands.

"Lord Darian! We call you forth to answer before the Maker on your own merits!" Jemson thundered.

And all at once, a flaming green vapor appeared in the air. It resembled the fox fire sometimes seen in Tamron Wood. It sent long tendrils out toward the humans in the room, as if looking for a host.

"Go home, Darian," Jemson said, in a voice that brooked no argument. "Be at peace. You do not belong among the living." He tossed the remaining water in the pitcher over the flames and they hissed out, leaving a faint scent of decay and a bone-deep chill behind.

"Is it gone?" Lila muttered, edging forward, her face a mask of revulsion.

"It is gone," Jemson said, swiping sweat-dampened hair from his forehead. "Thank the Maker."

"I have to say, I've seen more creepy scummer in the past year than in my entire life before that," Lila said, with a shudder.

Destin sat down beside Vega's bed again, while the others

withdrew to the margins of the room. The wizard had gone quiet and still, and it seemed that some essential spark had departed, leaving an empty husk behind. His skin purpled, blistered, and flaked away as evidence of his previous injuries surfaced. It was as if the demon inside him had kept them at bay, or hidden them under a glamour.

Something of the original man remained, because Destin could see the glitter of his eyes between slitted lids.

"I believe you're dying, Lord Vega," Destin said.

For a moment, it looked as if Vega was going to disagree, but then he coughed and cleared his throat, spitting blood on his wizard stoles. "I believe you're right," he said.

"Some say that confession is good for the soul," Destin said.

"Do you expect *me* to confess to *you*?"

"I say that revenge is even better," Destin said. "Perhaps you would like to give me the dirt on somebody else."

Vega laughed, harsh and wheezing. "Is there someone in particular you'd like to indict?"

"You can choose who you give up," Destin said. "The only stipulation is that it's true."

Vega snorted and fell silent, as if he meant to take all his secrets to his grave. Destin knew it was a long shot, but he had found over the years that the dying—even villains—are often eager to preserve their legacy by telling their story. And, clearly, Vega didn't see himself as a villain.

"How long have you been working with Arden?" Destin prompted.

"You misunderstand, spymaster," Vega said. "It's never been about Arden. Everything I have done has been for the church, and for the salvation of the wicked. Healing applies to more than flesh and blood—I have long dreamed of healing souls. Darian himself gave me the knowledge and the tools to do that when I was just a student." He paused and, when Destin opened his mouth to speak, snapped, "And yes, your theory was correct. That was in Aediion. He chose me to carry out his holy work here on earth. *He chose me.*"

By now, Vega was so disfigured by his injuries that he was scarcely recognizable.

"Unfortunately, I've had to work through sinners to do the will of God. I looked to Arden for assistance, but Gerard Montaigne disappointed me again and again. Even after I risked my life and my reputation to kill the Demon King and restore the—"

"Hang on," Destin said. "That happened a thousand years ago." Scummer, he thought. He's losing his mind. Please stay coherent long enough to give me something I can use.

"No, no," Vega said. "The reborn Demon King. The High Wizard, Alister. I knew that the empire—and the church— would never prevail as long as he was alive."

Jemson had been busy cleaning up the debris from the ceremony, but now he looked up. "You were the one who killed Han?"

"I conceived the plan, prepared the poison, and secured the assassins," Vega said, rather proudly. "The plan was to kidnap the boy—his son—and kill the father. That would prevent the boy from taking his father's place as the agent of the Breaker on earth. Instead, he would become the bargaining chip that would force the witch in the north to bend her knee."

"Brilliant," Destin murmured, while thinking, Not a chance. If you hadn't been so focused on paradise, you would have known the queen would never agree to that.

By now, every pair of eyes in the room was fixed on Vega. Destin looked from person to person, shaking his head to prevent any of them from interrupting. *Let him talk.*

"But the boy escaped," Vega said. "I was afraid he might have recognized me and would report me to the queen, but he simply disappeared. I knew that if I continued in direct operations, I would be recognized, sooner or later. I knew I needed more reliable help. Darian provided, once again. He taught me how to build a new army of Darian Brothers."

"How did Finn get entangled in this?" DeVilliers asked.

"He was curious about the Church of Malthus, and so I began to instruct him. He was an excellent scholar. He spent more and more time on spiritual matters. Soon, every winter, when Finn was supposed to be at the wizard academy, he was studying the word of Malthus at the Temple Church at Oden's Ford.

"The next summer, Finn came into the healing halls, near death. He was like a vessel that needed filling with truth and purpose. I took it upon myself to prepare him for his holy mission." With that, Vega exploded into a fit of coughing, spattering the bed with droplets of blood.

"Eventually, I took him to Aediion and the real war began. I was just the facilitator. Finn sul'Mander was the vessel through which the great saint worked to extend the true church throughout the Realms, even into the north. He deserves the praise of every follower of Malthus," Vega said. "I hope you'll tell the principia, Father Fosnaught, when you see him. Perhaps they can raise a monument to his sacrifice."

*I'm sure that will more than make up for what he's lost, you despicable bastard,* Destin thought. "Finn was my contact with the Darian Brothers at Oden's Ford," he said. "He called himself *Lord Darian*."

"Which, in fact, he was. He was the one who alerted us to Prince Adrian's presence there. But he wasn't involved in the sacrifice, because we worried that the prince would recognize him."

Destin rushed on, aware that he was running out of time. "How did Princess Mellony know that Finn was behind the murders of the prince and the queen?"

"Because Princess Mellony was behind Finn," Vega said. He shivered and closed his eyes, and it was like every muscle in his body went slack. Destin leaned forward, afraid the priest had expired, but his chest was still rising and falling, each breath a struggle to move air in and out.

"Mellony . . . was in on this?" Jemson said, unable to remain quiet.

"Yes," Vega said, opening his eyes. "Mellony saw no path to winning this war. She, also, was concerned about the spiritual health of the queendom."

Lila snorted softly.

"We conceived a plan to marry Finn to Julianna. They would ascend the throne as king and queen, and establish a kingdom of God here on earth, with Darian at its head."

"Except, unfortunately, there was already a queen, and a princess heir," Lila said.

By now, Vega seemed oblivious to his audience, so eager he was to tell his story. "There was. We assumed the princess had died in the attack on Chalk Cliffs, or would die in captivity in Carthis. When the prince planned a mission to rescue her, we couldn't take the chance that it would succeed." Vega closed his eyes again, as if it was too much trouble to keep them open.

"Which is why Finn sank my ship," DeVilliers said.

"And how Mellony knew about it," Lila said.

"Would the Montaignes hold still for that? An independent kingdom of God on their northern border?" Destin said. He was pretty sure he knew the answer to that.

"The new kingdom would, of course, be part of the empire. We knew that it would be difficult to win over the population at first, and so Arden offered an army to put down any resistance here in the north."

"Perfect," Destin said, thinking it was perfect for Arden. "How did it go wrong?"

"King Gerard died, Jarat ascended to the throne, and Mellony began dragging her feet, even after Finn opened the path to the succession. We decided to go forward with the marriage in secret. And you saw what happened."

We did, Destin thought. Mellony threw her new son-in-law off a cliff.

This latest burst of speech seemed to sap Vega's remaining strength. He lifted his hand, apparently meaning to make the sign of Malthus, but then it flopped down on his chest and Vega was done.

Destin took a deep breath, then let it out slowly. He scanned the room. The others looked positively pounded with mingled fury and sorrow.

"The question," Destin said, "is what happens now?"

# 51

# DISPERSION

Evan convinced the crew of *Destiny* to maintain their camp at the harbor so that they could repair their ship as quickly as possible. Also because he didn't really have a choice. Though he was eager to meet Breon—another of his magemarked brethren—he had no way to get to the mountain camp. None of the dragons would agree to carry him anywhere.

Flamecaster—the dragon Jenna called Cas—still had a serious grudge against him. The other dragons followed his lead. It was harrowing to look up from a book to find multiple pairs of dragon eyes watching his every move.

This was in contrast to the welcome the healer received. Cas gave him credit for removing the collar that he blamed Evan for. He was brother to the popular Lyssa Gray, whom Slayer had bonded with. And he'd freed the dragon named Goat from the ship's rigging.

When Evan asked Jenna for advice on how to win Cas over, she rolled her eyes. "You put a collar around his neck, locked him in a dark hold, and carried him across the ocean. Don't you think that might have been off-putting?"

Evan cast about for excuses. "He was wearing the collar when I bought him in the market."

"That's another thing. You don't 'buy' dragons or 'have' dragons or 'tame' dragons. Dragons are not weapons or airships. They are comrades. You partner with them, you bond with them—or you don't."

"He burned my ship," Evan said. "Doesn't that make us even?"

"'Even' is for enemies and rivals. You're going to have to give him more than that if you want him to trust you." Relenting, she added, "When you're trying to communicate with dragons, remember that they think visually. Show them what you mean, don't tell them, and you'll do a better job of making your case."

Still, the message was clear. *You're on your own.*

"How far away is the camp?" Evan persisted. "Is there a trail? Could I walk up?"

"Not where it is now," Jenna said. "We wanted a camp that the empress's soldiers wouldn't find unless they grew wings. So we moved it to the other side of the mountain." She paused. "Don't worry. Splash is coming with us. We're planning to bring Breon down here so that Adrian can work on the ship and tend to him, too."

"How is he doing?" Evan said. "Is he feeling better?"

"I think so," Jenna said. "We'll see. He still doesn't have his voice back, though he is making some sounds."

So Evan watched enviously as Jenna and the healer mounted Cas and launched from the quay.

That night, the two dragons returned, with Jenna and the magemarked boy riding double on Cas, and Adrian astride Splash.

Evan and Sasha rushed to help unload the patient.

"It's the busker!" Sasha exclaimed as he slid down the side of the dragon and into her waiting arms. "Thank the Maker."

The busker smiled when he saw Sasha and croaked a greeting.

"You know him?" Evan said, crowding in close.

"Yes," Sasha said, carefully setting him on his feet, but keeping a grip on his arm. "His name is Breon d'Tarvos. I captured the scummer-tongued scoundrel after Lyss was ambushed in Fellsmarch. I was his gaoler in Chalk Cliffs." Leaning down toward him, Sasha whispered, "Now, don't you dare spew on me like you did the last time."

"So," Adrian said, clearing his throat. "He must have some redeeming qualities?"

This sent the dragons into fits of laughter.

Sasha blushed crimson. "He's not really a murderer," she said defensively. "It's just that he was a razorleaf addict. He's quit it now, though."

"Bad news," Ash said. "He's been using it again, because he's going through withdrawal."

"Is that true?" Sasha tried to catch Breon's eye, but he avoided her gaze.

"Celestine must have given it to him," Evan said. "She's the biggest dealer along the coast." He tried not to stare at the musician—at his red-brown hair with a streak of glittering gold, his long-lashed blue-gray eyes. The musician's features stirred a deep memory that didn't quite make it to the surface.

"What is his gift?" Evan said.

"He has the gift of charm and empathy through sound," Sasha said. "The way he describes it is that he hears a person's song and repeats it back to them, which forms an immediate connection between them that is hard to resist."

Looks like it works, Evan thought, looking from Breon to Sasha. He couldn't wait to get a look at the busker's magemark.

The spellsinger was staring at Evan, frowning, as if trying to surface a memory of his own.

Evan reached out and took Breon's hand. "Hello, Breon," he said. "I'm Evan."

Breon smiled. "Ev!" he whispered.

The busker's voice was returning, hoarse, but improving every day. After supper, when it was too dark to work, he would sometimes play the jafasa, though singing was still too painful.

People said that scent is at the seat of memory; if it was, music was snuggled in beside it. The busker's music surfaced images that had been deeply buried until now.

The story Breon told was skeletal, halting, but, like all the others, his first memories were of survival on the streets.

Evan, Jenna, and Breon spent every spare moment together. They were like orphaned siblings reconnecting, trying to assemble the puzzle pieces of their memories and experiences into a picture that included all of them.

They debated endlessly. Were they all related to Celestine? Did she have a magemark, too? Was that why she was hunting them—so she could pry off their magemarks and steal their power? So she could eliminate rivals to the throne?

If so, why did she need them alive?

Was it possible that she just wanted to reunite her family?

"Blood is thicker than water," Evan said drily. "Ask the bloodsworn."

"Did she treat you like a prince?" Jenna asked Breon.

"Sort of," Breon said. "She dressed me up in fancy clothes and drowned me in affection." He paused, then added, "But she got me hooked on leaf again and took away my voice. She was really possessive—smothering, even. And bossy."

Reading the expression on the busker's face, Evan recalled the day he'd met Celestine, when he was crewing aboard his uncle's ship. The empress had dismissed him, had called him a ratling. Until she found out that he was a weather mage. And then, like the sun breaking through clouds on a stormy day, the weather changed.

*You carry Nazari blood—the heartsblood of the empire. You have a magical heritage that goes back centuries. Strangward wants to keep you to himself, but you belong at my side.*

"There's something else," Breon said. "She wasn't complete. It was like she had huge pieces missing."

Like a heart? Evan thought.

"What do you mean?" Jenna said.

"Her song," Breon said. "There were gaps that needed filling. It was . . . like a cadence with no melody. Or a melody without a rhythm." He sat back, looking pleased with himself.

Evan looked around at a circle of confused faces. Still, as if by mutual agreement, they left it alone. Though each person had his own history, his own quirks and desires and dreams, they were bound by blood and trouble.

Maybe, Evan thought, this is what it's like to have a family.

Evan, Adrian, and Sasha worked on *Destiny* from sunup to sundown, repairing and replacing her masts and spars, splicing her lines, doing whatever it took to make her seaworthy again. As Breon improved, he began to pitch in. Jenna and Cas brought materials from all over the island.

Days passed, and Evan's sense of urgency grew. The empress was in the Realms, and so was Destin. So was the young Gray Wolf queen. He needed to get back there, to find a way to salvage what he could. He needed *Destiny* seaworthy and ready to sail.

Annoyingly, doubts kept surfacing. Evan was a skilled ship's master, and his weather magery was most effective at sea. Even as a mage, would his entry into a land war make any difference? Was that the best way to defeat Celestine?

Two of the young dragons—Goat and Splinter—had taken to hanging around the quay, curious about what the humans were up to. Goat in particular wanted to learn more about the ship that had snared him. Soon, they began to help in a limited way—carrying lines up the masts, lifting the mainmast into place, and ferrying materials and supplies from ship to shore. Communication was a little awkward. The dragons could understand human speech, but only the healer could hear what they said back.

When the dragons grew tired of ship repair, they flew complex aerobatic maneuvers over the harbor, often joined in their mock battles by Splash. Sometimes Evan and Adrian stopped working to watch.

One of the three, Splinter, seemed to be having trouble keeping up with the others. He was visibly smaller than his brothers and sisters, and though he was smart and agile, he couldn't match their wingspread. The reason was plain to see—one of his wings was visibly deformed. Evan wondered whether he'd been born that way, or if he'd been injured.

If there was such a thing as the "runt of the litter" in a clutch of eggs, Splinter was it.

When Evan asked Jenna about it, she explained that the nest-
lings had been attacked by wolves. Splinter had survived, but
his wing had been badly damaged. Adrian had examined it, but
the injury was too old to remedy now.

Evan was no healer, but he did know a lot about using wind
and resistance to make things move. He began to give Splinter
a little extra help—for instance, a tailwind when he needed it to
outrace one of his nestmates, or an updraft to lift him above the
others so he'd own the "high ground" at a critical time.

The first time Evan did it, Splinter noticed. He hovered,
wings beating frantically, looking for the source of the sudden
rogue wind.

The third or fourth time he intervened, the dragon landed
next to Evan on the quay, fixing him with a look that said the
game was over. There was something else—a fluttering at the
fringes of his mind that he couldn't quite grasp. Was the dragon
trying to communicate with him?

"I think I can give you a better wing," he said to Splinter.

The dragon regarded him with what could only be defined
as skepticism.

Recalling what Jenna had told him about communicating
with dragons, Evan tried to visualize the fix he had in mind—a
kind of jib sail that would add surface area to the damaged wing
so that it would better match the other one.

Manufacturing it would be another matter. It would have to
be made of a flame-resistant fabric. And light, so the additional
weight wouldn't defeat its purpose.

Destin would have known exactly how to do it.

Evan heard that fluttering in his mind again.

Splinter stood, staring at him intently as if waiting for an answer, obviously frustrated with this deaf human.

"What's going on?"

Adrian had joined them on the quay and was looking from one to the other curiously.

"I think I can design a kind of sail mechanism that would compensate for Splinter's wing so that they match up better. Right now, he has to work really hard to make the adjustments that allow him to fly straight. I'm trying to sell him on it."

"He's asking you questions," Adrian said, nodding at Splinter.

Evan shrugged helplessly.

"If you're having trouble, it helps to be touching him."

*If I extend the hand of friendship, will he bite it off?*

"Remember—he can hear what you say to him, silently and out loud," Adrian said.

"Splinter," Evan said, feeling a little foolish, "is it all right if I touch you? That way I might be able to hear you."

The dragon lowered his head so that they were practically nose to nose. Evan could feel his skin tightening under the heat of his faintly sulfurous breath. That seemed to be a yes, or at least a maybe. He ducked under the dragon's jaw and rested his hand under his chin, where he wasn't as thickly armored.

A series of images slammed into Evan's head. The meaning was clear enough: *How can a flightless, wingless, rather puny creature help me fly?*

"Ships fly," Evan said, pointing at the ketch. It wasn't a great illustration, because her sails were still furled to the masts.

Splinter understood, though, because in response, he sent an image of a dragon skimming across the ocean, sending up a wake. *Ships fly on belly.*

"But you both use wind."

Once again, Evan visualized the rig he thought might work, though, admittedly, parts of it were rather sketchy.

*Try*, Splinter said, finally.

Evan was the architect, but all three members of the *Destiny*'s crew ended up working on the project after putting in a full day doing ship repairs.

They all gathered on the quay to watch as Splinter tried out his new gear. On the first try, he all but ended up in the harbor. By the third launch, he'd worked with it enough so that anyone could see that it was a huge improvement.

Day after day, the young dragon practiced. And day after day, he continued to assist in the repairs to the ship, as well as bringing Evan game and fish he'd caught while hunting. Evan made a few adjustments in the rigging, and before long, Splinter was nearly keeping up with the others, and obviously relishing his new mastery of the skies.

Destin would have built a better rig, Evan thought. Still, he couldn't help being pleased with himself. Especially because Splinter's endorsement turned out to be the key to winning over the other dragons, even Cas. With that success behind him, Evan turned to working with Jenna to make more and larger saddles and harnesses that would allow dragons and humans to fly together.

As the ship neared completion, the debate began—what now?

"Just before they left, the empress somehow found out who Lyss really is," Breon said. "Maybe that's why they left right then."

"It seems obvious that Celestine means to take advantage of Captain Gray's military skills," Evan said. "That's why they're heading back to the wetlands. That's where the war is now. The empress already controls the Desert Coast, with the possible exception of Tarvos. And your sister knows how to fight in the Realms. She's been successful there."

"I can't believe that Lyss would fight for the empress against her own people." Sasha added more ironwood to their campfire.

"The empress can be very persuasive," Evan said. "As Jenna pointed out, if the choice is between serving the empress as a bloodsworn slave, or serving the empress as a free person, nobody could blame her if she chose the latter. At least that way, there's the hope of escape."

"Wouldn't Celestine want to lock her up in a safe place?" Adrian said. "Wouldn't she be worth more as a hostage than as a military commander?"

"The empress has seen what Lyss can do," Breon said. "She doesn't have a lot of options."

"If Celestine takes Lyss to the Realms, you know they'll keep a close guard on her," Jenna said. "If she tries to escape, and fails, she knows what the consequence will be."

"I think Lyss will do whatever it takes to stay alive," Sasha said. "She's the only survivor of the Gray Wolf line. She'll fight tooth and nail to make sure it doesn't end with her."

"Now that she knows you're alive, Wolf," Jenna said, "she will also stay alive in order to see you again."

Sasha sighed. "I hate to say this, but I feel like Lyss has been getting farther and farther away while we've been stalled here. The ship still isn't seaworthy, and then it will take time to sail back home, even if we manage to avoid the empress's ships. I worry that we'll be too late."

"Maybe we don't have to *sail* back," Jenna said. When this was met with blank faces, she rushed on. "It depends on the dragons, of course. Whether they want to go to the Realms, and whether they are willing to fly us there. We have five people and six dragons."

"Have any of the young ones flown across an ocean before?" Evan said.

Jenna bit her lip, then shot a worried look at Splinter. "No. But they've been flying farther and farther every day since the stormwall came down. Some have flown nearly as far as the mainland of Carthis. . . ." She trailed off.

"Well, I'm not getting on a dragon," Sasha said. "No offense," she mumbled, looking down at her lap as if trying to avoid the dragons' eyes.

"Lyss is not afraid of dragons," Jenna said. "Lyss and Slayer flew together all the time. If you want to serve your queen, you must follow her example."

"If Lyss were here, and planning to fly across the ocean on a dragon, I would go with her," Sasha said. "Otherwise . . ." She shook her head.

"But if that's what you need to do to serve?" Jenna raised an eyebrow.

"You don't even know if any of the dragons are strong enough to carry me," Sasha said. "I'm twice as big as any of the rest of you."

In answer, Cas extended his wing to the ground, inviting her to climb aboard.

"Cas says he'll carry you," Jenna said. "Pricker will, too."

Sasha eyed them doubtfully, and Evan wondered if that was her real concern.

"You all can do what you want, but I'm not leaving my ship here," Evan said flatly.

Jenna's breath hissed out in frustration. "But—"

"Listen, you and Cas already burned up one of my ships," Evan said. "And I'm not sure whose banner my others are sailing under at the moment. This—" He swallowed hard, trying to quell the emotion welling up in him. "This is my first ship, and I'm not leaving her here."

In so many ways, *Destiny* had been the symbol of dreams made real—the acknowledgment that he had the right to hope for happiness. He and Destin had built it together. He was not ready to give up on it yet.

"Ships are too slow," Jenna said.

"If we go back to the Fells and into a war, the dragons can help," Adrian said.

"Anyway, Cas wants to go back," Jenna said. "The hunting is a lot better in the wetlands."

"You can all go back to the Realms," Evan said. "I'll stay here. I can sail a ketch alone, if need be. I sailed to the wetlands—twice—to warn you, and to try to prevent the empress from gaining a foothold there. I kept the empress from getting her hands on you, but I failed in everything else. I am not a soldier, or a diplomat. I'm a pirate, and my weather mage gifts are most useful on the water."

The back-and-forth went on a while longer.

"Look," Evan said finally, "Celestine has thrown everything into the war in the wetlands, because she assumes that the war is won here. I'm going to show her that it's not. Jenna, Cas, and the other dragons have destroyed her precious capital. I am going to reclaim her strongholds along the Desert Coast.

"When she finds out, it may cause her to pull some of her troops and ships back from the Realms. That would be more helpful to you than anything I can do in the mountains. Besides, I've discovered that I don't like cold weather."

"But—what if the empress controls Tarvos now?" Adrian said.

"I'm used to dealing with Celestine's crew. I promised my crew in Tarvos that I would come back, and I'm going to keep that promise. I'll welcome anyone who wants to come with me, though I'll tell you right now, it probably won't end well."

"I'll come," Breon said, surprising everyone.

"No!" Sasha said. "The empress brought you here for a purpose, and you don't want to stay and find out what it is."

"I'm not planning to stay *here*," Breon said, gesturing at the ruins of the marble palace. "The empress is in the wetlands. At least, I think she is. And the farther away I am from her, the better."

"You should come back with us," Sasha persisted.

"I'm a wanted man in the wetlands," Breon said, "and I deserve to be. I don't blame you for wanting me to come back and stand trial—"

"That's not what I want!" Sasha said. Then turned crimson as she looked around at the circle of faces. "I mean, I want you to come back and clear your name."

"I can't clear my name when I'm guilty," Breon said. "I would like to do something to make up for all the bad things I've done. I'd like to come back with you and kick the empress's ass. But . . . I'm not a soldier, either. I'm useless in a fight. And I don't want to see Evan stay here on his own. Maybe my gift could prove useful, in a pinch."

Evan looked from Sasha to Breon. "You can stay, Sasha, if you want. I mean, there is a chance that your queen is in Carthis."

"No," Sasha said, tears streaming down her face. "She isn't. I know she isn't. She's in the Realms, and I have to go there, even if it means riding on a dragon."

With that, the gaoler and her former prisoner embraced.

That's a strange friendship, Evan thought. But who am I to judge?

In the end, Splinter and Splash decided to stay with Breon and Evan. "Two dragons, a shadowcaster, and a stormcaster," Evan said. "Celestine's days are numbered."

In the days following, Breon joined Ash, Sasha, and Evan in a push to get *Destiny* as close to seaworthy as possible before they went their separate ways.

They had enough gear to equip three dragons for carrying passengers, and with only three humans flying, that was enough. Since there was no longer the need to wait until *Destiny* was ready to sail, the flyers prepared to go—Jenna and Cas, Ash and Goat, Sasha and Pricker. Slayer flew solo, carrying extra gear, ready to relieve the others as needed. The plan was that they would fly from the Northern Islands to Wizard Head, which was the shortest water crossing to the Realms.

The day of departure was bittersweet. All of his life, Evan had been surrounded by rivals, enemies, superiors, and subordinates. Except for his brief time with Destin, Evan had never had real friends—or even peers. This was as close as he'd come since, and now he was saying good-bye. He knew from experience that some good-byes were forever.

Evan removed the amulet that Destin had given him and

extended it toward Adrian. "You need this more than I do," he said.

The healer shook his head. "No. Keep it. I'll be in the north soon, where amulets are made. I'll be fine."

Evan and Breon stood on the quay to see them off. But Evan had one more ask.

"We've said that there is a chance that your queen—your sister—is in Carthis," Evan said. "If so, I promise I will bring her back to you." He paused. "But I want a promise from all of you in return."

"Which is?" Jenna said.

"Destin Karn is important to me," Evan said. "I want you to do everything you can to make sure he survives and thrives, no matter who wins."

Jenna's eyes narrowed. "I knew it! You were working together all along."

"Guilty," Evan said, without guilt. "Do I have your promise?"

And so it was agreed.

# REGIME CHANGE

Lila hadn't been in the great hall since she'd escorted the runaway prince back to the palace. Now it was transformed and swarming with activity. The Gray Wolf banners had been ripped down and replaced with the red hawk of Arden. The Ardenine colors and signia seemed to be everywhere.

The windows were open, admitting a welcome breeze on this warm evening.

To Lila's eyes, it looked more like a party or reception than a meeting or a tribunal. It resembled the king's more formal occasions in Arden—servants circulating, plenty of food and drink, everyone carrying weapons under their clothes. Shadow and DeVilliers had elected to stay away, after extracting a promise from Lila to give them a full report.

Lila, of course, didn't have a choice. Karn insisted that she come along.

It was a walking-around kind of a party, but Lila noticed that a table had been placed on the dais at the front of the room, elaborately set with royal regalia. Nobody was sitting there yet.

Lila plucked two silver cups of wine off a passing tray, noting that they carried the Montaigne M, and the hawk of Arden.

"How did all this fancyware get here so quick?" Lila muttered, handing one to Karn.

"Jarat brought wagonloads along with the military train," Karn said.

"I guess he was pretty sure of winning," Lila said.

"I guess you could say that," Karn said, nodding to several members of the King's Guard as they passed by. "It's easy to win if you fix the game."

"Are you sure I'm not going to be hauled away in chains?"

"I'm never sure of anything, but I put in a word for you. It helps that you are known to be a bannerless opportunist." Karn laughed at Lila's scowl. "Look, Jarat knows you're here. You'd already be in chains if he wanted you to be. He wouldn't waste his fine wine on anyone he planned to execute."

"What did you do with Vega's body?" Lila said.

"He's still dead," Karn said, raising his glass. "And he's where nobody will ever find him."

Lila peered into her cup and sniffed. "What are the chances this is poisoned?" she said. "Who's doing the pouring?"

"This is a new regime, remember?" Karn said. "It's all been vetted and tasted ahead of time, then locked up since."

"Well, then," Lila said, "bottoms up." She drained her cup and grabbed another. "There are a lot of people here," she said, scanning the crowd. "Including most of the nobility and the council members. Even the Manders are here! What's that about? Doesn't anyone know how to hold a grudge anymore? Isn't anyone in gaol?"

"I suppose you could say that the Manders have made a deal with the new regime. After all, they were playing with a poor hand, being the parents of a traitor and a murderer. The Queen's Guard is confined to quarters, those who are still alive. The wizards who weren't able to flee to Gray Lady are all collared. None of the copperheads have come down to the city."

Lila debated telling Karn about her specialized collars. Then decided she would tell him when and if he needed to know it.

At that moment, there was a stir at the front of the room. A trumpet played a fanfare, and an honor guard of blackbirds marched in. Next came Princess Mellony, elegant in a black silk gown, diamonds glittering at her neck and a diamond tiara on her head. After an awkward pause, Julianna Barrett arrived in a plain black suit with a gray shawl draped over one shoulder, subtly embroidered with—Lila squinted—fellscats.

"I've got to move closer to the front," Destin said, threading his way forward until he stood next to the dais. Lila followed him up to get a good view. Up close, she could see that there was some kind of a dispute going on between queen regent and princess. It seemed to have to do with clothes, because at one point Mellony tried to pull the shawl off Julianna's shoulder and the princess gripped her mother's wrist and hissed, "Leave me alone, Mother."

Ordinarily, Lila would have been glad she'd reserved a ringside spot. Glad of any drama that would draw attention away from her. But when she looked into Julianna's face, still black and blue under her makeup, her eyes puffy from crying and lack of sleep, she looked away, ashamed.

And finally King Jarat strode in from the wings, claiming his place center stage. He was the most brilliant bird on the dais, with his mother's raven hair and his father's icy-blue eyes, clad in a coat of deep blue silk. On his head, he wore the midrange crownlet the Montaignes favored for travel.

The murmur of conversation diminished as the crowd reacted, some elbowing forward, others dropping back as if to get out of range, all turning to face the stage.

Flanking the dais were the young general Eric Bellamy on one side, and Cedric Fosnaught, the principia of the Church of Malthus, on the other. Speaker Jemson mounted the steps and stood next to the southern prelate.

"I'm surprised Julianna is here," Lila said.

"They made a deal with Julianna, too," Destin whispered. "If she cooperates, Finn is buried with a clear name and military honors."

"I wonder what they are going to say about the wedding," Lila murmured.

"I'm guessing they'll say nothing at all," Destin said.

Another fanfare quieted the room, and Mellony stepped forward.

"This has been a difficult season for us all," she said, her voice carrying a slight tremor. "A season of unending grief, when losses come in twos and threes, allowing no proper intervals in which to mourn those who've gone. I would like to remedy that now. I've asked Speaker Jemson to call out the names of the recent dead and offer a benediction."

Good thing it's limited to the *recent* dead, Lila thought, or we would be here all night.

Jemson ushered Fosnaught forward. "In the interests of ecumenical harmony, I have asked Father Fosnaught to read the names, and I will offer the benediction."

I see what you did there, Lila thought. You don't want to sanction the list, you seditious scoundrel.

Fosnaught read from a list that Jemson handed him, his voice tolling like a bell. "Raisa ana'Marianna. Amon Byrne. Adrian sul'Han. Alyssa ana'Raisa. Sasha Talbot. Harriman Vega. Finn sul'Mander."

This announcement was met with gasps of surprise and disbelief, and then a cacophony of questions. Some of those present didn't know that Prince Adrian had been raised from the dead, and now was dead again.

It's hard to keep up, Lila thought. We should have a mourning briefing.

Speaker Jemson raised his hands, quieting the gathering in that way he had. "I know that all of you have questions about all that has happened. No doubt, your questions will be answered in the coming days. Tonight, I would like to remember the dead, recognize those still living, and consider how to honor our loved ones through our actions going forward. When we come to a crossroads, when it comes to making a choice, it would be useful to think, What would Queen Raisa have us do? How can we best serve her memory? Now. Let us pray."

When the benediction was over, Jemson exited to the right. The queen regent rose again, spots of color on her cheeks. "Now. In the midst of tragedy, there is reason for celebration. Weeks ago, when Princess Alyssa was missing, her fate unknown, the council took steps to assure that the royal succession would remain intact. Princess Julianna ana'Mellony was named as successor to Alyssa, should a successor be needed. Tonight, we celebrate the official coronation of Julianna ana'Mellony as queen of the Fells."

This was met with a brief silence, then scattered cheering and a whole lot of puzzled murmurs, especially among elder guests.

*This is not how it's done. What about the four questions? What about the temple service? Where is her bonded captain?*

"Kneel, Julianna ana'Mellony, blooded princess of the Gray Wolf line, and prepare to accept this burden," Mellony said.

Julianna knelt, her head bowed.

Mellony lifted the crown from the table and swiveled toward her daughter.

Jarat stepped in. "Let me," he said. He took the crown from Mellony's hands. "I, Emperor Jarat Montaigne, anointed sovereign of the New Empire of the Seven Realms, name you, Julianna ana'Mellony, queen of the province of the Fells." Gently, he placed the crown on Julianna's head.

*Province?* Lila looked from Mellony to Jarat, who was smiling like a fellscat on a carcass.

Jarat took Julianna's hands, lifted her to her feet, and kissed her. He scooped his glass from the table and raised it. "To the queen of the Fells!"

Mellony quickly raised her glass. "To the queen of the Fells!"

Lila lifted her glass with the others and murmured, "To the queen of the Fells."

Mellony reclaimed the floor. "There is more," she said. "Some of you have never known a world without war. It has cost us thousands of lives, and uncounted treasure. Tonight, it is my pleasure to announce that we have signed a peace treaty with Jarat Montaigne, emperor of the Realms. The war between us is over." She raised her glass again. "To an enduring peace!"

This was met with a mixture of more hesitant cheering and puzzlement.

"And, finally, to celebrate this new relationship between the empire and the province of the Fells, I announce the betrothal of Julianna ana'Mellony, queen of the Fells, to Jarat Montaigne, emperor of the Realms. With this marriage, the Seven Realms will be reunited, and ruled henceforth by their children."

Again, Jarat turned to Julianna, gripped her hand, and went to slip a ring on her finger. At the last minute, awkwardly, he had to switch hands because Julianna was still wearing Finn's ring on her ring finger.

Small rebellions, Lila thought, with a touch of admiration.

Mellony's lips tightened when she saw that, but she composed her face and raised her glass. "To the happy couple."

The crowd responded tentatively, like guests in an unfamiliar church.

A voice rang out from the rear of the hall. "You are not the queen of the Fells."

Everyone turned to see who spoke. It was a tall woman with a long gray braid, her bearing erect as any queen's.

"Who are you, old woman?" Jarat said.

"I am Magret Gray, a maiden of Hanalea, and guardian of the Gray Wolf line." The crowd parted as she walked forward. Behind her came wolves in every color of gray, their eyes glittering in the torchlight. They filled the hall from wall to wall, silent as ghosts, threading their way through the crowd.

Lila leaned toward Destin, who was staring, mesmerized. "Ah . . . humor me, but do you see any wolves?"

"What are you talking about?" Destin said.

"Never mind."

"Magret!" Julianna said, going paler than before.

"You are not the queen of the Fells," Magret repeated. "The true queen is coming with an army, and all who oppose her will pay a blood price."

"Queen Raisa is dead," Mellony said. "You're confused, Magret. Please. Someone help her." She looked around, but, of course, there were no bluejackets in the room, only blackbirds.

"I am not talking about Queen Raisa," Magret said. "I'm talking about Queen Alyssa ana'Raisa, the blooded queen."

"Alyssa!" Julianna said, directing a scathing look at Mellony. "She's alive?"

"Aye," Magret said. Now she stood in front of the dais. She pointed at Jarat, looking like the image of the Breaker on the day of judgment. "Boy, your days are numbered. Spiritgate has fallen. Ardenscourt has fallen. Delphi has fallen. And you, too, will fall under the blade of justice."

Jarat jerked his head at two of his blackbirds, and they closed in on Magret.

"Leave her alone!" Julianna cried, running for the steps, but her way was blocked by Jarat's guard.

Destin, too, moved toward Magret. Lila wasn't sure what the spymaster meant to do, but whatever it was, he was too late. Before he could get there, the maiden lay dead in a pool of blood, run through by one of the blackbirds.

With that, a howling started up, all around them.

"Magret!" This time, Julianna punched through the wall of blackbirds and ran to Magret's side. "Call a healer!" she cried, kneeling next to her, lifting her head and cradling it in her arms.

Nobody moved. Even at a distance, Lila could tell that a healer would do no good.

Even Mellony looked shell-shocked by how quickly things had gone south. "Julianna," she whispered. "It—it's for the best, don't you think? Magret was—was—"

"*Magret* was telling the truth, Mother!" Julianna shouted. "And died for it." She stood, her hands smeared with blood, and worked Jarat's ring off her finger. She flung it at him. It hit the table and careened out into the room. "I am not marrying you," she spat. "I am not marrying anyone."

# 53

# THE DESERT COAST

Evan leaned down along Splinter's head and called over to Breon, "There. That's them."

From this altitude, the shiplords resembled specks on the sand. Evan counted. Jasmina had done well. Four out of four.

The shiplords waited on the beach in a little cove south of Deep Harbor, probably wondering if they had been led into a trap. Jasmina had lured them here with the promise that the Stormcaster had a proposition for them and would provide a compelling argument to accept it.

No doubt they were well aware that a compelling argument can take many forms.

Evan was a little surprised they had accepted this invitation and his conditions. They must be really worried about what would happen when the empress returned to the Desert Coast.

Evan had insisted that they leave their weapons with their horses and gather on the beach unarmed. Not that shiplord weapons would make a dent in a dragon's hide, but Evan lacked that advantage.

"Do you see weapons?" he said.

*No*, Splinter said, after a moment.

Evan looked over at Breon, who gave him a thumbs-up.

"Let's go," Evan said. With that, Splinter folded his wings and plummeted toward the water. They came so fast that they were nearly at the surface before the shiplords could react. Just before they hit, Splinter snapped out his wings and they glided in and landed on the beach like a massive, ungainly gull.

The shiplords made a break for it, but Splash and Breon landed gracefully at the edge of the beach, between the shiplords and their horses.

The shiplords gathered into a jittery bunch, and all of their hidden weapons appeared, so that they bristled like a hedgehog. Evan counted noses again. Blazon, Ursula, Riggs, and Jasmina.

"Hang on," Evan said, sliding to the sand. "Don't go. You've not heard my compelling argument yet."

If the shiplords had been staring before, now their eyes nearly popped out of their heads. They clustered even more tightly together as he walked toward them, as if they could disappear in a crowd of four.

Splinter stretched out his neck so that he was looking over Evan's shoulder, his hot breath bathing the shiplords.

"This is Splinter," Evan said. "Sharp objects make him nervous, so I suggest that you put your weapons away." He paused and, when nobody moved, added, "They wouldn't do you any good, anyway."

Slowly, reluctantly, they returned their weapons to their hiding places. They glared at Jasmina, who had lured them into this trap.

Jasmina stood, hands on hips, staring at the dragons. "I've

heard stories about dragon riders in the past," she said, wearing an expression of frank admiration. "I thought those days were over."

Evan gestured toward Breon and Splash. "That's Breon d'Tarvos and Splash."

"Look," Blazon said, licking his lips nervously, "we had no idea Jagger planned to give you to the empress." Heads nodded all around.

"If we had, we would have told you," Ursula said.

"And Jagger's dead," Blazon said. "Jasmina killed him. And when Samara came to collect you, we wouldn't let him into the harbor."

"Really? I heard that Maslin and Kel wouldn't let them in," Evan said.

"None of us would," Ursula said. "We told him Jagger was running a rig on him, claiming he'd turn over the Stormcaster." They all nodded.

"I believe you," Evan said.

She blinked at him. "You do?"

"Shouldn't I?"

"Oh, yes," she said hastily, the other shiplords nodding agreement.

Riggs, who was probably the youngest of the shiplords next to Evan, was edging closer to Splinter. "Is it tame?" he asked Evan, reaching his hand toward the dragon. "Can I pet it?"

"No!" Evan said, and Riggs yanked his hand back. "I'm Splinter's friend and partner, not his owner," he said. He'd learned his lesson well. "If you want to touch him, ask him, not me."

"But . . . will it understand me?"

"They can understand you," Evan said. "Believe me."

By now Splinter was fuming. *Can I pet this young male?* Splinter asked Evan, glaring at Riggs.

"Splinter wants to know if he can pet *you*," Evan said to Riggs.

"Well," Riggs said, shifting from foot to foot, looking at the others as if they might bail him out. "I guess so. . . ."

With that, Splinter nudged him gently with his head, and Riggs fell backward onto the sand.

Splinter and Splash thought this was hilarious. Riggs scrambled to his feet, none the worse for wear.

*Can I pet humans, too?* Splash said.

"No," Breon said. "They're not used to being petted by dragons."

*Then they should keep hands to selves unless invited*, Splash said.

"I agree," Breon said.

The shiplords were watching these seemingly one-sided exchanges with growing alarm.

"The dragons have agreed to ally with us," Evan said. "They can burn an entire city in an afternoon. Ships are especially vulnerable, since they're almost entirely wood, and they have no place to escape to. Once we take one city, the rest will fall into line."

"What's in it for the dragons?" Riggs said. He, of all of them, seemed to be adjusting to this new way of thinking.

"They are looking for some concessions from us when it comes to territory and hunting grounds. In other words, they want us to leave the mountains to them, as well as allowing unmolested fishing in designated areas of the shore."

"So," said Jasmina, who was never long on patience, "I'm

with Strangward. Who else is with us?"

"What happens if we don't sign on?" Blazon said.

"You won't share in the spoils," Riggs said.

"Hold on," Evan said. "Nobody should sign on with an expectation of spoils. We're not raiding the cities of the Desert Coast, we are setting them free. What you do away from the coast is your business, but if you want to operate out of these ports, you can't be attacking them."

By now, they all looked crestfallen. "To answer your question, Blazon," Evan continued, "you may find it hard to stay neutral. If you align with the empress, your ship is fair game for any of us. If you manage to sit it out, you won't be involved in the council that makes the decisions, and you'll pay higher port fees from now on."

In the end, the decision was unanimous—everyone signed on.

"Now," Evan said, "we don't know when the empress will return to the islands. Tully Samara is here, though. When cities start falling, he'll notice. The last thing we want him to do is sail to the wetlands and alert Celestine before we have everything well in hand."

"So, if we see him, what would you have us do?" Riggs said.

"Take him alive, if that's possible," Evan said. "If not, kill him."

Deepwater Court was the largest, most important port on the Desert Coast, and the empress's most important stronghold along the Desert Coast. Evan's shiplords blockaded the harbor, demanding a surrender. The harbormaster refused, so the dragons flamed every ship at anchor.

When he met with the harbormaster, Evan said, "You think business is down now? Wait until the masters find out that Deepwater Court is where ships go to get burned to the waterline."

The harbormaster still refused to listen to reason, so Splinter burned the customhouse and the longest of the quays.

"You've seen fire," Evan said. "Next comes flood. Your entire waterfront will be underwater by tomorrow if you don't surrender now."

"You don't understand," the harbormaster said. "When the empress finds out I've given up the port, she'll turn me into a blood slave."

"Let me worry about the empress," Evan said. "You'd better worry about me."

Celestine's harbormaster surrendered.

The several hundred bloodsworn were more troublesome, lacking the instinct for self-preservation common to free men and women. When possible, Evan turned them with his own blood. When necessary, he killed them.

The result was that, without really meaning to, he was building himself an army.

An image came back to Evan—of him and Destin on the deck of the ketch, raising glasses, toasting themselves. *Ruthless.*

Within a week, Deepwater Court was a free port. Word spread as they moved down the coast, and the process became easier. Often, Celestine's free soldiers and administrators fled ahead of them. Everywhere Evan went, he asked if anyone had seen a Captain Gray, if anyone knew where she was. He also asked after Tully Samara.

He found neither. He hadn't expected to find the wolf queen.

He had expected to find Samara.

Where the devil is he? Evan thought. By now, if Tully were anywhere on the Desert Coast, he would have to know what Evan and his shiplords were up to.

Tarvos was the easiest "conquest" of all. In Evan's absence, it had remained a free port, under Kel's supervision, while Celestine was off adventuring in the west. Another week, and the entire Desert Coast was theirs, though there were isolated pockets of resistance to the east and in a few villages along the coast. The rapid conquest of the coast served a dual purpose—it diminished the empress's perceived invincibility, and hopefully it convinced the shiplords that Evan was not one to trifle with again.

He'd not seen or heard from Samara in that time.

They met in council in Tarvos, where Evan intended to reestablish his capital. Evan divided responsibilities among his shiplords. Jasmina and Riggs took Deepwater Court, a reward for her loyalty and in recognition of her abilities. Blazon and Ursula went to Endru, with the added responsibility of patrolling up and down the coast. Evan and Breon would be in Tarvos, for now.

They set some preliminary rules for the ports, and then moved on to a celebration. The only shadow over their good cheer was the knowledge that, sooner or later, Celestine would return, her armies swollen with wetland "recruits," hungry for revenge.

That's the whole point—to lure her back here, Evan thought. But he knew better than to share that with his new allies, who would prefer that she stayed on the other side of the Indio.

"Maybe that's where Samara is," Ursula said, having moved

from the cheerful to the glum stage of drinking. "Maybe he heard what's going on and sailed for the wetlands to tell Celestine."

"Maybe Celestine will turn right around and go back to the wetlands if she comes back to a free Desert Coast united against her," Riggs said.

"She will come back," Breon said abruptly. "She will return to the Northern Islands by midsummer, if not before."

Evan and Jasmina stared at him.

"Why?" Evan said. "Why do you think that?"

"It was in her song," Breon said.

Jasmina eyed him suspiciously. "Celestine . . . was singing?"

"Not out loud," Breon said.

"Can you sing it?" Evan said, quieting Jasmina with a look. His knowledge of Breon's gift was sketchy at best. He was the first spellsinger Evan had ever met.

Breon closed his eyes, as if searching out a memory.

*This is where it all begins.*
*This is where it all ends.*
*The shattering*
*The rejoining*
*Forged in the bleeding earth.*
*As it has been, it shall be again.*
*At midsummer,*
*When the sun pauses in the sky.*

This was met with silence.

"So." Evan cleared his throat. "That tells you that Celestine is coming back at midsummer? Whether the wetlands have fallen or not?"

Breon opened his eyes. "Yes," he said with quiet confidence.

"That's just a month away," Jasmina said. "How do you get that?"

"It's there," Breon said, brow furrowed, like he was surprised that they didn't hear it.

"What do you think that means?" Evan said. "'Forged in the bleeding earth'?"

Breon shook his head, as if to say, *I sang the song. My work is done.*

"Rivers?" Jasmina guessed. "Volcanos?"

"There are volcanos in the wetlands as well as here," Evan said. He didn't want to call Breon's prophecy into question, but it was making it harder to build a case. Fortunately, by now the shiplords were too deep in their cups to worry.

"To the Stormcaster!" the shiplords said, raising their glasses.

Evan raised his glass. "Ruthless," he said.

# KILLING SOUTHERNERS

It was good to be fighting southerners again, Lyss thought, even if it was under somebody else's flag, with somebody else's army. Most nights she was so exhausted that she fell into a deep and dreamless sleep. Other nights, she lay awake, worrying that she was helping Celestine to win control of the entire continent. Worrying that she was betraying her queendom for selfish reasons—her desire to keep her brother alive.

She'd lost her father, her sister, her mother, and countless friends. *Do I have to give up everything and everyone I love for this thrice-cursed line and star-crossed queendom?*

She would grip her brother's serpent amulet between her hands for reassurance. When energy flowed into her fingers, she wondered who had put it there—Adrian or her father.

Some nights, when she was falling into sleep, the amulet drew her attention, insistently, as if trying to pull her into a dream. Her father stood in the clothes he'd died in, but clean again, unblemished. He extended his hands, reaching for her, but there was too great a distance between them. She wanted to dive into the dream and leave the real world behind.

You need to live, and succeed, in the real world, she told herself. The Line won't end here.

As she'd expected, her bloodsworn army was much more effective in the relatively flat borderlands than it had been in the mountains. They made rapid progress to the west, following the river valley from Spiritgate toward Delphi. Lyss told herself that it was a good thing that Delphi was back in Ardenine hands. This way, when they took the city, they would be killing southerners instead of her countrymen.

Lyss's success pleased Celestine. She praised Lyss's skills on a daily basis, though much of her time was spent reflecting on her own good judgment in putting Lyss in command of the army.

Lyss was glad to share credit with the empress, even though she knew the blame would be all hers when things went wrong. "The first job of a general is to choose a battle she can win," Lyss said. "Then, when it comes to the actual fighting, she looks like a genius."

Her Highlander officers were relieved that they weren't fighting the Highlanders, but they found the behavior of their bloodsworn soldiers disquieting.

"They scarcely eat anything," Lieutenant Farrow said. "They don't seem to feel the cold. It's like they don't notice when they're wounded. They don't even go out to taverns or pleasure houses when we reach a town."

"So they're ideal soldiers, right?" Lyss said drily. "What commander doesn't dream of soldiers like this?"

"Me," Farrow said bluntly. "It's hard to care about them as much as I should, because they don't quite seem human."

"Just remember—most are unwilling recruits. And you

never know what's going on inside them. Maybe more than you think."

Jada Long Foot sauntered up and saluted in that lackadaisical way she had. "Some of the advance scouts just rode in. They say the road is fairly clear between here and Delphi. We should be there in two days."

Lyss had learned not to trust good fortune. "Where is everyone? It's like the entire countryside has been emptied out."

"The few civilians we can find say that one army after another has marched through," Long Foot said. "Many have hidden their food and their valuables and left the area."

Lyss groaned. They were moving too fast, in her opinion. The more quickly they reached Delphi, the more quickly she might be faced with marching north, through Marisa Pines Pass, and into the belly of the queendom.

At least Samara wasn't here, looking over her shoulder. Celestine had left him in Carthis, to keep an eye on things. She wished she could send Celestine east to join him. That would give her a bit more flexibility. Or a lot. She still wished she knew more about the blood bond, and if there was any way to break it.

And then, like a dream come true, Celestine was called away to the northeast. Since taking Chalk Cliffs, her armies had struggled to make any headway in the mountains. Clan warriors were decimating the bloodsworn in the mountain passes, and she'd lost several of her best commanders.

Lyss had worried that Celestine might pull her from the southern campaign and send her north to address the problems there, but she didn't. "This is one part of the war that is going well," the empress said. "Why would I interfere with that?"

Instead, she took Munroe Graves, one of Lyss's best Fellsian artillerymen, who'd been captured at Chalk Cliffs. "If we cannot get at these soldiers in the mountains," Celestine said, "we'll blast away their hiding places."

Good luck with that, Lyss thought, but didn't say it aloud, because she was glad not to be going herself.

When Graves asked for advice, Lyss said, "Say yes to everything she asks, but if you can get clean away, make a run for it. If you get away, find your way to General Dunedain and tell her what's going on. Tell them that my brother is probably being held captive in the Northern Islands."

"Yes, ma'am," Graves said.

"Be careful," Lyss said, swallowing hard, aware that tears were rolling down her cheeks. "Stay alive, and I'll buy you a drink when I see you again."

Impulsively, she embraced him.

She and Celestine had a parting conversation as well. "Just remember, Your Highness, that no one is irreplaceable," the empress said. "Serve me well, and you will be richly rewarded. But know that I deal with betrayal with a hard hand. I will find you, I will take you back to Celesgarde, and I will kill both you and your brother."

"I understand, Empress," Lyss said. "After I take Delphi, which way should I go?"

Celestine laughed. "As long as you keep winning, you can go whichever way you want."

How many times am I going to have to take this city? Lyss thought. She looked across the expanse of open land that surrounded Delphi. She knew for a fact that it was much better protected than it had been when she'd won it from Arden. She had taken advantage of its weaknesses, and then fortified the city so that it wouldn't be as easy for the next would-be invader.

She'd cleared the land surrounding the city fortifications. This way, any approaching army would be under fire from the walls for what would seem like an eternity.

"There's one odd thing," Long Foot said, pointing. "There's a new banner flying from the city walls. They've taken down the queen's banner and raised another, but it's not the Ardenine banner, either. I don't know whose it is."

Lyss shaded her eyes. "The emblem looks like a tree."

"That's my guess."

"Could it be a city banner?" Delphi had once been an independent city-state.

Long Foot shrugged. "Maybe. Or maybe one of Jarat's thanes is leading the invasion and claimed the city for himself."

Not for the first time, Lyss wished that Celestine gave the same attention to maintaining a network of eyes and ears as she did to her ships and her marble palace. Good intelligence saved soldiers' lives.

By now, everyone in Delphi must be aware that a massive army was camped just outside bowshot from the city walls.

She could just march around Delphi and head south for Ardenscourt. She didn't need yet another walled fortress, and, like any wolf, she preferred to go for the throat. Plus, a Delphi in Ardenine hands was one more obstacle on the road north, one more excuse not to go that way.

But Delphi sat astride the road from Spiritgate, blocking

supply lines from the coast. Celestine would—and should—question a decision not to take it.

In the end, she sent Demeter Farrow under a flag of truce to arrange a meeting.

They met under a canopy midway between the city walls and Lyss's army. For the empress, Lyss, Farrow, and Jada Long Foot. Two came from the city. Lyss scanned their faces.

"Fletcher!" Lyss recognized Brit Fletcher, one of the Patriots she'd partnered with when they drove Arden out of the city. The other was Yorrie Cooper, another Delphian freedom fighter.

"Captain Gray!" Fletcher said.

It was hard to say who was more surprised. It was hard to imagine the Ardenine empire choosing Fletcher as an emissary. As they quickly pointed out, it was hard to imagine the empress choosing Lyss.

"Since when do you fight for Carthis?" Fletcher demanded.

"Since when do you represent Arden?" Lyss shot back.

"Since never," he said, offended. "I represent the free state of Delphi."

Lyss looked from Fletcher to Cooper. "I'm confused."

"A lot has happened," Cooper said. "The king is on his way. He's running a little late."

"The *king*?"

"Aye," Fletcher said, like a cat with a bird in his mouth. "The king of Arden is here, in the free city of Delphi."

"What the hell is he doing here?" And why would he risk coming out here to negotiate?

"The king arrived in Delphi a week ago," Cooper said. "He's

getting ready to march north to Fellsmarch."

"He is, is he?" With what army? she wanted to add, in an echo of the childhood taunt.

Cooper nodded. "A few days later and you'd of missed him."

Then again, if the Highlanders and clans were concentrated in the eastern mountains, the road to the capital might be an easy one.

That will never, ever happen, Lyss thought, the wolf rising in her. Maybe her family was dead, maybe she wouldn't save her brother, maybe Celestine would win. But if Jarat Montaigne was trapped in Delphi with thousands of bloodsworn all around him. Lyss would make sure that he never left the city alive. That, at least, she could do.

She heard a challenge and response outside the tent, and the flap was pulled aside to admit a gray-haired man wearing a wizard's collar, followed by a person in an Ardenine military uniform—the person who must be the king.

Before she even focused in, she realized that the silhouette was familiar. Tall, broad-shouldered, erect. Somehow reassuring. Older than she'd understood Jarat to be.

She took in the gray-green eyes with their startling fringe of black lashes. The raven-wing hair flopping down over his forehead. The circlet of gold on his head, as simple and straightforward as the man who wore it. The grim expression on his face that said he knew he was hip-deep in scummer but would find a way to climb out of it or fight his way through it.

Lyss's heart flailed like a wounded bird, yet still the blood wasn't getting to her head, because she was totally stupefied.

Now she recalled where she'd seen that spreading tree signia before—the one now flying over a city that was not known for trees. It was on one of the occasions that she'd been confronted with a shirtless Hal Matelon. She'd noticed a tattoo on the inside of his forearm, where it wouldn't be too noticeable.

"What's that?" she'd said, resisting the temptation to grasp his wrist and turn his arm over to get a better view.

"This?" Matelon had traced the ink with his forefinger. "That's the spreading oak, the signia of my house. My sister, Harper, was afraid that I'd be killed in battle and my body would never be identified and they'd never know if I was alive or dead. She said that if I was dead, she was not going to spend the rest of her life waiting for me to come through the door. So she made me get this tattoo." He'd looked up at Lyss, his eyes crinkling at the corners. "You'd have to know her," he'd said.

And Lyss had felt guilty, knowing that, as his gaoler, she was the one keeping Hal apart from his sister, and recalling all those years she had waited for her brother to come back to her.

A voice broke through the haze of memory and confusion. "General? Ma'am? Are you all right?"

It was Farrow. The officer was peering into her face anxiously.

Lyss gave him a sharp nod, then turned to the king.

"Matelon," she said.

"Yes," he said, as if puzzled at being addressed in such a familiar fashion by a Carthian field commander. He looked her up and down, taking in the long, loose-fitting breeches, embroidered vest, curved blade, her head wrap draped around her neck. Then fastened on her face.

His eyes widened and he took a step toward her. "Gray?" he said, swallowing hard. He took a quick look around, as if to see whether she might be some kind of trick or apparition. Or whether Celestine was behind her, pulling her strings. They stood and gaped at each other, as voiceless as two big fish in a too-small jar.

"Do you two know each other?" Cooper said, pretending surprise. "Oh, right. You two met the last time you was in Delphi."

"This is our third go-round," Lyss said. "It seems that Matelon never gets tired of losing."

# MILITARY MANEUVERS

For months, Hal had been rehearsing what to say if he ever saw Lyssa Gray again. There were several different scenarios, but none of them turned out quite right. The truth was, his upbringing provided no framework for a story that centered on the two of them—at least, none with a happy ending.

In one, he dropped to one knee like a knight in a story, offering up his sword. *You have my sword, Your Majesty*, he would say.

She would roll her eyes. *Get up, Matelon. Nobody does that.*

Or she would growl, *I want more than your sword, Matelon.* And she would leap on him, somehow avoiding being cut in half.

In another, he lay mortally wounded on a battlefield, having driven Empress Celestine into the sea. Gray would drop to her knees in the muck and gore and cradle him in her arms. *You have saved the Seven Realms*, she would whisper. *From now on, it will be known as Matelonia.* And then he would die.

As it turned out, none of those scenarios remotely resembled what happened in real life. He could have daydreamed for the rest of his life and never conjured a scenario in which Gray showed up in desert horselord garb, leading an army of the empress's bloodsworn.

Ever since he'd watched the empress's ship sail away with her, he'd spent nearly every waking hour trying to help this queen-dom that he'd grown to admire, these queens that he respected.

And even though Gray had been totally unaware of all these efforts on her behalf, his gut reaction was betrayal. *After all I've done for you . . . you're fighting for the empress?*

Maybe it was just his bruised ego speaking, since this was the third time they'd met on a battlefield, and this was the third time she'd gotten the better of him.

She looked tired, a little beaten down, but he knew from experience that her battered surface hid a core of forged steel. Though he would have said it was impossible, she looked stron-ger, harder, more honed than before.

What had happened to her in Carthis? What could the empress have done to convince her to fight against her home-land? Against her own blood? Did she tell herself that since it was Arden she was fighting, it didn't really count?

Hal had limited experience with the bloodsworn, but one look at Lyss convinced him that she hadn't been bound. She was still a wolf to the bone. In a way, that made it harder. It would have been easier to accept if it weren't Alyssa Gray looking out through those brown eyes.

That first round of negotiations was like a card game between two stubborn people with losing hands, neither of whom would display or fold. They just kept on playing, while the stakes piled up on the table. So much to win, so much to lose. *Whose side are you on? How much should I reveal? Are we friends or enemies?*

Maybe it was more of a swordfight than a card game.

It didn't help that Gray began with, "So you've lost, again, Matelon."

"Not yet," Hal said.

She snorted. "Look around. You're surrounded."

She had a point, but Hal countered with, "So now you're a striper? That's new." *Striper* was the term used for mercenaries on both sides.

"What?"

"You're fighting for Empress Celestine?"

Gray's officers (all Fellsian) bristled, muttering among themselves.

"Not exactly," Gray said. She looked as if she had more to say on that topic, but thought better of it. "I'm told you've been crowned king of Arden. What does Jarat think of that?"

"I don't know," Hal said. "He's in Fellsmarch, with his army."

*That* drew blood, he could tell. Gray shot a questioning look at Fletcher and Cooper, and they nodded.

She swallowed hard, drew herself up, lifted her chin in that way she had. "What . . . Have you heard anything about . . . conditions in the city? About . . . casualties?"

Hal hadn't heard any news about bloodshed or body counts. Even if he had, he wouldn't—he couldn't—go in for the kill. Not this way. He shook his head. "I don't know. I don't have a network of eyes and ears, so I'm pretty much flying by the seat of my breeches." He paused, then couldn't help adding, like a cadet bragging in a tavern, "While Jarat's been busy in the north, I've taken Ardenscourt, and now Delphi."

"*Until* now, Delphi," Gray said. "And I hold Spiritgate."

Fletcher cleared his throat loudly. "Capt—Your Majesty, you

*said* you was fighting for the queen in the north," Fletcher said, jerking a thumb at Gray. "Were you telling the truth?"

Hal nodded. "Yes," he said, looking at Gray.

"Is that still true?" Cooper said.

"Yes," Hal said.

Gray frowned, looking from Hal to Cooper to Fletcher.

"Then what the hell are you two fighting about?" Cooper said, like a mediator in a schoolyard squabble.

"I'm not handing anything over to Celestine," Hal said. "So I need to know who *she's* fighting for." He pointed at Gray. "Looks to me like it's the empress."

"Well?" Cooper said. "Is it?"

Gray stood frozen, like a cadet called to recite who has nothing to say.

"You know," Fletcher said, "that shouldn't be a hard question."

That was when Hal noticed the tears pooling in Gray's eyes.

"Take it easy," he muttered to Fletcher. "I don't know what she—"

"Stop muttering!" Gray snarled. "If you have something to say, say it out loud."

They all stared down at the ground. Nobody had anything to say.

"Fine. All of you—get out!"

They all looked at each other, unsure what to do.

"General Gray," Farrow said, "would you like me to—"

"What's wrong with your ears? I said *get out!*"

As they began shuffling out of the tent, she gripped Hal's shoulder, spinning him around. "Except *you.*"

This prompted a chorus of objections from both sides.

"Your Majesty," Fletcher said, talking fast and low, "you don't know what she might do. She could be one of those bloodsworn I've been hearing about, bound to the empress. Even if you know her, she—"

"She's not bloodsworn," Hal said, thinking, If she kills me, she'll do it for personal reasons.

"Still. It's not worth the risk."

"You're wrong," Hal said. "It is worth the risk. If I end up dead, tell Robert he can be king. Then Harper. Wait outside."

They shuffled out, looking over their shoulders, and hovered just beyond the edges of the canopy.

"If you can hear this, you're too close," Gray shouted.

They edged a little farther away.

Gray swiped at her face with the backs of her hands. "Why am I crying, when you're the one caught in a trap?" she muttered.

"There are different kinds of traps," Hal said, taking a shot in the dark.

"What did you mean when you told Fletcher and Cooper you were fighting for me?"

"I meant that I've got your back. I saw what happened at Chalk Cliffs. I— When I saw the empress's ship sail away with you, I swore that she wouldn't win here. I tried to convince my father and the rest of the thanes that she was the real danger. I tried to persuade them to let me take an army north to help. They were too busy fighting with each other to listen. They said Ardenscourt came first. So I recruited my own army and took Ardenscourt. Then I followed Jarat north. And here I am."

"Impressive," she said. She'd stopped crying, but her eyes were still red and puffy.

"Lyss," Hal said. "What's wrong?"

She rose and started pacing. "Why isn't there anything to drink around here?"

"Don't drink. Sit. Talk," Hal said, gesturing to the camp chair beside him. He hadn't forgotten that time in Chalk Cliffs when Gray had learned that her brother was dead, and blamed Hal for it, and forced him into a drinking game.

She stopped pacing, glared at him, and sat. And then, as if she'd read his mind, she said, "Remember my brother, who died?"

Hal nodded.

"Well, he's not dead—at least not in the way I thought. Celestine is holding him as a hostage against my good behavior."

Scummer, Hal thought. "Are you sure? Did you see him?"

She shook her head. "She had my brother's amulet, which he got from our father," she said, touching a heavy pendant at her neckline. "Ash would never give that up willingly. So he's either dead, or a captive."

"Do you know where he is?"

"She said she found him in Tarvos, in Carthis, and was bringing him back to Celesgarde. I asked myself, What the hell was my brother doing in Tarvos, anyway? And then I realized—he must have been on his way to find me." She sighed. "I've said good-bye to him so many times, you'd think I'd get used to it. I mean, I haven't seen him since I was eleven years old. But he was the one who supported me after our sister died and I became the heir. I didn't want it, and I knew that everybody else was disappointed it was me instead of her, but he kept saying, *You can do this, Lyss.*" The tears were flowing again, and she swiped them away angrily.

It's not your fault, Hal wanted to say, but knew it would not make a dent in her guilt.

"Could it be a trick? That Celestine's holding your brother, I mean?"

"It could be." She swallowed hard, looking like the tears might overflow again. "He's all I have left," she whispered. "I know it's wrong. I know my first duty is to the queendom. I kept telling myself that if I could just get back to the Realms, if I could just keep fighting southerners, if—if—if."

"As you might recall, I was held hostage in the north," Hal began, "while—"

"You know I never approved of that," Gray said in a rush, but Hal put up his hand.

"Let me finish. I was held hostage in the north, while my mother and sister were held hostage by King Gerard. My point is, I know how you feel," he said. "Helpless."

"What happened—to your family?" she whispered, looking chastened. Looking as if she was bracing herself for bad news.

"I tried to rescue them, and they ended up somewhere in the north." When she opened her mouth to ask for details, he said, "It's a long story. Anyway. As far as I know, they're still in the north, if they're still alive. That's another reason I'm taking the North Road."

"I'm sorry, Matelon," she said. "You don't deserve any of this." She put her hand on his arm. Her palm was rough from hard work, the skin darkened by the desert sun and days at sea.

He put his hand over hers, resisting the temptation to pull her into his arms, to tell her not to worry, that everything would be all right. For one thing, he was very much aware of the audience standing a few paces away. More importantly, he understood that he could partner with Alyssa Gray, but there was no way he could protect her.

That didn't keep his heart from aching with the desire to close the distance between them.

"Look," he said, "I didn't want to be king. There are at least four thanes in Arden hot to sit on the throne, including my father. But I realized that if I didn't take it, I would be reporting to someone who would make my life miserable and keep the war going forever. It sounds like you didn't want the throne, either, but here we are. If we don't step up to this, the Realms don't have a future at all."

"I guess my situation is a little different," Gray said. "I didn't want to be queen at first, because I felt like I was just a fill-in for the person who belonged in that role. I was so different from my mother, and from my sister, Hanalea. But, gradually, I began to realize that, though I wasn't like my mother or sister, maybe I had something different to offer. Maybe I'm the queen they need right now."

"Maybe you are," Hal said. "What did Celestine offer you if you conquer the Realms for her?"

Gray laughed bitterly. "She said that my brother and I can rule the Fells together."

"With her as your friendly neighbor to the south?"

"Right."

"Do you believe her?"

After a long pause, Lyss said, "No," releasing the word in a whoosh of air.

"So where do we go from here? Are you really going to lay siege to Delphi and starve us out? That seems like a waste for two people who are basically on the same side."

It took her a good long time to answer. She shuffled her feet, picked a burr off her clothing. "It's just—she said she would burn him alive. I keep imagining her getting word that I'm no longer playing her game, and—and—"

"Gerard was going to hang my family from the city walls," Hal said, in a kind of bleak one-upmanship. "Look, we're smart, capable people. We've been doing well on our own. It seems like, together, we ought to be able to defeat just about anyone."

Gray frowned, thinking, and Hal knew she'd moved on from helpless frustration to planning mode. "My army is blood-bound to Celestine. Whatever we do, we need to keep them—and her—from finding out she's been betrayed until it's too late."

"Where's the empress now?" he said.

"Near Queen Court," she said distractedly. "She had to go up there to . . ." She trailed off, as if whatever she'd meant to say had been nudged aside by a new thought. She began to smile, the light of connivery in her eyes.

"Where's your army, Matelon?"

"We're camped up by the mines, in the headquarters up there," Hal said, figuring he wasn't giving anything away, since they'd be easy to find.

"I have an idea," Gray said. "But—so sorry, Your Majesty, you're going to have to lose again."

# 56

# BAD NEWS AND BAD NEWS

Just when you think you hold all the cards, Destin thought, somebody slips in the trickster. That's what happened to Jarat Montaigne—emperor, as he styled it, of the Seven Realms, conqueror of the stubborn northern queendom, military genius and peacemaker.

Destin would have the pleasure (and considerable risk) of delivering the news that at least some of Jarat's achievements were crumbling into dust behind him.

Jarat had convened a private meeting in order to devise a strategy to bring the rebellious (and disputed) queen of the Fells to heel. The attendees consisted of Destin Karn, spymaster; Mellony ana'Marianna, queen regent; and Jarat's traveling disciplinarian, executioner, and inquisitor, Bertram Olivette. Missing was the prospective bride, who, by all accounts, was not in her right mind.

Jarat was, apparently, all out of carrots, and had taken to wielding the stick. That was where Destin and Olivette came in. It seemed like the interview had been going on for hours.

"We had an agreement," Jarat said to Mellony, "and I expect the girl to honor it with suitable . . . enthusiasm."

"She's distraught, Your Eminence," Mellony said. "After all, she just lost her husband."

"A husband you never mentioned during our negotiations," Jarat snapped. "A traitor who tried to murder her. She should count herself lucky."

"She is *very* lucky, Your Majesty," Mellony said. "Very lucky indeed. It just may take her some time to recognize that."

"This was your idea, remember. You promised that you would dispose of the queen and princess heir and clear the way so that your daughter was next in line to the throne. Bring an army to Fellsmarch, you said. Marry my daughter and make her an empress, and I'll open the gates to you, you said."

"All of which I have done," Mellony said, without flinching.

Interesting, Destin thought. So Mellony was Jarat's "secret source" all along. These wolves can give the Montaignes a run for their money.

"And yet," Jarat said, "I find myself humiliated in my own hall, in front of my guests."

In Arden, humiliating the king is a capital crime, Destin thought.

"Have pity, Your Majesty," Mellony said. "Seeing first her new husband and then her nurse slain before her eyes—"

"Two things that should never have happened," Jarat said. "Is she unsullied, at least?"

Mellony's lips tightened. "I beg your pardon?"

"Was the marriage consummated? Am I bargaining for damaged goods?"

Destin spoke into the ensuing silence. "Your Eminence, as

I understand it, the wedding was interrupted when the groom tried to kill the bride. So it would seem that—"

"At this point, I would just as soon execute the girl as bed her," Jarat said sullenly. "The Seven Realms are teeming with women who would jump at the chance to sit the throne next to me."

Which made for a good question. Why was Jarat so fixed on wedding the heir to the Gray Wolf throne? He knew from experience that royal lines were easily disposed of. Why not start fresh with someone who didn't come with so much baggage?

Then it came to him. Destin remembered Jarat bragging back in Ardenscourt that he would marry a wolf princess. That meant that the negotiations with Mellony must have already begun. Jarat is bent on succeeding where his father failed—in every way. King Gerard failed to conquer the north, and he failed to wed the wolf queen. Jarat was checking those things off a list.

Fathers and sons. Mothers and daughters, creating generations of unfinished business. Gods, Destin thought. Please don't make me sit through any more of this.

Perhaps the gods were listening, because Jarat abruptly dismissed the queen regent. "Talk some sense into your daughter, Your Highness. I would very much like to commemorate our union of flesh and state and the end of the war with a magnificent celebration. But, if need be, I will drag her into a chapel by the hair."

The queen regent stood, curtsied, and swept out of the room.

When she was gone, Jarat turned to Destin and Olivette. "I want the two of you to visit my grief-stricken fiancée. If persuasion doesn't work, then do whatever it takes to bring her into line. Just don't leave any visible marks on her—understood?"

Destin and Olivette nodded.

"You may go, Olivette," Jarat said. "Colonel, stay a moment."

Scummer, Destin thought, watching the inquisitor's quick exit. Now the race begins.

"You've said that you had news from the south and east?"

"Yes, Your Eminence," Destin said. He paused, took a breath. "The rebel thanes have taken Ardenscourt and Delphi."

"Nonsense." Jarat folded his arms. "Who told you that?"

"I've heard this from several different sources," Destin said, "including a gaoler in Newgate who smuggled out this note from Charles Barbeau." He extended a sealed letter toward the emperor. "He's being held prisoner there."

Jarat snatched the letter, broke the seal, and unfolded it. He scanned the page, his hand shaking slightly. "This cannot be," he whispered, crumpling it in his fist. "Who the hell is leading them?"

"Halston Matelon," Destin said. "He's proclaimed himself king of Arden."

"It seems that treason runs true in that line." Jarat fingered the hilt of his sword. "I will spit that arrogant pretender like a suckling pig."

Destin held his peace on that. "All indications are that he means to march north, through Marisa Pines Pass."

"That makes no sense," Jarat growled. "Why would he do that? Doesn't he have enough on his hands with pacifying the south?"

"He seems to think that he can manage," Destin said. "There's more. The empress has landed an army at Spiritgate. They've taken the city and are marching through the borderlands toward

Delphi. They may be there already."

"No," Jarat said. "I have it on good authority that the empress is bogged down in the mountains, near Queen Court. She hasn't been able to break through the pass." Jarat always seemed to think he could change reality by arguing against it.

"Celestine's armies are growing all the time. She seems to think that she can fight on both fronts." Destin paused.

Wait for it. Wait for it. . . .

"This is *your* fault, Colonel," Jarat spat, never one to disappoint. "You call yourself a spymaster. We should have known about this sooner. We should have anticipated this and acted accordingly."

We did, Your Eminence, Destin thought. We tried to tell you, but you wouldn't listen, you were so hell-bent on showing up your father.

Destin eyed the furious young emperor, wondering whether Jarat still wore his talisman every day, as Destin recommended and Jarat's father, the king, had commanded.

Jarat's voice cut into his thoughts. "Colonel, I don't want to hear one word leaked about this to anyone. I don't want to give these northerners any reason to think they can drive us out."

"Yes, Your Eminence," Destin said, backing toward the door, eager to escape without being thrown in gaol. Bringing bad news to the king could be a capital crime, as well.

"One more thing." Still scowling, Jarat stalked over to the door and yanked it open. Outside was a swarm of blackbirds. Jarat motioned them inside.

Destin eyed them warily, his heart beating faster. Jarat opened a drawer in the sideboard and pulled out a glittering silver object.

Destin recognized it instantly. His gut twisted.

"Colonel, we have decided that it is important to handle our magical assets in a consistent fashion now that our numbers have expanded. It sends the wrong message to have an officer of this court walking around uncollared when we insist that all northern mages be restrained."

Destin tasted bitter defeat on his tongue as he eyed the king and his flock of blackbirds. Jarat wouldn't have made this move if they were not all wearing talismans.

"Consistency is an important principle, Your Eminence," Destin said quickly, "but—"

"We also believe that this will improve morale among our military mages," Jarat said, "and inspire a sense of comradeship with you, their leader. As you know, we've had serious attrition among our gifted forces."

And you think this will *help*? Destin thought. Gerard had been a cruel, vicious bastard, but he'd never put a collar around Destin's neck.

"You make a good point, Your Eminence," Destin said, thinking fast, "but have you considered the fact that this might limit my ability to protect you against magical attack?"

"Your ability to work magic will be unimpaired, so long as you remain a loyal servant of the crown."

"As I have been since I came into your father's service," Destin said. "Which is why I'm disappointed to have—"

"Besides, malicious magic will cease to be a problem when I have collared all of the gifted in the Realms. Without the witch queendom to serve as a sanctuary and support for them, we will extinguish the lawless practice of magic and assure that all mages serve the empire and the church."

Destin tried to keep the desperation out of his voice. "If in any way I've fallen short, I beg leave to try and correct this on my own."

"This is not a negotiation, Colonel," Jarat said, that sulky look reappearing. He extended the open collar toward Destin. "Kneel."

Destin looked around the room, seeking escape. It was tempting to blast a hole in the wall and flee through it. But where would he go? He had no allies and friends outside these walls, and few enough inside. There was only Evan, if he still lived.

Magery was power, but it was only one kind. A fugitive wields no power at court. He needed to be in the game in order to play it.

Destin sank to his knees, bitter tears stinging his eyes. Jarat fumbled a bit as he fastened the collar around Destin's neck.

He's nervous, Destin thought, and he should be.

"There, now," Jarat said heartily. "Not so bad, is it? You know much more about these collars than I do. But, rest assured, you have nothing to worry about as long as you serve me well."

"Yes, Your Eminence," Destin said, clearing his throat, clearing the murder off his face.

"You may rise," Jarat said.

Destin rose, by now confident that his face was as pure as any saint's. The blackbirds were all exchanging relieved looks, happy that the task had been accomplished without a magical standoff.

Jarat held up the key. "You may rest assured that I will keep this in a safe place," he said, tucking it into his waistcoat. "This in no way implies a lack of trust in you. In fact, this sacrifice on your part will result in your advancement. I expect that our gifted forces will vastly increase with the recruitment of north-ern mages. As general and commander of our gifted forces, you will play a key part in the pacification of the north and the protection of the empire." Jarat's expression said, *There, now! See what you get?*

I get a big fat fly on a pile of scummer, Destin thought. All my nightmares have come true. Is that the price of patricide? He'd spent a lifetime avoiding the traps his father had set for him, and then fallen headfirst into this one.

"Thank you for your confidence in me, Your Eminence," Destin said.

The boy emperor looked as if he might actually clap Destin on the shoulder, but at the last minute turned it into a salute.

Destin returned the salute. "Now, Your Eminence, if there's nothing else—?"

Jarat's triumphant expression faded as he possibly remem-bered that he'd just lost a deepwater port and his capital city. "Tell Bellamy I want to see him now," he snapped. "We have work to do. And don't forget—fix the thing with the girl." The emperor waved him out.

# THE WOLF AND THE HAWK

As he left Jarat's small council chamber, Destin seethed with anger, mostly directed at himself.

You're so damned smart, he thought. Moving pieces on the game board, believing you're one step ahead of everyone else, fully confident you've already won.

But he'd been ambushed like any farmer at the midsummer market, by a—how did the general put it—by a candy-assed boy who can't even dress himself. The general must be laughing himself silly in hell.

Ever since Destin had slipped free from the general's control, he'd sworn that he would never again be under the thumb of a tyrant. He would make his own choices, commit his own sins, for better or worse. It would be his call, his fault, his success or failure. He might serve the king, but he could, if he chose, serve another king. Or serve no one at all, accepting the consequences.

He touched the collar, still somehow shocked to find it there. He was trapped, once again, with no good choices on the table.

If Destin ran away to Carthis, the emperor could still reach across the sea and torture or kill him.

And now he was on his way to fix the thing with the girl. He had desperately wanted to get there ahead of Olivette, but he'd probably failed at that, too.

At least Jarat was not keeping his bride-to-be in the dungeons—not yet, anyway. But she *was* locked away behind several sets of doors in the family wing of the palace. As he got close, he could hear raised voices—an argument of some sort between the queen regent and Olivette.

Well, good, Destin thought. He was humiliated, smarting, more than ready to mix it up with someone.

"You will not take her!" Mellony shouted. "The emperor gave me orders to speak to her, and that is what I'm doing."

"I have orders from the emperor, too," Olivette said. "Let go of her or I'll call in the guard."

Nodding to the blackbirds outside, Destin slammed open the door to Julianna's chamber to find a tug-of-war going on between the queen regent and Olivette, the inquisitor. Between them was Julianna, like a child's rag doll. The contenders looked up as Destin entered.

"Colonel Karn, tell this man to leave us alone," Mellony said, her voice quivering with rage or fear or both. "He has no right to lay hands on the queen of the realm."

You're going to learn that queens have very little status or protection in the empire, Destin thought. Queen regents, even less.

"I'm taking her downstairs, Colonel," Olivette said.

*General*, Destin could have said, but it was a rank he had no interest in claiming.

"Let go of her and get out," Destin said.

"You heard the emperor," Olivette said, broadening his stance.

Torture and the threat of torture could be useful tools at times. But Olivette seemed more fond of the process than the result.

"I did hear the emperor," Destin said. "I heard the part about not leaving any marks on his fiancée. You'd better hope she doesn't bruise easily, or you're already in trouble." He pointed his chin at Olivette's grip on Julianna's arm. He hastily let go and Mellony drew her daughter into the safety of her embrace.

"The emperor said to use stronger measures if persuasion doesn't work," Destin said. "I'll definitely call you in if your specialized services are needed."

Olivette glared at him, as if debating whether to challenge Destin's version of events. Then finally descended to bluster. "If you weren't a mage, I would—"

"Happily, I am a mage, and I am losing patience," Destin said, fingering his amulet, hoping Olivette didn't notice his new collar. If he did, and made a comment about it, Destin might have another body to bury. "Now get out."

As soon as the door closed behind Olivette, Mellony said, "Thank you, Colonel. Your arrival was—"

"What's wrong with her?" Destin asked, putting two fingers under Julianna's chin and tipping her face up, looking into her blank eyes. "She looks like she's in a trance."

"She's been like this since—since her engagement announcement," Mellony said, guiding her daughter to a chair. "She hasn't spoken, smiled, or reacted to anything. I think she's just . . . overwhelmed or grief-stricken or—"

"Leave us," Destin said abruptly.

"Colonel, please, let me help," Mellony said. "Perhaps together we could—"

"No," Destin said. "I need to question her alone."

Mellony drew herself up. "It is inappropriate for the emperor's fiancée to be questioned unchaperoned by someone who—"

"Don't push me," Destin said. "I am not your swiving hero. The difference between me and Olivette is that he enjoys hurting people, and I don't. Usually. You and your daughter should count yourselves lucky that I am here. Now go, before I call the guards to carry you out."

She went.

Destin walked around the room, soundproofing it. Then he sat down opposite Julianna. He rubbed his chin, considering how to begin. "This is a dangerous game you're playing," he said.

She didn't move, didn't change expression.

"Jarat is cruel to the core, and Olivette is worse. He'll hurt you in ways you cannot imagine. It will be horrible and messy, and in the end, Jarat will get his way. That's no way to begin a marriage. It sets a poor precedent."

Julianna said nothing, though her lip might have quivered a bit.

Destin reached for her hands, gripped them firmly, and opened the channels between them. He was met by a torrent of rage, grief, and betrayal that all but made his hair stand on end. Sometimes that was the way it worked—like a dam bursting—in people who had been keeping secrets for so long.

"Tell me about Finn," he said.

Now tears spilled over and ran down her cheeks. "People

will think I was in on this—that I knew all along what they intended. But I did not. I swear by the Maker that I did not."

"I believe you," Destin murmured.

"I'm supposed to be the queen's spymaster, and I did not see this coming," she said, her voice thick with tears.

"Sometimes that happens." He, of all people, could attest to that.

"I loved Finn, and yet after he was wounded, it was as if he was two people. Sometimes he would be his normal self, and sometimes I would look at him and—see someone else." She shivered. "They tell me he did . . . terrible things."

"It wasn't his fault," Destin said. When she looked at him through narrowed eyes, he continued, "I'm serious. It wasn't. It's complicated, and there's no time to go into it now, but when this is all over, I'll explain it to you. In the meantime, it's all right to keep on loving him, and remember him the way he was before." After a long pause, he added, "But I can't say the same for your mother."

Julianna hung her head. "Blood and bones," she whispered. "She has always been so jealous of Aunt Raisa, though she hides it well. For some reason, she thinks every bad thing that happened to her, every loss along the way, was because of her sister. She was close to my grandmother Queen Marianna—closer than Raisa, the princess heir. I think she began to believe that she was better suited to the throne. At one point, when everyone thought Princess Raisa was dead, Mother came close to being crowned queen. I don't think she's ever forgiven Raisa for turning up alive.

"After I was born, she kept trying to reclaim what she'd lost through me. She was critical of Princess Alyssa, always comparing us and suggesting I would be a much better queen. I thought she had finally accepted the fact that I was happy in the role of diplomat and director of intelligence. And then to find out that, all along, she was plotting against her own family. That list of the names of the dead that she had read at the reception—I think she had a hand in all of those. It was as if she was reading a list of her victims. Except she should have included my cousin Hanalea and my uncle Han." Her tears were falling on their joined hands.

Destin had to ask. "Are you sure you didn't know? When people kept dying, didn't you ever suspect that Mellony had a hand in it?"

"I guess we find ways to ignore the things that would destroy us. Every once in a while, something would raise a question. But then I would let it go." She shook her head. "I'm so ashamed."

"Julianna. I learned a long time ago that it's not our fault if our parents are monsters. We can't take responsibility for that, or we're twice damaged. All we can do is try to go forward in a different way." He let go of her hands and sat back. "What you need to do now is agree to marry Jarat, wear his ring, appear in public with him, and pretend to be enthusiastic about the whole thing. That will buy both of us some time."

"No," Julianna said, folding her arms. "I can't."

"Lady sul'Mander, I realize how difficult this—" Destin broke off at her expression. "What is it?"

"Nobody's called me that until now. Everyone wants to pretend it didn't happen—that I never married Finn."

"Of course it happened," Destin said. "Now. Lady sul'Mander. How far are you willing to go to prevent this new marriage from going forward?" As it happened, he himself would go pretty far to ruin the emperor's wedding day.

"I would rather die," Julianna said. "I will never allow that arrogant, despicable boy to touch me." She sat thinking for a moment. "I have an idea—one that will prevent the marriage and ruin Jarat's wedding day and leave me alive at the end of it. But I'll need your help." Lifting her chin, she gazed at him, as if taking his measure.

"Believe me, Lady sul'Mander, I will do anything I can to further that agenda," Destin said.

She eyed him. "I must admit, Colonel, that I cannot figure out *your* agenda."

"That's the way I like it," Destin said. "Now, please." He gestured for her to go on.

"Here's what I have in mind," Julianna said. "But I'll need Shadow's help, and Speaker Jemson's, too."

# 58

# INTO THE VALE

It had taken some fast talking for Hal to persuade Fletcher and Cooper to raise Celestine's flag over the city of Delphi. It took more fast talking to persuade his officers to march north into the Fells with the bloodsworn army.

Fast talking had never been Hal's strength.

"We're just going to surrender without a fight?" Mercier had said, rubbing the back of his neck. "I know they've got the numbers, but the bulk of our army's up at the mines, and we have good walls between us and the bloodsworn. We can hold 'em off for a while, and our men on the outside can harry them from the north."

"You're right, but that pins us down here. We can't afford the time for a siege, and we can't afford to lose any of our men in skirmishes," Hal said. "Besides, it's not exactly a surrender."

"How is it not a surrender?" Fletcher folded his arms, scowling.

"Because the Patriots will remain in control of the city, with our military as support. The only thing that changes is we raise another banner."

Mercier shook his head. "I don't get it. Either we surrender the city, or we don't."

"Or you pretend to surrender the city," somebody said.

They all swung around in time to see Gray move into the lamplight.

"Gentlemen," Hal said, "I'd like to introduce Captain Lyssa Gray of the army of the Fells. You may know her as the Gray Wolf."

Their eyes went wide. Remy made the sign of Malthus.

"The Gray Wolf is a *woman*?" Marc DeJardin said, vastly amused. "She's not even a mage. What is the world coming to?"

Gray shook hands with each of them. "I got to know—and trust—your king while he was a captive in the north," she said. "After the empress took Chalk Cliffs, I infiltrated the Carthian army and was assigned to the southern campaign. Matelon and I have made a deal to join together to kick Jarat out of Fellsmarch and rescue the hostages. Then we will drive Celestine out of the Realms."

By now, Hal's officers were looking shell-shocked, and he didn't blame them.

Gray knew how to press an advantage. "It's important to keep Celestine in the dark about this as long as possible," she said. "Because my army is blood-bound to her, they have to believe that we are following her commands. Once she realizes that she has been betrayed, she will move swiftly. Her resources are all but endless. We need to handle Jarat before then."

"I love how you say, 'handle Jarat,' as if it's like swatting a fly," Remy said.

"Watch me," Gray said, with a grim smile.

Hal's officers looked at each other. He could tell that they were impressed with what she had to say. It didn't hurt that nearly everyone in the army of Arden had heard legends and tales about the Gray Wolf.

"We know a lot of the men fighting for Jarat," Mercier said. "The native-borns, at least. General Bellamy's a good man. I hate the thought of going up against them."

"We knew we were signing on for that when we joined up with Matelon," DeJardin said.

"And it's going to keep happening until we find a way to get to peace—on our terms," Hal said.

"I understand how you feel," Gray said. "I'm going to be attacking my home city. I have family there, if they're not already dead. If Jarat finds out I'm in command of this army, he'll target them to get to me."

"I'll be honest, it's going to be hard for our men to fight alongside the bloodsworn," Mercier said.

"Many of the bloodsworn were born here in the Realms," Gray said, "but they were unfortunate enough to be taken alive." She paused, giving that time to sink in. "I would love to have you in my chain of command. The bloodsworn tend to need a lot of direction. But I'll understand if you want to stick with your own men. The truth is, Celestine won't stop until she conquers the Realms from sea to sea. If we don't stop her, *you'll* be fighting against them, too."

"Will we be wearing those pirate outfits?" Mercier said, making a face.

Gray looked stumped for a moment. "First come, first served," she said. "Unfortunately, we don't have enough for everyone."

They all laughed. And, just like that, she'd won them over—men who'd never served with a female commander before. If Hal had forgotten, he was getting a quick reminder of why he'd pledged himself to the Gray Wolf queen after the fall of Chalk Cliffs.

Now, as they marched up the Way of the Queens toward the city of Fellsmarch, Hal realized that he had never been so close to the northern capital before.

It was eerie passing through the Vale without a challenge. No clan archers firing down from the heights, no magical traps awaiting them. Jarat hadn't bothered to secure the uplands, concentrating his strength on the flatlands, where he felt more at home.

The Vale was green and lush, with wildflowers blooming everywhere. The river Dyrnnewater flowed through it, filled bank to bank with snowmelt from the mountains all around. To the west was the snowy peak of Hanalea, wreathed in cloud. And to the north was the sullen face of Gray Lady, stronghold of wizards.

No wonder its citizens are willing to fight and die for this, he thought.

Back in Delphi, the empress's siren banner now flew from the ramparts, above the Matelon tree and the Delphian pick and hammer, in case any spying eyes were checking up on the empress's wetland general. In truth, the city was under the joint control of Matelon's men and the Patriots. Gray had sent word to Celestine that Delphi had fallen, and she was on her way to seize the northern capital.

Hal had been fighting for Arden since he was eleven years old; he'd been a captain since he was fifteen, but he'd never marched at the head of such a large army. It was ten thousand strong, of which only about five hundred were his own soldiers and officers. The rest of his men he'd left in Delphi.

The bloodsworn were tireless. They had to slow their pace to accommodate Hal's soldiers and their need to rest, eat, and sleep. Hal was impressed with the way Gray worked with them. As she'd said, they required a great deal of tending, being unsuited to decision-making on their own. She treated them with patience and respect and stubborn persistence, and Hal could see that they were responding to it.

They met a large force of Jarat's stripers midway through the Vale. Some fought bravely, but others ran like rabbits when they saw what they were up against. Mercenaries tended to do that when they realized that they were unlikely to survive to spend their blood money.

After that, the joined armies marched ahead unchallenged until they stood within sight of the walls of the city. Though it was late, the sun had not quite set, since it was nearly midsummer.

"It's . . . it's beautiful," Hal said, unable to hide his surprise. After all the tales he'd been told in his youth, he still half-expected it to be a dark, sinister place. But it was set like a jewel on the slopes of the mountains, temple spires reflecting the setting sun.

"Yes," Gray said. "It is." The closer they'd come to the city, the less she'd had to say. Now she sat on her horse, her Fellsian officers around her, the breeze teasing her hair out of its customary fighting braid. She was toying with the pendant that had belonged to her brother.

"Thank the Maker," her officer, Farrow, said. "I never thought I would see this city again."

"Any suggestions for how to proceed?" Hal asked Gray.

"Tell them we want to speak with the queen," Gray said. "See how they respond."

# 59

# RED-EYE FLIGHT

In consideration of the young dragons and their novice human flyers, Cas and Jenna planned a course consisting of short hops from island to island until they reached the westernmost of the Sisters, where they prepared for the final passage. They often flew at night, so as to avoid being seen by ships or spotters in the area.

The Weeping Sisters resembled dark scabs on the water, laced with jagged ribbons of light where lava leaked through the earth's dark surface like clotting blood from a wound.

Adam Wolf—Ash, as he now called himself—had said that his upland name was Speaks to Horses, reflecting his ability to communicate with them in a direct, visual way. The dragons were highly amused by the notion of a wolf speaking to horses, and he'd already developed an easy relationship with them. Goat in particular never forgot that first point of contact, when he was tangled in a web of rigging, and Ash had soothed him and then freed him. Now they were learning to fly together. If they survived this first water crossing, they would be great friends.

Goat was curious and intelligent, scrappy and impulsive. At times he forgot to make allowances for the limitations of his human passenger. When straight, direct flight grew boring, Goat would engage in mock aerial battles with his nestmates, with Ash hanging on as best he could. When fishing, he'd skim the water's surface, slicing through swells, sending up spray that soaked Ash to the skin.

"Don't get any ideas," Sasha said to Pricker. They were using Jenna's saddle and harness—the set she'd commissioned for Cas. On their first flight from Celesgarde, Sasha took a white-knuckled grip on Pricker's breast strap and squeezed her eyes shut. Fortunately, Pricker was calm and steady and not prone to airborne showing off, and Sasha gradually relaxed.

At first, they saw few ships, mostly fishing vessels and single-masted smugglers. During the last leg of their journey, from the westernmost of the Weeping Sisters to Wizard Head, they began to see more ships hugging the shoreline, most flying the empress's siren banner.

*Burn ships?* Cas said, dropping lower for a better look.

"Not yet," Jenna said.

They finally made landfall southwest of Fortress Rocks, where the mountains met the flatlands along the coast. After a long sleep, Goat and Slayer went hunting. Sasha mounted Pricker, and Ash and Jenna both mounted Cas. They flew along the eastern slope of the Spirit Mountains, looking for the war.

Jenna was learning to manage her response to the feeling of Ash's body against hers, his scent in her nose, his soft voice in her ear, his breath in her hair.

*You can't spend the rest of your life in a hammock,* she thought.

Still. She tightened her knees against Cas's sides and pushed herself back, into his embrace, into the welcome of his body. She could have that, at least.

They found the war in the pass that led from Wizard Head to Queen Court Vale. The eastern slopes were swarming with bloodsworn, so thick that it seemed as if the ground itself were moving. Their numbers were huge, but they were forced to funnel through the narrow pass under withering fire from upland archers on the heights. Unable to get through the pass, they flowed north and south like floodwaters seeking a channel.

These troops resembled a mob in search of a fight compared to the honed discipline of the Ardenine army. Then again, the battle-honed Ardenine army had always had trouble getting through these mountains, too.

The invaders had brought cannon up from Chalk Cliffs and were bombarding the escarpment in what appeared to be a random fashion, setting off a series of blasts at the base of the cliffs.

*Tunnel under mountains like moles?* Cas suggested.

"Maybe," Ash replied. "That should take a few hundred years."

Still, the empress had thousands of bloodsworn to fling at the pass, while every soldier the queendom lost was significant. Eventually, they would bully their way through into the flatlands of the Vale, where their numbers would be more effective.

The Fellsian forces were barely visible, both the Highlanders with their spattercloth uniforms and the clans in their earth-tone leggings and shirts. The leading edge of the bloodsworn was obvious.

"Do you think Lyssa is down there?" Jenna asked.

"No," Sasha said. "She's smarter than that." She closed her

eyes, as if searching with her sixth sense. "She's here, though, in the Realms. From what I can tell, she's far to the south and west."

"Hmm," Jenna mused, her eyes fixed on the ground. "They're fusing charges together and laying them against the walls of the pass."

"If you say so." Ash didn't bother to look.

"I assume they're trying to knock the archers off the heights," Jenna said. "I have an idea."

She leaned forward and whispered something to Cas. The dragon made a wide circle, passing over the western end of the pass.

"Keep your head down," Jenna said to Ash. "We're going to be flying through the pass at low altitude, and you aren't as well armored as me." She could feel her skin tighten and numb a little, signaling the appearance of her scales. They came on more quickly now, and more thickly at the prospect of a threat.

At first, they were skimming through the canyon, nearly level with the slopes to either side. Jenna found herself at eye level with a clan archer, who first leapt back in surprise, then recovered and nocked an arrow. Fortunately, they were far past her position before she could take her shot.

At the mouth of the pass, the bloodsworn had tied the fuses together so that they could ignite both sides with one bit of match. From her time as a saboteur and blastmaster in Delphi, Jenna knew the risks and benefits of that.

They crossed the no-man's-land between the Highlanders and the bloodsworn. By now, they were barely over the heads of the empress's soldiers, with Cas's wings stretching from wall to wall, Pricker following close behind. Some of them threw their arms over their heads, while others landed flat on their faces in the dirt.

"No flame until we turn," Jenna said. She and Cas were so accustomed to working together that it sometimes seemed that they were of one mind. Ash, Pricker, and Sasha needed a little more prompting.

Cas extended his clawed feet and snagged the fuse as they exited the canyon, dragging it behind them like a string of deadly beads, out of the canyon and into the midst of the battalions of bloodsworn on the slope beyond.

They continued eastward, nearly to the coast, made a turn, and came roaring back over the heads of the cowering bloodsworn.

"Now!" Jenna said. "Burn army. Cas to the left, Pricker to the right."

Cas bathed the troops on the left with flame, while Pricker swept the right-hand side, sending torrents of flame blasting into the massed soldiers.

"Up—up—up—up!" she shouted, and the two dragons gained altitude, their great wingbeats fanning the flames. Still, when the fused charges went off, the force of the explosions sent them tumbling tail over head so that Ash tightened his grip around Jenna's waist, struggling to hold on.

"Don't you dare fall off, Wolf," she said.

When they circled back, Jenna could see major holes in what had been a sea of bloodsworn. The soldiers still on their feet were running about like ants from a kicked anthill.

Sasha roared in triumph. The look on her face was nothing less than euphoric. "Take that, you gutter-swiving zealots! You're killable after all." She shook her fist. "Again!" she shouted.

Leaning sideways, Jenna yanked a battle-ax from a boot attached to Cas's harness. Her blood was up. Flames flickered over her skin, and her hair seethed and burned. This time, she would sweep in low and kill the bloodsworn up close and personal, so that their life's blood splashed over her.

Ash shifted behind her, reading her thoughts. "Jenna! Sasha! Hey, now. We've done a lot of damage already. It's better if the officers don't get a good look at us and send word to the empress."

"What?" Sasha growled, irritated at this unwanted interference. "I want her to know what happens when she kidnaps our queen and—"

"*Jenna*. Let's go and find the Highlander officers and find out what's going on. We don't want to accidentally kill our own soldiers. Also, they may be able to tell us where Celestine is. And if anyone has seen Lyss."

That finally penetrated through Jenna's bloodlust. "All right, Wolf," she said, searching for calm, feeling her skin change as the scales disappeared. "Let's go find your commanders and see what they know."

The Highlander camp was just to the west of the pass, in a place Ash called Queen Court Vale. To Jenna, it looked like the northern soldiers had converted the ruins of a falling-down palace to a field hospital, and a forest of tents had sprouted around it.

At the western end of the Vale was a refugee camp. A large corral held livestock of all kinds, and many of the residents appeared to have set up small workshops to supply items the army needed, take care of the livestock, and do whatever else civilians could do to help the war effort.

Cas and Pricker were eager to attend the meet-up, but Jenna persuaded them that a pair of dragons landing in the center of the Vale was likely to cause widespread panic and invite an immediate attack by their own side.

"We don't want to fight *them*," she said. "We want to fight the empress." So they landed in the mountains north of the Vale, as close as they could without being spotted. Ash, Jenna, and Sasha hiked the rest of the way in. They were still in the fringe of trees when they came upon three young women picking berries.

In an instant, they dropped their berry baskets. Two of them nocked arrows and aimed at the three newcomers. The third produced a wicked-looking knife.

"Drop your weapons," one of the archers said. "Or I will shoot you." She spoke Common, but she and the other archer were obviously clan. The girl with the knife had straight black hair braided and coiled clan-style, adorned with feathers, but she was too fair to be an uplander.

Ash, Jenna, and Sasha dropped knives, swords, and battle-axes to the ground.

"Harper," the spokesperson said. "Fetch the duty officer."

The knife wielder took off running.

Since neither of her companions seemed willing to speak up, Sasha said, "You can put your bows down. I'm Captain Sasha Talbot of the queen's Gray Wolf guard."

The young archers looked her up and down, taking in her Carthian head wrap, pirate slops, and sailor-knit sweater. "We will wait for the duty officer," she said.

The four of them stood in awkward silence. The spokesperson

looked familiar, and she kept eyeing Jenna, head cocked, as if confronting a puzzle piece that doesn't fit.

"Why are you picking bloodberries?" Ash said in Clan. He gestured toward the baskets.

The spokesperson blinked at him. "What?"

"They're poisonous," he said. "So I wondered what you planned to do with them."

Her chin came up. "How do you know our language, drylander?"

"Because I'm not a drylander," Ash said. "I was born in the Vale. I fostered at Marisa Pines and Demonai Camps every summer since I was a lýtling, working with Willo Watersong." He hesitated. "Tell me—is Willo Cennestre well?"

*Cennestre* was a title denoting wisdom in the uplands.

"She is well," the spokesperson said grudgingly. She lowered the bow, relaxing the string, but keeping the arrow nocked. "The bloodberries are for dye. They produce a long-lasting red."

"I always used bloodroot for red," Ash said.

"I used to, but now we can't get the mordant. I use burnt juniper to mordant the bloodberries."

Jenna shifted from foot to foot, impatient with this conversation about berries in a language she could barely understand.

"What are you dyeing?" Ash continued.

"Leather," the girl said. She pointed at Jenna and said in Common, "I made that jacket, months ago. See the red along the seams? It's still rich as the day it was made."

Jenna stared at the girl, the puzzle piece snapping into place. "You were in Fortress Rocks. You're . . . Sparrow."

She nodded. "You were with Shadow. You said your name

was Riley." The way she said it told Ash that she didn't believe it. "You were buying riding clothes and a harness for a—a gryphon." She smiled halfway. "How does your gryphon like his new clothes?"

At that moment, Harper burst out of the trees with six clan warriors at her heels.

Ash leaned toward Jenna. "Demonai warriors, elite fighters of the clans. That's Shilo Trailblazer, matriarch of the camp and commander of the upland fighting forces."

Trailblazer was a weather-beaten woman of middle age, her hair done up in tiny braids all over her head. She looked the three of them up and down, then fixed on Sasha. "Why are you dressed like that, Talbot?" she said. He gestured toward Ash and Jenna. "Who are they?"

"I'm Adrian sul'Han, son of Raisa ana'Marianna and Han Alister," Ash said. "Known as Speaks to Horses in the uplands."

"Ah. I see it now," Trailblazer said, studying him through narrowed eyes. "I heard you were dead."

"It's a long story. Can you tell me where I can find my mother?"

"She's in the command tent," Trailblazer said, pointing. "There."

"Is she well?"

"She grows stronger each day, thanks to you."

Ash turned and gripped Jenna's hand, tugging her toward the tent. "Would you like to meet my mother?"

Jenna dug in her heels, hanging back. "Don't you—mightn't you want privacy?"

"Come on," Ash said, pulling her forward.

"But . . . I can't meet a queen all windblown, flightworn,

and sweaty," Jenna said. *And I probably have bugs in my teeth.*

"She won't care. I've told her about you. She'll be anxious to meet you." He turned to Sasha. "Come with us. She'll want to see you, too."

Jenna resisted the temptation to drag her feet all the way to the command tent. Her history with royalty began with Gerard Montaigne, who came to Delphi and murdered her friends Riley and Maggi, then traded her to the empress in the east.

Ash spoke to the guards outside the tent, and they were immediately announced.

When they entered, they were met by a small clutch of people, a mingle of men and women, most in the spattercloth uniforms the Highlanders wore.

One of them, a smallish woman in spattercloth, stood frozen, her body canted forward, her hands opening and closing at her sides. Her eyes were a striking green under her shaggy cap of hair.

Ash leapt forward, pulling her toward him. She held back for a moment, then burrowed into the embrace. Her words were meant for Ash's ears only, but Jenna couldn't help hearing.

"I was afraid to touch you, for fear you would disappear," she murmured. "How many times are we going to do this?"

"I don't know, Mother," Ash said. "Hopefully this season of grief will soon be over, one way or another." He paused. "I didn't bring Lyss back, but I have news about her."

"We have news, too," the wolf queen said.

Behind her, a tall, grim-faced guardsman in a blue jacket studied Jenna in her flight leathers, the curved sword at her side. He eased forward until he stood between the two royals and Jenna.

"Who is this, Captain Talbot?" he said, nodding at Jenna.

"She's—she's—she's the one that saved us and brought us back here," she blurted. "She's like the busker—magemarked."

Ash turned back toward Jenna, smiling, taking her hand again. "Mother, Captain Byrne, this is Jenna Bandelow, Patriot of Delphi. An ally."

# 60

# IN THE EYE OF THE HURRICANE

We're dancing in the eye of the hurricane, Destin thought. We are dining on the deck of a sinking ship, and I happen to have a huge anchor around my neck. He slipped his fingers under Jarat's collar, as if he could somehow loosen it.

They were surrounded by Celestine's bloodsworn army, whose camp stretched as far as the eye could see. To call it a camp was being generous. Most of the soldiers didn't bother to pitch tents. They slept in the open, on the ground.

There had been an exchange of blustery messages and saber rattling. The empress's commander had demanded to meet with the queen of the Fells, and Jarat had refused. Jarat had demanded that the Carthians surrender, and they had refused. So everyone settled in to wait.

Meanwhile, plans proceeded apace for the wedding. The contents of the wagon train they'd muscled through the pass were deployed—linens and dinnerware, tureens, serving pieces, musical instruments, and livery for a string quartet and choir. Crates of Tamron wine and casks of Bruinswallow beer were carried to the great hall, along with wheels of cheese and tins of smoked oysters. Seamstresses altered Mellony's wedding gown to fit her taller daughter. Meanwhile, Julianna seemed as pliant and charming a fiancée as Jarat could have wished. She hung on his arm, agreed with everything he said, and accepted well wishes with a smile. It didn't hurt that she was spectacularly beautiful, which was rare in a political match.

"I don't know what you did to her, Colonel," Jarat said, smirking, "but in the future, when I'm confronted with an uncooperative woman, I'll know who to call."

Lila watched these preparations with a sour expression on her face. "I tried to leave, and you wouldn't let me," she said to Destin. "Now I'm trapped in a palace surrounded by swiving bloodsworn." She wasn't settling into her role as Destin's sidekick.

"At least you're trapped in a palace," Destin said. When she scowled at him, he said, "Oh, come on, Lila, look around. You know you love parties, and this will be the best party ever."

"Followed by starvation, torture, and entry into the ranks of blood slavery?" Lila raised an eyebrow.

"Just think of it as the price to be paid—like a major hangover." Destin looked forward, to where Jarat and Julianna were being lovely together. And alliterative. They were displaying the monogram to be used henceforth—two Js, entwined.

"I happen to know that the party will soon be over," he said.

"What do you mean?"

Instead of replying, Destin picked up a crate of wine, lowered it into her arms, then set a wheel of cheese on top of it. "They won't be needing this. I'm creating a private larder and wine cellar," he said. "You might want to do the same."

Lila staggered away under her burden.

Destin left the great hall, crossed the courtyard to the Cathedral Temple, and threaded his way through the maze of classrooms and offices behind the altar to knock on Speaker Jemson's door.

"Come," the speaker called.

The speaker was persona non grata since presiding at Julianna's first wedding without telling her mother.

Jarat, Destin thought, you don't know the half of it.

The office was tiny, packed floor to ceiling with papers and books.

"Colonel," Jemson said, leaning back in his chair. "This is a surprise."

"I'm sorry to bother you," Destin said, "but I need your help again."

"How can I help you?"

"This time, I need your help disposing of a body."

When Destin left the Cathedral Temple, one of his operatives ghosted up beside him. "Where have you been?"

"At church," Destin said, looking over his shoulder.

"There's someone who wants to see you," she said. "Says he's got some information for you. He gave his name as Claude Remy."

Remy. He was an officer in the Ardenine regulars who'd been reliable in the past. In fact, he'd been the one who tipped Destin off that the Matelon brothers were in Ardenscourt before the freeing of the hostages.

"Where is he?"

"He's outside, near the postern gate."

Destin sauntered outside, following the city wall until he reached the riverbank. He saw movement amid the shadows next to the gate.

"Remy?" he said.

The officer moved forward, into the light from the wall sconces, looking relieved. It seemed as if he'd seen hard times since last they'd met.

"What's happened to you?" Destin said, frankly curious. "You look like a refugee on the roadside."

"It's Matelon," Remy said, "and those swiving demon blood-suckers. That was the last straw."

Destin couldn't make any sense out of that. Was he talking about the Darian Brothers? What did Matelon have to do with them? "Come," he said, "sit down and explain." He drew Remy away from castle traffic to a bench next to the river. "What are you talking about?"

"I signed on with Matelon when he was recruiting for soldiers to march on Ardenscourt. He's always been a fair commander, takes care of his men, and I thought there was a good chance for promotion under the thanes. So we took Ardenscourt, and Matelon named himself king, so it was all looking good. Then we took Delphi, but after that, it all went wrong."

Destin was still lost. "Wrong? How so?"

"We ended up surrounded by the empress's army. Just like now. So the higher-ups had a meeting and Matelon agreed to surrender to the empress's commander."

Destin frowned. "He did? That doesn't sound like Matelon."

"That's what I thought, too. But the two of them—Matelon and the Carthian general—they claimed that it wasn't really a surrender, that they were going to team up and march on Fellsmarch. So half a hundred of us and thousands of bloodsworn hotfooted it all the way up here. We hardly took the time to take a piss along the way."

The pieces finally fell into place. "So . . . you're with the army outside?"

Remy rolled his eyes. "That's what I said. But I can't do this. I can't fight with the bloodsworn, and for the northerners. It's not how I was brought up."

Destin's racing thoughts skidded to a halt. "What? What do you mean, you can't fight for the northerners?"

"The commander of the empress's army is a northerner. A woman, come over from the Highlanders. She and Matelon seemed to know each other. They said they met when Matelon was a prisoner in the north."

Matelon, Matelon, Destin thought. What are you up to?

"What's this Carthian commander's name?"

Remy leaned in, as if worried he'd be overheard. "She goes by the name of Gray Wolf. She said she still has family here, and King Jarat can't know who she is, because he'd use her family against her. And she said the empress can't know we're working together, because she'll make the bloodsworn turn on us. And I don't want to be there for that." He shuddered.

Destin leaned closer. "So what do you intend to do, Remy?"

"I'm going to tell the king what I know. Hopefully he will use that information to persuade the northern commander to march her army away."

Destin thought it over. Considered his options. "I'm glad

you came to me with this," he said, putting a hand on Remy's shoulder.

Remy flinched. "So," he said, "can you take me to the king?"

"I'm sorry," Destin said, locking his elbow under Remy's chin and wrenching his head back, "but that won't be possible." He drew his dagger across the officer's throat, evading the fountaining blood, and dumped the body into the river. The Dyrnnewater was running high, so hopefully it would sweep Remy out of the city and far to the west. Destin rinsed the dagger, washed his hands, and dabbed at the blood that had spattered onto his sleeve.

Knives still work, he thought, with or without a collar.

He walked across the courtyard to the kitchens and descended the several sets of stairs that took him to his storeroom hideout, to the room that he kept locked behind layers of magical barricades. In his similarly protected travel bag, he located a small leather pouch. And, inside the pouch, a glass bottle, stoppered and sealed with wax. Holding it up to the light, he rocked it, and the contents sloshed. Still liquid, anyway. He put everything away, and threaded his way through the corridors to his secret guest quarters.

He knocked on Lila's door. There was a rush of activity inside and then Lila's voice on the other side. "Who is it?"

"Denis Rocheford."

"Ha," she said and opened the door.

In the time Destin had been dealing with Remy, Lila had accumulated a smoked ham, another wheel of cheese, and a small keg of ale. It was beginning to look like an actual storeroom again. Or a very small party, because

DeVilliers and Shadow Dancer were there as well, sharing in the bounty.

Good, Destin thought. Surely one of them will have the answers I need.

"Can I get you anything?" Lila said. "Wine, cheese, ham?"

Destin shook his head. "No, thank you."

Lila frowned, studying him. "Since when do you wear a scarf?"

"It's cold here in the north," Destin said, adjusting it.

"It's midsummer, nearly," Lila said. "What's that?"

"What's what?" Destin said warily.

"Under your scarf," Lila said. Quick as thought, she snatched away the black scarf Destin had added to his blacks. "You're wearing a *collar*? That's new." She reached for it, and he gripped her wrist. Hard.

"Leave it alone," he said. Releasing her wrist, he snatched up the scarf and reapplied it, struggling to knot the ends.

By now, Shadow had pushed to his feet and was nosing in, too. "Let me see. Is it one of ours?"

"I think so," Lila said. "I just need to get a better—"

"Leave me the hell alone!" Destin shouted, his voice echoing in the nearly empty storeroom, flame flickering around his body.

They stood, wide-eyed and staring, as if he'd set off a bomb. Which was kind of what it was like when he lost his temper. Destin dropped into a chair and put his head in his hands. He was mortified to realize that tears were leaking through his fingers.

For what seemed like an eternity, the room was absolutely silent. Then he heard little rustlings as people moved around

the room, chairs scraping across the floor. Somebody—Lila?—
shoved a cup under his nose. He breathed in the potent vapors,
took it and drained it, then hurled it against the wall. Happily,
it was metal, and ricocheted into a corner.

"So," Lila said, "is this about the collar?"

"I don't want to talk about the swiving collar," Destin said
through gritted teeth.

"Yes, you do," Lila said.

Destin looked up, crafting a blistering response, to find Lila
and Shadow smiling at him, a little smug, a little sympathetic.
That finally broke through his wall of fury.

"What?" he said, looking from one to the other.

"I made these collars," Shadow said, "and they have features
that King Jarat is unaware of." He reached into the doeskin
carry bag at his belt and pulled out a long-shanked key. The
kind of key used to open flashcraft collars.

Eyes fixed on the key, Destin swallowed hard and said, "If
Jarat discovers that I'm not wearing the collar, I'll go straight to
Executioner's Hill." It might be worth it, though.

"That's no problem," Shadow said. "Here. You can leave it
on. Let me show you how this key works."

At the end of it, Destin had a key in his inner pocket, and the
collar felt a thousand times lighter. "So all of those collars you
sold King Gerard . . . ?" He raised an eyebrow.

"In the north, we don't believe anyone should be enslaved—
not even mages."

"And enslaved mages, once freed—"

"Are likely to turn on those who enslaved them. Which
would be a shame," Shadow said.

"Do they know?" Destin said.

"Some of them do."

Which explains the attrition among the gifted forces, Destin thought.

"And, trust me, they'll all know before they engage the armies of the north."

"Thank you," Destin said simply. "If there is any way I can repay you—"

"We'll remember that, spymaster," Shadow said, winking. "I'm sure we'll think of something."

"A toast to the beholden," Lila said, and they clanked cups and drank.

I *will* find a way to repay them, Destin thought, though in what currency, only time will tell. Right now, he had other business.

"I'm hoping that you can answer a question for me," Destin said. "What can you tell me about a Fellsian officer—a woman—who goes by the name of the Gray Wolf?"

DeVilliers practically choked on her ale, then went into a coughing fit. Shadow's face flattened into a blank mask.

Destin was a practiced interrogator. Their reactions told him some of what he needed to know.

"Sounds familiar," DeVilliers said as casually as she could manage. "Why do you ask?"

"Because she's in command of the army outside," Destin said. "She and Matelon."

"What?" Shadow came up on his knees. He and DeVilliers looked at each other.

"Matelon?" Lila said. "Our Matelon?"

"He's no longer our Matelon, apparently. He's a king now."

"Who told you that?" Lila said.

"As I keep reminding you, I'm a *spymaster*," Destin said, rolling his eyes. "Do you know her, yes or no?"

"Yes," Shadow said.

"So what can you tell me about her?"

"I can tell you that she will win," Shadow said.

"Good," Destin said with a sigh of relief. Maybe the desperate plan he'd concocted with Julianna and Jemson wouldn't be needed after all. "I need an introduction."

# 61

# THE GRAY WOLF

Destin conjured up light on the tips of his fingers to illuminate the tunnel ahead. It seemed as if they must have walked to Arden by now. "Are you sure we're not lost?"

"Don't worry," Shadow said. "It's not too much farther. Hadley, Meadowlark, and I—"

"Meadowlark?"

"Princess Alyssa," Shadow said. "We used to play in these tunnels constantly when we were children. This is the tunnel that Alger Waterlow used for his trysts with Queen Hanalea. It runs all the way from her bedchamber to Gray Lady."

And, this time, it runs all the way to the Gray Wolf, Destin thought. The pouch with the bottle inside rested next to his heart, warmed by his body heat.

My work is nearly done here, he thought.

And, in an odd way, it was. The general was dead. His mother was at peace. Marina and Madeleine were out of the hands of the Montaignes. King Gerard was dead, and Jarat's days were numbered. Now it was time to go after his last great enemy. Destin knew he might not survive the night, but if he was going to die, he would die as a traitor to the red hawk.

The tunnel made a sharp turn and sloped upward, eventually merging into a natural cave.

"I told them to meet us here, at the end of the tunnel," Shadow said. "It's just up here."

Destin could see torchlight up ahead, and the silhouettes of the people waiting for them.

They stood in a little group, behind a magical barrier. Destin recognized their mage as Marc DeJardin, who'd served with Gerard's blackbird guard. He still wore a collar—no doubt, one of Lila's, now in use as an amulet. There was Matelon, the newly minted king of Arden, in the uniform of the Ardenine regulars with a spreading tree signia pinned on. And, finally, the Carthian commander, the woman Remy had outed as the Gray Wolf. She was of a sturdy build, though it was hard to tell much else about her given her desert fighting garb. She stood nearly as tall as Matelon, a cowl wrapped around her head and across her face so that only her brown eyes showed.

Shadow and DeVilliers were staring at her, too, and Destin could tell from their rapt expressions that he'd guessed right.

"Karn," Matelon said with a curt nod.

"Your Majesty," Destin said, bowing. "You've become extraordinarily flexible and nimble for a Matelon. Still, I never expected to see you fighting for the empress."

"I am not fighting for the empress," Matelon said. "I'm fighting for her." He nodded at his companion.

Destin looked from one to the other. "Such strange bedfellows," he said, which seemed to strike a nerve.

"So you're the notorious Lieutenant Karn," the commander said, in an unmistakable northern accent.

"I am." Destin fell to one knee. "Queen Alyssa, I presume?"
Everybody flinched.

"Get up," the wolf queen said, pushing back the cowl to reveal her braided hair, bronze skin, and a wide, good-humored mouth. "You do realize I'll have to kill you now."

"Maybe not," Destin said, "when you find out how useful I can be."

"Why should I trust you?" Alyssa said.

"Because we have a common enemy."

"Who? Jarat?" the queen said with an expression of contempt.

"No. Celestine."

She studied him, head tilted, brow furrowed. "How is she your enemy? I mean, aside from the fact that she's the enemy of everyone in the Realms, whether they know it or not?"

"It's a long story," Destin said, "but I intend to fight Celestine until the last breath leaves my body." He nodded toward Shadow and DeVilliers. "They can confirm parts of what I've said."

"Hmm," Alyssa said skeptically. "I suppose I'll have to hear you out, then. But first, I need a moment." Turning her attention to his companions, she embraced them. "I am so damned glad to see you two again," she said, her voice catching. All at once, it was as if a dam broke. Tears were running down everyone's faces.

Destin and Matelon stood around, like spouses at the army reunion.

"Let's sit," Alyssa said, finally, pointing to a scattering of cushions on the cave floor. Destin sat, trying to imagine sitting in a circle on a stone floor with Gerard Montaigne.

"Now," she said to Destin, "convince me that the benefit

of taking you on is greater than the risk. What do you have to offer?"

"I offer the gift of information," he said. "I can tell you who murdered your father, who betrayed your sister and your brother, and attacked you in Southbridge. Also who poisoned your mother and betrayed your friend Finn."

"Is that all?" DeVilliers muttered.

Alyssa leaned toward Destin, her hands on her knees, and Destin saw the wolf in the queen's face. The hairs on the back of his neck stood up straight, and he tasted metal on his tongue.

"If you were involved in those things, Lieutenant, you are digging your own grave," she said softly.

"I was not involved in those particular things," Destin said quickly.

"That's convenient," Alyssa said.

"Convenient and true. Gerard and Jarat worked directly with traitors in the north to see those things done. It wasn't until recently that I learned the truth."

"Which is? Briefly, please."

"Harriman Vega and your aunt Mellony were the major players."

She didn't blink. "I've always suspected Vega, but . . ." She trailed off, thinking. "Not Julianna?"

Destin shook his head.

"And you know this how?"

"I've asked her. Using persuasion, not torture," he said.

Alyssa considered this. "Even if I believed you, Karn, what's done cannot be undone. So this knowledge is of limited use to me now."

"Let's move beyond history, then, and focus on the future,"

Destin said. "Mellony has succeeded in putting a crown on Juli-anna's head, but she doesn't want it. Mellony intends to marry her to Jarat tomorrow. Julianna doesn't want that, either."

"Tomorrow?"

"Yes. Julianna, Lila Byrne, Speaker Jemson, and I have taken steps to prevent it from happening, but we could use your help. I can give you Jarat, and I can give you your city back. More importantly, I can help you drive the empress out of the Realms."

"Jemson!" the queen blurted. "He's mixed up with *you*?" The disdain in her voice was unmistakable.

"Lyss," DeVilliers said. "Karn is worth listening to."

Destin met the commander's eyes. *Thank you.*

The queen digested this. "Go on," she said to Destin.

Destin reached inside his coat, and both DeJardin and Mate-lon gripped his arms. He hadn't realized they'd moved in so close.

"Here," he said. "It's in my inside pocket. A small bottle. You fetch it, if you like."

DeJardin reached in and pulled out the bottle Destin had been saving since Evan had given it to him months ago. The mage looked it over, rocked it so that it sloshed, and held it up for Alyssa's inspection.

She wrinkled her nose. "It looks like blood," she said.

"It is. Your army is bloodsworn to the empress. That means that they will fight for you as long as they believe that they are serving her. If she finds out she's been betrayed, you're at high risk of being slaughtered."

Alyssa and Matelon looked at each other.

"We know that," Alyssa said. "But our free army is only five hundred strong. We need to work with what we have."

"Celestine is a blood mage," Destin said.

"Is that her blood?"

"No," Destin said. "It—it's Evan Strangward's."

"The pirate?" Queen Alyssa cocked her head.

"He was a blood mage, too," DeVilliers said. "His crews were bloodsworn."

"Stormborn," Destin said. "The empress hunted him up and down the Desert Coast for years. Evan had an ethical problem with creating new blood slaves, but he found that he could bind Celestine's bloodsworn with his blood. So they become what he calls 'stormborn.'"

"So his crews—the ones with purple auras—they're Celestine's bloodsworn . . . repurposed?" DeVilliers said.

Destin nodded.

"It sounds like you knew this Evan Strangward quite well," the Gray Wolf queen said, eyeing him thoughtfully.

"Yes," Destin said. "We were friends back in Tarvos." He paused, afraid he'd revealed too much.

"So," Matelon said, "what are you doing with a bottle of Strangward's blood?" The newly anointed king pointed at the bottle.

"He gave it to me when he came to Ardenscourt. He hoped I could use it somehow if the empress invaded the wetlands."

"Are you suggesting that we bind Celestine's bloodsworn to *Strangward*?" Queen Alyssa said.

Destin shook his head. "No. I'm proposing that they be bound to *you*." Seeing *no* in her face, he rushed on. "I suggest we mix a little of your blood with Ev—with Strangward's. Then we mix it in their water or their ale, or whatever it is they drink." Seeing the queen's revolted expression, he hurried on. "I don't know exactly what will happen, but I'm hoping Strangward's blood will loosen the bond and maybe they'll align with you, or at least be freed of the empress. Though I don't know how it will work since—now that—he's gone." Saying it out loud made Destin realize how unlikely this plan sounded.

"Hang on," Alyssa said. "I must have missed something. This pirate—Strangward—he's dead?"

DeVilliers cleared her throat. "Strangward came with us to try to free you from the empress," she said, "but he and Sasha and Ash were lost when my ship went down."

Queen Alyssa flinched, as if she'd been struck. "*What?*"

"I'm sorry, Cap—Your Majesty," DeVilliers said, staring down at her boots. "It seems like I am always bringing bad news."

Alyssa sat motionless, her hands on her knees, her face bleak. Matelon reached for her, drew his hand back, then finally rested it on her shoulder.

The queen cleared her throat. "Are you sure they are dead? The empress claimed that she'd found my brother in Tarvos. She had his amulet for proof." Reaching into her neckline, she pulled out a distinctively carved snake pendant. "Was Ash wearing this aboard *Sea Wolf*?"

DeVilliers stared at it, then nodded.

"How would Celestine have this if they went down with *Sea Wolf*?"

"I—I don't know, unless his body washed up on the shore. . . ."

"In which case, how would they have identified him?"

Alyssa said. "I assume you weren't wearing Gray Wolf regalia."

"No, ma'am," DeVilliers said.

The queen bit her lower lip, as if thinking. "Celestine claimed that Ash had come to Tarvos looking for me and wanted to strike a deal."

"You didn't see him before you left?" Shadow said.

Alyssa shook her head. "She said she'd sent someone to fetch him back to Celesgarde. We sailed right after she told me that."

Hope welled up in Destin—he couldn't fight it down. If the northern prince had survived and made it to shore, was it possible that Evan had, too?

"Did Celestine mention anyone else?" he said, trying to hide his eagerness.

"No. Just Ash." She frowned. "Though it's odd. I keep seeing Sasha in my dreams, telling me that she's alive, telling me that she's coming for me." She shrugged. "I don't know what to make of that."

"Sasha is your bound captain now, Your Majesty," DeVilliers said. "I stood in for you at the binding ceremony since . . . since you couldn't be there. Jemson had some blood of the Line on hand."

"So—you're saying that Sasha is bound to me? And that might explain the dreams?"

They were all looking at each other as if this were an important clue.

But something else DeVilliers had said caught his attention.

"What's all this about a 'binding ceremony'?" Destin said. Nobody would meet his eyes. Obviously, this was a secret that they didn't want to share.

"Look," Destin said, "at this point, we're going to live, or die, together. You may as well trust me. I swear on my mother's grave that I won't betray you."

The queen's brown eyes met his own. "Fair enough, Karn, but if we're not convinced of that before we're done here, you're a dead man."

Destin nodded his assent to what he already knew.

The queen held his gaze for a long moment, then said, "The blood of the Line is used to bind the captain of the Queen's Guard so that he has to act in the interest of the Line, no matter what," Alyssa said.

"How are they bound? What do you do with the blood?"

"The captain drinks it, mixed with water from the Dyrnne-water." She wrinkled her nose. "So, I guess, though I've never considered myself any kind of mage, in that way, I guess I am."

"Does this binding diminish intelligence, decision-making, any of that?" Destin asked.

"No!" the queen said, looking horrified. "I would never do that. Nor would I want a captain who was . . . diminished."

"There's the difference between you and Celestine," Destin said, feeling a spark of hope. "So—leave Strangward's blood out of it. Use the blood of your Line to bind the bloodsworn. If it doesn't work, no harm done."

"No," Alyssa said flatly. "I don't like it."

Funny how people can shed blood all day long, but draw the line when it comes to *drinking* it, Destin thought. Including me.

"You're using them now, aren't you?" Destin persisted. "Are they here of their own free will?"

"No," she admitted.

"And you're tricking them, because they think they're fighting for the empress, when they're really not."

"I am," she said, scowling, as if she knew she was losing this argument.

"Many of the bloodsworn are from the Realms," Destin persisted. "Wouldn't they be better off under your command? Whom do you think they would rather serve?" He paused again. She said nothing, and kept scowling. "You mean to tell me that you're willing to risk the outcome of this war, the lives of your free soldiers, and the citizens of the Fells because you're squeamish?" He watched the queen wrestle with this, thinking, A ruler with principles? How inconvenient.

"Your Majesty," Matelon said, "maybe we—"

"Celestine doesn't care about them," the queen said miserably. "She spends them like their lives are worthless. She . . . she holds these despicable tournaments for entertainment. . . ."

When a person is talking herself into something, Destin knew enough to keep quiet. So he did.

"All right," Queen Alyssa said, rubbing her forehead wearily. "We'll try it."

"Can you do it tonight?" Destin said, pressing his luck. "Tomorrow will be a busy day."

# 62

# DEAD WEDDING

Lila Byrne found herself attending Julianna's second wedding within a month. Though it was larger than her first wedding, Lila, Shadow, and DeVilliers were among the few repeat guests. Many who'd attended the first wedding were dead, or related to the dead groom. Most of Jarat's relatives were dead, too, many murdered by his father. His mother and sister were hiding out in Hunter's Camp to the east, but hopefully he didn't know that.

Since the wedding guests had to be chosen from among those who'd taken refuge inside the city, the guest list was less upscale than might have been expected for a royal wedding. The queen regent dug up a few cousins to attend the bride. Jarat enlisted some of his foul young thanelings.

Collared wizards lined the sanctuary—pretty much all of the wizards still left in the city, along with those that had come up with the Ardenine army.

Lila spotted Destin in the gallery, walking the perimeter, watching and waiting.

DeVilliers was subdued, and Shadow was somber, dressed in

a coat embroidered with a subtle design of aspen trees and fells-cats. Aspens for his fiancée, fellscats for his mother.

"Should you really be wearing your funeral coat?" Lila murmured.

"These flatlanders have no idea what kind of a coat it is," Shadow said. "But Owl will know."

Apparently, Owl was Julianna's upland name.

The groom waited at the front of the Cathedral Temple with Father Fosnaught. That's appropriate, Lila thought, that the swiving principia of the swiving Church of Malthus should preside over this mess. The mother of the bride took her place at the front of the church, positively glowing in champagne-colored satin.

A string quartet played music from all over the Seven Realms, in recognition of their joining. Thunder rumbled, far to the north, unusual this early in the season. The air was thick, portending trouble. The wind picked up, and the candles guttered, the light flickering on the walls, sending shadows prowling like wolves along the— Stop it! Lila thought.

Trumpets sounded a fanfare, and the bride appeared at the front of the nave, carrying a cascade of maiden's kiss, lilies, bloodberry, and rowan, a circlet of rowan and bloodberry on her head. Odd choices for a bride. Appropriate for a blood sacrifice.

As she walked up the aisle, thunder crashed again, and the wind rose, swirling around Julianna, ripping petals from the flowers she carried, teasing her hair free from its binding.

A murmur ran through the crowd. *Hanalea breathes.* The quartet played louder.

Jarat gestured impatiently to the blackbirds, and they

struggled to close and latch the shutters, but the shutters ripped free and kited away.

Now the howling began. It seemed to come from both inside and outside the temple, inside and outside of Lila's head. Lila hunched her shoulders, shuddering against the sound.

Shadow put an arm around her. "Are you all right?" he whispered.

"Make it stop," Lila moaned.

"When Hanalea speaks, we must listen," he said, stroking her hair.

She wanted to burrow her face into Shadow's shoulder, but she couldn't take her eyes off Julianna.

The bride walked forward slowly, deliberately, chin up. By now, the din of wind, thunder, and howling was deafening. Julianna had nearly reached the altar when she staggered, and the crowd sucked in a breath. She dropped to her knees.

"Julianna?" Mellony said, practically shouting to be heard over the noise. "What's wrong?"

Still on her knees, the bride lifted her arms, palms up, her face bathed in torchlight. "For Hanalea the warrior!" she cried. She slumped forward onto her face and lay still, what was left of her bouquet scattered on the stone floor.

With that, the storm died.

"What the bloody hell?" Jarat said into the sudden silence.

Clutching her skirts in her hands to keep from tripping, Mellony raced back down the aisle and knelt beside her daughter, slapping her cheeks, picking up a limp wrist to feel for a pulse. Sitting back on her heels, she wailed, "She's dead!"

"No," Jarat said, descending from the altar and striding toward the women. "I have had enough of overwrought, hysterical women." Gripping Julianna by the arm, he tried to drag her upright, but she was a dead weight. Mellony leapt at him, but two blackbirds gripped her arms and dragged her back.

The congregants watched in shocked silence. Then, from the gallery above, someone began to sing in a loud, clear voice.

*We are children of the north,*
*Born among the trees.*
*We will not take the collar*
*And we will not bend the knee.*

Lila looked up. Above, on the gallery, stood a tall, grim-faced woman in spattercloth, a sword in her hand, her long braid falling over her shoulder.

Spattercloth—the uniform of the Highlander army of the Fells.

Hal Matelon stood beside her, wearing the buff of Arden.

What the—?

The quartet picked up the tune. Around them, people joined in singing. More and more spattercloth soldiers stepped forward, out of the shadows, lining the entire gallery, longbows aiming down at the wedding guests. Outside, now, could be heard the sounds of a pitched battle. Some of the wizards in the room slipped out through the doors to join in.

*We will fight you in the winter snows*
*And in the summer mud,*
*And the slopes of Hanalea*
*Will be watered with your blood.*

Blackbirds swarmed toward the steps. Overhead, bows sounded, and the blackbirds dropped in their tracks. More spattercloth soldiers stepped in through the doors on all sides, preventing anyone from exiting. Jarat's thanelings drew their ceremonial swords, only to be cut down by arrows from above and swordsmen on the ground.

Julianna's attendants were singing along with the crowd.

*We are children of the north*
*And we do not fight alone.*
*Our mothers fight beside us*
*To protect the mountain home.*

*From mountain camp to upland vale*
*You'll hear our battle cry:*
*You think you've come to conquer.*
*Instead, prepare to die.*

Mellony threw herself across her daughter's body, sobbing.

"Mages! To me! Protect your king!" Jarat shouted, seeing soldiers closing in on all sides.

The remaining mages stood along the perimeter, arms folded, faces stone-like.

"Karn!" Jarat shouted, looking around for his spymaster/ mage wrangler. "Where are you? Make them obey." Karn was nowhere to be seen.

The sounds of fighting outside had subsided. The entire hall had gone quiet, everyone waiting to see what would happen next.

Jarat stared up at the gallery. Somewhere along the line, he'd lost his elaborate crown. Quite suddenly, he was very much alone.

"Who the hell are you?" he said to the singer.

"I am Alyssa ana'Raisa, the Gray Wolf queen," she said. "Who the hell are you and what are you doing in my hall?"

"I am Jarat Montaigne, emperor of the Seven Realms."

Very deliberately, Alyssa looked from one side of the hall to the other. "I think you are mistaken," she said. "I believe you are my prisoner."

Mellony's head came up when she heard this exchange. She pushed to her feet, moving away from Jarat. "Alyssa! Thank the Maker." She pointed a shaking hand at Jarat. "He murdered Julianna."

Just then, the doors to the hall opened with a bang, and Destin Karn strode in. He came and stood next to Jarat. "The fighting's over," he said. "We've driven the enemy out of the close."

Jarat drew himself up. "Thank you, General. Now." He looked up at Alyssa. "You have made a grievous mistake. It is my custom to be merciful, especially when it comes to young women, but this is impossible to forgive. You have ruined my wedding and killed my bride."

Lila took a moment to be amazed at how people will lie about what happened in a room full of witnesses.

Then Jarat pointed to Alyssa and said to Karn, "Kill her."

Karn merely looked at Jarat, as if perplexed. "Oh. Didn't I tell you? I've changed sides. The wolf queen has won the day. Not you." Quick as thought, Karn looped a garrote around the king's neck and drew it tight.

Jarat's eyes bulged, he kicked and struggled, desperately

clawing at his neck, then pawed at his wedding coat, trying to reach an inside pocket.

Eventually, Karn forced the emperor to the floor, pinning him. Jarat thrashed and drummed his heels on the floor, the sound echoing through the candlelit sanctuary. Gradually, his movements became erratic, slowing until they finally stopped. Karn gave it another few moments, just to be sure, then sat back on his heels.

That's Destin Karn, Lila thought. Always willing to tie up those loose ends.

Mellony gaped at this, horrified. Then looked up at Alyssa, raising her hands beseechingly.

"Aunt Mellony," Alyssa said, "I am so very disappointed in you."

"Wh-what are you talking about?"

Alyssa didn't reply, just kept staring down at her.

"I— Please understand," Mellony said finally. "I know what you're thinking, but we really had no choice. General Dunedain took her army east, leaving us defenseless. After Arden took the city, we had to do what was necessary to survive. Jarat was determined to marry a queen, and so . . ." She trailed off. "And now—I've paid the highest price imaginable. I've lost my daughter. And you've lost your cousin, who loved you."

This is sort of like the child who kills his parents and then asks for mercy because he is an orphan, Lila thought. Only the other way around.

"No," Alyssa said, her voice tremoring a bit. "This doesn't work for you, not anymore. I probably don't know everything, but I know enough—about Vega, about Finn, about my father and my sister and my mother. They loved you and trusted you.

I loved you and trusted you. And you betrayed us all."

Mellony looked around, at the room full of soldiers and the wedding guests who hadn't already fled. "You're hurt and upset," she said. "I understand that. Perhaps we should discuss this in private. What's said can't be unsaid, and we'll need each other more than ever now."

"I have no intention of taking anything back," Alyssa said. "And I want everyone to hear what you have to say for yourself. The biggest mistake my mother ever made was taking you back after you tried to take her throne the first time."

The first time? Lila thought. When was that?

For a moment, it seemed that Mellony would go on pleading. But maybe the "queen regent" realized that it would do no good, because she changed tactics. She stiffened, lifted her chin, and said, "What I did, I did for the good of the realm. Julianna would have been a far better queen than you. She was so graceful, so lovely, so well-spoken, and so very smart. Everybody loved Julianna. You've always been big and awkward, never knowing how to act in social situations, always picking fights with everyone. You used to drive your poor mother to distraction."

"I do make people uncomfortable," Lyss said. "When I see something wrong, I call it out. I ask hard questions. And I do pick fights with people—because some things are worth fighting for." She put her hand on the hilt of her sword. "This is my weapon of choice. I don't stab people in the back or put poison in their wine."

"If you're suggesting that I did such things, that's a shameful lie," Mellony said. "It's a good thing poor Raisa didn't live to see this day. She would be mortified to hear how you've treated me."

"Actually, my mother is alive and well," Alyssa said. "We'll sit down with her one day soon and you can tell her all about it."

For once, Mellony had nothing to say. She stood, fists clenched, surprise and horror on her face.

"Together, my mother and I, and you and Julianna could have accomplished so much," Alyssa said softly. "Sometimes, it seems the bonds of blood and history are not enough."

She nodded to her soldiers, and they ushered Mellony away.

By now, the sanctuary was empty except for Highlanders, bluejackets, and the queen's inner circle. Julianna had been carried into the side chapel that the string quartet had vacated. Shadow and DeVilliers were with her. Lila sat down, too.

Julianna did look like a sleeping princess in her wedding gown, pale and beautiful, a purple bruise blossoming on her forehead where it had hit the floor.

Lila leaned in to take a closer look. "What was it you gave her?"

"Bloodberry," Shadow said. "It's a nerve poison. Taken in a small dose, it depresses breathing and heartbeat and so mimics death. Clan children get into them sometimes. That's why we always sit vigil with the dead for three days before we burn them."

Everyone in the Seven Realms must have a personal stash of poison to draw upon, Lila thought.

"How is she doing?" Queen Alyssa said from the doorway.

"She's coming to, I think," Shadow said. He stood, pointing to the place he'd vacated. "Sit," he said.

Julianna groaned, turning her head from side to side. Reached up and fingered the bump on her head, wincing in pain.

Shadow leaned in and whispered, "Time to wake up. It's over."

"I have the mother of all headaches," Julianna said. She cracked her eyes open. "Am I married?"

"No," Alyssa said.

Now Julianna's eyes snapped wide open. "Lyss! Thank the Maker. It's true—you're not dead."

"You're not dead, either," the queen said, stroking her hair. "But Jarat is."

Julianna struggled to sit up, then gave it up. "What about my mother?"

"She's still living," Alyssa said. After a pause, she added, "She's locked up. I haven't decided what to do about her."

"I never wanted to be queen," Julianna whispered. "I loved the job that I had—diplomacy, collecting information and analyzing it, solving problems. I don't blame you if you don't believe me, but—"

"I believe you," Alyssa said. "I've misjudged you. I was jealous of how smart and capable you are, and I mistook your mother's ambition for your own."

But Julianna plowed on, as if bent on convincing her. "I am not fierce enough," she said. "I am not the wolf that you are."

"It's not enough to be fierce," Alyssa said.

"It's not fair," Julianna said, tears running down her face. "I am . . . so very sorry. Karn said that it's not our fault if our parents are monsters, but I still feel responsible. If I could trade my life for—for Uncle Han's, or for Hanalea, or—"

"I would love to have them back," Alyssa said, taking her cousin's hands. "But I don't want to make that trade. I'm going to need you."

# 63

# HUNTING IN THE VALE

As Ash had anticipated, the Highlanders' reaction to their new winged allies quickly transitioned from fear and suspicion to fervent enthusiasm as the dragons became powerful partners in fighting the empress's armies. The bloodsworn's advantage was numbers, strength, and stamina. As long as soldiers were meeting on the ground, Celestine could both overwhelm the enemy and replenish her armies. But the dragons fought above the fray, immolating entire columns in one swoop. The fact that the empress's soldiers were funneled into the pass only made that job easier. Since immolation was one of the few effective ways to kill the bloodsworn, that turned the tide of the fight.

Gradually, the dragons and their human partners forced the empress's army back, past Fortress Rocks, past Alyssa Peak, leaving thousands of dead behind. Ash took little joy in this, since so many of the bloodsworn had begun as northern soldiers.

The news from the Vale wasn't as good. Scouts brought reports that Jarat's army had marched north through Delphi and taken Fellsmarch. Since Sasha claimed that Lyss was still alive, and somewhere to the west, Ash worried that she might be in the path of Jarat's advance.

Ash and Sasha met with the queen and her military commanders to ask for permission to fly into the Vale to try to find her.

General Dunedain raised an eyebrow. "Who is 'we'?"

"Goat and me, and Sasha and Slayer," Ash said. When Dunedain frowned, he hurried on. "That leaves you with Cas and Pricker. Jenna said she would stay and fight with you."

"You're sure Alyssa is there?" Queen Raisa said.

"I *think* she's somewhere in the Vale," Sasha said. "I can't be sure. I'm new at this. Look, if she escaped and came back to the Realms, she'd probably circle around Chalk Cliffs and try to make it back home through the borderlands. She would have no idea where we are."

"Can you tell if Alyssa has been turned?" Queen Raisa asked. "Is it possible she's fighting for the empress?"

"I'm convinced that Lyss is still Lyss," Sasha said flatly. "She hasn't been turned. So I don't see how she could be fighting for the empress."

"My children keep following each other into danger," Queen Raisa said, with an air of resignation. She embraced Ash. "Be careful."

And so, on a beautiful late-spring day, Ash, Goat, Sasha, and Slayer flew over the fringe of mountains that marked the eastern edge of the Vale, following the Firehole River. Plumes of vapor marked where streamlets fed by hot springs met the cold river. Major obstacles in the landscape looked like crinkles on a map. He'd never seen his homeland from this vantage point before.

The dragons were fascinated by the lush landscape, so different from Carthis.

*Green*, Goat said. And, then, *Good hunting?*

"Yes," Ash said. "Good hunting."

At Sasha's direction, they turned north, following the Way of the Queens toward Gray Lady.

"She must be near the capital," she said.

Who else is in the capital? Ash thought. Who, if anyone, is sitting on the throne? Jarat Montaigne? The idea turned his stomach.

As they neared the city of Fellsmarch, they could see what appeared to be an ocean of soldiers surrounding the city. If that was Jarat's army, the young king of Arden seemed to have brought the entire empire with him. Is that how he managed to take the city? Was Lyss trapped inside the walls?

*Bloodsworn*, Goat said. *Same as before.*

"Bloodsworn?" Ash's heart sank. Was Celestine just going to keep sending soldiers until everyone in the Realms was dead?

*Don't be sad. More to kill.*

"I'd like to stop killing one day," Ash said. As they circled, losing altitude, he could see that most of the soldiers were dressed in the familiar desert warrior garb. But they were *not* the same as before.

It was their auras. They weren't the purplish color the bloodsworn wore, nor quite the ruddy color of Strangward's stormborn. They were so faint that in the bright sunlight, they scarcely showed.

"Lyss isn't in the city," Sasha called. "She's somewhere north of it. On Gray Lady."

The "bloodsworn" soldiers slopped partway up Gray Lady's

sides. Amid the desert warriors were splotches of buff—a few hundred Ardenine dirtbacks.

Ash's heart sank. Had Jarat and the empress teamed up against the queendom? Was Lyss hiding out, somewhere above?

*Go lower,* Slayer suggested. *Catch her scent maybe.*

They descended in slow spirals, until dragon eyes could pick out details on the ground.

"It seems like she must be right below us," Sasha said. "Do you see her?"

A handful of people had emerged from a gash in the mountainside—what looked to be a cave. They began picking their way downslope toward the soldiers' camp.

Ash squinted, but he couldn't see anyone who resembled his sister.

The group walked out onto a ledge that overlooked the gathered soldiers.

*Officers maybe,* Goat said. *Good target?* The dragons had embraced warfare tactics and terminology with a will.

"Maybe," Ash said. "Can we go lower?"

One of the officers began to speak to the assembled soldiers, her voice ringing out over the valley. Ash couldn't make out the words. But Goat could, and transmitted them to Ash.

"You all have until tomorrow to make your decision. Some of you are from the Fells, some of you are from the downrealms, and some of you are from Carthis. All of you are welcome to stay, and pledge to me and join the fight against the empress. But if you're from the south, I must warn you that our winters are a lot colder than yours."

Laughter rolled through the massed soldiers. Bloodsworn laughing?

"So. See your field commanders and let them know if you are staying or going home. If you go, take your personal gear with you. You'll need it for the journey home."

An officer in Ardenine colors came up beside her and addressed his soldiers. "I expect my brigades to stay. Once we establish order in the city and determine what we need here, we'll deploy east, toward the fighting on the coast."

The two officers looked at each other, then said in unison, "Dismissed."

All at once, Slayer said, *Lyssa Wolf!* He folded his wings and plummeted toward the ledge with Sasha hanging on for dear life. Goat instantly plunged after him. When the people on the ground spotted them, they screamed out a warning, scattering and looking for cover, but there was none to be found on the bare ledge.

The dragons landed between the ledge and the cave, so that the humans were trapped. Two of them were mages, and they stood their ground in front of the others, firing volleys of flame at the dragons, which had no effect on their armored hides. Ash and Sasha slid to the ground and took cover behind them.

*Puny mage flame*, Goat said.

"Don't retaliate," Ash said quickly, for fear the dragons would give them a demonstration.

*Not stupid. Find Lyss, then retaliate.*

Slayer extended his head toward the cowering humans. The officer in buff had thrown himself down on top of the officer who'd spoken first. She appeared to be trying to squirm out from under him.

*Lyssa Wolf!*

"Slayer!" she cried. And "Matelon, get off of me!" to her

would-be protector. She finally freed herself and sprinted toward Slayer, pressing up against the dragon's side, doing her best to embrace him. "No, no, no," she said, when he glared menacingly at the soldier, who was advancing toward them. "He was trying to help me, not hurt me."

Ash got an up-close look at his little sister for the first time.

First of all, she was no longer little. She was nearly as tall as Ash, and had lost every bit of girlish padding on muscle and bone. Her hair was the color of November hay, and done up in little braids, clan-style, but she was dressed like a desert warrior, like one of the bloodsworn he'd been fighting in the east. Her complexion was a burnished copper—closer to their mother's—and she'd inherited her grandfather's brown eyes. He knew all this, and yet—it was as if it were laid over the frame of a different person. Her face was almost the same, with her stubborn chin and broad forehead, but her cheekbones and jaw were more sharply angled.

She moved like a warrior, too, with a predatory grace and economy of movement.

*Lyssa Wolf,* Ash thought, his heart heavy with regret. My little sister is gone forever. I have missed so much.

Lyss turned away from Slayer then, distracted by shouts of alarm from the soldiers below. Some of them had begun scrambling up the mountainside toward them. Slayer extended his head over the edge of the promontory, ears flattened, preparing to attack.

"No!" Lyss shouted. "Slayer, no! Those are my soldiers. Everybody—just stand down a minute!"

The soldiers scrambling up the mountain quit scrambling and stood in place.

Slayer looked shamefaced. And confused.

*Lyssa has bloodsworn, too?*

"Not exactly. I'm hoping that what I have now is a free army." She turned to speak to the soldiers once more. "Everything is all right," she said. "These are my friends. They surprised me, is all."

"Dreki?" One of the officers pointed at the dragons, as if Lyss hadn't noticed who she was embracing. Both the dragons and the bloodsworn were questioning Lyss's choice of companions.

"Yes," Lyss said. "But I know them. I trust them." With that, Sasha peeked out from behind Slayer's body. "Lyss?"

For a long moment, Lyss stood staring, dumbfounded. "Sasha?"

"Yes, ma'am," Sasha said, reverting to long habit.

Lyss looked from Slayer to Sasha. "What the—how did— Are you with Slayer? Were you—actually—riding on a dragon?"

"I actually was, ma'am," she said. "I mean, Your Majesty." She fell to one knee, presenting her sword. "Captain Sasha Talbot, reporting for duty."

"Talbot," Lyss said. "It is so damned good to see you. Put that sword away so that I can give you a proper welcome."

Sasha sheathed her sword and they embraced.

Slayer was hanging back but practically dancing with impatience, thrusting his nose in close. Eventually, Sasha noticed.

"Your Majesty, Slayer has something for you. It's from all the dragons—and Jenna. They all helped. They planned to give it to you back in Celesgarde, but you left before they could." Sasha ran up the dragon's side and unbuckled the leather pannier he was carrying. Moments later, she was back on the ground, with a package wrapped in more leather. She thrust it into Lyss's hands.

Lyss carefully unwrapped it. The contents glittered between her hands like a handful of stars.

"Try it on," Sasha said. "It's dragon-scale armor."

Lyss stared at it for a long moment, letting it slide through her fingers. She looked up at Sasha. "Is this my jacket that disappeared?"

*Jacket better now*, Slayer said.

Lyss slid her arms into the sleeves and fastened it down the front. The scales were a variety of colors, like quicksilver in the sunlight.

*Now Lyssa Wolf looks like Lyssa Dragon*, Slayer said. *Hard to bite, hard to flame.*

"I love it," Lyss said, fingering it. "Thank you," she added, dabbing at her eyes with the back of her hand.

Each small reunion seemed complete and perfect in itself, requiring time to savor. Ash hated to intrude, but he just couldn't wait any longer.

Ash stepped away from Goat and said in a hoarse voice, "Lyss?"

She turned toward him, her hand on her curved sword, that familiar impatience on her face. "Yes? Sasha, who's this? Do I know you?" Her eyes swept over his features, swept over them again. "Hanalea's blood and bones," she whispered, with an expression of mingled hope and disbelief. "Ash?"

"Lyss," he said again. He'd planned out what he would say a hundred times. And changed it a hundred times. Now the words seemed wooden. Inadequate. "I'm sorry I broke my promise to you." He swallowed hard, never taking his eyes off her. "I told you once that you might be the queen we needed. And you are."

Goat nudged him forward, all but knocking him into Lyss. And then Lyss grabbed him and held on. Her strength was amazing—and reassuring.

She was crying—laughing and crying—and squeezing in words here and there. "The empress . . . said she had you . . . said that she would burn you alive if I didn't . . . I didn't want to, but she had your amulet, and you were— I have lost you so many times already."

She pulled the serpent amulet out from under her shirt. "See? She gave it to me—told me to wear it to remind me of what would happen to you if—"

They both closed their hands over the amulet, and flash rocketed through them. And, again, their father's voice.

*It was worth it. You are worth it.*

Lyss's eyes widened, filled with wonder. She looked down at the amulet and up at Ash. "Did you—is that—"

"I saw him," Ash said. "I talked with him. And so when they took the amulet from me, I thought I had lost our connection with him forever."

Lyss lifted the chain from around her own neck and slid it over Ash's. The amulet rested just above his collarbone, where it belonged.

"He is really, really proud of you," Ash said. "We'll go and see him, I promise, and he can tell you himself."

For a long moment, Lyss said nothing, only studied his face intently, as if trying to recall the brother she'd followed around years before. "You've changed," she said finally. "When—when I thought you were dead, I always wondered who you would have turned out to be."

After a long pause, she seemed to wrench herself back to the present. "Where have you been?" she said. "Where were you coming from, when you—"

"I've been in the fighting east of the Spirits," he said. "With Mother, Captain Byrne, General Dunedain, and—"

"Mother *is* alive, then? Thank the Maker. I've heard so many different stories, I didn't know what to believe." Lyss jammed her hands into her breeches pockets. Familiar. Ash was beginning to see remnants of the girl he remembered, like tiny gifts from the past.

"Hadley is here," Lyss said. "And Shadow. They're back in the city. And Lila Byrne—I think you know her. And Destin Karn."

Reflexively, Ash gripped his amulet. "What the hell is Destin Karn doing here?"

"It's complicated," Lyss said. "One thing you can say about Celestine—she's brought the Realms together."

"Excuse me, Your Majesty," someone said.

Lyss turned. It was Matelon—the soldier who'd tried to protect her from the dragons.

"I'm sorry to interrupt, Your Majesty," he said, "but Mercier, Lereaux, and I are going down to camp to answer questions from the men. And women," he added awkwardly. "I will get used to that, I promise." He glanced at Ash, then back at Lyss. "I don't suppose you want to come with us."

"No," Lyss said. "I'll talk to them tomorrow morning."

Matelon turned to Ash. "I'm Hal Matelon," he said, offering his hand.

"The son of the thane? The army officer?"

"Yes," Matelon said.

Ash had seen the elder Matelon in Ardenscourt, at the

ill-fated dinner where the Thane Rebellion began. He could see the resemblance of son to father. Matelon was looking Ash up and down, as if taking his measure.

"I'm Adrian sul'Han," Ash said. "Lyss's brother. Which, from the looks of things, is how I'll be known from here on in."

"I know the feeling," Hal said. "I've lost Delphi to your sister. Twice."

"Don't forget Queen Court," Lyss said.

"How could I?" Matelon said. "Since you bring it up daily."

Ash laughed. "She's always hated losing," he said. "Even when she was little, she'd find a way to win."

"Matelon is the new king of Arden," Lyss said.

"Really?" Ash looked south, toward Fellsmarch. "What happened to Jarat?"

"He's dead," Lyss said, her jaw tightening. "Lieutenant Karn did us that favor."

Karn? Ash's racing mind stumbled over that.

"I think it's General Karn now," Matelon said.

"He told me he's done with the army," Lyss said.

I wonder if I'll ever catch up, Ash thought.

"What's going on with the bloodsworn?" he said. "These seem . . . different than the ones I've seen before."

"We may have found a way to loosen their bond to the empress," Lyss said, brushing her fingers over a healing wound on her forearm. "It may be too soon to tell, but my officers think there's been a change, that they're showing more initiative, more self-reliance. I hope that isn't just wishful thinking."

"I told them to be careful what they wish for," Matelon said. "They may miss having soldiers who do what they're told, don't ask questions, and never complain."

Lyss laughed.

Matelon saluted Lyss and went to turn away.

"Kings don't salute," Lyss said, arching an eyebrow. "Do we need to send you to king school, Matelon?"

Matelon waved that comment away. Then he and his officers walked down the hill.

Ash looked after them, a little jealous of their easy camaraderie, then turned back to Lyss.

"So. This Matelon. Do you trust him?"

"Yes," she said simply. She broadened her stance and lifted her chin as if ready to do battle on the southerner's behalf. In that, again, he saw the sister he remembered.

"What about Karn?"

She rocked her hand. "As he says, we share an enemy. The empress. And he's been a gold mine of information about conspiracies at court."

Ash was confused. "In Ardenscourt?"

"No," she said. "In Fellsmarch." When he opened his mouth to ask more questions, she shook her head. "We'll talk about that later. There's so much to tell, so much that I still don't know."

It seems like we all have a piece of this puzzle, Ash thought.

But Lyss had already moved on. "So you're alive, and Sasha is. How about the pirate Strangward? I'm told he sailed with you to Carthis?"

Ash nodded. "Strangward saved me and Sasha after our ship foundered. It turns out he's magemarked like Breon. When we left, he and Breon were sailing for the Carthian Coast. They intended to give Celestine something to worry about back home."

Lyss smiled, as if relieved. "You'll have to tell Karn that. He's convinced Strangward is dead."

Ash recalled what Evan had said when the flyers left for the Realms.

*Destin Karn is important to me. I want you to do everything you can to make sure he survives and thrives, no matter who wins.*

"There's so much to say," Lyss whispered. "If we had a hundred years, we still couldn't say it all."

"But we can make a start," Ash said, "right now."

# 64

# BETRAYAL

As midsummer approached, Breon became obsessed with identifying bolt-holes up and down the coast where he could take refuge when the empress returned. Each morning, he would climb to a rocky plateau above Evan's house and meet Splash and sometimes Splinter for the day's adventures. They even crossed the straits to the Northern Islands, making some of the first detailed maps of that region, hidden for so long behind violent storms and high seas.

Evan would have loved to go with them, but he found himself hip-deep in disputes between his client shiplords and other up-and-comers who saw the free ports as an opportunity to carve out fiefdoms of their own. Horselords and pirates had short tempers and, it seemed, shorter memories. Pledges and agreements burned off like mist in the midday sun.

After a day of hand-waving arguments and posturing, Evan was ready to board a ship—any ship—and sail away. He was still down on the waterfront when Splash and Splinter dropped from the sky, landing hard on the quay beside him. This was unusual. The dragons tended to avoid the harbor front, with its forest of tangly masts and excitable humans.

"Did you get tired of waiting?" Evan said. "I was just heading home."

*Breon stuck in cave*, Splash said.

Breon, Splash, and Splinter had flown south to Midden Bay to explore and map some of the sea caves there.

"What do you mean, he's stuck?" Evan said.

*In cave, won't come out*, Splash said.

"And you're too big to fit?" The dragons were frustrated, sometimes, that the humans could go places they couldn't. This wasn't the first time that Breon had gotten so involved in exploring that he forgot the time. "Did the tide come in? Was there a rockfall? Is he hurt?"

*Stuck. Evan come help.* Apparently, Splash thought that was enough of an explanation.

"All right," Evan said, thinking that flying away on a dragon was almost as good as sailing away. "Let's go up to the house and I'll get some gear. We need to go now if we want to get there before dark."

They flew south along the coast, Evan riding with Splinter and Splash carrying ropes and tackles, medical supplies, and clothing and camping gear in case they needed to stay over. To the west, the sun was beginning its descent, but they had several hours of daylight left.

Midden Bay was one of the best places to hide a ship between Endru and Tarvos. It was surrounded by tall cliffs and riddled with fissures and caves that often filled with water at high tide. It was unsuitable as a port, since the only way to off-load cargo was to winch it up the cliffside to the high plateau at the top. The plateau was also the only good landing place for a dragon.

Evan unloaded the gear and carried it to the edge of the cliff. A rope had been tied to a tough, gnarly juniper lodged in a niche just below the plateau. It passed through a tackle and snaked down the cliff face nearly all the way to the water.

"Did he climb down here?" Evan said, turning to look at the dragons crowded in behind him.

*Down rope, into cliff.*

Evan sighed, pulled on his gloves, wrapped the rope around his body, and backed off the cliff's edge. He rappelled down the stone wall toward the water. Who knew that his long days of climbing in the rigging of sailing ships would prove useful on land as well? Near the bottom, he found a gash in the rock large enough for him to slide into. He swung his feet into the cave, then turned and looked up to where the dragons were peering over the edge.

"Here?" he said.

*Yes. Don't get stuck.*

The floor of the cave was wet, with puddles of seawater here and there, so Evan knew it must flood at high tide. "Breon?" he called. His voice echoed against stone, but there was no answer. From the sound of it, the cave went back quite a distance into the cliff. Evan picked his way forward over a floor littered with fallen rock and fissured with cracks and crevices. It would be easy to twist an ankle or fall. He could hear the sound of waves crashing against rock ahead, so he knew there must be other outlets to the sea. Perhaps Breon had gone all the way through and come out on the other side.

Evan heard something—a sound farther on that might have been a moan. It was getting brighter again, so he knew he must be approaching the other entrance to the cave. He rounded a corner and saw shadows moving against the wall.

And then something solid crashed into the back of his head. He fell forward, trying to break his fall with his hands, but his forehead hit an outcropping of stone. He must have bitten his tongue, because at once, his mouth was full of blood. His vision swarmed with black spots, then everything went dark.

Evan awoke, conscious of tightness around his neck, something hard and metallic and suffocating. He tried to reach for it, but then discovered that his hands were bound tightly. His head hurt like fury in two places. A few feet away, he heard water lapping on stone. He cracked his eyes open and saw that he was lying on his side on a rock ledge, in a stone chamber lit by flickering torches.

He turned his head, and saw another trussed-up captive— Breon. Breon with a metal collar around his neck—one of the kind used to control mages in the wetlands. The kind Cas had been wearing when Evan bought him at the market.

*What you cast out to sea will eventually wash up on your shore,* Evan thought. A sailor's proverb.

A small boat was tied up nearby, and shadows moved through the darkness, stowing away supplies, apparently in preparation for departure. Barnacles and algae lined the walls to a point high above their heads, which meant that the cave must be underwater at high tide. It appeared that the tide was coming in, though high tide was probably an hour or two away.

"Stormcaster!" a familiar voice said. "I was beginning to think I'd hit you too hard. And that would be a shame, because the empress wants you alive."

It was Tully Samara, planted at the water's edge, arms

folded, smiling broadly. "How do you like your new collar? The empress brought them back from the wetlands. She said they should make it much easier to get you two safely back to Celesgarde."

"You're going to Celesgarde?"

"Yes. The empress has taken the stormwall down."

"Actually, I was the one who took the stormwall down. And then we took the city down. You sure you want to go there? It's not much more than a ruin."

Samara eyed him suspiciously. "What's your point?"

"My point is that you don't want me for an enemy," Evan said.

"I'm not worried," Samara said. "Without the dreki, and without your stormcaster magic, you're just scummer on my boots." The shiplord took a sounding in the channel, then nodded to his crew. "Put them aboard. It's time."

Samara's bloodsworn crew picked Breon up by his hands and feet and swung him aboard the jolly boat. Evan was next.

With that, Breon spoke for the first time. Or, rather, sang:

*This is where it all begins.*
*This is where it all ends.*
*The shattering*
*The rejoining*
*Forged in the bleeding earth.*
*As it has been, it shall be again.*
*At midsummer,*
*When the sun pauses in the sky.*

It was odd, hearing Breon's voice without the element of

magic in it. It sounded somehow plain, undecorated.

"What's that, a prayer?" Samara said.

Outside, a clamor arose as the dragons began keening their displeasure and frustration.

Samara flinched and looked toward the entrance. The flicker of flame was visible in the distance, glittering on wet stone.

"They usually like my singing," Breon said, shrugging. Evan could see his eyes glittering in the light from the torches.

"You can sing for the empress in a little while," Samara said, stepping into the boat, setting it to rocking.

"Slayer, Sprinter!" Breon called. "Don't forget. We're sailing for Celesgarde, in the Weeping Sisters. Look for the bleeding earth."

"Tell them to write it down so they don't forget," Samara said, rolling his eyes. With that, the crew cast off and the force of the current spun them away from the ledge and out toward the open sea.

# 65

# THE PRICE OF WINNING

Since the recapture of Fellsmarch, Hal had been able to establish limited communication with Robert in Ardenscourt.

The downrealms were restless, testing the resolve of the new regime. The royal army was still in the Fells, still unpaid, and the royal coffers were empty.

It seemed that his brother was holding his own against the ambitious thanes and their intrigues. Either that, or he didn't want to burden his brother with southern politics. To hear him tell it, he spent most of his time fielding marriage proposals.

"You can have your pick, Hal," he said. "Every thane in the kingdom has a daughter, and they all want to marry her off to a Matelon. You, preferably, but I'll do as a second choice."

There were so many reasons to stay here in the north, doing what he was good at. That's the thing about winning, Hal thought—eventually, you have to quit fighting and govern. He knew a lot about fighting, and very little about governing.

Still—it was better than losing.

It wasn't like he even had good examples to go by. The kings of Arden won their thrones through connivery and force of arms, then ruled by fear and favor, populating the government with friends and family. The army was not immune to that. Blood and loyalty were more important than talent or training.

We might have won this war a long time ago if we'd done things differently.

When he was military governor in Delphi, he'd avoided involvement with civilians and their problems, preferring to focus on what he knew. And that had turned out to be a mistake.

He was realizing that he had a lot to learn from these northern queens, especially if he wanted to travel a different path from his predecessors.

Though Lyss claimed that she had little experience with governing, she did have experience with a good government. To his surprise, and to the disapproval of some, she allowed him to sit in with her as she assembled a new government from the remains of the old. With Jarat gone, some of the queendom's longtime administrators emerged from hiding and went to work. She put Julianna Barrett in charge of logistics, with the help of Matelon's quartermaster, Jan Rives. Micah Bayar resumed his role as High Wizard, then immediately hurried off to the war in the east. Demeter Farrow took charge of the city garrison.

After some debate, discussions with his officers, and a heart-to-heart with Eric Bellamy, Hal kept the royal army with him, under Bellamy's command, and sent his loyalists home to Ardenscourt to back up his brother. He didn't intend to make the mistakes that Jarat had by failing to protect his rear.

Now it was time to rejoin the war. Hal and his army began the long march east to Queen Court.

Lyss, Ash, and Sasha had flown on ahead with Goat and Slayer, so that the royal siblings could reunite with their mother and update the commanders of the war in the east with happenings in the west. Hal was happy to hand off the task of explaining everything to someone else.

He also wasn't sorry to miss yet another happy reunion, since he hadn't managed to locate his own family. He'd been disappointed that nobody in the capital of Fellsmarch seemed to know where the hostages had ended up. Could they have been intercepted on their way north? Could their ship have been lost at sea? Captured by pirates? There were so many possibilities in a world at war—most of them bad.

Lila Byrne, Shadow Dancer, and Destin Karn traveled with Hal and his army from Fellsmarch. Hal wondered if Shadow was there to keep an eye on Hal and Destin Karn and their southern army.

"Why do you think she trusts us?" Destin asked Hal one night as they sat outside the command tent after everyone else had climbed into their bedrolls. Karn and Matelon had become Destin and Hal after nightly conversations by the campfire.

"Why does who trust us?"

"Queen Alyssa," Destin said.

"Does she trust us?" Hal raised an eyebrow.

"She's letting two southerners travel through her queendom with an army," Destin said.

"I think she's taking a chance on us because she knows that the only way to defeat Celestine is to unite the Realms. She's spent more time with the empress than any of us. She knows what we're facing."

Now Queen Court Vale spread before them, a green oasis

amid the gray granite of the mountains. At the western end lay a sprawling military camp, with tents, corrals, field kitchens, and the like. So the empress's armies had not broken through. They must still be stoppered up in the pass that had held against Hal's green troops when General Karn had sent him here to fail.

After his defeat at Queen Court, Hal had dreamed of returning to the scene of his schooling with the kind of army that could win. His dream was coming true in ways he'd never have imagined. He led an army comprising Ardenine regulars—some of the best soldiers and officers he'd ever commanded—and recovering bloodsworn whose stamina and strength somewhat compensated for their lack of experience and mental edge.

In a way, it mirrored the strategy he'd proposed and the late General Karn had rejected—to partner experienced soldiers with his green recruits. Day by day, it seemed, the former bloodsworn improved. He hoped he wasn't just seeing what he wanted to see.

At the center of the Vale lay the ruins of Queen Court, the meeting place of the queens of the Seven Realms. The place where Hal and Lyssa had kindled something that had smoldered ever since. The memory of that night had lodged next to Hal's heart, or wherever such memories are kept. After everything that had happened, did she ever think of him in that way? Would it ever amount to more than that—a sudden spark in the dark?

She's a queen, a voice in his head said, and you're just a—you're a king, he had to keep reminding himself.

Alyssa Gray was somewhere down below.

As they descended into the Vale, Pricker flew out ahead of them, soaring over the valley, calling out a challenge. Three specks appeared in the skies to the west, flying over the shoulder of Mount Alyssa and hurtling toward them. There followed a spectacular aerobatic and pyrotechnic show that left the uninitiated stunned and gaping.

Given the dragon early warning system, by the time they reached the relative flat of the valley floor, a welcoming committee of sorts had been assembled. Alyssa, the queen emeritus Raisa, Captain Byrne, Sasha, and General Dunedain. Ash, Jenna, Cas, and Goat were apparently flying reconnaissance missions east of the pass.

"Welcome, Your Majesty," Raisa said to Hal. "Congratulations on your recent coronation." She looked him up and down, as if searching for any surfacing signs of kingliness.

"Thank you . . ." Hal hesitated, then finished with, ". . . ma'am." He still couldn't understand how Lyss was queen when her mother was still very much alive.

She noticed. "You can call me Raisa Cennestre. It's a title of honor in the uplands."

"Thank you, Raisa Cennestre," Hal said, trying it out.

"I understand that we owe you our thanks for assisting in the liberation of our capital," she said. Hal had the sense that she was choosing her words carefully so as not to delegate any power in the queendom to him. She turned to Destin. "And you, Lieutenant Karn—thank you for uncovering the treason at the heart of our realm."

Destin inclined his head. "I take no pleasure in being the bearer of bad news," he said. "In Arden, we're always alert to betrayal by family, because it's a way of life."

That's true, Hal thought. For instance, Destin had killed his own father.

Raisa smiled. "We'll talk further." She turned away.

Alyssa took over. "I've told General Dunedain to work with Lereaux and LeFevre to get your soldiers settled. Right now, you and Karn need to come with me to the supply tent."

"To the supply tent?" Hal and Destin looked at each other.

"You both need some new clothes," she said, eyeing them critically.

We're in an army camp, not a salon, Hal thought, brushing at his uniform. Maybe it wasn't as fresh as it had been, but he was surprised that Lyss would make an issue of it. "I have other clothes," he said. "I just need to find a place to change."

"We've been a week on the road," Destin said, "but I was planning to bathe as soon as we arrived."

"That's not sufficient," Lyss said. "Follow me." She strode off, with Hal and Destin following, exchanging mystified looks. Was it the fact that her mother was there, and she was embarrassed by the stinking king of Arden?

When they entered the supply tent, it was filled with the familiar scent of leather, wool, and saddle soap. Three girls in clan garb were working behind the counter, pounding rivets and eyelets into leather and stitching pieces together. One of them rose and came to the counter to meet them. Her black hair was woven into a thick braid that reminded Hal of Lyss's, but when she looked up at Hal, her eyes were a striking gray-green. Familiar.

"May I help y— Hal!" His name came out in a shriek of joy.

It was Harper. She vaulted over the counter and into his arms.

"They kept telling me you were alive, but I wasn't ready to believe it until I saw you with my own eyes," she said. "You're scratchy," she added, brushing her fingers over his chin.

"Harper," Hal said with his usual eloquence. Gripping his arms, she danced him around the room, while everyone else watched, with mingled amusement and amazement.

"I had no idea you were a dancer, Matelon," Lyss said.

"This must be your brother," one of the other leatherworkers guessed.

"It is, it is! Hal, this is Sparrow, and this is Flicker Silvertree. They are geniuses. I've been learning so much."

"Is Mother here, too?" Hal said.

"She's up at Hunter's Camp," Harper said. "She's been working with the matriarch there, Willo Cennestre, helping in the healing halls."

Finally, Hal thought, I get the reunion I wanted. He veered from thanking all of the saints and the gods in the Seven Realms to new concerns about keeping them safe. A king's family was another point of vulnerability that could be exploited by his enemies.

Harper caught sight of Destin Karn, who was lurking near the door. "Lieutenant Karn! Destin!" Releasing Hal, she embraced the spymaster, who looked rather startled at first.

"I never got to thank you for saving me from that despicable Granger," she said.

"Ah. Lady Matelon," Destin said, his confusion clearing. He bowed and kissed her hand. "You were the one who saved yourself, along with the rest of the hostages. I am in awe of you."

Sparrow and Flicker stared at Harper, clearly impressed.

"Why didn't anyone tell me they were here?" Hal looked accusingly at Lyss.

"As long as Jarat was on the move, we didn't want anyone to

know where the hostages were," Lyss said. "Especially because we suspected that someone on the queen's council was feeding information to Arden. We didn't want Jarat coming to collect them. We had enough to contend with here."

"Come on, Hal," Harper said, pulling at his arm. "Let's ride to Hunter's Camp and see Mama. It's not far."

As he and Harper walked toward the horse corrals, Hal couldn't help thinking, What if the empress makes it through the pass? What then? Nearly everyone he cared about was right in her path.

# 66

# BLINDSIDED

This is a different kind of warfare, Jenna thought. She'd never served in the military, but in her role as a saboteur, she'd worked alone, mostly—up close and personal, setting the charges, laying the fuses, then igniting them. Though she watched from a safe distance, she was often close enough to hear the *boom* as the powder caught, feel the reverberations through her feet, and breathe in the musty, sulfuric smoke from black powder.

Now, she spent much of her time soaring over the carnage on the ground, descending only to contribute to it, then flying away. This seems wrong, she thought. When a predator makes a kill, she is engaged in an intimate dance of death. This is too easy.

An infantry, no matter how fierce, presents little risk to armored flyers swooping down on them, spouting flame and dropping boulders on them from above. The dragons' role in reconnaissance also made it nearly impossible to ambush or outmaneuver the joined armies under Hal, Alyssa, and General Dunedain. The dragons scanned the ground, looking for the telltale glow that signified Celestine's presence. Eventually, the empress learned to cloak herself, or take cover under a ledge or other obstacle to hide her presence. Still, Jenna's magemark responded whenever she was close enough.

*So, Celestine. How does it feel to be the hunted for a change?*

Her luck can't hold out forever, Jenna thought. But luck runs both ways.

Celestine was the only weapon that threatened the dragons themselves, although a skilled archer might be able to pick off one of the riders. Along the Desert Coast, weapons had been developed for use against dragons who preyed on livestock. *It's only a matter of time,* Jenna thought, *before they ship in more firepower through Chalk Cliffs*—cannons that shot weapons-grade steel shrapnel that could penetrate the dragons' armor; mammoth crossbows transported on wagons whose bolts were launched with such power that they could deliver a killing blow.

The joined armies of the Realms finally broke through the pass between Queen Court and Alyssa Plateau and pushed the empress's troops east, toward the coast. The addition of Hal's Ardenine regulars and the "reborn" bloodsworn made a potent difference on the plateau. Lyss had been training her soldiers for just this sort of fight, and they were able to counter the physical strength and stamina of the bloodsworn.

Jenna and Cas took to hunting at night. Not only were they harder to see from the ground, it was easier to spot the ruddy glow of bloodsworn magery in the dark. The empress's army never knew when a dragon was going to hurtle out of the night sky, spewing flame.

One night they were soaring over the dark eastern end of Alyssa Plateau, just to the west of Wolf's Head, when they saw what appeared to be a troop of horse soldiers riding hard for the coast. In their midst, they saw one small wagon with a canvas cover, pulled by four horses. And from inside, a telltale glow, like a ground-bound firefly.

Was it Celestine, with her bloodsworn escort? Gifted prisoners?

They circled lower, but even with Cas's sharp eyesight they couldn't tell whose side they were on. The riders all wore the fighting garb from the Desert Coast, but then, so did Lyss's reborn soldiers. It could be a scouting party under the queen's command.

"Can we go a little lower?" Jenna said.

The riders still seemed oblivious to their presence. Jenna's magemark hadn't responded, either, but it could be that they were still too far away.

Finally, several of the riders cried out and pointed at the sky. The horse troop stopped, forming a circle around the wagon. This seemed promising, but Jenna was still unsure. It could be prisoners in the wagon.

"Can you get close enough to rip off the covering, Cas?" Jenna said.

Cas made a wide circle, then swooped in low, crossbow bolts rattling against his armor, clawed feet extended to catch the tarp. As they closed in, the canvas rolled back, revealing not the empress but a cannon, primed and ready to fire. A trap.

"Up—up—up!"

Cas was already climbing, but too late.

*Boom!* Instinctively, Jenna closed her eyes and pressed her face against the saddle padding as a projectile exploded against Cas's armored head at close range. Cas screamed, a heart-rending cry that sliced deep as his fear and pain muscled their way into her head. Jenna was coughing, eyes streaming, face burning, until her scales emerged, deadening the pain somewhat.

Afraid to open her eyes, Jenna felt rather than saw the dragon's counterattack—blistering heat and the scent of burning flesh. And then Cas was climbing again, powering skyward with strong thrusts of his wings. When she opened her eyes, they'd passed the coastline, and she could smell the scent of the sea. Her eyes still stung and burned.

*Ocean?* Cas said, his desperation arrowing through the both of them. *Smell ocean. Is that ocean?*

"Yes," Jenna said, bewildered. "Can't you—?"

*Jenna hold on.*

She had time to take a quick breath before Cas plunged into the cold sea, driving salt water up her nose. The young dragon plowed forward, slicing through the surface before he broke free and launched skyward. Water streamed off them. Jenna coughed, trying to clear her throat of salt water.

Cas careened wildly sideways, all but dunking them a second time, then skimmed along the water's surface, allowing the water to sluice over his head. Jenna could feel the panic rising in him.

"Cas! What is it?"

*Eyes hurt. Can't see.*

Jenna pressed herself against Cas's scales and looked out through the dragon's eyes. She saw only a white haze.

*Can't see—can't see—can't see!*

He careened sideways into the water again—this time, close to the rugged shoreline, in water so shallow that he could stand up, the water just breaking over his back. Still, he flailed his wings, splashing water everywhere in his panic, bucking and twisting so that Jenna could barely keep her seat.

*Can't see. Can't see*, Cas whimpered, over and over. Jenna understood. While dragons had excellent hearing and sense of smell, they were primarily visual creatures. Like birds, they relied on their vision to locate prey from high above, to find enemies and prospective mates. A dragon without eyes wouldn't survive for long.

And then, when it seemed that things couldn't get any worse, Jenna's magemark began to burn.

She looked shoreward and saw several small boats launching from the spit of sand at the base of the cliffs. Jenna didn't need to see their auras to know that the boat crews were bloodsworn—nobody else would row a small boat toward a flailing dragon.

And there, at the top of the cliff, stood the empress, her silver hair twisting in the onshore winds, her stormcoat whipping around her body.

"Jenna!" she called. "Don't worry. Leap free of the beast, and my crew will pick you up."

Jenna looked past her, still blinking away tears. When she scanned the clifftop, she saw something most humans would never have noticed—Celestine's soldiers muscling two massive cannons toward the cliff's edge.

She saw the plan immediately—as soon as Jenna leapt clear, they would fire down on Cas from the safety of the heights and finish him.

Rage welled up in Jenna, her skin going numb as more scales surfaced.

*Jenna jump?* She could feel the dragon's racing heart, every heaving breath.

"I'm not going anywhere," she said. She crept forward, over

the dragon's collar of spines and onto his head, grateful for her body armor, as there was no part of his head and shoulders that wasn't stippled. She carefully positioned herself between his two largest spines, keeping most of her body weight on his neck and shoulders. She wrapped her arms around his neck and lay flat, so that she was just even with his eyes.

"Use my eyes, Cas," she said. She had to repeat it several times before it penetrated the panicked dragon's mind.

"Jenna!" the empress shouted, anger and impatience creeping into her honey voice. "I *said*, jump before you get hurt. Be sensible."

Meanwhile, the boats were drawing closer, though they seemed at risk of capsizing in the roiled waters.

Taking a deep breath, Jenna dove into the dragon's mind, merged with it, let go of Jenna Bandelow to help her friend in the only way she could.

Cas's flailing slowed, stopped. His heart steadied. And then they were one mind, one fierce heart, one pair of clear eyes. Their vision was better than Jenna's, maybe not as good as Cas's, but . . . enough.

They devised a plan. *Burn boats. Fly. Burn Silverhair.*

They looked up. By now, the cannon were just peeking over the rim. The boats were close now, cautiously nosing forward, the crew preparing to toss a rope to Jenna.

*Burn boats.*

They put their feet down, raised their head, and sent flame sheeting over the water's surface, enveloping the oncoming boats. Then they plunged toward shore, smashing through the burning flotilla, through a school of struggling bloodsworn, seeking shallower water so that they could get a running start.

Humans shouted; heavy wheels creaked as the guns rolled forward. The silver-haired human called, "Don't shoot! I want the girl alive!"

*Fly.*

They pushed away from the ground, reaching for air, soaring up, up, up—out over the ocean as they gained altitude.

*Burn Silverhair.*

They made a wide circle, then sped back toward the cliffs, the tiny figures at the top growing larger as they hurtled toward them. Humans scrambled, diving into holes, behind rocks. Except the one with the silver hair. She stood frozen for a moment, like a star caught on the edge of the firmament, staring at them as if captivated. Then she raised her arm and sent flame screaming toward them. They rolled sideways to avoid it, and by the time they came around again, she was gone.

Furious, they scorched the clifftop until the cannons were reduced to puddles of metal and the white chalk of the cliff was charred a smoky gray. Below, in the water, the remains of the launches still smoldered.

*Go back. Heal eyes.*

It was a prayer as much as a plan.

# 67

# ARRIVALS AND DEPARTURES

Destin looked up as the healer crawled out of the tent they'd erected over Flamecaster's head. By then, it was full dark, the only light coming from the hearth and the wizard lights set around the perimeter. "Well?" he said, setting his plate aside. "Does the face guard help?" Destin had devised a cage-like headgear to protect the dragon's injured eyes.

Prince Adrian—Ash—rocked his hand. "It works really well when we can keep him from scraping it off," he said. "The only way he'll tolerate it is if he's stone drunk." He paused. "He's sleeping now. Thanks for the turtleweed and brandy. It did the trick." Ash scrubbed his hands thoroughly before he sat down by the fire.

"Let me know if you need any more," Destin said, passing him a jacket of ale and a full plate.

Lyss had established a separate camp for the flying battalion—the dragons and their human companions. It prevented unfortunate incidents between the armies of the Realms and their winged allies. It had become a habit for Destin and Hal to walk down at dusk to dine with the flyers—Jenna and Ash, and sometimes Lyss and Sasha, when they could get away.

On this night a pall hung over the camp because of Cas's injury. Ash sat next to Jenna, obviously trying to soothe her, but she was all but inconsolable.

Jenna came up on her knees, hands planted on her thighs. "What about his vision? Is there any improvement? Is he going to be able to see?" Her tone suggested that there was only one right answer to that question.

The healer hesitated. "I hope so," he said. "It seems to have been some kind of caustic chemical. It's lucky he was smart enough to keep rinsing his eyes, or it might be even worse."

"How could it be worse?" Jenna muttered. "He needs his eyes."

"He could be dead," Ash said. "*You* could be dead."

"The empress should be dead," Jenna growled, her hair flickering around her head like flames, her skin shimmering with heat. "I'm going to kill her."

She was fierce in the Ardenscourt dungeon, Destin thought. She's even more dragon-like now.

"I don't care who kills Celestine as long as somebody does," Sasha said, reaching for another biscuit. "Sooner rather than later."

It had been two days since the attack. Two days during which Ash and Jenna traded off tending to Flamecaster while the other dragons tried to help. All day, they'd bring small offerings—meats and quail eggs and fish and precious baubles, sea glass from the beach. Bits of armor and weapons from recent kills. Cas just roared at them until the brandy took effect. He was not a very good patient.

"It's my fault," Jenna said, poking at the fire until it sent up sparks. "I told Cas to go close so we could get a better look. I was careless, overconfident." She thrust her stick into the flames so hard that it broke. "And now he's paid an awful price."

"If it's all the same to you," Lyss said, "I'll blame the empress."

The other dragons were still out hunting. It seemed a shame that after a day of fighting, they had to go out and hunt their own dinner. The young dragons required huge amounts of fresh meat daily.

Destin watched the dragons with wary fascination. From what Jenna said, Evan had managed to win them over. But then Evan was warm and charming. Destin couldn't say the same for himself.

"Look," Hal said. "We've been gaining ground every day. Before long, we'll push them into the sea."

"We've burned most of their ships," Sasha said. "There aren't enough left to carry them all home. Anyway, we don't want to send Celestine's army back to her."

"We can't leave them to roam the countryside," Hal said. "Most didn't join the empress's army of their own free will."

"Quite a few of them are northerners," Lyss said, picking at a scab on her arm. After a long pause, she added, "I suppose I have a little more blood left."

Destin raised an eyebrow. "After your initial reluctance, you seem to have climbed aboard the blood mage wagon."

"As an alternative to slaughter, yes," Lyss said, lifting her chin and looking him in the eye.

Don't irritate the monarch, Destin thought. Especially the one who affiliates with dragons.

"Anyway," Jenna said, shifting on the ground. "We haven't

won yet. That's where I made my mistake—thinking we'd won." She paused. "I think we're missing something."

"What are we missing?" Ash said.

"The empress. I'm worried that she's left the Fells," she said. "My magemark burns when she's close." She rubbed the back of her neck. "It's gone totally cold."

That stopped the conversation in its tracks.

"Well, good," Sasha said unconvincingly. "Maybe we've driven her off."

"Why would she go and leave her army here?" Hal said finally.

"She doesn't care about her soldiers," Lyss said. "In her mind, they are totally expendable. She can always make more."

"But . . . if she wants to win here, she has to stay in the game," Destin said. "She can't fight a war from Carthis." Even as he said this, worry kindled in his gut. *If Evan's still alive, he's in Carthis.*

"All I can figure is that she has business elsewhere," Jenna said.

"Maybe she's found a way to hide her presence," Ash suggested.

"Maybe," Jenna said. "Or maybe the attack on me and Cas was a last-ditch effort to take me with her."

"But it doesn't make sense," Hal persisted. "Who's leading the bloodsworn, if not Celestine?"

"General Gray?" The voice came from beyond the light of the campfire, startling them, sending them scrambling for their weapons.

Sasha stepped in front of Lyss, sword drawn. Destin stepped up beside her, his hand on his amulet.

"It's Munroe Graves." The speaker came forward, into the light, hands in the air. He looked to be a Carthian officer, dressed in the garb of a horselord.

"Graves!" Sasha let the tip of her sword drop a bit. "What the hell are you doing here—dressed like that?"

Lyss stepped around her brace of would-be guardians and embraced him. "Thank the Maker! I kept looking for you on the plateau. When I didn't see you, I was afraid you might be dead."

"The empress has been keeping me on a tight rein," Graves said, "especially since the tide of the fighting began to turn against her."

"Who is this, exactly?" Hal said, stowing his sword, but keeping his hand on the hilt.

"Graves was an artilleryman in the Highlanders," Lyss said. "He was captured at Chalk Cliffs and ganged into the empress's army as an officer, serving under me. Celestine took him with her when she came up here to find out why her armies weren't making any progress."

"How were you able to break away tonight?" Jenna asked.

"The empress hasn't been seen for three days," Graves said. "It took me that long to decide that it wasn't some kind of trick. I went down to Wolf's Head today. She's been keeping her flagship moored there, out of sight, and out of the line of fire. It's gone, and so is her regular crew."

Jenna looked around at the others, collecting silent apologies.

"Where do you think she's gone?" Lyss said.

"If I had to guess, I'd say she's gone back to Carthis," Graves said. "Or Celesgarde."

"Why would she up and leave now?" Sasha said. "Aside from the fact that we're kicking her ass."

"I'm guessing it's a strategic retreat, more than a rout," Hal said.

"What's that?" Jenna was looking toward the sky.

After a moment, Destin heard it, too. The beating of wings, the screams of multiple dragons. Here they came, like so many shooting stars. One—two—three—hang on—*four*? He glanced over at Cas, as if he might have crept away and joined his brethren when they weren't looking.

The others heard now, and stood, all except Graves, who took off running into the night. Goat's scream split the air as he spiraled down and landed way too close, moving so much air that he nearly put out the campfire. The others followed, circling, landing.

The newcomer was the last to land. It crouched, head drooping so that its chin nearly touched the ground. It appeared totally spent.

"Splash!" Jenna said. "What are you doing here?"

"Splash?" Destin looked to Ash.

"She went to Carthis with Breon and Evan," Ash said.

The implications of that hit Destin like a fist to the gut. This dragon had been with Evan, and she'd come back alone.

"What's happened?" Jenna said. "Where are the others?"

There was a long pause while the dragon delivered an explanation that Destin couldn't hear. The growing horror on Jenna's face told him that it wasn't good news.

Jenna swore. "How long ago did this happen?"

Another pause.

"Maybe that's why the empress left," Ash said.

"But how would she know about it?" Jenna said. She turned back to Splash. "Where's Splinter?"

There was another, longer wait. Ash had pulled out a small journal and had begun taking notes.

At the end of it, Ash and Jenna turned to the others, who had been watching the one-sided conversation with growing alarm.

"One of the empress's shiplords, Tully Samara, captured Strangward and Breon in one of the sea caves along the coast. The dragons couldn't get in, but they listened to the conversation," Jenna said.

"Apparently, Samara is taking them to Celesgarde to meet the empress," Ash added. "Splinter followed them, while Splash came to warn us."

"And—and Breon sang a song and told the dragons to remember it and repeat it to us." Jenna looked at Ash, who read from his notes.

*Followed ship. Samara tricky maybe. Spellsinger sang song, said sing to you, you come help.*
*This is where it all begins.*
*This is where it all ends.*
*The shattering*
*The rejoining*
*Forged in the bleeding earth.*
*As it has been, it shall be again.*
*At midsummer,*
*When the sun pauses in the sky.*

They all looked at each other.

"What the hell does that mean?" Destin snapped, every muscle taut as a bowstring.

"I remember that," Lyss said. "He sang it when we were together in Celesgarde."

"That's Breon's gift," Sasha said. "He captures people's songs, and it gives him some power over them."

"What does that mean—the 'bleeding earth'?" Hal said. "A mineral spring? A clay-stained river?"

"Most of the rivers in Carthis come from snowmelt in the Dragonbacks," Destin said. "They are clear trout streams."

"What about in the Northern Islands?"

"There's not a lot of fresh water there," Jenna said. "It's pretty active volcanically."

Goat seemed to be trying to get Ash's attention, poking his head in front of his face, then nudging him when that didn't work.

"Hang on. Goat thinks he knows what it means. Does anyone have a map of the Northern Islands?" Ash said.

Lyss did, and they spread it out on a flat rock. "There." Ash traced the spot with his forefinger. There were sketchy lines across one of the islands, the one closest to the mainland. Destin leaned close, but he could barely make out the text. *Demon's Wounds.*

"That has to be it," Jenna said.

"That has to be what?" Hal said.

"The bleeding earth. We flew over it at night. The islands looked like scabbed-over wounds, the lava flows like blood."

"I think this is important," Lyss said. "Breon kept warning us that the empress would be coming back to Carthis at midsummer. Like in the song."

"When's Midsummer's Day?" Destin said. "I've lost track."

"It's three days away," Jenna said.

Destin stood, clenching and unclenching his hands, body canted like a racehorse at the gate. "I need to get to the Northern Islands before then," he said. "Do you think one of the dragons would take me there? Is there something they might want, a reward I could offer? Is there something that I could do for them in return?"

Though Destin tried to make it cool, transactional, he knew that he sounded like a desperate man.

Jenna reached out and put a hand on his shoulder, and he flinched.

"Why don't you ask them?" she said.

He looked up, met her eyes. "Just speak to them," she said softly. "Make your case."

Destin faced the dragons, who were watching him curiously. He licked his lips, like a student at a recital. He wasn't used to asking for anything. Bargaining, threatening, deceiving, yes.

"I wondered if . . . one of you might be willing to carry me to Celesgarde." He waited. They crowded in closer, but he stood his ground.

"They can hear you," Jenna said. "But if you want to hear them, you need to find their voices. It helps if you make physical contact, the first time, anyway."

"One of them, or . . . all of them?" Destin said.

"Start with one," Jenna said.

Destin edged closer to Splash, planted his feet, took a deep breath, and said, "Is it all right if I touch you?"

Splash tilted her head toward him, all but putting her chin on the ground. Destin laid his palm against the dragon's shoulder and asked again. "Would you take me to Evan and Breon on the bleeding island? I want to help them. I want to save them." He swallowed hard. "In return, if there's anything you want, a service I can do for you . . . ?"

*Scratch my head. Behind horns.*

Destin blinked at her. He glanced at Ash, wondering if he might have misunderstood, and Ash nodded. "Go ahead," he said.

Destin reached for a lightly armored spot just behind her horns. He rubbed it gently, then scratched the scaly places where horn met flesh. Splash reacted like a cat, contorting herself so that Destin could do an even better job.

Destin looked into the dragon's emerald eyes and murmured, "You are beautiful."

*Splash sleep. Then fly to bleeding island with sad Destin.*

Pricker nudged Splash aside. *Splash too tired. Pricker fly to bleeding island with sad Destin.*

"Why are they calling me that?" Destin said, looking up at Ash and Jenna. "Sad Destin, I mean?"

"Dragons read emotion along with whatever you're saying," Jenna said. "That's why it's never a good idea to try to lie to them."

"Oh," Destin said, flinching, wishing he could close the doors to his private thoughts.

"So they can tell that you are worried about the pirate. They can tell you care about him, and—"

"All right," Destin said quickly. "I get it."

Ash cleared his throat. "If you're going up against Celestine and her stormborn, you're going to need another wizard along," he said. "I'll come with you."

Destin stared at him. "But—you and your sister just reunited. You're a prince of the realm. You—"

"I'm expendable," Ash said. "I'm the spare, remember?"

"You are *not* expendable," Lyss growled.

"Your Majesty, requesting permission to go to the Northern Islands," Sasha said. Everyone turned and stared at her, and she flushed crimson. "If Pricker will take me, I mean. I'm good with a sword, and I'm not critical to the war effort here. Prince Adrian is a member of the royal family, and should not go off without a guard."

"I *think* I see what you mean," Lyss said. "I'll allow you to go, Talbot, on the condition that you come back alive."

"I'm going, too," Jenna said. "This is my fight. It's been my fight from the beginning."

"That's a bad idea," Ash said. "Celestine has been hunting you for years, and now you want to walk right into her hands when's she's holding two more magemarked?"

"*I've* been hunting *her*," Jenna said. "I chased her all the way to Carthis and back again."

"Does she know that?" Ash said, raising an eyebrow.

For a moment, Jenna seemed to be at a loss for words. Then she said, "She'll know I was there when she gets to Celesgarde and finds it destroyed. Anyway, I don't *intend* to walk right into her hands."

"If we both go, who's going to look after Cas?" Ash said.

It turned into a free-for-all, with all the dragons and most of the humans wanting to come along.

Destin looked from person to person, ambushed by their willingness to join with him. He'd been the enemy of some of them for years. Some others he'd just met. They had a war to finish here, rebellions and governments in shambles all over the Realms, deaths to mourn, crimes to punish. Granted, Celestine had proven to be the enemy to both Arden and the Fells, but dealing with an enemy across the sea is more easily deferred than any close-up crisis.

"Look," Destin said, "I hoped at least one of the dragons would be willing to come with me, but I never thought to draw more volunteers. For those of you who haven't been to Carthis, it's not exactly the garden spot of the world. Plus, we'll probably all die."

"The Northern Islands are worse than Carthis," Jenna said. "Just being honest," she added.

"Well, we can't all go. There *is* a war to fight here," Lyss said. "But I think this mission is important to the Realms, beyond our—beyond our desire to get our friends back. We have every reason to believe that Celestine is hunting the magemarked because they make her more powerful. We can't afford to have her come back stronger than before. So. We need to choose those best suited for the job."

"It doesn't make sense for Queen Alyssa or Mat—ah—King Halston to go," Sasha said. "You're both needed here, to lead the armies now and to rule when the war is over."

"I should go," Jenna said. "For reasons already mentioned."

So, in the end, it was decided that the team would comprise Destin and Splash, Jenna and Ash with Goat, and Sasha and Pricker. Lyss and Slayer would care for Cas and work the war in the Realms, along with Shadow and Lila.

# DOMUS NAZARI

Evan Strangward hadn't been seasick since he was a boy—during his first year serving under Latham Strangward. He'd sailed some rough waters since then, but the remedy for rough waters was always his skills as a ship's master and weather magery. Now both he and Breon were locked in the hold of Tully Samara's ship as it pitched and rolled in the currents off Carthis Head, and Evan was horribly, humiliatingly sick. He felt sorry for Breon, having to put up with it. He didn't even want to be with himself.

He tried to calm the winds and quiet the seas, but it was like trying to force water through a closed spigot. With the collar locked around his neck, he couldn't find the ocean currents, nor grab the air flowing through his fingers, nor pull lightning down from wherever it lay hidden until he called it.

Samara made no effort to relieve the discomfort of his unwilling guests. Apparently, the empress's sole stipulation was that they arrive alive before midsummer's day. Locked in the hold as they were, there was no chance they would spook the crew or throw themselves overboard.

Breon didn't try to engage Evan in conversation. He spent

most of his time sleeping or daydreaming or singing softly. Even without his spellsinger gift, his voice was soothing.

Eventually, the seas subsided, the ship steadied, and Evan's stomach quit churning. He assumed that meant they'd crossed the channel into the shelter of the islands. Soon after that, he heard the rattle of the chain as they dropped anchor.

"Well," Evan said, "it seems we've arrived." *When Celestine sees what's happened to her new capital, maybe she'll kill you outright.*

They heard voices approaching—Samara's silky baritone and the familiar voice of the empress. The hatch to the hold was lifted away, casting a square of light onto the floor.

"What is that stench?" Celestine demanded, pressing her gauntleted arm across her nose.

"It seems that the Stormcaster cannot stomach a channel crossing," Samara said scornfully.

The empress leaned in, casting her long shadow across the floor. When she saw Evan and Breon, her face went chalk white and her eyes darkened from a lavender to a bruised plum. "How dare you allow Nazari princes to lie, bound hand and foot, in their own sick and scummer?"

"Y—Your Eminence," Samara said, his arrogance sliding off him like a seal from a rock, "I thought you would be pleased that I—"

"They are blood of my blood, born to restore this lineage to its former glory." She sat back on her heels. "I have been too long in the wetlands, it seems. When I left you in charge of my holdings here, I assumed you were up to the task. Now I return to find the entire Desert Coast in rebellion, my capital in ruins, and my line disrespected."

Samara seized on the last piece of that. "But . . . they are disloyal connivers. The Stormcaster admitted that he destroyed your new capital. The spellsinger will betray you the first chance he gets."

"Of course he did," Celestine said. "Of course he will. That's what we do. That's what keeps the Line fresh and strong. This is how we win back the empire."

To see the shiplord's expression was almost worth the price of admission. Clearly, he believed that the empress was not playing by the standard rules of royal fratricide.

"Cut them loose," Celestine said. "Get them fresh clothes and a bath. I'm not bringing them aboard my ship in that condition. Mind that you tread carefully, Captain. I will demand from them a full accounting of their treatment." And then she disappeared again.

It wasn't easy for Evan to get into the tub after days of lying on the floor in one position, but Samara assigned two of his bloodsworn crew to assist. The hot water did wonders for Evan's muscles and joints. Getting rid of his filthy clothes did wonders for his mood. When he scrubbed under the silver collar, his fingers found his magemark and he realized that it hadn't responded to Celestine's presence.

When they emerged on deck for the first time, he saw that they were anchored in the familiar harbor at Celesgarde, surrounded by the ruins of the city. The *Siren* was anchored nearby. Evan saw no signs of life along the waterfront or among the buildings on the shoreline. It looked much as they'd left it when they'd departed for Carthis, down to and including the remains of their camp next to the tumbledown palace. Yet the empress seemed more energized than angry about it. To a point, Evan could sympathize with Samara's confusion.

But only to a point.

The empress sent a skiff to fetch them back to her ship. Samara wasn't invited. It was just her bloodsworn crew and the three of them. When they were almost to the ship, a shadow fell over them. The crew pointed, shouting, "Dreki!"

Evan looked up and saw a dragon fly over the harbor, its flight just a bit erratic. Familiar. Recognition pinged through him. Splinter. He must have followed them after they left the cave.

Before he could react, or shout a warning, a greeting, anything, Celestine launched a bolt of lightning, sending the dragon tumbling tail over head, disappearing into a clump of trees. Evan kept watching the spot where he'd gone down, hoping to see movement, signs of life.

Nothing. Evan's heart clenched, hoping the young dragon wasn't one more casualty in this endless hunt.

As soon as they boarded, the *Siren* raised anchor and left the harbor, sailing southeast before the wind. Evan and Breon moved as far forward as they could, enjoying the wind in their faces after so long locked up in the hold.

At first, Evan thought they might be returning to Carthis, but instead of sliding between the two southernmost islands and into the straits, *Siren* turned sharply east, circling the easternmost of the islands and slipping into a protected harbor on the far side.

I know this place, Evan thought. Scent and sound dragged him into the past. Memories flickered through his head—of he and his brothers and sisters packed into a small boat, sliding through the cove in the dark. Then there came a clamor of alarm on the shore, a flotilla of boats giving chase, plunging through a storm, the rain and seawater mingling with the tears on his face. Crying for his sister. Crying out for his brother, Jak. Crying for the only home he'd ever known.

As soon as they dropped anchor, Celestine came forward and found Evan and Breon huddled together in the bow, both crying, overwhelmed with loss.

Celestine looked perplexed, even alarmed for a moment, and then her eyes fastened on Evan's collar. "Ah," she said, ruffling his hair. "It's all right. You don't need this anymore. You're home now." Kneeling, she fished a key from her carry bag, unlocked and removed their collars. "You won't be needing those here," she said, dropping them onto the deck. Extending her hand, she helped first Breon, then Evan to his feet.

The first thing Evan noticed was his magemark. Now that the collar was gone, it was pleasantly warm, sending soothing tendrils of heat over his shoulders, deep into his muscles and down his arms. It radiated calm, up through the base of his skull, down through his body to the soles of his feet so that he felt like a tree taking root. All of the aches and pains from the voyage here faded away, replaced by a sense of peace and well-being. Breon, too, looked smitten. He fingered the back of his neck, his face lit up with wonder.

Celestine smiled at their moonstruck expressions. "It's lovely, isn't it?"

Evan was enchanted by the beauty all around him—the small, round pebbles on the rocky shore, the peaks, partially clothed in evergreens, that rose from the sea, the waterfalls cascading down from high valleys, plumes of spray at their feet. The colors of the pines, the sea, and stone so vivid they hurt his eyes. So vivid that they smothered the whispered warning in the back of his mind.

Next to the shore stood a high-roofed longhouse built of red timber and gray stone. Clustered around it, brightly painted houses reflected in the still waters of the cove.

The air was intoxicating, perfumed with flowers and a hint of sulfur. The scent penetrated to the bone, in the way of memories from childhood. Evan felt relaxed, almost floppy—embraced. When he looked over the gunwales, the water below the keel of their ship was crystal clear and seemed to go down hundreds of feet. What would it be like to dive into the water and keep swimming down?

"It's an old volcanic crater," Celestine said, noticing him staring down into the water.

"Where are we?" Evan asked.

"We are home," she said simply. "This is the ancestral home of the Nazari, where our stories have always begun and ended," she said, echoing the song Breon had been singing. "It is the foundation of our power, the seat of our legacy."

"It's nice," Evan said, his murky mind unable to come up with anything more descriptive than that. "I feel like I know this place."

"We were all born here," she said. "We lived here together until you were taken away from me."

"Who took us away from you?" Breon said.

"Enemies of the Nazari line," Celestine said. "They trapped me here and took you away. At midsummer, six years ago."

Being trapped here wouldn't be so bad, Evan thought.

Loosing the bindings on the skiff, Celestine swung it over the side and cranked it down into the water.

"Come," she said. "Let's go ashore."

Breon looked back toward his cabin. "Should we bring our—?"

"No," Celestine said. "Everything you need is here." She disappeared over the side.

Everything we need is here, Evan thought. But Breon scooped up the silver collars and slid them inside his coat.

I should tell Celestine about the collars, Evan thought. But he wasn't going to rat on his brother.

They climbed down the ladder after Celestine and found seats on the center thwarts. She handled the oars. They were languid passengers. Evan trailed his hand in the water.

A small crowd of bloodsworn stood on the shore, waiting for them.

"Welcome back, Empress," they said, hauling the skiff onto the beach. "Welcome, Princes."

Princes, Evan thought. We're princes. He could smell the scent of roasting meat emanating from one of the smaller buildings. His mouth watered and his stomach growled. He'd eaten next to nothing on Samara's ship, and now he was ravenous.

Celestine led them into the longhouse. It was as beautiful inside as it was on the outside. It had high, beamed ceilings and a massive stone hearth at the center open on four sides with a chimney at its center that stretched all the way to the roof. The sides of the Great Hall were lined with curtained-off sleeping benches. At one end was a passageway to a barn. At the other, a hallway with bedrooms and a library, each with hearths of their own.

Breon and Evan followed Celestine down the hallway to their rooms. "Rest and relax for now," she said, "while I prepare for tonight."

"What's tonight?" Breon said.

"It is Midsummer's Eve, when the Nazari magic comes closest to the surface." She took their hands. "Can you feel it?"

Magic seethed through all three of them, a connection, unbreakable, inviolate. They were a chain of magic, with Celestine at the center.

So this is what it's like to have a family, Evan thought, his heart full to bursting. Yet a memory flickered in the back of his mind, like a warning beacon on a faraway hill.

"You see?" Celestine breathed. "We belong together. We always have. After tonight, you will never be alone. Tonight, you join the Nazari line. Tonight, we rise." She paused. "Say it with me now, in the tradition of the Nazari. 'Tonight, we rise together.'"

"Tonight, we rise together," they recited, like speakers at the temple.

"You'll find suitable clothing for the ceremony laid out in your rooms. The attendants will come for you when it is time."

And she walked away, back toward the great hall. Evan listened until the sounds of her footsteps faded, feeling a profound sense of loss.

Evan went into his room, sat down on the bed and ran his fingers over the clothes. Silk and wool, he thought. Silver and blue, to match his hair. Dress clothes and smallclothes. Very fine, and they looked like they would fit.

He opened the trunk at the foot of his bed. It was empty. There was just the one set of clothes.

It hadn't occurred to him to ask how long they would be staying.

It hadn't occurred to him to ask any questions at all.

Strange. He was usually a curious kind of person. Now it was an effort for him to keep moving.

This is home, he thought. This is where your story began.

He slipped to the floor and walked out into the hallway. Breon's door was open. The spellsinger was lying on his bed, staring up at nothing, opening and closing one of the silver collars, as if fascinated by the soft *click* the latch made.

"Why did you bring that along?" Evan said. It made him uneasy for some reason.

Breon eyed it, looking a little perplexed, as if having trouble remembering. "Silver is valuable," he said. "Silver sells for a good price at the market." He ran his fingers over the buffed surface. "Aubrey always said that once you get your hands on some silver, the rest comes easy." His face clouded. "Aubrey," he whispered.

Evan had no idea who Aubrey was, but it didn't matter. "Everything is here," he said. "This is where it begins."

"This is where is all ends," Breon recited, as if the words had lost their meaning. "The shattering, the rejoining, forged in the bleeding earth . . ." His voice trailed off. "I forget the rest."

"Let's go look in the library," Evan said. "Maybe there's a book."

Breon shrugged, rolled off the bed, and followed Evan across the hall. They stood, side by side, in the arched entrance to the library. The walls were lined with shelves of leather-bound books, enough for a lifetime of reading.

As if in a dream, Evan ghosted along the shelves, scanning the bindings. He could make out most of the words, although the titles were in a language more akin to Fellsian than the language spoken along the Desert Coast.

Breon wandered over to a large, round table, with an elaborately bound book lying on it.

"Evan. Look at this."

Evan left off reading book spines and came to see. Breon traced the title of the book with his forefinger. It was stamped in gold—*Domus Nazari*. House Nazari.

Under the book, embedded into the top of the table, was a large metal device under glass—a disk made of what appeared to be copper, gold, silver, and precious stones. It was centered by a human figure, surrounded by five segments spoking out—copper, red, blue, silver, and gold. Each segment was inscribed with symbols. The emblems on the silver segment resembled wind and wave and cloud. The blue reminded him of a geometric puzzle knot. The copper was a rune like a many-headed beast.

"It matches our pendants. See?" Breon set his pendant on the tabletop. The gold segment of the disk in the table matched Breon's fragment, down to the harp engraved on it.

Evan pulled his pendant from under his shirt and laid it beside Breon's. The fragment he had matched the silver and blue segments, though the pendant wasn't colored. It was plain, time-darkened silver.

Silver and blue, like the streaks in his hair.

Evan scooped up his pendant and opened the book.

One of the first pages was an engraving—a gathering of celebrants on an arching bridge over a river of flame. One of them, larger and more resplendent than the rest, seemed to be dangling a child over the railing.

It looks like some sort of ceremony, Evan thought, a sacrifice, maybe.

Breon leaned in. "Looks like it must be hot up there."

Evan began leafing through time-yellowed pages written by many different hands. It appeared to be a genealogy of sorts, with one generation to a page. But with each generation, there was a reproduction of the disk in the table, with names inscribed in the segments and dates by the names. Some of the dates seemed to be so old that they came from a calendar he'd never seen.

In the first half of the book, all of the segments of the disks on each page were filled with names and dates. In later sections, most were blank.

Evan flipped to the back of the book, to the last page that was filled in.

*Iona Nazari* was written in script at the top of the page. Next to her name, the puzzle knot symbol.

Immediately below her name, Celestine Nazari, with the complete disk symbol next to her name. Two segments of the disk were filled in with names. *Jak Strangward. Claire Slavesh.* The other three segments were still blank.

Below Celestine's name was a heavily illuminated family tree, with Iona at the top and names written across, underneath.

Harol Strangward and, next to his name, the stormcaster symbol.

Branching down from him, two names:

Jak Strangward, and a date, and the knot symbol.

Evan Strangward, the knot symbol, and the stormcaster symbol. There was no date.

Another name. Karf Bandelow. Next to his name, the many-headed beast. Branching down from him, Jenna Bandelow, also with the many-headed beast. No date.

Next, Jaheen Alfarsi, with a harplike symbol next to his name. Below, Breon Alfarsi, with the same symbol, and no date.

Omar Slavesh, with a lightning-bolt symbol. Below him, Claire Slavesh, with the same symbol, and a date. Two years ago.

"Breon Alfarsi," Breon whispered. "Son of Jaheen Alfarsi."

"Jak and Evan Strangward," Evan said. "Sons of Harol Strangward. Jenna Bandelow, daughter of Karf Bandelow."

"Celestine said she was my sister," Breon said. "We have the same mother. Iona."

"Iona was the empress before Celestine," Evan said. "But we must be half brothers and sisters, since we have different fathers." But Jak and I had the same father, he thought. Harol Strangward. Evan fingered his magemark, still warm, and vibrating with power. Did Jak have the same magemark as me?

"Look at my magemark, Ev," Breon said abruptly. "I think some of these symbols are in it." He leaned forward, bracing his hands on his knees, so Evan could get a better view.

"Here's the harp," Evan said, tracing it with his fingers. "The same as Jaheen Alfarsi's."

Breon straightened. "Do you think the symbols represent the gifts we've inherited from our fathers?"

"Maybe." The longer Evan looked at it, the more convinced he became it was true. Each father brought a different gift. A shape-shifter. A spellsinger. A blood mage. An elemental mage. Each child inherited at least one gift. Almost as if the fathers had been chosen specifically for that purpose—for the gifts they brought to the Line.

He studied the page. "Where's Celestine's father?" Evan muttered. "There's nobody listed for her."

There was something Evan should be remembering, but, try as he might, he couldn't get his mind around it, or even conjure up much desire to solve it. It was distant, academic, as if someone had dumped a box of puzzle pieces on the table, and Evan's reaction was, "Huh. A puzzle."

He closed the book, thinking, "Maybe I'll take a nap until it's time to get dressed for dinner."

He heard Breon fumbling with something, but he paid no attention until he felt cold metal on his neck and heard the soft *click* as the collar latched. He jerked away and landed hard on his tailbone on the library floor. Instantly, all of his aches and pains flooded back, along with a deep-seated, unreasoning terror.

Evan reached up and fingered the collar. "What the— Why did you do that?"

"I shouldn't have taken both of the collars," Breon said. "Silver is valuable, and this one belongs to you. So I gave it back." He extended his hand to help Evan up, but Evan shook his head. He remained splayed on the floor like a starfish as fragments of memory surfaced from the fog of tranquil wonder that had immersed him since their arrival. Since his collar came off, anyway.

He recalled the day he'd first met Celestine Nazari while crewing aboard Latham Strangward's ship. She'd claimed that Strangward's brother, Harol, had caused a falling-out between her and her mother and they had imprisoned her on this island.

*My mother loved me. Your thrice-damned brother turned her against me after Jak died.*

After Jak died. Harol was Evan's father—and Jak's, too.

*We were all born here,* Celestine had said earlier that day. *We lived here together until you were taken away from me. . . . They trapped me here and took you away. At midsummer, six years ago.*

There was something else—when they'd met that day off Tarvos, Celestine had had Claire's pendant. She said that Claire had given it to her. Something about the conversation left Evan thinking that Claire was dead, too.

And Jak and Claire were two pieces of Celestine's puzzle disk that were filled in.

Captain Strangward had said, *I have my faults, Celly, but at least I don't make war on children.*

The engraving of the ceremony on the bridge. The lake of fire below. Midsummer—when the Nazari magic comes closest to the surface.

Their magemarks were the emblems of the gifts they brought to the Nazari line, courtesy of their fathers. There was something about this place—and their magemarks—that rendered them docile, going like lambs to the slaughter. And prevented them from remembering the danger they were in.

But Celestine had miscalculated. She'd used the collars so that he and Breon couldn't use their gifts against her. She hadn't realized that the collars rendered the magemarks ineffective in other ways as well.

That's when Evan knew, with startling clarity—his father had tried to save them. He'd tried to save them all.

Tonight is Midsummer's Eve. Tonight we rise. And after tonight, Celestine would be stronger than before. A tsunami of danger was rushing at them, and they were pointing and saying, "Look! A wave."

"Evan? Are you all right?"

Evan looked up to find Breon still peering down at him. The spellsinger extended his hand again, and this time, Evan took it. "I'm sorry," Breon said. "I didn't mean to startle you."

Just then, Evan heard boots on the tile in the corridor outside. "Don't tell her I'm here," Evan hissed. "If she sees me in
the collar, she'll know you took them." He dove behind a cart
stacked with books, layered in dust.

"What are you doing here?" Looking out through gaps in the
stacks, Evan could see Celestine in the doorway, frozen midstep.

Evan prayed to all the gods he knew, and some he'd only
heard of. Please. Help him pull this off.

"I like books," Breon said, totally without guile. He waved
a hand at the stacks. "There are lots of books here." Then he
added, almost defensively, "I read a little, though mostly I look
at the pictures."

Celestine smiled. "I like books, too," she said. "I used to
spend hours here in the library, reading about the old ways. I
knew more than anyone, even my mother." She walked to the
round table, picked up *Domus Nazari*, cradling it in one arm.

"What's that book?" Breon said.

Evan's heart all but stopped.

The empress's grip tightened, knuckles whitened. "Just a
history of our family," she said. "I need it to prepare for the
ceremony. You'll learn all about it tonight."

"I can't wait," Breon said.

Celestine frowned, looked around. "Where's your brother?"

Breon shrugged. "He was here a little while ago."

"Why don't you choose a book to read and take it back to
your room," Celestine said. Then she turned and walked out.
Evan shivered as beads of cold sweat broke out all over him.

When he was sure she was gone, he stood, mopping his face
with his sleeve.

"Let's go back to your room. Hurry."

# DEMON'S WOUNDS

Several times during the flight over the Indio, Destin would awake in a panic, his head full of troubled dreams. How could he possibly fall asleep riding a dragon on his way to the fight of his life?

But the warmth of the dragon's body seeped into him, and the rhythms of flight were soothing, and for long periods they were above the clouds, so there was little to see and no real sense of altitude. He couldn't see the others who were spread out behind them, but he could "hear" fragments of conversation, mind-to-mind.

Destin and Splash, Jenna and Ash with Goat, and Sasha and Pricker. Destin still couldn't quite believe that they'd all come to help him free Celestine's captives.

Communication with dragons turned out to be easy and natural, once he'd broken through the initial barrier so that he could hear their voices. They were easier to hear than humans, in fact, when flying in formation.

The others were letting Destin and Splash take the lead, since Splash, at least, had an idea where they might be going.

*Sleep now, Sad Destin,* Splash said. *See Spellsinger and Pirate soon maybe.*

"Maybe."

They'd seen no sign of the dragon called Splinter so far.

They were descending through clouds now. Destin's ears seemed to pop several times. And then they were below the clouds. It was Solstice Eve, and they were far to the north, so the sun was still visible over the western horizon. He recognized the northernmost piece of Carthis, known as the head, from maps he'd seen in the past.

Splash turned north, following the coast up until the first of the Northern Islands came into view. This should be the island that Jenna had identified—the wounded island, where the blood of the earth broke through the surface.

But what if they were looking in the wrong place? he thought. What if Celestine had taken her prisoners to Deepwater Court, or Tarvos? What if they were already dead?

*Spellsinger and Pirate not dead.*

"Stop listening in my head."

*Stop shouting in my ear.*

For a person used to keeping secrets, a friendship with a dragon was challenging.

They circled high over the island whose peaks were shrouded in cloud.

Destin squinted down at the matted clouds. "Do you see anything?" he said.

*Go see.* With that, the dragon folded his wings and plummeted toward the ground, through layers of damp cloud. As soon as they broke into the clear, he spread his wings and shot across the island. Destin had time to see a protected harbor empty of ships, a kind of lodge, lit from within, and long streaks of lava, like angry orange fingers stretching down the mountain. Then, wings beating strongly, Splash gained altitude again.

*Did not see Spellsinger or Pirate.*

"No," Destin said, fingering his midsection to see where his stomach might have ended up, "but they might be inside that building. Let's take another look over the rest of the island. Then land on the far side and figure out what to do."

The far side of the island showed no signs of human activity. Splash found a relatively flat place on the side of the volcano to land. The other two dragons followed suit. But Pricker (with Sasha aboard) was carrying a struggling human in his talons. When he neared the ground, he released his hold, and the unwilling passenger dropped like a stone. He was immediately surrounded by three dragons and four armed humans.

Being bloodsworn, their prisoner got to his feet and tried to smash his way through the circle, but Pricker knocked him down and planted a foot over him to pin him in place.

"We picked him up in the harbor area," Sasha said. "I thought we could interrogate him and find out what's going on."

Destin and Ash closed in on the horselord.

"Be my guest," Ash said, "but I don't think persuasion will work on him."

Destin knelt next to the prisoner, but the man's eyes were fixed on Jenna. "Princess," he said. "I didn't know you were coming."

Jenna had removed her leather flying gloves and was fingering the back of her neck, a bewildered expression on her face.

"Yes," she said. "I am here. Where are the others?"

"They are near where you found me," the man said eagerly.

"They have been in the temple, feasting with the empress, but by now they may be on their way to the bridge."

"The bridge?" Jenna said. "Where's that?"

"Near the temple. I can show you, but we must hurry. We don't want to keep the empress waiting."

"No," Jenna said. "We don't." She ran lightly up Goat's side and settled onto the dragon's back. Then leaned down, extending a hand toward the horselord. "Come on. Fly with me."

"Jenna," Sasha said, gazing up at her, shifting from one foot to the other. "I don't think you—"

"Follow us!" Jenna said with a brilliant smile. "We'll all go."

Goat leaned down, gripped the horselord's coat in his teeth, and dropped him onto his back behind Jenna. Then launched himself from the mountain.

What just happened? Destin thought. And then, Scummer.

"Healer!" Destin shouted. "Ride with me. Hurry." He and Ash ran up Splash's wing and settled onto the dragon's back. Splash took off after Jenna. Sasha followed on Pricker. But by the time they circled the shoulder of the mountain, Jenna and Goat were out of sight.

Back in Breon's room, Evan carefully fastened the other collar around the spellsinger's neck. As soon as it snapped shut, Breon's eyes widened. "We've got to get out of here! She's running a rig on us—I can smell it."

"Don't panic," Evan said, gripping Breon's shoulders. "Let's think. The magic here seems to interact with our magemarks to keep us docile. The collars must interfere with that, the way they do with wetland magic. That puts us in a box, though. With the collars on, we can't use our splinter magic to fight back. If we take them off, we won't see any reason to fight."

Breon raised an eyebrow. "And you're saying we shouldn't panic?"

"Right now the empress thinks we're on her magical leash—that she can lead us to slaughter. If she sees the collars, though, she'll know something's up. Since we can't use our gifts, surprise is our best weapon." He fingered the beautiful coat Celestine had provided for the festivities. "These jackets have high collars. Let's dress for the dinner, hiding the collars underneath, in case she sees us. We'll walk down to the harbor, steal a boat, and row out to the *Siren*. Even with just the two of us, we ought to be able to get out of the harbor and hopefully beyond the reach of the enchantment."

"It couldn't extend out too far," Breon said. "It wasn't like this at Celesgarde. The empress had to use leaf to keep me under control."

"Maybe the spell is only strong enough at Solstice," Evan said. "Either way, we'll keep the collars on for a day or two, until we put some distance between us and her. Then we'll sail for the mainland and the free cities."

Hurriedly, they dressed in the finery Celestine had provided. Evan found that by settling the silver collar at the base of his neck, the fine linen shirt and the jacket hid it completely. When they were both ready, they walked casually along the seaside gallery, heading for the quay.

They stopped in their tracks. *Siren* was gone, along with the skiff they'd taken into shore.

"What now?" Breon murmured.

Evan considered alternatives. If whatever was going to happen had to happen today, maybe they could hide somewhere on the island until the critical period had passed. That, at least, would give them more time. But when they turned back toward shore, Celestine was striding toward them, elegantly dressed in an emerald-green jacket and divided skirt, a gossamer cowl studded with jewels covering her head.

"There you are," she said. "I was afraid you'd gotten lost. It's time for dinner." She ushered them into the longhouse, then halfway down to a table next to the central hearth. It was set for three with elegant dinnerware emblazoned with N and heavy silver. Evan half-expected Breon to start sliding silver into his jacket pockets.

Servants filled their glasses and served the first course. Evan didn't touch his wine and noticed that Breon didn't either. He wasn't sure what influence one blood mage could have on another, but he was taking no chances. Besides, they needed to keep their wits about them.

Celestine seemed to be in a festive mood, however, and refilled her own glass several times.

"Did you find a book?" she said, fixing on Breon.

"A book?" Breon blinked at her.

"In the library?"

"Oh. Yes. Lots of books. Lots and lots."

"Where were you hiding?" she asked Evan. His heart stuttered, until he realized that she was joking.

"I was buried in a book," he said.

The awkward conversation continued. Neither of them ate much, either, though Evan had been starving not long ago. Celestine noticed.

"Is it not to your liking?" she asked. "Should I have the cooks prepare something else?"

"No," Breon said quickly. "It's just—my stomach hasn't settled from our time in the hold."

"Ah, too bad," Celestine said. "Would you prefer some soup?"

"No, thank you," Evan said. And then, to change the subject, he said, "You were going to tell us about our family? I've always wondered."

Celestine's head came up. She eyed them, looking from Breon to Evan, but Evan maintained an eager, curious expression.

"Of course," she said. "As you know, the Nazari have always ruled a large part of the world, sometimes more, sometimes less. That is because we have always collaborated rather than competed. In the wetlands, families such as the Montaignes tear each other apart, while we find that there is strength in unity."

Something told Evan that she was being technically truthful but misleading.

"How many brothers and sisters do we have?" Breon said.

"My mother, Empress Iona, had five splinter children, plus me," Celestine said. She seemed to be putting herself into a different category.

"We . . . um . . . we all seem very different from each other," Evan said.

"You are nearly all half siblings by different fathers," Celestine said. "You mustn't think of your mother as a libertine. Iona chose your fathers very carefully for the benefit of the Line."

Evan tried to figure out how to ask his next question without giving anything away. "Are any of us full siblings to you?"

"No," the empress said. "The true heirs to the empire are born through a splitting process, without benefit of a father. It is important that the Nazari line remain pure, so that there is no question as to who inherits the throne."

"We aren't pure, so we don't inherit," Breon said, with no hint of rancor.

"That's the beauty of it," Celestine said. "You are a part of it, because you are critical to the viability of the Line. You see, the Nazari empresses are born without splinter gifts. The heir's half siblings are born with one or more gifts from their fathers, which they can then bequeath to the heir. She becomes more powerful than she ever would be through simple inheritance from two parents, and the bloodline remains clean."

Well, Evan thought, yesterday, I knew nothing about my family. Today, I know too much.

"So," Breon said, "if we *bequeath* our gifts, does that happen after we're dead?" It was as if the spellsinger was bent on bringing every aspect of this ugly deal into sharp relief.

Celestine studied them over the rim of her glass, as if watching for any flicker of resistance. Evan worried that the busker had cut too close to the bone, but eventually, the empress gave a little laugh, drained her glass, and said, "Exactly. And your names will live on in our archives as heroes to the Nazari line."

"To our legacy of magic." Breon raised his glass, and he and Evan found themselves toasting their own deaths.

"You told us that we were taken away from you," Breon said, pouring the empress more wine. "Who did it? How did that happen?"

Celestine's face darkened. "It was that pirate, Harol Strangward. Iona discarded her other consorts as soon as they had fulfilled their purpose. But there was something about Harol that stayed her hand. He kept coming back. Eventually, he fathered not just one, but two splinter children." Celestine's glass was empty again. Her voice was low, bitter, the words a little slurred.

"Mother would not allow me to claim my legacy. She was afraid that it would drive her lover off. So I took matters into my own hands, on Midsummer's Day."

She smiled fondly, fingering a silver pendant. "Jak went willingly into the flame. He gave me a precious gift—the gift of blood magery."

And my father, Harol Strangward, had a problem with that? Evan thought, fighting to maintain his "quarterdeck" face—calm, confident, without a hint of fear or indecision.

Maybe none of the other fathers knew.

He slid a look at the empress—serene, confident, a trifle tipsy. This must be powerful magic, Evan thought, if generations of splinter mages have gone cheerfully to their deaths.

"Come," Celestine said. "It is time." She clapped her hands, and a large group of bloodsworn appeared. Their "attendants," apparently.

They moved through the gardens surrounding the longhouse like a large swarm of bees with three queens at the center. And Celestine is the queen who eats her rivals, Evan thought.

What would happen if we killed her? Evan thought. What would the bloodsworn do?

How would we accomplish that while wearing these collars?

They'd reached the edge of the garden and were turning onto a path up the mountain when someone called from behind. "Empress! She has come. The princess has come."

They turned. It was Jenna Bandelow, with a bloodsworn escort.

Rescued! Evan thought at first, but then he realized that

Jenna wore the same vacant, moonstruck expression they'd worn when uncollared. Why was she here? How had she stumbled into this?

If Celestine was happy with Breon and Evan, she was delighted with Jenna.

"You've come back to me!" Celestine cried. "How did you come here?"

"I flew," Jenna said.

When she said that, Celestine looked momentarily confused, then hunched down and scanned the skies nervously. Apparently seeing nothing, she must have decided that this thing had better be accomplished sooner rather than later. "Come," she said, sliding an arm around Jenna. "You're just in time. We're going up to the bridge."

"What's at the bridge?" Jenna said.

"Immortality." Any pretense to a processional was abandoned, as the three of them were hustled up the mountain in a forced march. As they climbed, the smell of sulfur became more intense. Soon, they were walking along the top of a ravine that grew deeper and steeper as they moved along. Heat and fumes boiled up from below, and Evan realized that they must be walking parallel to a river of lava that flowed from a fissure up above.

Eventually, the trail turned and hugged the side of the volcano. As promised, they came to a lovely arched bridge over a thrashing pool of lava below. Recalling the image in the *Domus* book, Evan suspected that, whatever kind of ceremony came before, the empress's plan would have all three splinter mages in that pool before the night was out.

Except for one thing. Planted in the middle of that lovely arched bridge was a dragon, ears pasted back, coiled to spring.

"Splinter!" Evan cried involuntarily.

The apparatus Evan had rigged to repair the young dragon's damaged wing was broken, dragging on the ground. He had other injuries as well. One of his forelegs was oddly crooked, and scales had been torn away here and there.

"Move, dreki," the empress ordered, launching torrents of flame toward him.

Splinter answered with a withering gout of flame that struck the bloodsworn straight on as they charged onto the bridge. When they kept coming, like a battalion of charred scarecrows, he smashed his head into them, sweeping them off the bridge and into the boiling pool below.

As if directed by one mind, Evan and Breon launched themselves at Celestine, knocking her backward onto the bridge deck. They pounced on her, trying to wrestle her to the edge, while Jenna stood staring at them, as if unable to process what was happening.

Celestine was remarkably strong, and it was difficult to hold on to her while she was spraying them with flame, burning away their sacrificial clothes. Unfortunately, the collars seemed to make them less resistant to direct magic than usual.

Evan saw movement out of the corner of his eye, and then the bloodsworn were dragging him and Breon away from the empress.

As soon as she was free, Celestine took hold of an unresisting Jenna, lifted her high, and flung her over the side of the bridge and into the lava pool.

From overhead came a heart-stopping scream.

And then, "Jenna!" A human cry of anguish, the voice familiar.

Evan looked up and saw Goat, with Adrian sul'Han mounted on his back, reaching out his open hands as if he could drag her back.

The empress gazed into the fuming boil. Then, finally satisfied, she looked up in time to see Ash and Goat bearing down on her. Ash shifted forward in his saddle, gripped his amulet, and bathed the empress in flame. It charred her clothes but accomplished absolutely nothing else.

Healer, Evan thought. Not a good time to forget that the magemarked are resistant to direct magic.

*Jenna gone?* Goat said. Goat and Adrian swept back and forth across the lava pool, looking for signs of life.

"Bring the princes," Celestine ordered the bloodsworn.

They dragged their unwilling prisoners forward. But Splinter still crouched in the middle of the bridge. He extended his head, opening his jaws for the attack. But seeing Breon and Evan in the midst of the bloodsworn, he hesitated.

"Dreki," Celestine commanded. "Stand aside. I am your mistress now."

Splinter didn't move, didn't stand aside. He looked from Celestine to Evan to Breon. The only way to describe his expression was *puzzled.*

"Do it, Splinter," Evan shouted. "Open fire." He reasoned that if he had to die, he'd rather not be responsible for enhancing Celestine's power. He braced himself for an onslaught of flame.

Celestine stared at him, as if suddenly realizing that her remaining siblings were not going like lambs to the slaughter. Evan heard screams from high above, felt the air stirring around him, and knew more dragons were circling.

He looked up. It was Pricker and Sasha. Then Splash. That's

when Evan realized that she must have flown all the way across the Indio to fetch the others, turned around, and flown straight back.

"Dreki!" Celestine cried, extending an imperious hand toward the circling dragons, palm out. "I am Empress Celestine, heir to the gifts of my sister, the shape-shifter Jenna Bandelow. I order you to seize my magemarked brethren and drop them into the pool to join our sister."

Pricker circled, losing altitude. Sasha seemed to be arguing with him, pleading with him not to listen. Goat hovered on the hot gases rising from the lava pool, eye to eye with Celestine, Adrian flattening himself along his back. One by one, the other dragons joined him, their attention fixed on the empress, their hot breath stirring her hair and garments. Even Splinter dragged himself toward her.

"Splinter, no!" Evan said, wondering if he should be taking cover. Given the dragons' eyesight, he would be ferreted out in no time.

He was unsure how strong the connection was between empress and dragons. With Jenna, it had been more of a bond of friendship than a compulsion.

Celestine stamped her foot impatiently. "Dreki! I am now the mistress of dragons. I command you to obey."

The dragons drifted in closer. *Mistress? Of dragons?* Goat said.

*Commands us to obey?* Splash cocked her head.

*Killed Jenna?* Splinter slapped his tail on the bridge.

*Blinded Cas?* Pricker said, flame trickling ominously from his nostrils.

Celestine, of course, didn't hear any of this. If she had, she might have had a clue as to what was coming.

Goat launched forward like a viper and seized the empress in his jaws. He rose on the updraft, wings fluttering lazily while she wriggled and squirmed, still screeching orders. Then he dropped her, flailing, into the boiling pool. It foamed up, as if it might spit her back out again, and then subsided.

New power rippled through Evan, knocking him back on his ass, his skin pebbling and burning.

"Feel that?" Breon said, extending a hand to help him up. "I guess shattering and rejoining works both ways."

Evan shuddered. He wasn't sure that he wanted anything of Celestine's.

Then again, it was really a legacy from their dead siblings, Claire, Jak, and Jenna. A way they could live on.

It wasn't much of a consolation.

The dragons weren't finished. One by one, they pitched the bloodsworn off the bridge to join their mistress.

Adrian slid to the ground and raced to the bridge abutment, turning to try to scramble down the slope to look for Jenna, but Goat blocked the way.

*No. Wait. Dangerous.*

Adrian tried to find a way around the dragon, but Goat was having none of it.

Evan didn't try to stop them. Instead, he ran to Splinter's side and threw his arms around the dragon's neck.

*Splinter follow you.*

"I know," Evan said, stroking the dragon, his tears falling, sizzling when they struck the dragon's scales.

*Splinter help.*

"You did," Evan said. "Thank you."

"Pirate," someone said. "You've thanked the poor dragon.

Why don't you help me move him off the bridge so we can have a look at his wounds."

The voice carried a familiar note of irony, that element that had always kept Evan off balance, at arm's length.

It didn't work this time.

He looked up to see Destin Karn, wearing a black leather flight coat, snug riding breeches, and an expression of mingled relief and joy.

"Destin!" Evan flew into the spymaster's arms, and this time there was no resistance. Destin held him tightly, pressing him into his chest as if he would never let him go. Evan could feel his heart beating madly, and he was trembling. He smelled of fresh air and dragon flame and hope.

"I thought you were dead, pirate," Destin whispered, stroking his hair, cradling his chin, then kissing him slowly and thoroughly. "I would think that a pirate would have a better sense of—"

"Shut up," Evan said and returned the kiss.

Destin slid warm fingers under the silver collar, raising gooseflesh across Evan's shoulders and down his arms. "I must admit, this is becoming, but do you want me to—?"

"Please."

Destin unfastened the latch and opened the collar. Evan was a little worried that he might feel an impulse to leap pell-mell into the lava pool, but nothing happened. The true heir was gone, after all.

Together, they helped Splinter off the bridge and onto solid ground, where Destin examined Splinter's makeshift prosthetic wing. "This is . . . pathetic," he said, lips twitching. "Who the hell made this?"

"It was better before it got smashed," Evan said. "I'm hoping you migh . . ." He cut off, staring past Destin. "Saints and martyrs," he whispered.

A tall figure had appeared at the edge of the ravine. It was a girl from the shape of her, wearing no clothes, but covered in glittering scales from head to toe. Her hair was like spun metal, streaked with red and orange and gold, her eyes golden, too, her scales glowing a sullen red from the heat of the lava pool.

It was Jenna Bandelow.

The dragons—all of them—screamed out a welcome.

"Jenna!" Adrian charged forward, opening his arms to embrace her, but then stopped short. Heat waves rippled off her, and she glowed like a banked fire. Any direct contact would have cost him a layer of skin.

The dragons, of course, had no such reservations. While the healer looked on jealously, they twined around her like cats, nudging her with their great heads, sheltering her in their coils as she gradually cooled.

"What the hell happened?" she said. "I feel like I'm coming off a four-day drunk. I dreamed that I turned into a dragon, and I was swimming in a lake of fire. It was like I was living within Flamecaster's skin." She looked around at the staring circle of humans and dragons.

After a long pause, the healer said, "That's sort of what happened."

As some of the scales began to fade, it became more and more evident that she was naked. Ash peeled off his jacket and put it around her. "The empress is dead," he said.

"Huh," she said, rubbing the back of her neck. "After all this trouble, I hope I had a hand in it, at least."

# ON THE BRIGHT SIDE OF TROUBLE

When Hal finally returned to Ardenscourt, he was happy to find that Robert was still alive. He hadn't fought any duels, and neither one of them was betrothed to anyone.

Look on the bright side, Halston. You're the king!

Some in the Thane Council questioned the fact that Hal had marched north, taken Delphi and the capital at Fellsmarch, and then marched back south again, leaving the old borders in place. Some said the northern queen must have bewitched him. Since Hal had returned with a larger army than he'd left with, there wasn't too much saber rattling from the thanes. They had seemingly discovered the pleasures in returning to their estates and putting their fallow fields back into production.

Most of the thanes had no idea of the catastrophe they'd avoided when the combined armies of Arden and the Fells had driven the empress's armies into the sea. Only a few, who had holdings near Spiritgate, knew what the stakes had been. They were among Hal's most ardent supporters.

While Hal had been gone, fighting in the north, Robert

had discovered that either Jarat or his father or both had socked away an immense store of money and treasure. Hal canceled the levies imposed on the thanes to fund the Montaigne grudge match against the queen in the north. That made him the most popular king in a long time.

Not that the Montaignes were much competition.

Not that it would last.

Happily, his father eventually seemed to accept the fact that Hal was not going to wrest estates and titles away from Jarat's supporters and add them to the Matelon holdings. Hal did return the Scoville Estate at Whitehall to his mother, with the stipulation that it go to Harper when his lady mother passed on. And he rewarded Robert with some of the choicest Montaigne titles and estates. He put Eric Bellamy in command of the army, to the displeasure of some who'd answered his call to the rebellion at Temple Church. But he believed in promoting talent—he knew it would make his job easier in the long run. And he expected that Bellamy would offer him the same loyalty he'd given the Montaignes.

Not everyone was happy. Hal cut free the Church of Malthus from involvement in the government, and ruthlessly stamped out any tendrils that slithered back in. He made it plain to the principia and everyone else that people in Arden were free to worship as they pleased, or not to worship at all. Mandatory tithing was done away with. Discrimination against the gifted was forbidden.

Hal knew he couldn't change attitudes overnight, but he was not going to put the force of government behind any one church. The great saint would have to earn the hearts of his adherents like anyone else. Most people stayed with the church they'd grown up in, but a few other faiths emerged from underground.

Any kind of change creates winners and losers, and Hal was under no illusions that his royal honeymoon would last forever. Some predicted trouble when he gave more autonomy to the downrealms. He knew that might happen, but he hoped a looser kind of confederation would work.

He missed Queen Marina and Princess Madeleine. They'd moved back to Tamron, where Marina established a small court of her own. It became a popular stopping-off point for travelers between Arden and the Fells.

Hal encouraged Destin Karn to stay on as spymaster. He agreed to do so in the short run—on the condition that Hal accept Harper's petition to join the intelligence service. Hal had been putting that decision off for months. He knew she was well suited for that work—maybe too well suited.

"Didn't you tell me that you believe in promoting talent?" Destin said. So Hal reluctantly agreed.

At least *she* got the job she wanted.

Destin and Evan were disposing of the Chambord estate in Tamron. They planned to return to Carthis and settle in Tarvos once that was done. Hal hoped the Stormcaster and spymaster wouldn't choose to target Ardenine shipping. One of them was bad enough—the two of them together would be unstoppable.

Hal had never wanted to be king, and he didn't enjoy it now, especially knowing that this was probably the best it would ever be. But Hal was a Matelon, and so he did what needed to be done. Though he missed the camaraderie of army life, he would not be the sort of ruler who left the work of governing to others while he rode after the hounds or played at war or squandered his legacy at the gaming tables and clicket-houses. He would not start a war simply because it was something he was good at.

Robert said it was no wonder Hal didn't enjoy being king—he'd sworn off all the pleasures of the office.

Truth be told, Hal had unfinished business in the north. He'd been working on a plan for some months now. But he was finding it easier to plan than to execute.

Lyss had been frantically busy putting her queendom in order and sieving out the traitors at the Gray Wolf court. The queendom had been at war for decades, too, with fewer resources to draw upon than the empire. That's the hidden cost of war, she'd told him once. The young people who don't grow up and create the future. The schools and libraries that don't get funded, the roads and bridges that never get built. It would take a long time for them to catch up.

Hal grew more and more restless as another winter solstice celebration approached. It marked the end of an eventful year and, to his mind, the beginning of many years of unrelenting drudgery. During his time as an army officer, he'd always celebrated Solstice at court with his family, making awkward conversation at parties, trying to remember the names from the year before, and making up for nine months of privation by eating and drinking too much. As the eldest son of a thane, and a well-respected military officer, he'd attracted attention in the marital market in a third-tier kind of way. He didn't look forward to being the main course at a feast of ambition.

What he really wanted was to celebrate quietly with his family at White Oaks. But his family insisted on celebrating at court.

Then Queen Marina invited him to a Solstice celebration at a summer cottage at Swansea.

"I'm planning a very small gathering," she wrote. "I promise that there will be people you know, people that you want to see."

The smaller the gathering, the better, Hal thought. On impulse, he decided to go.

His mother and father were savagely disappointed, this being their first chance to show off their son the king.

"But we're hosting three parties, and we're invited to six more," Lady Matelon said.

"Good," Hal said, folding clothes and stuffing them into his bags. "You'll have something to do."

"Everyone's looking forward to seeing you, son," his father said.

"I'm here all the time these days," Hal said. "Why doesn't anyone throw a party in February?"

"Swansea is so far away. Couldn't Marina have her party at Tamron Court?" Lady Matelon said. "Who has a winter solstice party at a summer cottage?"

Hal said nothing but continued packing.

"You have to stay, Halston," Lady Matelon said, in a last, desperate plea. "Your dance card is already full."

"Give Robert my dance card," Hal said. "He's the better dancer, anyway." He kissed her. "Happy Solstice, Mother. Let's each celebrate in our own way."

So it was that Hal found himself riding hard from Ardenscourt to Tamron Court to Swansea on Solstice Eve. You're nineteen years old, and you're running away from home, he thought.

Swansea had long been a resort town for the Tamron nobility. Most of the homes there were "cottages" with broad front porches, quaint names like Gull's Rest, and "only" fifteen to twenty rooms. His destination had a typical name—Snug Harbor.

He asked directions in the village and rode south along the coast road, battling sheets of cold sleet coming in off the ocean.

Who has a Solstice party at a summer cottage?

He turned off at a tumbledown stone gate with a rusting sign—*Snug Harbor.*

The cottage was on a bluff overlooking Leewater. It was more modest than he'd expected—built of stone, with a tile roof, a small barn, and a path down to the water. Smoke rose from the chimney, but no servants rushed out to greet him. He checked his invitation again. Yes, this had to be the right place. Was he early? Was he late? Was he the butt of some kind of joke? Or, worse, the target of a coup? Here he was, the king of the realm, riding alone to a deserted spot in the borderlands. His hand found the hilt of his sword.

He dismounted in front of the barn and led Bosley inside. There were six stalls, but only one was occupied—by a mountain pony.

A small gathering, indeed, Hal thought. He rubbed down the stallion, put him into a stall, and forked hay into the bin. Then, shouldering his bags, he walked around to the front porch.

Swags of greens and berries were pinned up around the door. He tried it, and it was unlocked.

A pair of clan-made boots sat in a puddle of water just inside. A fire burned on the hearth in the front parlor, releasing the aroma of cinnamon and spiceberry. In front of it, there were a settee and a table set with two glasses and a jug of wine. All around the room, maps of the Realms were pinned to the walls.

Setting down his bags, Hal removed his boots and hung his coat on a hook by the door. Then walked around the room, studying the maps. Some were very old, dating from before the Breaking, when the Realms were all one queendom. The others were more recent, with varying borders, depending on the outcomes of an endless string of wars with the north and with the downrealms.

"Hello, flatlander."

Hal spun around.

It was Queen Alyssa. She wore close-fitting leggings over her muscular legs, and a thick wool sweater. She was barefoot, and her cheeks were pinked up from the cold. For once, her hair wasn't braided. It was pulled back from her face into a kind of knot, but then flowed freely down her back.

"Happy Solstice," she said. "We're having a very small party tonight."

"Oh!" Hal said. He looked at the table in front of the fire, then back at her. Hope rose in him like a spring tide. "It's just us?"

"The others are set to arrive tomorrow. Sasha, Breon, Destin, Evan, Hadley, Shadow, and Lila are riding in. Ash, Jenna, Cas, Splash, and Goat are flying in from the northern Heartfangs." She paused. "Maybe you've heard—they've established a dragon homeland there."

"I have heard that," Hal said. "How has that gone over with the residents in the area?" He recalled the reaction of Ardenine citizens to the mere rumor of a dragon.

"Nobody lives in the highest peaks year round," Lyss said, "but the clans do hunt the slopes in summer. We've worked out an agreement with the dragons regarding who and what they can hunt. And they're close enough to the sea to go fishing."

With so many dragons coming, Hal could understand why this meet-up was happening on a coast that was mostly empty of people in the winter.

"What about Queen Marina?"

"Marina's at home, at Tamron Seat," Lyss said. "This is actually my party. It may be the last time we can all be together, for a while, anyway."

She padded over to the table, yanked the cork with her teeth, and poured two glasses full. He loved the way she moved, like a restless predator. "Here," she said, gesturing toward the settee. "Sit."

Hal sat, pressing his suddenly sweaty palms against his thighs.

Alyssa sat beside him, only inches between them—a distance that thrummed with tension.

To ease his nerves, Hal continued spitting out questions. "How is Cas doing?"

Lyss rocked her hand. "Ash is still treating him, but it looks like his vision is never going to be what it was. Meanwhile, he and Jenna fly together every day, always working on how to use his other senses to compensate. More dragons are moving to the homeland, and Jenna and Ash have recruited some of them for an air corps and courier service. She's been training war orphans to partner with them."

"It sounds like they're busy," Hal said, realizing that he was jealous.

Lyss nodded. "It's a good kind of busy, though. Breon is working with Speaker Jemson and Raisa Cennestre in the Briar Rose Ministry and the temple schools. As the army shrinks, veterans need new ways to make a living."

We're facing the same issue, Hal thought—what to do when we're not making war.

"Does Breon plan to stay in the Fells?" he asked.

"I think so," Lyss said. "He and Sasha are walking out."

Walking out. The northern term for a serious relationship. That was a matchup he'd never have predicted.

Maybe there was hope for the one he had in mind.

"Your mother is well?"

"She is," Lyss said. "I can't tell you what it's meant to me to have the counsel of my parents, especially since my experience is in fighting, not governing. It's the way it should be, and yet—"

"Hang on," Hal said. "The counsel of your *parents*?"

Lyssa laughed. "It's a northern thing. We're not very good at respecting boundaries of *any* kind."

Clearly, she wasn't going to say any more about that, so he lobbed the first shot over the wall.

"So," Hal said, "why are we here?"

She gestured at the maps on the wall. "Speaking of boundaries," she said, "I'm hoping that we can make some changes."

"Yes," he said solemnly, his eyes fixed on her lips. "I've been thinking the same thing."

The Gray Wolf queen looked a little flustered. "And . . . uh . . . so, I thought it was best if we did that before the others arrive."

She set down her wine, stood, and crossed to one of the maps. "These were our borders at the time of the founding of the New Line of queens," she said.

Hal stood, walked over, and studied it. "Mmm-hmm," he said, clasping his hands behind his back.

"And here . . ." She walked over to another map. "This is the border that you're defending now, after years of encroachment, including the seizing of the port of Spiritgate."

"Hmm," he said.

"So this . . ." She traced an area along the border with her fingers. "This is disputed territory."

"I wouldn't call it *disputed*," Hal said. "I mean, it's belonged to Arden for my lifetime. Actually, for more than two hundred years."

Alyssa waved a hand, dismissing the two hundred years. "That's a blink of the eye in the history of the Realms," she said. "We want—we need—the copper mines back"—she pointed— "and our port. But we're willing to negotiate timber rights for the area north of Fetters Ford, and give you access to the harbor. The thing is, we want to protect the watershed for the—"

"Why would I give you your port back?" Hal said, digging in. "Let alone the mines. We won them fairly. I'm not asking for Delphi back, and we controlled it for years." It was odd to find himself in the position of defending the actions of previous kings of Arden, when he was the usurper who'd pushed the Montaignes off the throne.

"Delphi isn't mine to give," Lyss said. "It's a free city. Aren't you the one that offered them autonomy in exchange for their help against the empress?"

"My *point* is, you cannot turn back the clock and stop at a point that's advantageous to you."

Lyss's chin came up, and she fisted her hands at her sides. "Really, Matelon? Do you think I'm being greedy?"

"Look, you bring me here, ply me with wine, and then demand a one-sided giveaway of assets that we spilled blood over."

"Fine!" she said, in a tone that meant that it was not fine at all. She began pacing back and forth, talking with her hands. "Just forget it, Matelon. I merely assumed that, as a friendly neighbor to the south, you might be open to negotiation."

"That's what I'm doing," Hal said. "Negotiating."

"You call that negotiation? Claiming I'm greedy? In fact, I'm being highly restrained. The Gray Wolf line once ruled all of the Seven Realms. If I were *greedy*, I'd demand that we go back to that."

"I never said you were greedy," Hal said. "I'm saying that borders would be less important if there were closer ties between us."

"If you want closer ties, this is not the way to—"

"I have two proposals." Hal walked back to the map on the wall—the current map—hoping she couldn't tell that his heart was flopping around like a fish.

"First off," he said, "I'd be willing to establish your southern border *here*, under certain conditions." He traced a line from Southgate to Watergate—the southern border of Arden.

She stared at the map, then frowned at him. "I don't get it," she said.

"When King Gerard of Arden proposed to your mother, Queen Raisa, he suggested they 'marry their kingdoms together,' with him in charge, and succession through their sons." Hal knew he was taking a chance bringing that up, but he had a point to make.

"I think it was more than a suggestion," Lyss said.

"Nonetheless, she refused."

"Smart," Lyss said, folding her arms, tapping her foot.

"Very smart," Hal said. "I propose that we marry our realms

together, with *you* in charge, and succession through our daughters."

"Our . . . daughters." Lyss rubbed her forehead. "I think I missed a step somewhere."

"To put it a different way, Alyssa ana'Raisa, queen of the Fells, will you marry me?" Hal said. "As my dowry, I offer Spiritgate and the copper mines."

Lyss gaped at him for a long moment, then exploded. "What is it with you southern kings? Why are you so hell-bent on marrying us? Do you think we're trophies to hang on the wall? A notch in your swiving sword belts? The ticket to bragging rights in the—?"

"No, Your Majesty," Hal said. "Mind, I'm speaking only for myself. I want to marry you because you're the most remarkable woman I've ever met. I learn something new every day we spend together. I think we can go through the rest of our lives and never run out of things to say. Plus you've kicked my ass on the battlefield three different times, and I like to have talent on my side."

"Well," Lyss conceded, "I don't know if that third time really—"

"If it helps, think of it as fighting alongside an ally who will always have your back. I'm in love with you, and I want to marry you. I'm under considerable pressure to get married, and I don't want to marry anyone else."

"This sounds like a—a—"

"I realize that a good negotiator would never display his hand so plainly," Hal said. "A good negotiator would tell you that there's a faction that wants to marry me off to Princess Madeleine, King Gerard's ten year old daughter, because that would give me a stronger claim to the throne." That was, in fact, true. "As you can see, I am a miserable negotiator. But I have other redeeming qualities." He looked into her eyes, very directly.

Color stained her cheeks. "Oh, you do, do you?"

"Aye," he said.

Alyssa crossed to the hearth, poked at the fire. It sent up sparks, burnishing her skin to gold. "How do you think your thanes would respond to living under a queendom?" Alyssa said.

"It might take them some time to get used to it," he said. "Hopefully, they'll have time before our daughters come of age. I think it will help if we raise our princesses to wield a sword, to lead an army, and to form alliances with dragons."

"Huh," she said. Dropping the poker, she swung back around, studying him, chewing her lower lip. "You've come a long way, Matelon."

He nodded, acknowledging the compliment. "In the interest of full disclosure, I should tell you that I've been negotiating a looser confederation with the downrealms. So if you had dreams of becoming queen or empress of all Seven Realms, that's not part of the bargain. I offer my heart, my kingdom, my sword, and, of course—most importantly—the port and the copper mines."

"I see," Alyssa said. Her lips twitched, and Hal knew he was gaining ground. "You—ah—said you had two proposals?"

"I do," Hal said. "I knew that it was a possibility that you would decline proposal one. For one thing, it would plunge the two of us into some messy politics at the outset of our marriage, when we have enough to contend with in our home realms. So my second proposal is that we marry, thereby strengthening the bonds between our realms, but maintain our own territories intact. We could split our time between Ardenscourt and Fellsmarch. Or we could build a new palace in the borderlands." Or find a cave in the mountains.

"Either way, we'd get married?"

"Either way," Hal said, feeling a squirm of fear in his belly that this requirement might kill the deal.

"Either way, I'd get Spiritgate and the mines?"

"Either way."

"And what do *you* get?"

"I get you," Hal said. "I get a friend—something I really need right now. I get a sparring partner, of sorts. I get good counsel—something that's impossible to find at court. I get the truth when everyone around me is lying. I get *this*." Gently, he cradled her chin between his two hands and kissed her. Her lips were warm, still tasting of wine. When she opened them, he extended the kiss, drawing her close, her breasts pressing into his chest, his body on fire from hips to shoulders.

When they broke apart, she stood, flushed, breathless, speechless.

"Nobody does that, Matelon," she said, swallowing hard.

"Does what?"

"Marries for love."

"I would cite the example of your parents," Hal said. "If it's against some sort of rule, we should ask forgiveness, not permission. We can plead inexperience." He took hold of her hands. "Now. With your permission, I would like to kiss you again."

Her eyes narrowed. "What are you saying—that your kisses

are so powerful that I'll lose my head and agree to whatever you propose?"

"Not at all," Hal said. "I'm giving you fair warning that kissing is a feature of these proposals, and you may need more data in order to decide whether you want to sign on for it."

He could tell that her anger was fading. In fact, she seemed to be having trouble maintaining her scowl.

"I'm also saying that I'd like to kiss you again."

"Fair enough," she said.

"Is that a yes?"

"That's a yes, you arrogant flatlander," she said. She gripped his lapels and pulled him in for another, fiercer kiss that left his lips bruised and tingling. Pressing her hands into his shoulder blades, she rested her head beneath his chin until her breathing normalized.

They stood like that for a long moment.

"Hmm," Lyssa murmured, kissing his neck and nibbling his ear until he thought he might explode. She pushed him down on the settee and back against the pillows, kissed him again, then said, her brow furrowed, "More data, please." She pulled his shirt free from his breeches, burrowed her head under, and planted a series of incendiary kisses on his chest and stomach.

Eventually, the two of them rolled off the settee, landing hard on the rug, coming close to spilling the jug of wine.

Now he was on top, pinning her. "If we cannot come to terms," he growled, "we must not give up. We must, of course, continue negotiations until we do."

It turned out that their negotiations required many more kisses, flinging of clothes, wrestling, and the rest of the wine. Later, as they lay entwined on the rug in front of the fire, Lyss said, "Blood and bones, Matelon, I had no idea that you could be this persuasive."

"Hal," he said softly. "I think you can call me Hal." He stroked her hair, leaned down, and brushed his lips over her ear. "Are there any particular points you want me to go over again?"

"No." She smiled faintly. "Well, yes, but I think we'd better get some sleep before tomorrow."

"I am, as always, your obedient servant, Your Majesty."

"Lyss."

"Lyss."

She lay silent for so long that Hal thought she might have fallen asleep. Then she said, "Hal?"

"Hmm?"

"I'm older than my mother was when she married, but I'm still young."

Hal nodded. "I know."

"There is still so much to do, so much rebuilding, so many decisions to make when trying to heal the queendom and take care of my people. It would be especially hard to announce a betrothal so close on the heels of Jarat's plan to marry Julianna and absorb the queendom into the empire. People who have sacrificed blood and sweat and property to keep the queendom free would be understandably rattled, no matter how we tried to explain it. Ardenine kings are not well regarded in the north."

"I understand. I didn't plan on pressing my suit this soon, but, well, you started it."

She laughed. "I did." She stopped again, as if debating whether to go on. "We have so much in common, and yet we're so different in temperament—like we complement each other."

Hal said nothing, not wanting to interrupt the queen's conversation with herself.

"And—and your kisses—they—I mean, there's that."

"Yes," Hal said. "There is that."

"Maybe a marriage between us could work," she said.

"Maybe it could," Hal said. "It may require some time to reach an agreement."

"And negotiations," Lyss said. "Lots and lots of negotiations."

She laughed, and they began kissing again, so it was some time before they slept.

REALMS
FROZEN SEA
Invaders Bay
Grey Lady
THE VALE
Fellsmarch
Wizard Head
Chalk Cliffs
Marisa Pines Camp
Marisa Pines Pass
Firehole R.
Fortress Rock
Way Camp
Hunter's Camp
Queen Court
Alyssa Plateau
Wolf's Head
The Harlot
Spiritgate
Delphi
KINGDOM of ARDEN
Heartfang Mtns.
Middlesea
North Rd.
Temple Church
White Oaks Keep
Bittersweet Keep
Ardenswater
THE INDIO OCEAN
Ardenscourt
East Rd.
Baston Bay
Ardenswater
Heartfang R.
Bright Stone Keep
Bitter Springs R.
Watergate
Grypnon Pt.
The Claw
The Wastes
WE'ENHAVEN
Hidden Bay